THE VATI...

David Leadbeater has published more than forty novels and is a million-copy ebook bestseller. His books include the chart-topping Matt Drake series and the Relic Hunters series, which won the inaugural Amazon Kindle Storyteller award in 2017. *The Vatican Secret* is the first book in the new Joe Mason series, and David's first book with HarperCollins.

www.davidleadbeater.com

DAVID LEADBEATER

THE
VATICAN
SECRET

avon.

Published by AVON
A division of HarperCollins*Publishers*
1 London Bridge Street
London SE1 9GF

www.harpercollins.co.uk

HarperCollins*Publishers*
Macken House, 39/40 Mayor Street Upper,
Dublin 1, D01 C9W8, Ireland

A Paperback Original 2022

6

First published in Great Britain by HarperCollins*Publishers* 2022

A catalogue copy of this book is available from the British Library.

ISBN: 978-0-00-847111-8

Typeset in Sabon by Palimpsest Book Production Limited, Falkirk,
Stirlingshire
Printed and Bound in the UK using 100% Renewable Electricity
at CPI Group (UK) Ltd

For Erica, Keira and Megan.
'One life, live it.'

And for the readers who supported me from
the beginning – this is for you.

Chapter 1

They came together in a derelict hotel just outside Marrakesh: a thief, a monarch, two killers, an infiltration specialist and a communications expert.

The monarch, a man named Marduk, spoke first: 'Do you believe in God?'

The men and only woman present shifted in discomfort, but made no reply as Marduk appraised them. The thief was easy; she was his daughter, Nina, and far more than just a streetwise pickpocket. She had been trained by the world's criminal elite in the fine art of thiefcraft to be a cat burglar extraordinaire. The infiltration specialist was a man named Luke Hassell, the killers known only by codewords: Ash and Base. The communications expert was known as Mac. All except Marduk's daughter had been supplied by a renowned underworld kingpin.

'Gido tells me you're the best,' Marduk said. 'You will have to be.'

'We work better with people we know,' Hassell said, throwing a pointed glance at Nina.

'Rest assured, my daughter is your equal in every way. She has my complete trust, and will not fail you.' Marduk paused before adding, 'And you will not fail her.'

Hassell acquiesced with a brief nod.

Marduk took a breath, considering his next words. They needed to know only the pertinent points of their mission. As he deliberated, he cast a long look around the abandoned lobby, taking in its derelict appearance: the crumbling walls, the rotting wood and broken glass, the musty odour of mould. Where his feet moved, they shifted through piles of dirt, debris and old, broken syringes.

'I'll make this quick,' he said. 'As you know, Gido is a criminal kingpin, a great underworld figure, but *we* command his services for free. We, the Amori, of which I am the Monarch, the head of state. You now work for the Amori, an age-old entity which understood that the Crusades against the Holy Land would lead to thousands of years of religious war. They understood even then that the Church and the Vatican would become their greatest enemy. We were there at Babylon and still we flourish.'

Hassell looked at his team before frowning. 'You said this was gonna be quick?'

Marduk showed no emotion. Years of leadership and this new hour of opportunity overrode petty displays of irritation.

'The Church, and the Vatican, will be destroyed. To this end, you will steal the *Vatican Book of Secrets* from the Apostolic Archive. I am told you are unequalled in what you do – and Nina will handle the theft itself – which gives us the best team in the world.'

'There's a *Vatican Book of Secrets*?' Hassell asked. 'I never knew.'

'The Church has many foul secrets,' Marduk said, struggling to quell the vehemence in his voice. 'From the time of the false messiah Jesus Christ to the present day. But the book contains at least one secret that, if revealed, would bring Christianity to its knees. I tell you this only to ensure you grasp the full importance of your mission. Understand this – you will never undertake anything of more significance.'

Marduk appraised their reactions, the most honest of which shone through the eyes of his daughter. Nina had trained for this auspicious moment for years. The others appeared to need more convincing.

'The secret is immense; it will shake the world, and you are incredibly fortunate to be the early engineers of its *revelation*. Just as the Gospels were the early engineers of our enforced concealment. *She has become a dwelling place of demons,*' Marduk recited. '*A prison of every unclean spirit, and a prison of every unclean and hateful bird.*' Underneath his black cloak his hands clenched into painfully hard fists. He took a moment to exhale and calm down. Shows of emotion did not befit his standing.

Hassell was staring at him. Marduk resumed control of the situation. 'You have been selected for your skillsets to help retrieve the *Book of Secrets*.'

'To recap then,' Mac, the IT expert, said with a touch of sarcasm. 'You people are some kind of ancient enemy of the Church. You want *us* to steal a dusty old book full of dirty secrets so that you can raze Christianity.' He grinned. 'I'm down with that.'

Marduk considered issuing a future kill order on Mac for his insulting trivialisation of his prime goal. His monarchy came with many such perks, but it also attracted a responsibility to put the Amori's goals first, above all else. Without thinking, he touched the red symbol emblazoned on the right side of his jacket, seeking calm from the ancient symbol designating the Amori.

Hassell watched him.

'We are allies of humanity, not enemies. *They* called us harlots and abominations in their Bible . . . in the *lies* that they call scripture. But this secret will undo them. The proof will unravel two thousand years of inaccuracies and manipulation.'

'Moving on,' Hassell said. 'I'll be devising the actual

robbery. I'll be sending your daughter into the lion's den, so to speak. No good plan survives contact with the enemy. We need to be fluid and flexible in there. Are you happy for me to take full command of Plans B and C too?'

Marduk nodded. 'You were brought here because you are the best. I defer to your abilities. Build in as many contingencies as you like. The book is the only thing that matters.'

Hassell looked unconvinced, glancing at Nina before turning back to Marduk. 'Breaking into the Vatican and escaping unnoticed will be no easy task, even for us.'

'We will have an insider, though he does not yet know it.' Marduk waved the doubt away. 'A member of the Swiss Guard. During the robbery I will listen in through systems you establish and will act accordingly if help is needed.'

Hassell nodded his agreement. Mac looked bored. The two specialist killers, Ash and Base, followed the conversation without once opening their mouths. Their eyes roamed the ruin and decay surrounding them as if the rustlings of hidden animals held the keys to their existence.

Nina's face held that shrewd look he knew so well. Standing there, she was assessing every shift in their bodies, every nuance of speech. Too much depended on the outcome of this mission to ignore even the slightest sign of disaffection.

Thousands of years of work, sacrifice and planning, to be precise.

Marduk looked up at the ceiling as several mini-waterfalls found their way through and struck the ground in regular drumbeats, a rhythmic indicator of a light rain outside. It was cold and miserable here, not the ideal place to initiate the Amori's paramount mission, but the perfect place to start it clandestinely.

One final warning. 'We are everywhere,' Marduk said. 'In every government, bank and security service, every school, energy conglomerate and oil consortium. We own people in every major city's police force and many more. Nobody hides from us. Not you, not even Gido. Double-cross us and we will kill you, your family and every friend on your Facebook page. I hope I make myself clear.'

Hassell coughed. 'Crystal. We done here?'

'Almost. How long will you need to plan?'

'For *this* job?' Hassell whistled. 'I'd say a year but I'm guessing you don't have that long?'

Marduk didn't say a word, letting the force of his stare answer for him.

'All right then.' Hassell cleared his throat. 'Six months. Maybe seven.'

'That is not acceptable.'

'You want this doing right? Flawlessly? I'm gonna say six months. You want this doing competently, but with minimum stuff that can go wrong? Three months, minimum.'

'Three months it is then.' Marduk smiled. 'I'll see you again in three months.'

'So we're done now?'

'You are. Any further information will come from Nina. For anything else, I can be contacted through her alone. And now you will go make history. But . . . I have to say . . . not one of you answered my earlier question.'

Hassell narrowed his eyes whilst the others looked blank.

Marduk smiled slyly and repeated it. 'Do you believe in God?'

'Processors, bandwidth and ghostware are my gods,' Mac said. 'Hallelujah to the mainframe.'

Both Ash and Base raised their weapons in answer, smirking.

Hassell looked away as if contemplating private demons that beset him. 'No,' he said at length. 'A benevolent god would never tolerate the shit I've seen in my life. Or allow what happened to me.'

Marduk remained impassive as he said, 'That is good. Because, in the coming months, the believers will question their place in the world. They will question their faith, their entire lives that they built around reprehensible lies. They will collapse in the streets, in their homes and across their false pews in their disingenuous places of worship.'

The Amori, he thought, *will . . . finally . . . win.*

Chapter 2

Joe Mason bobbed and weaved before the heavy leather punching bag, then jabbed with a powerful left, rocking it to the right. It felt good tonight. The rhythm in his head, the rock and the roll of the bag, the measured shuffle of his feet. Even the smells were right – stinging antiseptic mixed with fresh sweat, old sweat and blood.

It was all here tonight in the boxing gym, the place he'd frequented for half his life and the only place where he could escape the unrelenting terrors that fought to engulf him.

Those who could, trained under the bright lights; and the old men who couldn't sat around watching, their rheumy eyes bright with memories of younger, fitter days.

Mason absorbed the atmosphere. Real life receded. These nights came around once, maybe twice a year.

It was late, almost closing time. Mason dropped a shoulder and pummelled the bag once more as the thought struck him that only those who led broken lives would train and sweat at this time, in this place. And there were many here.

He stepped away from the bag, taking a breath. The gym resounded with the grunting of men and women, the pounding of gloves on pads and bags. Mason bent down to pick up a towel and wipe the sweat from his face as he scanned the place.

He felt comfortable here. As a skinny youth, he'd turned to boxing to help deal with the bullies. Now, it served as an outlet and a way to numb the mind. He nodded at Washington, the old pro who ran this place, and gave the bag one last punch before removing his gloves.

There were no changing rooms here, no showers. Lockers lined the walls. Mason crossed the floor to his and caught a reflection of himself in the scratched, worn mirror that clung precariously to the door. He was wiry rather than bulky; strong, but not obviously so. Short blond hair offset piercing blue eyes, and an unlined, youngish-looking face didn't reveal the hell he'd been through, which made Mason a man who was often underestimated.

He opened the door just as his phone rang, surprising him. Without checking the screen, he answered the call. 'Yeah?'

'It's me.'

'Patricia? Have you seen the bloody time?'

'It's close to midnight, Mason, and I know I didn't wake you.'

'You still at work?'

'Why else would I be calling you at this ridiculous hour?'

A good point. Patricia Wilde was his boss.

'All right, Patricia.' Mason grabbed his bag, slammed closed his locker with a metallic clang and headed for the exit. 'What's so important?'

'New job.' She got straight to the point. 'And it's got your name written all over it.'

Mason paused with his hand on the door handle. 'What does that mean?'

'Unique. Engaging. Away from the UK but no war zones. Right?'

That was the ideal scenario he'd presented Patricia's private security company with when he'd agreed to work for them. 'Sounds great.'

'It's seven days' work, but you need to be in Rome by morning.'

Mason cleared his throat. 'You mean *this* morning? The morning that starts in about twenty minutes?'

'Yeah, that's the one. Is it a problem?' Patricia's tone was amused.

Mason totted up the minutes it would take him to drive home, shower, pack and get to a London airport. 'No, shouldn't be a problem. You're gonna have to talk to me while I get ready though.'

'Okay, as long as you don't take me into the shower. The last guy I brought up to speed in the shower slipped and broke his ankle.'

Outside, Mason felt the night air strike his face, laced with sleet. The cold was refreshing and welcome, the rain not so much. A single bare light shone across the parking area, illuminating a flurry of hail, whipped up by a rising wind. Mason hurried over to his car.

'Simple gig,' Patricia was saying. 'You're accompanying a Professor Pierce Rusk and his daughter, Sally. The guy's wealthy, the daughter born with the proverbial silver spoon. Anyway, she rebelled, fell in with some wrong 'uns, and disappeared off the grid for a while. She's back now, but Rusk doesn't take chances. Especially with this.'

Mason started the car. 'With this?'

'He's been granted access to the Vatican Apostolic Archive. Apparently, he's well respected among cardinals and regularly gets this kind of access. For security reasons they always confirm last minute though, which is why you're against the clock.'

Mason waited for his phone to mate with the car's Bluetooth system as he pulled onto a rainswept London street and then said, 'I go with them?'

'Hey,' Patricia said. 'You work for one of the most respected private security firms in the UK. Of course you go with them. Both Rusk and I are counting on you,' she added.

'Ah, I see. Sounds like a tame gig. You need me to be at my best?'

Patricia didn't answer immediately. After a minute, she said: 'Is your head in the game, Mason?'

'You tell me.' Mason put up a solid front. 'I've been working for you for over eighteen months now, which makes it two and a half years since I left the Army, since Zack and Harry died on my watch. By making me take this job you forced me through a wall of guilt, Patricia. What do you think?'

'I think you're still counting the days. The hours since Mosul. Maybe you need more time.' She hesitated.

Mason sighed. 'Protection. That's what I do now. It helps me cope. So let me protect.'

'I know that's what you *think* you need,' Patricia said. 'But it hasn't worked out well so far, Joe.'

'You mean Hannah? The split was mutual. We're still friends.'

'I don't mean your wife, Joe, I mean since *Mosul*.'

Mason gripped the steering wheel until his knuckles turned white and the wet streets to both sides receded. He was suddenly alone in London, in the south of England, in the world, and trying, desperately, to hold on.

Patricia's voice brought him back. 'Are you still there, Joe?'

It was a profound, poignant question, and one she clearly didn't intend to have a double meaning.

'Joe?'

'Yeah,' he said, stopping for traffic lights that illuminated his windscreen with twin red smears. 'I'm right here. Is there anything else?'

Patricia gave him the name of Rusk's Rome hotel and a meeting place. She promised to email the Rusks' background information across, so he could better plan his protection detail.

10

By the time Mason had pulled up and parked outside his house, entered and locked the front door and was dragging his old, durable backpack out from under the bed, Patricia was winding up.

Mason sensed she wasn't quite finished though. 'You done? I really need that shower.'

'All done. Just collect Banks from the Heathrow Hilton by eight a.m. and you're good to go.'

Mason froze. 'Wait! What? Who?'

'Oh, didn't I mention?' Patricia sounded apologetic, though Mason knew the game she was playing. 'The client asked for a double guard. Male and female. Roxy Banks will be going with you.'

'Now wait a minute—'

'Hey, she's fine. She's good. I know she's got a reputation, but—'

'I don't give a damn about her reputation. I work alone.'

'Not this time, Joe,' Patricia said with an air of finality. 'The client is like the customer. Always right.'

'The client's usually an idiot,' Mason said, irritated. 'Is there no way around this?'

'Two guards, one female, and Banks is all that's available at short notice. I sent her to the Hilton before I called you, so she knows you're coming.' Patricia reeled off a room number.

'Roxy Banks is a loose cannon.' Mason changed tack, trying to find a way around the issue.

'She's a legend,' Patricia countered. 'They whisper about her in the office. Nobody knows the truth of what she was and what happened to her. And I know you don't trust reputation, good or bad. You'd rather trust your own abilities.'

Mason closed his eyes, thinking she couldn't be further from the truth.

'And if she . . . ?'

'That's my problem, not yours. Don't listen to office gossip, Mason. Roxy hasn't touched a drop in years. At least, so she tells me. You two will make the perfect team.'

Mason, unconvinced, ended the call. The dim green glow of the bedside clock told him it was 0.21 a.m. and the bed looked inviting. Maybe it was the rain lashing at the window. Maybe it was the comedown after hours of hard work at the gym. Mason set his alarm for 5.00 a.m., hoping the nightmare memories wouldn't come crawling out of the dark cave where the physical exertion had chased them.

His hope was short-lived.

Mason sat with his head in his hands for an hour before dragging himself off the bed and running the shower until it was scalding hot. After that, he waited to roll out, sitting with all the lights blazing to keep the darkness at bay.

You trust your own abilities, Patricia had said.

Not for a long time, he thought, but he would never tell her so.

Chapter 3

Three months passed before they met surrounded by the sparkling blue waters of the Indian Ocean. Marduk was choppered in as befitted his regal standing, the helicopter landing with a soft touch on the superyacht's helipad.

Once cold meats, salad and drinks had been served in an opulent stateroom, Marduk sat back, adjusted his jacket and faced Hassell, Mac and the two killers, Ash and Base.

'Who's in command?' he asked.

'I'm leading the operation.' Hassell sat forward.

'They'll follow your every direction?'

Hassell nodded. 'They will.'

'You've had your three months. I trust you're ready?'

'As much as we can be.' Hassell looked unhappy. 'It's just not long enough to plan the perfect crime.' He hesitated. 'Is Nina joining us today?'

'I will apprise my daughter of what's required of her. Do not worry. And let's be clear: I do not care who you hurt, who you kill or what you have to blow up.' Marduk made a dramatic gesture with both his arms. 'The book is all that matters.'

'But I do,' Hassell said. 'My job is to make it look like we were never there. To leave no clues. And no killing.'

'So what are these two for?' Marduk indicated Ash and Base.

'Purely muscle,' Hassell said. 'Gido insisted we bring them along.'

Marduk narrowed his eyes, wondering how well Hassell knew his boss. The Gido Marduk knew would happily agree to a no-killing policy whilst arming Ash and Base with AKs, rocket launchers and poison gas on the side.

'Tell me,' he said.

Hassell nodded at Mac. 'He's done the lion's share. I'll let him explain.'

'Smoke and mirrors.' Mac spoke quickly as if itching to wrap this up and get the hell off the ship. 'That's the trick. I started with multiple vector attacks, trying to gain access to their system. It's well guarded, but human stupidity always gives hackers an edge. They always say their system's foolproof.' Mac grinned. 'But I'm no fool.'

Marduk smiled despite himself. 'Go on.'

'I bombarded them with emails, malicious files and cookies to compromise their data systems. After that, you mine that data for valuable information. Passwords, user-names, that kind of thing. It's not about getting access, it's about getting *undisclosed* access without detection. The attacks are methodical and take a long time to fully implement. It's like an army testing a castle's vulnerabilities with a small contingent of men, night after night for a year, instead of a full-on bloodcurdling assault. Anyway, I breached the system in the second month. After that, I used my own malware programme to mine the security data and gain access to their cameras, their alarms and sensors.'

'I thought the Vatican would be harder to crack,' Marduk said.

'Oh, let's be clear. I'm giving you the dumbed-down version.' Mac stared around the stateroom wide-eyed, as if troubled by the lavish trappings, the golden mirrors, sparkling chandeliers and expensive paintings lining the oak-panelled walls. 'But their firewalls are weeks out of date.'

'Weeks?' Marduk frowned. 'That doesn't sound too bad.'

'In the cyberworld a week is worth a year when a world-class hacker has his claws into you. You see, a computer receives data packets from millions of emails. In an encrypted injection attack, I can gain backdoor access by a method you probably know as phishing.'

'The Vatican employs no cyber-security team to ward against this?' Marduk asked.

'Sure they do. But they're not in my league.'

Hassell spoke up. 'Mac has access to their security,' he said. 'He can lock them out both digitally and physically. That was the hard part. I've engineered the rest of the smoke-and-mirrors attack, giving their security teams plenty to think about when the moment comes.'

'Their sensors? Pressure pads? Alarms?' Marduk recalled everything he knew from books and television.

'All hooked up to their system,' Mac said. 'And ours to manipulate.'

'And that's an issue,' Hassell put in. 'We haven't had time to test and find out if they're employing anything *old*. Some outmoded security device that *isn't* hooked up. It can happen, especially in old buildings.'

Marduk thought about the book and the delicious, deadly secrets it held. 'Nothing can go wrong,' he said.

Hassell stared at him. 'Then give me three more months so that I can arrange a closer look, possibly even an on-site check.'

Marduk and the Amori had waited long enough. Now that the moment was at hand, he was almost salivating with anticipation. 'I won't give you three more *days*. Do you have the best equipment?'

Hassell sighed and sat back. 'Laser cutters. Military grade

glowsticks. Nina will even have a carbon bodysuit with mask. Gido enjoyed spending your money.'

'Then he'd better be worth it,' Marduk said. 'And so had you.'

'We are the best,' Hassell said. 'But we can only work with the time we're given.'

Marduk eyed them all. The nervous Mac, who was probably used to nothing more luxurious than his mother's basement. The killers, with their scarred hands and faces and unreadable expressions. And finally Hassell, the man Gido had put in charge, confident but wary, tough-talking but weak in vision. Of course, he couldn't hope to understand the colossal importance of the book and what it meant to the Amori.

'When?' he said.

'In two days,' Hassell said. 'If luck is on our side, we'll breach the Vatican secret archives in two days.'

Chapter 4

Mason was late. He strode across the hotel's spacious, airy lobby, its polished floor awash with bright light. The facade to his right was a wall of windows against which a stormy darkness pressed. He settled the backpack across his shoulders as he reached the lifts and called Roxy's room for the third time in fifteen minutes.

Still no answer.

Mason cursed under his breath. They hadn't reached the plane yet and she was already causing complications. He stepped into the lift and jabbed the button for the fifth floor, blinking, his eyes adjusting to the artificial brightness after leaving the dim, pre-dawn murk of the world outside.

A long, bland corridor greeted him outside the lift, the same bloody corridor that ran thousands of miles along a hundred other hotels all over the world. He'd seen too many of them. Two minutes later, he stopped outside Roxy's door and decided to give her an uncompromising double whammy.

He knocked loudly at the same time as calling her number.

And waited.

A minute later, cursing, he tried again. Then he checked his watch. He was running out of options. Maybe he could leave her behind. Gain a couple of days before she . . .

Something smashed inside the room. Mason came alert in an instant. First, he checked left and right along the passageway and then kicked the lock.

At first, the heavy door didn't budge, but it made a crunching sound on his third attempt.

Mason used his shoulder to force his way in, alert for whatever was happening on the other side. The door slammed back against a wall and rebounded. Mason ran inside.

The room's lights were blazing, illuminating a possibly naked Roxy Banks sitting up in bed, wrapped in a white sheet, holding the corner with one hand and a military knife in the other. It was an odd contrast, a surreal scene.

Roxy was raven-haired and American, a thirty-three-year-old, six-foot-two, stunning fusion of grace and muscle. She moved to a sitting position, holding the knife's blade between finger and thumb.

'The only reason you're still alive is because I know your face,' she said, her American accent thickened by sleep and a bad hangover.

'I called you,' he said. 'You're late. If I wasn't a team player, I'd have left you behind.'

As he stepped forward, he smelled the thick perfume of rum surrounding her. 'Is that you?' Mason tried not to breathe in the fumes. 'Did you spill a whole bottle in here?'

Roxy tried not to squint. 'I soak my sheets in rum,' she said. 'It helps me sleep.'

Mason could tell she wasn't joking – not just by the smell, but by the grave look on her face. 'Get dressed,' he said.

'You wanna know what happened to the last man who told me what to do?'

Mason sighed and eyed the knife. 'Look,' he said. 'We're flying to Rome in about . . . eighty minutes. You're lucky I'm a—'

'Yeah, yeah, a team player,' Roxy said caustically. 'I feel blessed.'

Mason saw only a hard facade in her black eyes, in the severe set of her face. Deliberately, he turned his back on her.

'Apologies,' he said. 'Now, either put me out of my misery or, *please*, get dressed.'

There was movement from the bed. Mason half-winced, not expecting a knife in the back but not convinced he was entirely safe.

'Your misery, eh?' Roxy said, starting to pull clothes on. 'I've heard of you, Joe Mason. Office gossip. Some of the women think you're cool. Me? I don't go for scrawny, babyface boys. I want a man who looks like he's lived, loved and lost.'

Mason had been underestimated before, many times. He stayed quiet.

'What's your misery, Joe Mason?'

He held back a retort, checking the time. They had seventy-five minutes to make the plane. Roxy walked across his eyeline, making for the door, fully dressed in black jeans and a white T-shirt and carrying her backpack. Mason made to follow her.

She turned. 'Don't listen when the Devil's calling,' she said. 'Words I try to live by. You know what I mean?'

'You're referring to the words in our heads,' he said. 'Our inner demons.'

'That's right, Babyface. Now, are you coming? Because, apparently, according to my unusual wake-up call, we're late.'

Mason followed her out of the room.

It was a short flight. Roxy slept the entire way. Mason used the time to go over their mission. The wealthy Professor Rusk required protection for himself and his daughter during their seven-day trip to Rome, most of which would be spent inside the Vatican Apostolic Archive – their secret archives. A short, no-nonsense email furnished him with snippets of background information on both Rusk and his daughter, the stand-out facts being that the Professor was a world-renowned historian and Sally a county champion fell runner. Mason was more impressed by the latter. From what he knew, fell running involved negotiating long, steep and unmarked courses and featured arduous descents.

Mason had received a message from Patricia Wilde, assuring him all four of them had been granted access. He had been worrying that he and Roxy might have to wait in some far-flung vestibule while Rusk and his daughter disappeared underground. There was only one way to protect a client, in his opinion, and that was eyes-on, twenty-four-seven. And his only impetus these days came when he was actively protecting clients.

He fired off a quick message to Patricia, questioning the Vatican's apparently relaxed acceptance of the two body-guards. He was worried that the Vatican might change its mind when the four of them turned up. He finished off with the words: *If I can't protect them unconditionally, I won't protect them at all.*

Patricia soon returned his query, stating that the professor *had his feet firmly under the papal altar.* Rusk was well liked at the Vatican and was engaged on an ongoing body of work.

Nice easy money and a week in Rome, Patricia signed off.

Mason sighed, studying the people around him. The plane was packed with men and women in business suits, with families, with excited day-trippers. Mason sat in an aisle seat, Roxy to his left.

The American looked serious even in her sleep, the hard lines of her face never relaxing. Mason wondered briefly what manner of creature haunted her dreams. What horrible experience stopped her from moving on? He knew very little of her past. Nobody did, except perhaps Patricia Wilde.

At that moment, she woke and stared straight at him. 'That's twice,' she said. 'And it's still morning. You gonna keep on waking me up?'

Mason spread his arms.

'I see what's behind those pretty blue eyes,' she said. 'You're thinking – this loudmouth American, this loose cannon, is she gonna get me killed?'

Mason held her stare and ignored several fleeting glances of concern from nearby passengers. 'I like the fact that you speak your mind. But we're a team and we need to act like one. Hey,' he shrugged, 'it's just seven days babysitting in Italy. What could possibly go wrong?'

Roxy winced. 'Well, hearing you say that means you're not superstitious. Which I like. And don't worry; if required, I'll back you up despite the rumours to the contrary.'

Mason nodded, accepting her assertion. 'They're our responsibility from the moment we meet them,' he said.

Roxy nodded back. 'You normally work alone, I'm guessing?'

Mason gave her a slight smile. 'Does it show? The truth is, I get along with people, the *right* people, but when I took this job I vowed to keep moving forward. Never stand still.' He repeated it like a mantra. 'Stay busy.'

But she isn't like that, he thought. Roxy was right there, large as life, a force of nature and as confrontational as anyone he'd known, but at the same time he could tell she was lost. Roxy was searching for something.

'Plane's descending,' she said, looking up, feeling the slight shift before he did.

Mason was ex-British Army, a veteran of countless flights, and took that awareness as a good sign. He settled back into his seat.

Either way, he imagined, with Roxy along, the next few days should be interesting.

Chapter 5

Rome, a city sometimes defined as the capital of two states, was one of the oldest continuously occupied cities in Europe. Mason knew that because, since he was about to meet two archaeological stalwarts, he'd taken the initiative to bone up while on the plane. But by the time he stepped out of Leonardo da Vinci Airport just after 11.30 that morning, the glacial snap of an icy February squall had become the full focus of his attention.

'Residenza Paolo VI,' Mason told the taxi driver, knowing the journey should take about thirty minutes in normal traffic. 'And please put your foot down. We're late.'

Roxy climbed in the other side, shivering in her T-shirt. She dragged the backpack in and placed it on her knees. 'The plane was late,' she amended. 'Not us.'

Mason didn't answer, revelling in the hot blast from the car's heating system. He watched the streets unwind as they made their way towards the Vatican, the movements of locals and tourists, the hard frosts coating every pavement and window, the heavy skies like molten lead hanging with dire warning over the bustling city below.

Thousands of starlings created dynamic sculptures in the air, clouds of birds flinging themselves back and forth in perfect sync, which only made their driver hiss and complain at the mess they made.

Thirty minutes later, they were outside once more, staring down the same cold currents of air and hurrying towards the lobby of the Residenza Paolo VI, a four-storey boutique hotel on the edge of St Peter's Square. Mason got within three metres of the front door and a reprieve from the cold before it was opened by a tall, stern-looking man with a bushy beard.

'Watchtower?' he asked by way of greeting.

'Yes, sir. I'm—'

'You're late,' the man said in a voice markedly colder than the weather. 'You're Mason and Banks, I know. We're Rusk and Rusk. Shall we go?'

Mason had wanted to spend at least ten minutes talking, trying to get a feel for his clients' wants and needs, and where exactly they might feel crowded by his and Roxy's presence. But to the professor the plane's late arrival was an imposition, and Mason didn't want to start their relationship on the wrong foot. Client harmony was as important as anything else.

'Let's walk and talk,' he suggested, standing aside so that the professor and his daughter could pass.

'Best be quick,' Rusk grunted. 'We're minutes away.'

'They do coffee?' Roxy asked. 'The Vatican?'

Rusk blinked at her as if she were an alien. His daughter let out a snort of laughter. 'I bloody well hope so,' she said, holding out a hand. 'I couldn't work an hour with this old fruit-and-nut bar without it. Hi, I'm Sally.'

First Roxy and then Mason adjusted their backpacks and shook her hand. Sally was a five-foot-five brunette. At twenty-eight, she had deep worry lines on her otherwise smooth face that Mason wouldn't have associated with a wealthy professor's daughter. In addition, faint dark-blue tips to her shoulder-length hair displayed a hint of rebelliousness.

'Great to meet you,' he said. 'We'll discuss the security setup later.'

'He's trying to assert his authority.' Sally nodded at her father's back. 'As a professor, a teacher and a mentor it's something he's had to do all his life.' She sighed and nodded at Roxy. 'Let's go get that coffee, shall we?'

They crossed St Peter's Square, making an unwavering beeline for the Basilica. They passed the unmarked Egyptian obelisk, the centre of the square, to the right. Sally noticed Mason scanning its impressive forty-one-metre height.

'The only obelisk in Rome never to have been toppled since ancient times,' she said. 'All the way from Egypt to Alexandria and the Circus of Nero. The ancient gilt ball on top was once thought to contain the ashes of Julius Caesar. But all they found inside was dust.'

Mason nodded as Roxy licked her lips and continued to talk about coffee. Considering her arms were still exposed to the raw weather, Mason thought she did well to keep her teeth from chattering.

The square was broad and open to the elements. Incessant, hungry winds scoured its dark paving. Tourists stared at Roxy as if she were mad, or very brave.

Mason studied the huge Doric colonnades to either side, four columns deep around the square, the embracing arms of the Church designed by Bernini in the seventeenth century. They walked into them, the main facade and dome of St Peter's Basilica becoming more detailed as they approached.

Mason's judgement told him to stop Rusk, to slow the man's stride and lay down the strict protocol of the security detail. Everything he'd been taught told him it was the right thing to do, but Rusk's insistence on haste and the close proximity of the well-protected basilica held him back.

A constant and thorough examination of their surroundings, and of the people milling around the square, gave him assurance and confidence. A cursory assessment of Roxy's attention to the scene also put his mind at rest.

'All good.' She'd noticed his glance.

Mason nodded. They would save the rules for later discussion. Yes, Rusk might flail and flap at being told what to do of an evening. Some clients performed for attention, others did it because they felt they should, but if Rusk wanted protection, he would have to deal with the restrictions it entailed.

St Peter's Basilica's front elevation loomed over them, giving Mason a faint, ominous chill that had nothing to do with the weather. This sanctuary, this ancient temple, was the man-made embodiment of an age-old, sacred and holy trust. Did its current inhabitants possess the conviction inherent in its long-standing foundations? Mason assumed that they did.

Rusk veered to the right, looking back and giving them a vague wave. 'Did you think we'd enter through the front door?' He shook his head.

Mason cursed silently. He was responsible for the guy's safety. Frivolous behaviour should be off the agenda. What was Rusk scared of anyway to need protection? His daughter's old acquaintances?

To the right, a noisy queue bent towards the entrance to the basilica. Rusk made his way through it, then passed between the massive stone columns that defined the right-hand side of the piazza.

Mason remembered that the tiny state of Vatican City lay in a group of jumbled buildings to the left of the cruciform church. Rusk led them that way, stopping before a guard wearing a blue doublet and beret.

'The Swiss Guard,' Roxy said. 'I thought these guys were famous for wearing something a bit more colourful.'

'Sworn to protect the Holy See.' Sally had overheard Roxy's words and replied in what Mason was starting to assume was her normal casual fashion. 'The blue, yellow, red and orange uniform has a Renaissance look which is in keeping with the pontifical banner, but is kept for ceremonial occasions.'

Rusk presented some credentials. The Swiss Guard used a shoulder-mounted communications system to speak to some higher power.

Less than two minutes later, a man in flowing robes approached them, and Mason realised that Rusk had serious juice. It wasn't every day a cardinal came out to greet a professor and his security team.

'Vallini,' the man said by way of introduction before smiling at the professor. 'Pierce,' he said. 'It is good to see you again.'

For the first time, Mason saw Rusk smile. It was genuine, and transformed his entire face.

Vallini smiled back, his own careworn features creasing into a genuine beam of pleasure. He spoke with compassion and sincerity, but his walk was careful and slow, as if he were dealing with hidden health issues or a problem of balance.

Mason kept his eyes on their surroundings for the most part as the men exchanged their brief but warm greeting. He expected to see nothing untoward and got his wish.

'Cardinal Vallini is an administrator of the archives,' Sally told them. 'My father and he have met many times.'

'Your father carries out a lot of research here?' Mason asked. 'Some kind of special access for study, is it?'

Sally nodded. 'Researchers are granted access to see the true face of the Church through documents which provide the Holy See with over one thousand years of memories. Documents that cover more than fifty miles. Archivist training is required to handle these rare and fragile papers. And all this is allowed whilst we stand over the bones of the apostle Peter.'

Mason nodded, knowing she was referring to the tomb, found at the west end of a complex of mausoleums, that was said to contain the bones of the first vicar of Christ.

He waited whilst Rusk showed Vallini the appropriate documentation for his visit – something required even between friends – and then followed the pair inside. He and Roxy waited for a while in a warm, carpeted corridor, stamping the cold from their feet, while Vallini facilitated their entry.

'They will ask you to place all personal items in a locker outside the main research area,' Sally forewarned them. 'We are allowed a laptop and a digital camera. You will also be given white gloves in case, for whatever reason, you handle any of the documents. It's tightly controlled down there, as you can imagine.'

'You're allowed to just wander around?' Roxy asked. 'Like in a library?'

Sally shook her head. 'No, not at all. You're made to submit a written request for materials days before you arrive. Those materials are then brought to your table downstairs.'

'But these are *secret* archives,' Roxy said with half a smile. 'How do you know what to request?'

Sally didn't answer, which prompted a speculative look between Mason and Roxy. In any case, it wasn't their business. Now that they were here, inside Vatican City, Mason knew their presence wasn't really necessary. Still, this was the job, and passing it in the confines of the Vatican archive was inestimably easier than trudging through a war zone.

The last thought sobered him. Over two years had passed since Mosul, but the passage of time hadn't smoothed the sharp, jagged edges of that dreadful memory one bit.

Thirty minutes later, Vallini led them down a short flight of stone steps. The walls were lined with works of art and Mason was conscious of passing beneath the ageless gazes of saints, martyrs and the Madonna. They emerged onto a landing of sorts and walked eight feet before stopping in front of a lift. To the right of the nondescript metal door, a single white button glowed.

'It's pretty well protected,' Mason said as the group stood in silence. 'This place.'

'Regrettably, it must be,' Vallini responded, his voice tinged with the sadness of a man who has seen the worst in people. 'Explosives, chemicals, weapons, infections . . . it has all been tried. We live in an age where religious repudiation manifests in violence. *The exercise of justice is joy for the righteous, but is terror to the workers of iniquity.* Have you read your Bible, Mr . . . ?'

'Mason. And no. But I have seen terror first-hand.'

Vallini nodded as the lift came to a halt and the doors opened. 'As have I, Mr Mason, as have I, although I suspect not in the same context.'

The lift car descended several floors, discharging them into a glass-walled vestibule where two guards waited.

Mason's fleeting impression of the archives beyond the vestibule was of a random but neat collection of long aisles formed by high racks of shelving, all lit by stark white striplights. An untold number of manuscripts filled the shelves and stood in piles around the floor.

Vallini caught his attention and asked them to stow any valuables and their backpacks in specially selected lockers. Then he showed Professor Rusk to a side room where a rectangular desk sat, its surface dotted with several note-pads, pens and two reading lamps. A cart loaded with documents stood to one side.

On seeing the pile, Mason made a face, assuming a long day lay ahead.

Roxy must have had similar thoughts for she leaned in and whispered, 'Did we bring food?'

Mason's stomach grumbled.

Chapter 6

Mason, tired of standing, plonked himself into a chair. The professors, young and old, were engrossed in their research, sifting through fragile documents and scribbling whole essays in their notepads, occasionally making use of their digital camera.

The two Guardsmen stationed outside the room didn't bother them, and the view beyond of tedious, unending rows and rows of documents had long since grown old.

At one point, Roxy, already seated, leaned over to whisper in Mason's ear, 'I'm starving. You think there's a McDonald's down here?'

Mason winced. 'I think the very thought is blasphemy, and you should keep your bloody voice down.'

'You British.' Roxy laughed. 'So uptight.'

'You Americans,' he hit back. 'So . . . oblivious.'

'Oblivious in the right ways,' she replied thoughtfully. 'This is good. New memories. A new life.'

'Distraction?' Mason thought about the rum-soaked sheets.

'Not distraction,' Roxy said. 'Rebirth.'

'But the Devil still calls,' he said in reference to her earlier statement.

'Every damn night,' Roxy said. 'We have this . . . appointment I can't shake.'

'I'm sorry,' Mason said, lowering his head.

'What about you?' she asked, eyeing him from under her raven locks. 'What keeps you awake at night?'

Death, was his immediate thought. *Blood. Guilt. Shame.* 'The thought that I may lose a client,' he said. 'Which is why, once we're out of here, we need to lay down some ground rules with our slightly naïve professors.'

Sally, overhearing his last comment, looked up and smiled, the mutinous blue tips of her hair belying the academic presence she and her father radiated as they discussed their research.

Mason saw a standoffishness in Sally when she was addressed by her father, a reserved demeanour more suited to an assistant than to a family member. He wondered what had transpired between them in the past.

The hours wore on.

Mason checked his watch at four, then five and then six, unable to fathom why the Rusks weren't craving any form of sustenance. Roxy tried to nudge their appetite to life, talking about local pastries and various spaghetti dishes and, naturally, pizza, but both Rusks were fully absorbed in their research.

Mason wondered if there was a specific closing time, but decided the professor accrued more privileges than your average scholar in that regard.

Roxy was growing more miserable as the day wore on. 'They do know we're here for seven days, right? I thought this job sounded too good to be true.'

'You'd rather be protecting a politician? A general? A movie star?'

Roxy turned bored eyes on him. 'At least the distractions would pass the day. It's not like they actually need us down here.'

Mason was inclined to agree. There were only so many times you could study a tapestry, a defunct marble fountain and a frieze. Only so many times you could walk a room 25 feet by 15 and stare out of its internal glass windows at two doubleted Guards.

'The client is . . .'

'Always right?' Roxy finished. 'Don't tell me you believe that bullshit Patricia spouts?'

Mason didn't. He nodded in apology. Maybe it was time to address the professor. He checked his watch once more and noted that it was past 7 p.m.

'I'm sorry.' Sally looked up and saw his face. 'This is taking longer than either of us expected. We're starting to think the information we need is in the restricted archives.'

'Isn't *this* the secret archive?' Roxy said. 'The true face of the Church, the cardinal said.'

'Yes, but there are still restricted archives,' Pierce Rusk said. 'Some of the documents they possess would alter history, and not in a good way. And then there are those we're better off not knowing about.' He clammed up, as if realising he'd spoken out of turn in the guestroom of a benevolent landlord.

Sally shook her head at her father's awkwardness. 'He doesn't get out much,' she said.

Mason turned away as Rusk threw his daughter a pained look; he didn't want to get in the middle of their conflict. Then he noticed that both Guards were leaving their posts, walking very slowly.

'Hey,' he said. 'What's going on?' The movement was more noticeable because neither Guard had shifted more than a muscle all day.

'Give the guys a break,' Roxy sighed. 'They're probably going for a—'

'Together?' Mason raised an eyebrow.

With surprising swiftness, Professor Rusk slid out of his chair and crossed the room to rap on the glass. One of the Guards turned with a frown.

31

'What are you doing?' Rusk held up both arms with palms outstretched.

If Mason had learned anything in thirteen years with the armed forces, it was how to spot genuine emotion. Whatever had caused the Guards to move away, it had them rattled. One of the men was speaking urgently into his shoulder mic.

'Come away from the window,' Mason said, jumping to his feet, and sensing Roxy at his side.

Sally was staring at her father as if he'd gone mad. 'Father,' she said. 'I really think—'

'They stay put,' her father said. 'Usually. I've never seen . . . Wait, what's that?'

Beyond the glass, Mason saw the Guards come to an abrupt halt along the nearest narrow aisle. The harsh strip-lighting illuminated high racks of shelving which stretched as far as the eye could see. Even squinting, he couldn't see the far end. Rusk's attention had been grabbed by a figure.

'What's that . . . ?'

'Don't worry,' Sally said. 'It's another Guard.'

'No . . .' Rusk frowned and bit his lip in speculation. 'Whoever it is, they're coming up all the way from the far end. They probably set off an alarm which they knew would alert the Guards. There's only one item stored down there, and nobody should be anywhere near—'

The Guards shouted a challenge.

Mason saw the source of their agitation. The approaching figure was dressed all in black and wore a black mask.

One of the Guardsmen yelled into his shoulder mic, while the other strode forward and reached for a weapon.

Mason wondered for one moment what the professor meant by *only one item stored down there,* and then the gunshot rang out.

Mason acted instantly. The sound was hideous, stoking a conflagration of slumbering nightmares. He grabbed the professor and bore him to the ground. Roxy manhandled Sally out of the way.

The window shattered as bullets smashed into it. Mason raised his head a fraction to see the Guardsman with the gun slumped on the floor, blood pooling towards the metal racks.

Reaching for a weapon, he remembered he didn't have one. Unfortunately, Patricia's security firm wasn't yet one of the chosen few that had firearms agreements with the Italian authorities.

Surely somebody had heard the shots. But right now, that didn't matter. It could be several minutes before help arrived.

The second Guardsman abandoned his shoulder mic and reached for his own gun. Mason winced, knowing he was way too slow.

The black-clad figure was running up the aisle, gun held out in front, and now fired again. Three bullets tore into the second Guard.

Mason glanced at Roxy. In here, there was no protection. No way of defending themselves. The small room was a death trap.

'Watch them,' he said.

Sliding across the wooden floor, he reached the shattered window and glanced over the frame.

A bullet hit what was left of the timber surround, splintering it. A wooden shard drew blood from Mason's right cheek. He wondered if he'd be able to reach the nearest Guard and grab his weapon.

Touch and go. And you'd be exposed the minute you stepped out of here.

Mason readied himself, knowing that he'd have to do something, but at that moment Professor Rusk leapt up from his huddle in a surprising burst of energy.

Expecting a rant about the madness of firing weapons

33

inside the Vatican, about exchanging gunfire over the bones of St Peter himself, Mason raised his arms and turned Rusk's way, trying to calm him.

But Rusk ran straight for the door.

Mason cursed and dived for the man's legs. Sally screamed and tried to run after her father. Roxy knocked her to the ground.

Bullets smashed through the wooden door of their room, missing the professor's head by inches before destroying an alabaster statue mounted on the far wall.

Rusk tore open the door. 'You can't have it!' he screamed.

Mason put his shock at Rusk's actions aside and leapt at the man.

Using his wiry strength, he grabbed Rusk by the waist and wrenched him aside. Holding Rusk like that, he felt the bullets slam into the man's chest and stomach, both above and below Mason's own arm. Rusk cried out, his body driven back and over Mason, crashing to the floor.

Which left Mason exposed, in the firing line. He crouched in the doorway, expecting to see the shooter, but saw only the Swiss Guards lying prone, unmoving, both surrounded by growing pools of blood. The black-clad figure was bolting back down the aisle from which it had appeared, running away from him.

Escaping? Or raiding? Seeing no further threats, the person had chosen to flee.

Mason had been under fire many times. Thinking fast, he saw just one option. He couldn't let the killer escape. Roxy could take care of Sally.

The killer ran and glanced back, and Mason flew to the left, entering an aisle parallel to the one where the dead Guards lay, giving the killer something else to think about rather than the people back in the research room.

Behind him, Sally Rusk screamed.

Chapter 7

Mason figured he had the opportunity to put on some speed.

The killer was running, no longer aggressive; a good thing since it told Mason reinforcements were on the way. But that was conjecture, not something Mason could rely on. The only way forward was to nullify the shooter.

Mason ran down the aisle, staying low. His view was restricted by the endless shelves filled with books and manuscripts, and he could see only a little, through intermittent gaps.

At last he found a break between racks of shelving. He took the chance to slow and peer through into the killer's aisle. He glanced back towards the office as Sally's screams grew in volume. He could see Rusk's lower torso – unmoving.

Down the other end, the black-clad intruder was on one knee, gun pointed, taking aim at him.

Mason was still at least thirty steps away when the gun fired.

Bullets struck sparks off metal shelving and thudded into thick manuscripts as Mason flung himself backward into cover. Pausing for a three-second count, he dropped to his stomach and shuffled back to the aisle.

The shooter was gone.

Cursing, Mason was about to run and grab one of the dead Guards' guns when Roxy emerged from the far office at full speed. Mason blinked twice to see that she was chasing Sally.

What now . . . ?

The pair raced up the aisle, bypassing the dead Guards, where Roxy stooped to check pulses and collect a gun. They stopped just in front of Mason, who stayed on constant lookout for the killer.

Sally's hands were covered in her father's blood. Droplets fell to the floor. Roxy shook her head. 'The Guards are dead,' she said matter-of-factly. 'The professor went almost instantly.'

Mason couldn't console Sally and chase a killer at the same time.

Sally's face was grief-stricken and agonised sobs were wrenched from her throat. 'What did you do?' she kept saying, looking back to where her father lay. 'What did you do?'

'Do we stop this?' Mason said.

'Depends what *this* is,' Roxy said.

She was right.

Mason reached out a hand towards Sally. 'Why did your father do that? Why did he confront the killer that way?'

Roxy was standing close to Mason's shoulder. 'They just called the office phone,' she said quietly. 'The Swiss Guard, cardinals, whatever. They called us. Said they can't get down to help us. Someone's locked them out. Disabled the elevator. Booby-trapped the staircases. They told us to wait there.'

'We're okay.' Mason pointed at the ceiling. 'CCTV will show what happened.'

Sally gestured angrily. 'No, that means the person responsible for killing my father will escape.'

Mason scanned the aisle again, wary of the black-clad figure's return. 'Whoever did this,' he said, 'is highly capable.

Professionals at the top of their game. The Vatican . . .' He sighed. 'Is heavily guarded.' It felt like an understatement.

'Clearly, they didn't come in through any of the floors above,' Roxy said.

'Sally,' Mason said, trying to grab her attention. 'What was your father trying to protect?'

His sense of prudence was prickled by guilt. There was no blame here, but he couldn't help but see the extent of his failure laid out in that office, framed in blood. He blinked hard to drive old shame back into the shadows.

Roxy touched his back. 'There was no foreseeing this.'

Mason saw only black spots before his eyes. 'I've knelt over the dead before.'

'As have I. Only *I* did the killing.'

Mason leaned back on his haunches and looked up at her. 'I'm sorry, Roxy. But why did you both run up here?'

Sally's sodden eyes stared at Mason as her mind refocused on something of great magnitude. 'Because my father died trying to save the *Vatican Book of Secrets*.'

Mason watched as Roxy shoved the Guard's gun into her waistband. 'The what?'

'Wait.' Sally raced back to the office, looking only at the table, picked up her laptop, stuffed it in its bag, and dashed back, securing the bag over her shoulders. Roxy, annoyed, had started to give chase but stopped when Sally quickly re-emerged.

'What's that—' Mason began.

'Move,' Sally said. 'We have to stop them. Move *now*!'

She ran past Mason, leaving him cursing in her wake and questioning why a second Rusk was running past him towards danger this evening.

They raced down the aisle towards its far end with Roxy at their backs.

Sally gave a running commentary as she hurried along. 'At the far end of this aisle is a secure room. Its windows are obscure, veiled. Its contents unknown except to a select few. If there ever was a secret that the Vatican guarded, *that* is it.'

'A book of secrets?' Mason said as they ran faster. 'Isn't this place full of them?'

'Despite all the access,' Sally said, 'restricted areas still exist. Look, I'll explain more about the *Book of Secrets* later. We just *can't* allow it to be stolen.'

Mason guessed her anxiety welled up from a source beyond the murder of her father, something far deeper. A wedge of darkness shifted ahead, a figure near the racks. They were already halfway down the aisle. Sally ran faster. Mason could see the far end now and the fleeing figure. He sped up, overtaking Sally.

'Slow down,' he said. 'The Swiss Guard and gendarmes will be here soon. This is their jurisdiction.'

'Will they?' Sally panted back. 'I don't hear them. But if the thief gets that book . . .' A grimace of fear contorted her face.

Mason understood. Every second they hesitated gave the murderer and potential thief more breathing space. And they were gaining. The wedge of darkness had stopped running and now clung to the racks like a large black spider, an eerie vision in the vast vault. Its head swivelled towards them and then it began to climb. Mason shouted a warning and put on a burst of speed, hoping to catch the figure before it started to climb. Roxy was a step behind, so close he could hear her breathing.

As he drew close, the killer started to scramble upward. Mason jumped, reached out a hand, and brushed a boot that swiftly drew away. The shelves rattled and shook. A ream of manuscripts spilled out and burst across the floor. The figure climbed fast, swarming up the metal framework.

'Stop him!' Sally cried.

Mason leapt to the second shelf and lunged again. The

38

whole shelving array swayed ominously, but he focused on his target. He managed to wrap one hand around an ankle and pulled hard.

The figure twisted gracefully in his grasp and kicked out with its free foot. Mason felt sharp pain as a boot mashed his fingers, but held on. This was their chance to prevent the theft, to avenge Professor Rusk's murder and give Sally a little succour.

Mason's right boot slipped on the metal shelf. This wasn't his speciality, not by a long shot. The thief slammed a boot time and again against his knuckles and the back of his hand. Mason swung out from the rack, unable to gain any purchase. The thief hung on with remarkable confidence.

'I will shoot you,' Roxy said softly.

The thief's head swivelled, fixing on a point below Mason. The figure froze for a moment as if trying to decide what to do next. At that moment, Mason's grip gave way.

He fell to the floor, landing hard and folding. A stab of pain shot through his left ankle. When he looked up the thief was gone and Roxy was still aiming her gun.

'What happened?'

'I'm not that killer anymore. I can't be.'

'They're getting away,' Sally cried, and started quickly past them both.

'Wait . . .' Mason leapt to his feet, wincing as his ankle protested. Sally raced off further down the aisle. He and Roxy gave chase, gaining speed, but soon, and with a gasp of fear, Sally started to slow.

Ahead, the far wall of the archives loomed and, built against it, a square brick structure no larger than a garden shed. The door was made of heavy steel, four inches thick, and stood wide open.

A bright spotlight inside illuminated a five-foot marble pedestal. Atop the pedestal was an empty book stand.

'Is that it? Is it missing?' Mason asked.

'I've never actually seen it before,' Sally said. 'But I do know it was kept inside this structure under the strictest of security measures. Bypassing them would take some kind of genius.'

Mason motioned for everyone to stay quiet. Assuming the thief had spent some time breaking into the building, they couldn't be too far away.

'Strictest of measures?' Roxy waved at the open door. 'Nothing's safe. It's all about motivation.'

'And skill,' Mason added. 'You need world-class skills and a hotshot team to break into here. Now, give it a minute.'

He placed a finger to his lips. They all listened.

Raising his eyes to the tops of the shelves, where a small gap separated them from the ceiling, Mason spotted a large shadow leaping expertly and swiftly from rack to rack maybe twenty feet in front of them.

'Go,' he said. 'I see him.' He'd been part of ops like this. Ops requiring deniability, stealth, total secrecy. They brought in the best tech guys and system hackers to lay it all out like a jigsaw puzzle.

The shelving didn't extend all the way to the far wall, which created another aisle running along the back of the archive. He led the way at a run, a stone wall to his left. Unlike every other wall he'd seen so far, this one was unadorned.

Mason moved fast, expecting the others to keep up, a thorny conundrum gnawing at his brain. They were walking into blind danger with their one remaining client. They should be protecting Sally, keeping her away from danger, rather than taking her towards it.

Mason shot a glance behind. 'We ought to take cover and wait for the gendarmes.'

Sally's eyes flared. 'No,' she hissed. 'These bastards planned this to the very last detail, clearly. They'll escape. My father tried to save the book, and for good reason; now I'll finish what he started. For him.'

Roxy made a surreptitious gesture at Mason, a flexing of an arm that said: *I could force her to stop.*

'No.' Sally saw the motion. 'You *can't* stop me trying to avenge my father's murder.'

Mason ground his teeth together. As much as he hated to admit it, her conviction appealed to his sense of ethics. The perception that she wanted to stop the killer and avenge her father, who had died trying to help others, was a principal belief of his own. One that dragged him out of bed every morning.

'There,' he said without further comment, seeing another fleeting movement of shadow.

They moved faster, still racing down the aisle. Mason had always kept fit and breathed easy. Roxy was probably fuelled by rum fumes. Sally ran on adrenalin.

'I transcribe my father's writings,' she said. 'Every scribble. Every essay. Something I started doing when I . . . came back. It helped me focus.' She paused for a breath as Mason's gaze trawled the high shadows.

'Everything goes to the cloud.' She laughed without humour as if recalling a conversation. 'My father didn't have a clue what the cloud was, but he knew the importance of recording observations. It's how I know about the *Book of Secrets*. It's utterly hush-hush and vitally important to the Catholic Church. Or rather—'

Mason signalled with a slashing motion of his hand for her to stop talking. They were closing in on the far wall.

At this end of the archive, where the northern wall met the western, beyond the stacks of shelving, several towering, disorderly piles of documents attested to the fact that the Vatican was undermanned. One of the unstable heaps had collapsed.

Mason saw a high shadow move and then a gunshot rang out.

The bullet ricocheted off the shelving to Mason's right,

nowhere near them, pinging twice before disappearing into the archives. Ducking, he saw Roxy grab Sally and then glanced up.

Just in time to see a black-clad figure duck into a square ventilation shaft.

Chapter 8

'Up,' Sally said.

'Are you joking?' Roxy groaned as she peered upwards. 'My head spins at ground level, let alone fifteen feet high.'

'That'd be the alcohol,' Mason said.

'Hey—'

Sally rushed at the wall and used a stack of documents to clamber upwards. Mason reached out a hand to stop her, and pointed at the walls.

'What are those?' Sally asked.

'Suction cups; probably secured by a fast-patch resin,' Mason said. 'See how they're shaped? This burglar's an expert climber.'

Eight textured wall grips led up to the exposed vent shaft. Mason started up first, reached the square hole, felt around the steel edge, and hauled himself up. Scrambling sounds echoed along the shaft. He leaned out. 'Hurry. And Roxy, stick with Sally. We have no idea what this killer will do next.'

Leaving the others to climb, he started along the steel-lined tunnel. It was a tight fit, the sides rubbing against his shoulders. Mason's physique allowed him to push forward where a bulkier soldier might have got stuck.

As he heard Sally enter the shaft at his back, he reflected on how easily his mind had reverted to military imagery.

The truth was, even revisiting this fraction of his old self was energising. Sally had swayed him easily. Working for Patricia and the security firm did not often result in this kind of action.

'I'm in,' Roxy whispered from behind Sally.

Mason increased his speed. The shaft led downhill, with an incline so steep at one point that Mason was forced to press his knees against the smooth metal sides to keep from sliding.

A flat stretch followed where he crawled on his knees. The minutes passed. This was taking too long. The killer was fast and resourceful. Any slackening in pace would allow them to escape.

Mason reached the end of the shaft, noticeable because of the halo of light surrounding it. Slowing, he moved to the opening and looked out.

A short drop led to a rough concrete floor. Craning his neck, he saw more of the textured grips attached to the wall and reached for one to take his weight.

'Some kind of tunnel below,' he said. 'Nothing more than a rough passage. The good news is that it's one way. The bad news: I can't see a thing past three or four feet.'

'How can you see that far?' Roxy asked.

'Glowsticks,' Mason said. 'Whoever this is appears to have planned for a quick escape and scattered glowsticks along their escape route. It's easier to run by the light of glowsticks than with a torch.'

He climbed down easily, then turned and held out a hand as Sally followed. She grabbed his arm. 'Hurry,' she said and then dashed into the tunnel, making him and Roxy chase after her.

Mason exchanged a resigned look with Roxy. 'Why are we here?' he asked.

'Here?' she asked, indicating the tunnel. 'Or . . . *here*?' She meant working for Patricia Wilde. 'We're all here fighting our demons. Using the company as a kind of passive therapist while we maintain our secrets.'

Mason stored that for later and turned his attention back to Sally.

The tunnel seemed more of a bore hole than anything serving a purpose: rough walls extending for an indeterminate distance and holding a killer prowling in shadows. Apart from the glowsticks, no debris littered the floor; there was no sign of human life whatsoever.

'Where the hell are we?' Roxy asked.

Nobody answered.

They ran along the tunnel as fast as they dared. Sally allowed herself to be overtaken by Mason, but then forged ahead when he slowed at the end. At first, Mason was taken aback by her fitness and ability but then recalled that she was a champion fell runner. She'd probably match him pace for pace.

A four-foot-high rough archway greeted them. The tunnel changed in composition here, continuing at a sharp angle, its floor strewn with fragments of shale, stone and rubble.

Sally slid into it boots first. Mason followed at speed, trying to restrain her but knowing that the fire inside her belly would not be extinguished by anything except capturing their quarry.

They found themselves in an entirely different environment.

The passage, illuminated by more glowsticks, had dark, greyish, crumbling walls. It had been cleaved out of the rock in a narrow arch shape, and shored up every twenty feet or so by thick timbers.

'Just like the Appian Way,' Sally breathed back. 'We're in the catacombs now.'

Mason didn't like the sound of that. 'Catacombs? How far do they run?'

'Most are separate burial chambers,' Sally said. 'Maybe thirty or forty throughout all of Rome. But some are connected, and others remain undiscovered. They may transect all of underground Rome.'

Mason had noticed that when she elucidated on archaeological topics, Sally's voice and demeanour became relatively calm and deliberate, as if she wanted to prove herself, to show that she was as hard a worker as everyone else. She was making up for what she considered was a privileged background.

'Any maps?' Roxy asked.

'Phone won't work down here,' Mason said. 'Let's not get lost.'

'It's one way,' Sally pointed out, head down and still moving at pace. The passage was too narrow for Mason to overtake her.

Mason noticed recesses for tombs in various places along both walls, as well as faded frescos and other wall art. He slowed, fascinated by the ancient subterranean graveyard despite their urgency.

Roxy jabbed him in the spine. 'Get a move on, Babyface.'

He glanced back. 'Hey, there's no call for that youthful insolence. I'm a year older than you.'

Roxy attempted a laugh, but the sound didn't match the emotions wrestling across her face. Mason wondered again what afflicted her.

Sally was several steps ahead, picking her way through rubble in the dim light.

A shadow shot out of a recess and lunged at her, knocking her to her knees. The bag she'd been carrying fell off her shoulders and the laptop that had been inside it clattered out and away.

Mason saw their black-clad quarry punch out, striking Sally in the head and the side of the neck and heard Sally's tortured voice.

46

'You *murderer* . . . you . . . murdered . . . my father . . .'
Sally curled up, covering her head as best she could.

Mason lunged and threw a punch as he loomed over Sally.

Sally's attacker was deft, nimble, and twisted away before striking back, connecting solidly with his chest. Mason felt the blow but ignored it. Sally was in the way, preventing him from manhandling her attacker to the floor.

The figure was clad in tight-fitting black, and this close up, Mason realised his opponent was a woman.

Shadowy eyes peered out of the face mask.

Sally screamed about her father's death as Mason unleashed a flurry of punches. The woman blocked them with her wrists and arms, twisting left and right.

Roxy uttered sounds of annoyance at his back. She carried their only gun, a thought that made Mason wonder why the killer hadn't used hers.

Sally reached out for the thief's legs, but the woman was incredibly agile. A swift kick to Sally's chin sent her sliding backwards into the stone wall but Sally showed her toughness by retaliating immediately. This time she grabbed the thief's right leg and dug her fingers in, bringing forth a yelp of pain. The thief kicked out at Sally's arm with her left boot, smashing the heel down onto Sally's wrist. Sally cried out and let go. The woman shrugged off Mason's next attack by rolling away from his grasping hands, then turned and ran.

Mason dropped to Sally's side. 'Are you okay?'

Roxy leaned over the top of their bodies, gun in hand, and fired twice. The weapon boomed in the confined space, hurting his ears, but there was no sound from the woman. Roxy cursed into the darkness.

'I had her. *I bloody well had her.*' Tears sprang from Sally's eyes. Fury twisted her face. 'That *bitch*.'

She shoved at Mason and made to run after the woman, but he stood in her way. 'No,' he said. 'We're the bodyguards. She could have killed you back there. We go first or we end this pursuit right now. Understand?'

Sally scowled but nodded and picked up her laptop, scanning it for damage.

Mason checked her injuries as Roxy pushed by. 'I'll lead,' she said in a hard-edged voice.

They resumed their pursuit, able to hear the thief as she picked her way through the rock-strewn passage ahead. The tunnel bent sharp right a little further on, which probably accounted for why Roxy's bullets hadn't found a target.

They passed one fading glowstick and another. Mason slowed when, ahead, an impenetrable cloying darkness filled the passage.

'She's started to take them with her.' Roxy swore. 'To slow us down.' She held up her phone and took a moment to switch on the torch. Holding it in front of her, she led the way through the ancient catacomb.

'Why didn't the killer shoot us?' Sally asked quietly.

'I was wondering that,' Mason said. 'But it could be simple. She lost her gun or ran out of bullets.' He shrugged and followed Roxy, keeping an eye on Sally. The route curved left and then right before taking an eastern turn underneath the city. The air was dry and cold, the darker spaces filled with unidentified rustles, like the fleet scurrying of claws. Dust motes swirled before their eyes.

Mason stayed watchful, expecting another attack at any moment. The woman knew they were close.

He wondered where she'd stashed the book during her sneak attack, but then realised she'd probably hidden it further along the passage before doubling back to deal with them.

Roxy kept the momentum going. Some time passed before the catacomb ended in a solid wall.

'She went up.' Roxy aimed her phone at the ceiling.

In the bright light, Mason picked out two vertical rows

of wall grips rising about ten feet in height and leading to what appeared to be a black wrought-iron grate. The grate was closed. Hopefully, it would not have been secured.

One way to find out.

Mason gestured for Roxy to raise her phone as high as possible, and started up the wall.

'What's so important about this book anyway?' he heard Roxy ask as he climbed.

'I don't know a great deal, but my father once described it as the spark which could ignite the powder keg modern Christianity sits on. He said it ought to be destroyed, but tradition, history and custom forbade it. The Church is balancing a double-edged sword over its own neck on shaking fingertips.'

'What's *in* it?' Roxy asked.

'Very few people know. By tradition, the book is revealed to each new pope after their inauguration. Every pope has read it, and every pope has added to it.'

'Surely someone evaluates the contents,' Roxy said. 'Otherwise . . . it's little more than a book of speculation.'

'Yes, someone has to keep it up to date, to properly assess the subject matter, old and new. That task has been handed down to just a few trusted individuals through time. One archivist per pope is granted access.'

'I still don't understand why they haven't just burned it,' Roxy said.

'Then you don't understand the Catholic Church. The sheer weight of some of those secrets can't be trivialised. The—'

Mason pushed at the grate, found it loose, and took the weight on his shoulders. Slowly, he rose, lifting it with him until he clambered out into the night and a blasting, frigid wind.

A suburban street met his eyes. Houses marched in two directions. Cars splattered with bird excrement were parked outside their residences, narrowing the wide road to a single lane. The dark shadows of trees waved to and fro in a steady gale. Mason was happy to breathe fresh air.

Scanning the street, he spotted his target running in an easterly direction, passing under the bright pool of a street-light, and he called down to the others, 'I see her.'

'Go!' Sally cried out. 'Don't lose her. Please!'

Mason would have preferred to wait until Sally was safely out of the hole before giving chase, but the raw emotion in her voice spurred him into action.

He crossed the road and sprinted along the pavement, trying to close the gap, assaulted on all sides by wind, hail and a biting cold.

The woman looked back, saw him and accelerated.

From behind came the sound of running feet as both Roxy and Sally escaped the catacombs. Roxy replaced the grate with a deafening crash, reminding Mason there was nothing subtle about the raven-haired American who was now his partner.

But there was no time to think, to hesitate, to pause for even a second. The thief was a good eighty feet ahead, lithe, fast and determined, and now Mason could see the backpack hooked over her shoulder.

For him, the book didn't matter. He only wanted to apprehend someone who thought murder was an acceptable way of achieving her goals.

Mason avoided a row of refuse bins toppled by the woman, leaping over two and moving around a third. He slid across the bonnet of a parked car when she crossed the road, losing little momentum. Oncoming cars dazzled with their headlights, momentarily blinding him, but he kept her in sight. Slowly, he reeled her in.

Sirens wailed in the night, coming from the direction of the basilica. Mason kept his mind on the prize. The woman crossed the road once more as a howling gale blasted at their faces, spattering them with sharp pieces of hail. Mason ran under a row of trees, ignoring the unbridled branches waving frantically above his head like spindly arms against a macabre sky, a dark and ghoulish nightmare.

The woman slowed, and a wary Mason slackened off as she pulled out her gun.

Mason ducked in front of a parked car, watching through the windscreen. She didn't fire, but instead ran in front of an oncoming car, pointed the gun at the windscreen and held up a palm to order the driver to stop.

Mason gritted his teeth as Roxy and Sally joined him.

'She's stealing a car,' Roxy said.

'Yeah, I noticed. Make sure you get the plate.'

'You get the first bit, I'll get the second,' Roxy said.

'Is your memory that bad?'

'No, but alcohol causes short-term memory loss. I read it somewhere.'

Mason watched the carjacking, too far away to do anything about it. The thief pulled out the driver, a young woman, and then dragged out a baby seat, complete with tiny occupant. Unwilling to stand by and watch the unfolding scenario, Mason rose and broke into a run. He yelled, attracting his target's attention.

The figure dropped the baby seat. The female driver scrambled over and grabbed it, pulling it clear of the car. The thief jumped inside, slammed the door closed, and pushed the accelerator pedal, screeching towards Mason.

He saw her masked face close up, those impersonal eyes staring at him, and dived for cover.

The car roared by just two feet to his left. For half a second he felt relief, but then an alarming thought sliced at him like a cut-throat razor.

Sally won't let her go.

Mason leapt up. The vehicle's rear lights blazed red. Sally was running headlong at the car, Roxy reaching out for her just a step behind.

The car swerved hard, deliberately, just missing Sally, who staggered headlong in its wake, pounding the hard road.

Mason turned to the young mother. 'Are you two okay?'

The woman nodded, understanding English but unable to speak, cradling her infant in the baby seat.

Mason ran towards Sally. 'Don't worry, I got the plate.'

'You *got the plate?* That's no good. We can't let her go!'

Mason checked himself. 'Well, I'm all out of chase vehicles. Maybe—'

'There!' Roxy cried.

Mason turned to see a taxi idling at the kerb about a hundred yards away. The driver was helping an old lady to her front door and carrying enough weight in bags to sink a battleship. Mason knew they had seconds to decide.

'You work for me now,' Sally said. 'And I take full responsibility. Yes, it's for my father, but it's for the book too. Once the Church gets involved, the authorities will understand.'

Mason cursed aloud, torn between two obligations.

Roxy grabbed hold of Sally and hustled her towards the still-running taxi. 'You coming?' She shot a keen look back at him.

'We're really gonna regret this.' Mason rushed towards the car.

Chapter 9

Mason slid in behind the wheel. Through the windscreen, further down the road, he saw the killer's car turn sharp right. The car – a white SUV – slewed as it swept around the corner, its back tyres sliding.

Mason waited for the taxi's back doors to slam shut before starting his pursuit. Tyres screeched. The engine roared. Mason saw the taxi driver in his rear-view drop his double armload of bags and try to give chase.

He caught Sally's eyes in the mirror. 'We just committed a crime.'

'For the greater good,' she said, dark eyes flashing. 'I'll vouch for you.'

'Doesn't make us any less complicit,' Mason said.

'Oh, and tell me you never broke the rules in whatever war they sent you to fight.'

Mason was taken aback, forced to recall events that had redirected the course of his entire life. He was also reminded that this increasingly reckless pursuit had cleared the junk from his head until now.

'This isn't *war*,' he said. 'You can't quantify actions in war.'

'Unless you're a politician,' Roxy said, looking like she wanted to say more.

Mason distracted her by throwing the car around a corner, then accelerating hard. They raced up a side road, parked cars to either side, flashing past the glowing curtained windows of hundreds of homes.

The SUV was up ahead, its driver clearly aware of their pursuit. She blasted her horn, encouraging obstacles to get out of her way.

Mason drove more cautiously, mindful of civilians.

A wing mirror, clipped from a car up ahead, flashed past the side window, bouncing in their wake. The SUV ripped along a three-car line, denting metal and shearing off valuable plastic or carbon sections, littering the road.

Mason tried to avoid them, but space was limited. He used the woman's poor driving skills to move closer.

The one-way road branched at a junction. Mason had a split-second view of headlights coming in both directions before the SUV swung left, cutting off another vehicle.

Mason kept going, speeding up to avoid the affronted slewed car, then found a narrow gap just in front of another on the opposite carriageway, and turned.

Headlights loomed large in his mirrors, the driver of the car behind gesturing and shouting, but Mason didn't react. He was too focused on keeping up with the SUV.

They swept along a new tree-lined road, both engines roaring as they swerved from side to side, one seeking to escape, the other to keep up.

On the pavements, some people stopped to stare, others raised already active mobile phones and snapped pictures or video.

Mason inched as close as he dared to the SUV's rear bumper.

'If she brakes . . .' Roxy warned.

'We'll take her out,' Mason said. 'Just make sure your seatbelts are secure.'

Another junction flew by, this one mercifully empty.

Beyond that, blinking lights marked a pedestrian crossing. Mason saw two people using it; a couple with their arms around each other and no other cares in the world.

The SUV screeched and swerved to miss them. Mason did the same.

The kerb came up fast. If they struck it sideways at speed, they might conceivably roll their cars, but both the thief and Mason managed to keep control, steering back into the centre of the road.

The next road was well lit with bright, round streetlamps chasing the shadows back to their alleyways, and more populated. Mason slowed, giving the thief space and hoping she would do the same, but, if anything, the SUV accelerated.

'It's becoming too dangerous,' Mason said. 'I'm sure we're on course for some major streets. But I'm not sure she's doing it on purpose.'

'She's too good not to have a plan,' Roxy said. 'This woman definitely has a destination in mind.'

Mason tended to agree, but that didn't make it any less dangerous. Both Sally and Roxy held on in the back as he made another tight turn.

'This is the Via Marcello Prestinari,' Roxy said, her accent stripping the street name of any glamour.

'She's headed for the Tiber,' Sally said.

'Wait . . . what . . . the *river*?' Mason half-turned.

'Eyes on the road, Babyface,' Roxy prompted. 'Just because she's headed for the Tiber doesn't mean she wants to swim.'

'Why do you call him Babyface?' Sally asked, though, from the look in her eyes, Mason knew she'd already figured it out. He ground his teeth, stopping the retort.

The SUV was four car lengths ahead. The one-way street was bordered by large trees to their left and buildings to their right. On-street parking areas were full, some with cars waiting to pull out. The SUV shot past, blasting its horn. Mason flew by a few seconds later, having to swerve just once.

A tree-lined view gave way to a bridge spanning the river. Their cars shot onto a new road, curving round towards the entrance to the bridge. Mason gripped the wheel tight.

The SUV powered onto the bridge, the dark waters of the great river to either side. Mason followed.

Ahead, oncoming cars protested at their speed, flashing blinding lights and blowing horns. Those in front tried to get out of the SUV's way. One veered, then clipped and mounted the pavement, swinging towards the concrete barrier which protected it from the long drop to the muddy waters, but mercifully ground to a halt before hitting.

Mason tried to get alongside the rear of the SUV, a police tactic popping into his mind. If he could shove the car at an angle from the rear, it would swing around sideways and come to an abrupt stop.

The SUV accelerated further, perhaps sensing his intentions. Mason backed off, loath to push the thief into an accident. It was only a little after half-past-eight and there were still plenty of people around, a fact which he put down to the Italian fondness for late nights and socialising.

They sped off the bridge, onto the Viale delle Belle Arti, the road deserted at this time of night, and pushed further east.

Mason's concentration was fixed firmly on the chase. It was Roxy who fished her phone out of her jeans pocket and stated that she would call the cops.

The longer they continued their hot pursuit, the more trouble they'd be in with the police, he knew. But surely this *could* be justified? Mason thought their reasoning was sensible and that the Vatican would support them.

As long as they got that book back.

Mason juiced the accelerator, shooting up behind the SUV. Roxy found the keypad symbol on her phone. Sally sat as far forward as her seatbelt would allow, glaring at the figure in the car ahead as if willing her eyes to shoot lasers.

A smear of dull red crossed Mason's field of vision. It came from the right, a cumbersome, slow-moving delivery truck that ambled out of a side street and into their lane without indicating. The collision was unavoidable.

The white SUV slammed into the rear wheel of the truck, scraping down the side.

Mason hit the brakes hard, but still struck both vehicles with a shuddering impact.

The taxi came to a sudden stop. The white SUV squirmed in the wake of the still-moving truck, swerving towards the front of a gothic-style church.

Mason saw a courting couple standing in front of that basilica, in the path of the out-of-control car. His heart leapt into his throat.

The couple were too deeply involved in each other to hear anything above their own heavy breathing. Framed by a pool of light that illuminated the front of the basilica, they didn't see or hear the car veering towards them.

'Don't look.' Mason's words were for Sally, but the white SUV smashed into a stubby row of concrete bollards set before the basilica with a thunderous crunch of crumpling metal. The couple leapt apart, faces twisted in shock, both yelling, and were rooted to the spot in terror at the sight of the crashed vehicle.

Mason let out a long breath, trying to slow the intense beat of his heart. Their own car had suffered damage to the passenger side which was preventing Roxy from jumping out. Mason held onto the wheel, jarred by their impact.

'Are you okay?' he asked Sally.

'Just go. *Get the book!*'

Galvanised by her panic, he threw open the door. Ahead, the delivery truck was coming to a grinding halt. Mason, mindful of the thief and her gun, kept the bulk of the taxi between himself and the wrecked SUV, and scooted around the back.

The courting couple were his first concern. He ran towards the basilica, staying as low as he could.

'Hey,' he shouted, waving at the pair as if scattering birds. 'Get out of here.'

They stared back, apparently not understanding a word he was saying. Mason kept his focus on the car and the thief but gestured wildly for the couple to run away. He could see that the SUV was badly crumpled around the bollards.

'*The book!*' Sally's cry was muffled by the car, her voice shot through with anxiety.

Mason was torn. His nature leaned instinctively towards protecting people he could see were in shock. A few seconds ago, they'd thought they were going to die. He needed to make sure they were okay.

With quick gestures he reassured himself that they were unhurt before whirling back to the SUV. Maybe forty seconds had passed. Roxy had scooted across to the taxi's driver's seat, and Sally was scrambling out of the same side, clutching her laptop.

We need that book.

Mason started forward. The SUV's engine was still running, a tortured, rattling sound betraying its condition. The driver's door was hanging wide open. Mason ran to the rear of the car, ducked, and then peered around the side.

The first thing he saw was blood.

Not pools of it, but enough to tell him the person who'd been driving was injured.

To his left, Roxy had a better view. The American was already striding forward, a sign that the car was empty.

'She got away,' Roxy said, no emotion in her voice.

Mason ran to the open door and peered inside. The inner shell that suffered the impact was crumpled but not too badly. The doorframe and window were covered in blood spatter, revealing that the driver hadn't been wearing a seatbelt. If that were so, Mason imagined her skull had probably bounced hard off the doorframe on impact.

An airbag hung loosely, having been deflated, Mason assumed, by the thief. The doorhandle was smeared with blood, and several drops were pooled outside the car as if the woman had leaned out and hung her head for several seconds.

'She's struggling,' he said, more to himself than anyone else.

Sally ran up. 'She's gone? Is the book still here?'

Mason was already checking. Roxy hit the boot switch and ran around. Mason swept his eyes around the front and rear of the interior, checking footwells and storage compartments and feeling underneath the seats. Thirty seconds later, they turned back to Sally.

'It's gone.'

Mason wasn't ready for the wan pallor that settled across her face, the way her legs wobbled. He reached out a hand to steady her. 'Hey, you okay?'

'Oh God,' she said, her voice trembling. 'What have we done? What have *they* done? The world . . .' She held their eyes. 'It will never recover from this.'

Chapter 10

'She's limped away,' Mason said. 'Can't have gone far.'

'She's . . . injured?' Sally asked.

'Yeah, can't you see the blood?' Roxy scanned the street.

Sally looked down for the first time. 'That's good. Let's track her. Can you do that?' She looked at Mason.

Roxy grinned at him. 'Yeah, can you?'

'Not without growing another two legs and a tail,' Mason said. 'The rain's already washing it away.'

Though they had slackened since the chase began, sporadic wintry blasts of wind and sheets of hail still swept up and down Rome's streets. Mason stood unmoving in the bright beam of a streetlight, studying the shadows enfolding the nearby buildings.

'First things first,' Roxy said. 'Let's put some distance between ourselves and this crash.'

Mason shook his head. 'That's basically an admission of guilt. We've done nothing wrong.'

'Agreed, but do you want to spend the next eight hours explaining that to an irate Italian policeman?'

Mason weakened. 'Well . . .'

Sally clutched his arm. 'Please,' she said. 'They killed my dad. They . . .' Her voice broke for the first time, telling

Mason that she was losing her battle to hold in her grief. 'Look . . . it's no secret that my father and I clashed. I hated being born with a silver spoon. I rebelled, and lived off the grid, doing time at a soup kitchen. But I came home on the proviso that my father and I work together, doing what we love. I may hate the self-serving rich, but I saw how I was ruining my own life and I changed it.' She turned her face to the sky, rain pattering off her skin in the glow of the streetlight. 'We couldn't live together . . . but we worked together *very* well. *I know what I'm talking about.*'

Mason felt compelled to help her avenge her father's death as he tried to atone for the mistakes of his past. He cradled her arm and steered her across the road, away from the wreckage, the basilica and the shellshocked couple.

'All my life,' Sally said, 'we've been at odds. We fought every day. I didn't want any of it . . . not one gilded scrap of the affluent life I was born into. But lately . . . archaeology brought us back together. A shared interest. A shared love . . .'

Roxy was behind them. 'Don't worry, people,' she said. 'I'll come too.'

'When I ran straight for the couple instead of the thief,' Mason explained, 'I couldn't help it. I couldn't fail them.'

Roxy answered quickly. 'Hey, we're *not* bad people,' she said, as if it were a mantra that she recited every night. 'We can make up for all the ruthless shit we were forced to do.'

Mason studied her, recalling the rum-soaked sheets, the bad-girl reputation, the silent struggle playing behind her eyes like a harrowing puppet show.

'I hope you're right,' he said and turned to Sally. 'We'll help you find the book and the killer. For now.'

'But first.' Roxy pulled a shiny black coat out of the rear of the crashed SUV and handed it to Sally. Mason became aware that he too was shivering in the inclement weather and ran over to the taxi, logically thinking that a taxi driver would be prepared, and opened the boot. Inside, a blue bomber jacket lay on top of a clearly well-used, oily grey hoodie. They would have to do. He threw Roxy the bomber and shrugged the hoodie over his head.

They continued across the road and started down the pavement before cutting through a thick stand of trees to another street.

Sally seemed lost and spoke up. 'How is this helping?'

'It's distancing us from the crash,' Mason said. 'Keep going.'

Ten minutes later, they stopped again. Sally was fretting, peering into every dark recess they passed as if hoping the thief would jump out, brandishing the book like a weapon. 'I still don't see how—'

Mason produced his mobile phone. 'We can't track her,' he said. 'Not by sight, or smell,' he added ironically. 'But we do have other options.'

As Sally looked intrigued, Mason placed a call to Watchtower. The office was manned twenty-four hours a day.

'You're thinking Patricia can help?' Roxy asked, wiping rain from her face.

'The company's plugged into all the right places,' he said. 'Security businesses have to be.'

'Maybe in London,' Roxy said dubiously. 'But here?'

'To help keep her clients and employees safe and secure all around the world, Patricia employs only the best . . . computer personnel . . .' Mason said, aware that Roxy would know he meant hackers. 'The best private security organisations work hand-in-hand with law enforcement in many countries. Often, it's merely a question of how many influential board members they have but, sometimes, it's mutual respect and give and take. Watchtower is intertwined with dozens of governments. Let's hope one of them is this one,' he added for Sally's benefit.

Roxy made a face. 'I think *intertwined* is an unfortunate

choice of words. Gives the impression they're in some kind of sordid relationship.'

Mason gave her an ironic smile but didn't answer. Patricia Wilde had picked up the phone, most likely after recognising his number.

'This had better be good, Joe.'

'Nice to hear your voice too, Patricia.' He gave her a brief, diluted view of what had happened.

'Watchtower doesn't lose clients,' Patricia said.

Mason took a moment to figure out how best to expedite the information he needed. 'The situation is still unfolding,' he said. 'And we need your help.'

'You have the daughter?'

'Yes, *Sally* is here with us. You know Gheel and Green?'

'Our resident solicitors. Yes.'

Mason hid a grim smile. Gheel and Green, who to the uninitiated might sound like a firm of lawyers, were in fact the agency's best hacker team. 'We need their expertise. We're chasing someone.'

'Why? You just told me you have the asset.'

Mason closed his eyes briefly. 'Yes, Miss Rusk is safe but . . . her father's murderer took something of great importance that *must* be recovered.'

Patricia coughed down the phone line. 'Let me get this straight. She's with you and you're pursuing her father's killer on your own, trying to retrieve a stolen item? Are you insane?'

'The truth? I think your best employees do have a dose of insanity in them, Patricia. Our past experiences broke us all to varying degrees. But the insanity keeps us razor sharp, operating on a knife edge. And, Patricia, that's where you need us.'

'Right . . .' She seemed at a loss for words. 'Right . . . I get it. You're in the field. You make the call. I hope to God you're making the right one.' She was walking now.

Mason could hear the fast clip of her high heels and the change in her breathing. 'Green!' she shouted. 'Gheel! Look lively now, boys. What do you need from us, Joe?'

'CCTV,' he said, then reeled off everything they needed, confident that the 'boys' were good enough to hack any CCTV system, and Patricia was practised, skilled and connected enough to grease any wheels she needed to.

'It's gonna take some time,' she said. 'Whether you like it or not. The boys have to be super careful.'

Mason already knew that. 'Just get back to me as soon as you can.'

He ended the call, cutting short any cross-examination Patricia might have attempted. Both Roxy and Sally regarded him with expectant eyes, their faces streaming with water, their hair plastered down. Sally had placed her laptop under her new coat and was holding it through the material.

'What do you say we find some shelter?' he said. 'We should hear something within the hour.'

Sally bit her bottom lip. 'Will they locate her?'

'Rome's closely monitored,' Roxy said. 'Watchtower is an old, respected agency and they're well hooked up. If anyone stands a chance, they do.'

Sally didn't look entirely comforted. Mason checked his watch as the warbling sounds of sirens drew closer, and then led them into the trees, fighting an uneasy feeling that this night was far from over.

Chapter 11

Something terrible had happened. Marduk was sure of it.

All communication from his daughter Nina had ceased over thirty minutes ago. She'd escaped with the book, an act that sent ripples of fiery anticipation through Marduk's body, but something had gone wrong.

Marduk beat down the temptation to seize the communications system Gido's team had established and start issuing orders. Such an act didn't befit his standing. Gido's team was the best. They had already pulled off the impossible, and they had a whole raft of secondary protocols.

Marduk respected them, for now. Employing Mac's unmatched expertise, Hassell's infiltration skills and an unwilling insider, they had accomplished the theft of the *Book of Secrets*.

The tome was so close after so long that Marduk could feel his fingers flexing, opening and closing in expectation of holding it. But it was the anticipation of possessing the secrets within that made his blood simmer, an anticipation that encompassed thousands of years of jealous rage.

A handheld radio sat upon his desk, cradled in a charger. Marduk couldn't take his eyes off it. The room was deliberately dark, the paintings, statues and tapestries adorning the walls all cast in shadow to help Marduk focus. There was only one dim light in the room, and that was focused on the radio.

It crackled. '*Come in, Seven. Come in. This is One. Are you there?*'

The team leader, Hassell, was asking Nina to respond. Marduk leaned forward, holding his breath.

Seconds passed, laced with a deepening disappointment. Hassell spoke again, asking similar questions from the safety of his hotel room somewhere across the city. The only response was an empty line that felt like a kick in the teeth to Marduk.

Nina? Of all people I did not expect you to fail me.

But she *had* been successful in stealing the book, he reminded himself. Mac had bypassed their CCTV and alarm systems, creating looped feeds, false warnings in other sections of the basilica, and a device that detected and negated their bespoke infra-red capabilities.

Hassell had engineered a distraction outside the main entrance, some flares and coloured smoke that diverted attention for ten to fifteen minutes. That was their window.

But something had happened inside. Nina had lifted the book from its pedestal and, right then, something alerted the Guards. Something Hassell and his team had missed. A small failsafe perhaps. A pressure pad connected off the main system. Marduk didn't know, but Nina had done exceptionally well to kill the Guards and still escape with the book. Marduk paused then, almost snarling at an image that swept through his mind.

Pedestal?

How dare they? Keeping something that amounted to a global religious incendiary device mounted on a reverential stand only served to demonstrate their inhumanity, their ignorance of the state of the outside world. They kept obliviousness wrapped around them like a comfort blanket.

The Church was unworthy of a position it had stolen from the Amori a long time ago, unworthy of the position it held.

Marduk lifted his head as the radio crackled again.

'This is Seven. Are you there?'

Nina!

Marduk shot towards the radio, his hand snapping out towards it before he remembered that he'd been asked to remain silent. That had been the deal this team insisted on after informing him of their innumerable contingency plans.

On your heads be it, he'd said, and meant it.

'Seven?' Hassell sounded immensely relieved. 'Are you okay?'

Marduk couldn't stop an annoyed breath escaping through gritted teeth. The idiot should be asking about the book. Did she still have the book? Where the hell had she been for the best part of an hour?

'No,' came the jolting reply. 'I'm hurt.'

'Bad?'

'Yeah, bad enough. I need . . . your help.'

'What happened?'

Marduk was practically dancing on the tips of his toes in expectation. Unable to help himself, he reached for the radio, but then Nina spoke and answered the question lodged in his throat.

'I have the book,' she said to his relief. 'But when I killed the Guards, I had to kill some old guy. Whoever he was, his daughter and bodyguards gave chase through the catacombs.'

'Did they see your face?'

'No.' Nina let out a groan of pain. 'Nothing like that. There was an accident, a car crash. I escaped but . . .' She moaned again, this time a low whimper. 'You have to hurry.'

'We will. Do you need medical help?'

'I . . . think so . . . yes.'

'That's a problem,' Hassell said. 'But we'll work something out. Where are you?'

'Rendezvous C.'

'Good. Sit tight. We'll be there in twenty.'

Again, Marduk was forced to restrain himself from taking hold of the radio and urging Hassell to act faster, to make recovering the book his highest priority. The Church would still be brought to its knees on his watch, despite Nina's stupid mistakes.

'Sit tight?' His daughter's voice came through the handset, tiny not only due to the cheap speaker but as a direct result of the pain she was suffering. 'I can barely move.'

'Try to stay awake.' Hassell sounded concerned. 'We're en route.'

Marduk waited, calming himself by pressing his fingers against the red symbol of the Amori on his cloak. The Amori had waited thousands of years for this moment, they could wait twenty more minutes. But Marduk's face twisted with hatred as he recalled the way they'd been painted in the early days, when the Church was asserting its grip.

For this reason, in one day shall come her plagues. Pestilence, mourning and famine. And she will be burned up with fire; for the Lord God who judges her is strong.

No more shall the ashes of the past remain undisturbed. No more shall the downtrodden remain voiceless. The secrets will out . . . and then . . .

And ever since, either unknowingly or purposely, the Church had banished the Amori to the shadows.

Filled with jealous rage, Marduk poured himself a good slug of bourbon. It wasn't just the Amori who would benefit from this – he would too. Everything he'd ever done had been to further the Amori's sphere of influence but his status would also grow. *Perhaps,* he thought surreptitiously. *Perhaps I will become the most important leader in the world.* It sounded good, strengthening his will and straightening his shoulders. He went to the window, plucked at the curtains, and peered out. *Perhaps I will tell them all what to do.* An icy rain battered the windows and thrashed the streets, and the impenetrable darkness of a crypt hung overhead, split only by uniform rows of lonesome street-lights. Nobody should be abroad on this harsh and in-hospitable night.

But many were.

Marduk imagined the thieves and the cutthroats, the pure evil stalking the unsheltered byways tonight. The bourbon sank into the pit of his stomach like a warm promise, and he was just contemplating another shot when the radio crackled once more.

'We're here,' Hassell said, no doubt for his benefit. 'Split and explore. We're not taking anything for granted.'

Marduk waited, throat dry.

'Approaching the door.'

At this point, Hassell switched to his throat mic, a live blow-by-blow feed that Mac had set up for just this kind of emergency. The team were moving fast; Marduk could tell as they rapped at the door in question.

'No answer,' someone said.

Marduk clenched his fists.

'It's unlocked. Going in,' Hassell said.

Marduk held his breath.

'Hey, put the gun down. It's us.' Hassell's voice seemed to catch. 'Shit, Nina, that looks bad.'

Marduk fidgeted, desperate for news of the book, fearful that they would squander this one and only chance to pluck it from the Vatican's greedy fingers.

The sound of running, shuffling boots reached his ears and then a door slammed shut. The entire team were in the room. Marduk heard a curtain being pulled, one way or the other, and the sound of a bottle cap being twisted off.

'Drink,' Hassell said. 'Try to sit up.'

'She's going nowhere,' either Ash or Base said in a deep, ugly voice. 'Bitch is mostly dead.'

Marduk snatched the radio from its cradle and thumbed the speaker button. 'The book,' he snapped. 'The book. Is it there? Is it unharmed?'

Hassell's voice was thick with emotion. 'It's here, but your daughter's badly injured. Could be a skull fracture. She's vomiting, losing consciousness. She's . . . in a bad way.'

'Will she slow you down?' Marduk asked.

'Well, yes, of course. She needs a hospital.'

'Is the book intact?'

'Yes. We have it right here.'

Marduk was starkly aware of four vital points. One: the Amori had never been this close to success. Two: the book mattered above all else. Three: the leader of the Amori always put the interests of the Amori first.

And four: his daughter had been brought up inside the Amori, was privy to all its secrets and aware of everything they were about to do. She knew the risks of failure.

'Make it quick,' he said. 'A bullet to the back of the head.'

After several seconds of silence, Hassell responded in horror. '*What?* No, we'll be safely on our way once we've helped her.'

'The Amori come first,' Marduk said. 'Above all else. It is an entity that does not *wait* for the doctor, does *not* risk misfortune, and does not brook failure. You will do as I say.'

'Nina didn't *fail*.' Hassell sounded like he'd been punched in the gut. 'No plan survives contact with the enemy. It's war theory, and fact. She's accomplished something incred—'

'Others are listening,' Marduk interrupted, referring to the two killers, Ash and Base, who were with Hassell. 'You two are there to kill. So do your job.'

Marduk heard Hassell swearing and the intensifying sounds of a scuffle. Harsh words were exchanged between Hassell and the killers, forcing Marduk to step in.

'Stand down,' he ordered. 'This is my operation. I am

in charge. You will all do as I say.' As he finished, breathing heavily, the faint questioning tones of his daughter's distressed voice could be heard, asking what was happening.

Hassell replied with compassion in his voice. 'Don't worry. Everything will be okay.'

Then Hassell addressed the killers. 'You two, take the book. I'll sort this out.'

A voice came back: 'Hey, he asked us to smoke the bitch, man. I've no problem with that.'

Hassell said, 'It's not right, but I'll do it. You two leave *now*.'

Marduk clenched his fists in anger as the argument heated up. In the end, he snapped. 'Just let him do it. Get going. Who cares who fires the killing shot? I don't. Get a goddamn move on.'

Seconds later, a gunshot rang out. Hassell's voice returned, breathing heavily. 'She's done,' he said. 'I'm moving.'

Marduk stared blankly into the clinging darkness as the sound of the gunshot sent the radio's tinny speaker into a series of pops, cracks and sizzling static. After that, there was a profound silence.

'Take the book,' Marduk said into the radio. 'And bring it to me.'

The Amori would have their glorious future.

Chapter 12

Mason answered the call on the second ring.

'Patricia?'

'We may have something.'

Mason nodded at Sally's questioning gaze. They had taken the shelter offered by a dark, arched recess in a stone wall, gnarled trees to their other three sides. The rain spattered the ground inches from their boots, throwing water across the leather uppers, and the rampant wind tugged at their coats and jackets with a glacial enthusiasm.

Through the trees and greenery, Patricia directed them to the Via dei Monti Parioli, another suburban street maybe ten to fifteen minutes' walk from the crash site.

Mason led the way through the rain, keeping the phone cradled between his shoulder and his right ear, worrying that the hour they'd lost waiting for Patricia's call would severely hamper their search for the thief.

The debate as to whether they should call the police had risen again, but Sally seemed genuinely concerned that no one except representatives of the Vatican should be allowed to take possession of the book. If this continued, Mason was going to have to hear some persuasive extracts from the *Vatican Book of Secrets*.

'You see the camera to your right, at the top of the streetlight?' Patricia said in his ear. 'We have footage of your thief from that. Brief footage. Moving north at an odd pace.'

'An odd pace?'

'She's weaving and ducking but not like she's trying to hide from anyone. I'd say she'd partaken of one too many Merlots if I didn't know she'd been in a car crash.'

Mason started down the road, tracking the thief's route.

'Now,' Patricia said. 'You see that other camera, nestled in the eaves of the building across the road?'

'I see it.'

'The feed catches her passing about forty minutes ago. After that, she doesn't reappear.'

Mason stopped and studied the way ahead as the drizzle continued to coat his face. The street was empty. 'And where is the next camera?'

'Approximately three hundred yards further on.'

Mason conveyed the information to Roxy and Sally. Together, they eyed the buildings on both sides of the road.

'At least eight possibilities.' Mason blew water from the end of his nose. 'Come on.'

Roxy held him back. 'We're doing some good here and I can get on board with that. But there's a line we can't cross.'

'I'll go alone then,' Sally said obstinately and started past them.

'I think we have to do everything that we can to apprehend the architect of Rusk's murder *and* the Vatican thieves,' Mason said. 'I really do.'

'This won't help rectify past mistakes,' Roxy said. 'Believe me, I've tried.'

Mason stared at her for almost half a minute before turning away. Failure was a nemesis he warred with every hour of every day. Ignoring Roxy, he pushed forward.

'Check every door,' he told Sally. 'The woman was bleeding badly. Check the entrance steps and frames. Most of the residences' doorways are inset, sheltered, so maybe the rain won't have washed the evidence away.'

Mason approached the first, finding a solid oak door nestled under an overhanging concrete lintel. The door itself was dry, the guttering above redirecting the water. He tried the handle before moving to the windows but found not even the thinnest sliver of a gap to peer through.

'That's a private residence,' Roxy said, stalking past. 'We're better off looking for flats.'

He liked her thinking and that she was being a team player even when she didn't agree with him. To be fair, he thought, judging the hour, she was probably suffering from a mega rum withdrawal. He watched her cross the street and continued with his own investigation.

Minutes later, Roxy caught his attention and waved him over. Mason crossed to her side, closely followed by Sally.

'Blood on the door handle.' She pointed to a brass knob smeared in dried crimson. 'And there, and there.'

Mason saw a red handprint on the concrete door frame. It was at a low height, as if the person who made it had hunched over and taken a few seconds to rest. There was also a dark stain in the centre of the door, which told Mason that somebody had rested their head or shoulder against it.

Roxy pointed out a multi-unit doorbell and announcer panel. 'There are six flats.'

'Shouldn't be too hard to find the right one.' Mason tried the door handle, finding it locked.

'Yeah, Einstein, I already tried that.' Roxy rolled her eyes.

'Didn't they teach you how to pick locks in your previous life?' He slipped a hand into his back pocket.

'Sure they did. But I don't have my tools on me.'

'Crap.' Mason felt an empty pocket. 'Neither do I.'

'Every second we waste,' Sally fretted, 'increases the chance of the book disappearing.'

'Yeah, yeah, we get it,' Roxy grumbled. Mason had the impression her reply would have been far more scathing if Sally's father hadn't just died.

'Pizza delivery?' Mason ventured.

'Go for it.' Roxy nodded.

On the fifth of six attempts, Mason was buzzed in.

The building consisted of two floors, three rooms per floor. They scanned the lower level but saw no signs of blood. Mason started up the stairs, dripping water all over the thick, dirty grey carpet. A faint musty odour reached his nostrils as he climbed and a minuscule crack in the landing window admitted a thin, bitter gust of wind. Mason stopped opposite the first door.

Not only was there blood on the handle, but the door was ajar.

Mason gave Roxy a questioning glance and received a nod in return. He crossed the landing and gave the door a gentle push, allowing it to glide open.

Sally stayed behind them, her instincts making her act as part of the team.

Mason watched the room's interior unfold as the door swung open. 'Oh, no.'

The black-clad body was slumped sideways on the floor in front of the sofa, head down, the ashen face turned towards them. Mason rushed inside, telling Sally to close and lock the door behind her. He reached the woman and bent down.

'Is she dead?' Sally asked.

Mason checked for a pulse and studied the body. 'Yes. It must be blood loss or internal injuries perhaps. There are no other wounds. Don't touch anything, and wipe that door handle down. Judging by the blood I'm guessing that our killer expired a short while ago.'

'We're dealing with some really sick psychopaths,' Roxy said.

'The book?' Sally asked.

Roxy was scouring the apartment. 'Gone,' she said. 'Unless it's very well hidden. But judging by the state of her . . .'

Mason nodded his agreement. The thief's facemask, partly askew, was concave on the left side of her skull. Dried blood encrusted it and had dripped down to her shoulders.

'They left her to die?' Sally had walked over and was staring down at the body. She gripped the bridge of her nose to assuage the rich coppery stench of fresh blood saturating the air. 'Don't get me wrong, I hate her, but she was a master thief, and completed a task some would say was impossible.'

'Tying up loose ends,' Mason said. 'The people who perpetrate these crimes – they are not like you and I, Sally. Life means nothing to them. They didn't care that she would die a slow death, alone.'

'I hate to say it,' Roxy said, making sure she was standing clear of the pool of blood. 'But if the book's gone, we're done. Patricia won't risk helping us again with CCTV without a local police sanction. At least, I doubt it.'

Mason took in the entire room: the dusty old prints on the walls, the pockmarked wooden flooring, the chipped and stained furnishings.

'Impersonal,' Roxy said, reading his mind. 'I've checked the drawers and wardrobes. All empty. This was, at best, a backup safehouse.'

'Which indicates a larger team,' Mason said. 'Who came to help our thief and then abandoned her. Wait. What's this?'

On turning back to the body, his eyes had alighted upon the top edge of a piece of paper nestled behind a cushion on the sofa where the woman had slumped in death. Carefully, he reached across the body and plucked the paper from its resting place. In their melancholy, neither Sally nor Roxy seemed interested.

'To find book, find Amori,' he said.

Sally whipped her head up. 'What?'

'That's what it says. I'm guessing she wrote this before she slid to the floor, wanting us to find it. The paper is blood-smeared.'

'She wanted *us* to find it?' Roxy asked dubiously.

'Sorry, bad phrasing. She wanted *someone* to find it, and she knew we were closing in.'

'To find book, find Amori,' Sally mused. 'Written in haste. Written . . . possibly as an act of vengeance? I mean, why else do it?'

'They left her here to die,' Mason agreed. 'Which, obviously, she was aware of. But what's the Amori?'

Sally pursed her lips. 'A secret society. My father wrote about them more than once. I'd have to refer to his—'

'Wait,' Mason said. 'There's more.'

The way the thief's body was slumped facing the door had obscured more lettering. 'She wrote something on the floor in her own blood as she died.' He leaned over.

'What is it?' Sally asked eagerly.

Mason couldn't make it out. 'She's obscuring most of it. I see V, A, R and Y. If we want it all, we're gonna have to move the body.'

'Where do we draw the line?' Roxy asked.

'We can't stop now,' Sally insisted. 'Even *she* knew the value of the book.' She pointed at the thief. 'Even *she*, the person who stole it, knew it had got into the wrong hands. Why else would she leave the message?'

Mason reached down and gently rolled the body before letting it settle back once more. 'The entire word she wrote is "Calvary",' he said. 'In her own blood.'

'Calvary? Amori?' Sally pondered it, rolling the words around her tongue.

'Betrayed by her own team,' Roxy shook her head, looking down at the thief. 'I kind of know that feeling.'

Mason blinked at her. He hadn't imagined her words came from deeper anxieties.

The raven-haired woman shrugged at him. 'It doesn't matter now.'

Mason was about to dispute that, maybe get her to speak openly, but Sally spoke up.

'It's a riddle,' she said. 'A clue. The Amori are a secret society who hate the Church. That much I recall. I'll have to check my father's writings for more. But it has to be them, right? They stole the *Book of Secrets*.'

'Let's not get ahead of ourselves,' Mason said. 'Where does Calvary fit in?'

'I don't know,' Sally said. 'Yet. Look, the thief is saying the book may be gone but the Amori are discoverable. She wanted to write it all on the note, maybe, but wasn't strong enough to hold out. That's why she wrote just one word, "Calvary", in blood. At least, I think so.'

Mason thought her premise feasible. 'So what are you saying? That the book's still close by?'

'I'm saying,' Sally turned towards the door, 'that we need to put our research heads on and delve deeper.' She hesitated. 'Which is exactly what my father used to say. I never thought I'd miss him saying that, but . . .'

Mason took a last look at the body and the blood pooled around it. The sight of death and gore didn't bother him, which was worrying. He'd taken the security job to avoid scenes that reminded him of Mosul.

What have we got ourselves into?

Whatever it was, it felt huge. And with Sally pushing them, he was sure their night wasn't going to get any easier.

'You want to go after that book?' Roxy asked.

'If not us, who else?' Sally answered. 'The Vatican police

don't have these clues. We do. And we're all personally invested.'

'But your father,' Roxy said. 'Won't the Vatican people be calling you? Looking for you?'

'They are.' Sally nodded. 'That's why I removed the chip in my phone and threw it away. Please.' She gazed at them. 'Please help me save the world as we know it.'

Mason wondered if she were exaggerating just to get them on board. But his mother and father were both Christians. He hadn't seen them in years, but knew how deep their faith ran, how precious their beliefs were. And they were but one couple in a wider church of millions. Was Sally dramatising the situation? Probably, but Mason didn't want to dissuade her, for his own sake. Discouragement felt too much like failure. Also, the Amori were clearly violent extremists capable of killing anyone who got in their way. Mason had encountered their like before and knew they shouldn't be allowed free rein.

'Why us?' he asked.

'Because we can,' Sally said. 'And we should. We were there at the beginning of all this, and we'll be there at the end.'

Mason didn't doubt it. He just hoped they'd still be alive.

Chapter 13

In the darkened lobby of a twenty-four-hour hotel, in a dim corner where nobody would bother them, Mason, Roxy and Sally ordered coffee and snacks from the bar and shrugged their wet coats and jackets off, letting them fall to the floor.

Roxy selected a long leather sofa and put her boots up; Mason chose a well-padded armchair; and Sally knelt on the thickly carpeted floor, her laptop set on the low table before them. They waited for refreshments to arrive before proceeding, each trying to process the events of the last few hours.

Roxy eyed her coffee, clearly wishing it were something stronger. 'Technically,' she said, 'we're off the clock, right?'

'I'm not carrying you out of here,' Mason said. 'And I'm not dragging you out of a rum-soaked bed again. We're on the clock until this thing is resolved.'

Sally eyed them both. 'I didn't realise you two were a couple.'

'Eh?' Mason choked. 'No, we bloody well aren't.'

Roxy pouted. 'Thanks, Joe. You really needn't sound so aggrieved about that. Besides,' she winked at Sally, 'Joe's married.'

Mason glared. 'I didn't think you knew that.'

'Water cooler gossip, that's all. You know what it's like down at the office. I'm sure there're plenty of stories starring yours truly.'

Mason tried to repress a smile. 'One or two.'

'One or two?' Roxy snorted. 'Yeah, right. I'm told Mason and his wife are the spitting image of each other.'

Mason frowned. It was a long-standing joke. 'You mean blond hair, blue eyes, wiry and young-looking? Maybe. She's a bit shorter.'

'That sounds rehearsed.' Roxy sipped her coffee and made a distressed face. 'Tell us something original.'

'We're separated,' Mason said under his breath as he reached for his own coffee. 'Hannah and I separated after Mosul. Two years ago. She's met somebody else now.'

Roxy stared at him, blinking, lips working but unable to deliver a comment. Sally fiddled with her laptop. After half a minute Roxy rose, swore and said she was heading off to order three straight rums. Mason stared after her, worried.

'She'll be fine,' Sally said. 'Let her cope in her own way.'

'I have no problem with that. As long as her way doesn't compromise us.'

'First time working together?' Sally ventured.

'How can you tell?' Mason looked back at her. 'Sorry. What have you got?'

Sally paused with her fingers above her laptop and looked up at him, tears hanging in the corners of her eyes. 'I want that book,' she said. 'My dad died trying to save it and the Vatican. The thief was killed by her own team. The car chase was crazy. The police certainly have their hands full.'

'The Vatican have their own police force,' Mason said. 'Though admittedly, I don't know if they'll get jurisdictional control. If not, they'll still be well represented in the hunt for your father's murderers.'

'Which raises another dilemma,' Sally said. 'How did the thief gain entry?'

'Inside job,' Mason said, knowing she already knew the answer. 'The more elaborate version of that statement being – secret societies survive through infiltration. If the Amori are as old as you think, they'll have insinuated themselves in all the big organisations. The government, the banks, the stock exchange, not to mention the Vatican.'

Sally tapped the table to emphasise her next point. 'Which means we can't trust anyone. What we do next we do alone.'

Roxy rocked up then, a tumbler in each hand. 'I was thinking,' she said, 'that, technically, our job here is done.'

'Technically?' Sally looked up at her. 'Technically? You wanna quit so you can swim to the bottom of another bottle?'

Roxy stared at Mason. 'What have you told her?'

'Never opened my mouth.' He shrugged. 'In any case, I don't *know* anything.'

'About me? Nothing from the water cooler?'

'I don't hang around water coolers. Whatever your demons are – and I'm assuming they're *powerful* – I can't help you.'

'But I can,' Sally put in as Roxy sat down and knocked back a shot. 'You work for me now. You're both contracted for at least three more days.'

'The circumstances of our agreement have changed—' Mason thought he should make it clear.

'I know, I know, but I will inherit my father's estate. I have the power and the sway.' Sally's face dropped as she spoke, taking on a haunted expression. 'Shit, I can't believe I just said that.'

'You and your father didn't get on,' Mason said gently.

'Not for a long time. His wealth embarrassed me. All the privilege, the self-serving, back-patting, conniving freaks who came calling every day. I saw the corruption, how the poor suffer for the evolution of the rich. I was courted by men who never saw *me*, just my name. And my father . . . well, he was born into it and embraced it.' Sally shook her head. 'Probably the fault of his own parents, but I couldn't do that. My father never knew real struggle, so I fought for everything. I was the first in and the last to leave school and then college, and when I turned twenty-two, I left. Went off the grid and stood on my own two feet. I fought, worked for the underprivileged . . .'

As she spoke, Mason saw that she was not only engaging both him and Roxy but tapping away at the laptop, already advancing their research.

'Respect for my skills, my work ethic, my integrity, that's what I want. And I thought working with my father would, ultimately, help me to attain that level in this field of work. Maybe it will.'

'You don't have to prove yourself to us,' Mason said. 'We're just bodyguards.' He wanted to keep things as detached as possible, worried that Sally might be latching herself too tightly to them. 'I'm sure there are people better suited to this task that you can hire.'

Sally stopped tapping for a moment as if considering. 'You're involved,' she said. 'The Amori murdered my father in the act of stealing the *Book of Secrets*. You were there. You were captured on camera. You chased the thief through the catacombs and then across Rome. I'm sorry, Mason and Roxy, but you have to see this through.'

'The Catholic Church,' Roxy said, 'has beaten powerful enemies, old and new. I would guess it comes under attack every day. What makes this day so different?'

'A great question,' Sally said. 'And one I'm trying to answer with this laptop right now. I've accessed my father's journals and have used the search term "Amori".'

Mason leaned forward, interested despite himself. 'And what have you found?'

'It's rifling through reams of material. As I mentioned

before, I've been converting decades of notebook ramblings into usable data. My father's notes, the Rusk Notes, as I call them, were vague and scribbled at speed, but I can decipher them. Look, are you willing to help me?'

Wondering why she referred to them as the Rusk Notes, alienating her father in a way, Mason took a deep breath. 'Roxy?'

The raven-haired American stared through the bottom of her empty glass. 'What?'

'We'd be going against company protocol if we help Sally.'

'You mean rebelling?' Roxy grinned. 'Yeah, I'm all up for that.'

Mason had been hoping for something more constructive but, in truth, he was still trying to deal with old mistakes and the only way forward was to make up for the lives he believed he had cost.

By saving new ones.

'What do you have?' he asked Sally.

Chapter 14

Their little corner of the lobby was bordered on two sides by bare windows. Mason looked up as the rain lashed at the ten-foot panes, striking the glass with an icy fury that refused to be ignored.

'The Amori,' Sally said, 'as I recalled, have been mentioned several times. Of course, the Catholic Church has had many enemies during the last two millennia. Conspiracy theories are rife, and secret society threats from the infamous Illuminati to the Knights Templar and the Freemasons. The Amori, however, are a different animal altogether.'

Mason already knew why. 'Yeah, I've heard of all the above.'

'They're the Church's greatest enemy. The society yearns to destroy Christianity.'

'How do you know this?' Roxy asked.

'My father encountered them several times during his research. Historical fact is the *only* absolute in his notes. I doubt that he ever made a speculative comment in his life. Anyway, they are an ancient entity, founded around the time of the birth of Babylon. Some say they established the first settlement where Babylon was later constructed.'

'In other words, they were here way before Christianity?' Roxy asked.

'Oh, yes, Babylon can be traced back to the eighteenth century BC, although its earliest mention appears on a small clay tablet from around 2340 BC. I guess you would call these facts mere annotations, footnotes to history that my father nevertheless catalogued thoroughly as his job demanded. The real interesting part comes much later.'

Mason flicked his eyes to the windows, distracted once more by the angry squall and powerful gusts of wind that tested the integrity of every plastic frame and layer of mortar. The streets would be scoured clean tonight.

'You mean in history?' he asked. 'Or your father's writings?'

'Both. For untold years, the Amori were content to exist in the shadows, the puppet-masters of humanity without challenge. But through the centuries they saw how Christianity flourished, how it defied and tested all that had come before.'

'What do we know about them?' Roxy asked.

'Well, that's the problem. Even among early Christians the Amori were a well-kept secret. They were a name muttered in anger and then ignored, never discussed. Talking about a group, or a person, or anything, gives it visibility, power and purpose. For instance, in these days of social media, an obscure conspiracy theory can turn viral in hours, thus empowering the real virus – the people behind the fake news – and spreading speculation to the point where even sensible people become confused.'

'You're saying the Vatican's view was the less said about them the better?'

'Exactly. Keep them buried and out of sight. The Amori have been seeking a way to legitimately break free of their shadows.'

'And so we come to the *Book of Secrets*,' Mason said. 'And the explosive power it may contain.'

Sally nodded. 'Let's not forget that the Amori are intertwined with the shadows that have controlled humanity's governments for centuries, and still have great sway. Whatever they choose to reveal, the coverage will be extensive.'

'Going back to the thief's message,' Roxy said. 'We're being directed to find this Amori. Is that even possible?'

'I'm not sure that it's ever been tried. Well, actually, *somebody* tried. Hence the clue "Calvary". But the real information is inside the book.'

'Do you have more?' Roxy waved at the laptop.

'Don't confuse my father's research with the *Book of Secrets*. He never got to examine it. All we have are his notes concerning other matters that may cross-reference.'

'And that doesn't sound like a whole lot.' Roxy finished the last of her drink as a machine-gun clatter of rain spattered the windows.

'It's not,' Sally agreed. 'But like I said – there are a lot of notes here. You need to be patient.'

Mason raised an eyebrow in Roxy's direction, assuming patience wasn't one of her strong points. 'At least we're warm and relaxed,' he said, settling back in the chair and feeling anything but the latter.

Roxy grimaced in his direction before heading back to the bar. Mason let his eyes roam the lobby for a few seconds but saw nothing untoward. A thin haze of weariness settled over him. He closed his eyes for a moment, letting it wash on through.

'We have a lead,' Sally said. 'At least, I think so.'

Mason looked up. 'On the Amori?'

'Not exactly. But there's mention of a man here, an archivist and academic who has researched both the Amori and the *Book of Secrets*. As you know, the book is shown to each new pope after their inauguration but also, crucially, *one academic per pope is tasked with the book's upkeep.* A trusted individual updates it, adds new information when it arises. You don't rely on a pope to do that, you rely on a qualified professor and researcher.'

'And the current pope . . .' Mason prodded.

'Took office in 2013. Pope Francis took over after Benedict XVI renounced the Papacy in February 2013.'

'Which means this academic, this . . .' He paused.

'Mateo DeVille.'

'. . . won't speak to us. He'll have signed the Vatican equivalent of the Official Secrets Act.'

'Maybe.' Sally bit her lip. 'Maybe not. My father's been hanging around the Vatican for years.'

'Is that a good thing?'

'No, I don't mean like a perv or anything.' Sally gave him a disbelieving glance. 'What I mean is, he probably knew this Mateo DeVille. There's every possibility that they worked together, both being professors and researchers. And if I explain what's happened . . .'

Mason saw credibility in her words. Sally Rusk might well be the only person Mateo DeVille would talk to outside Vatican City. A conflicting mix of excitement, apprehension and restraint churned inside him.

'If it's a way to redress your father's death,' he said, 'then I'm in.'

'In where?' Roxy returned, another tumbler in each hand.

'We're going to talk to a man named Mateo DeVille,' Sally said.

'Does he own a Dalmatian?' Roxy blinked.

'No, no, he worked on the *Book of Secrets* with Pope Benedict up to 2013.' The jest flew over the top of Sally's head. Quite rightly, in Mason's opinion.

'You're making the assumption that the *Book of Secrets* mentions the Amori,' Roxy said, sitting down.

'No,' Sally assured her, 'I'm not. I'm hoping that Mateo, a Vatican academic, will be able to throw some light on the thief's message. *To find book, find Amori.* And then just *Calvary.* If the thief used the *Book of Secrets* to define that message . . .'

'Then Mateo should have some ideas,' Mason said. 'Technically, Mateo doesn't even have to break any vows. All we need is a nudge in the right direction.'

'We need more than a nudge.' Roxy sighed. 'But I'm willing to give it a try.'

Sally was already on her feet. 'Good,' she said. 'Because we can't shy away from this. The Church has always fought the most terrible of enemies. The Amori might just be the worst.'

Chapter 15

The *Book of Secrets* had been with Marduk for many hours now. On delivery, a smear of blood had daubed its front cover, blood that had not yet fully dried by the time it reached Marduk's sweating hands.

His daughter's blood.

Marduk had wiped the book clean with a tissue and thrown away the blood-smeared rag. He'd held the book at arm's length, studying this grand unicorn, this legendary tome which was both the work and the ruin of the Amori's greatest enemy. For two thousand years, they had sought the best path to Christianity's destruction.

Marduk would be the monarch glad to walk it. And breaking the shackles with which the Vatican had restrained them was important to *his* future too. If he were to be the world's most significant leader, to rule governments and increase the Amori's global influence, then his most devious rivals needed hammering to their knees.

After laying the book on his desk, Marduk had summoned his top aides into his study. Archgenerals Kuthu, Leland, Arcady and Masterton. Kuthu was a brute of a man, relentless and vicious. Arcady was craftier and far more bloodthirsty, an astute woman with a deadly hand.

Leland was the subtlest of the three, often speaking with a forked tongue but useful because he knew how to get things done. Masterton was the trickiest to handle – he was older and set in his ways, on the cusp of being retired, but something both valuable and challenging in his Archgenerals that Marduk found came with age was *connections*, and Masterton had too many to upset. At least for now. All four had proved their loyalty to the Amori, and had been tested beyond their limits.

They entered together and took seats without being asked. Kuthu spoke first, his voice deep and thick. 'Is that it?'

'Yes.' Marduk regarded the book. 'Not much to look at, I grant you.'

The *Vatican Book of Secrets* sat about five inches thick. It was wrapped in a hard, frayed crimson jacket and bore only an old form of the Vatican City's coat of arms, an addition that must have been made after the fourteenth century, Marduk knew, since that was when the arms originated.

The cover's edges were creased, the pages misaligned and tatty. They were not uniform, as if many archivists had added new pages in haste through the years. Or maybe they just hadn't cared for the book's upkeep. Either way, it was a messy volume.

'And that tatty thing will destroy the Church?' Arcady asked, sitting back and crossing her legs.

Marduk reached out. 'Let's see, shall we?'

'Yes, let us see if thousands of years of Amori narrative will pay off,' Leland said.

Marduk didn't doubt it for a minute. 'I do hope that's a general comment, Archgeneral. We do not cast doubt on our ancestral origins.'

'Ancestral? Inherited? We know only what we're told. For all we know the book could destroy the church *and* the Amori.'

Marduk froze, his hands inches from the book, and eyed his Archgeneral. 'Do you doubt the word of the Creed?'

'Another book we've never seen,' Leland snapped.

'The original was lost thousands of years ago,' Marduk admitted. 'But you have seen copies of our bible.'

'Are they copies?' Leland challenged. 'Or are they part of someone's new agenda?'

Marduk felt something dark like curdled poison churn deep in his belly. 'The Creed is the Amori. It defines our ethos, our belief system. Do you question it?'

'No,' Leland said with less confidence than Marduk was comfortable with. 'It's the arrival of this vile book. It has me in doubt.'

Marduk held the man's gaze. It was earnest, open. Clearly, Leland thought he was dealing with a confidante, a figure with whom he could discuss his misgivings. Marduk glanced quickly into the faces of Kuthu and Arcady. Both appeared in shock, and were looking at Marduk to see what he would do.

'I also have to ask,' Masterton put in softly, 'was it absolutely necessary to order your daughter shot to death?'

Marduk ignored him. 'You doubt the Creed, the Amori?' he said, trying to keep his voice even. 'This omniscient society.'

'The world's oldest society,' Kuthu put in, maybe trying to defuse the situation. 'We are hundreds of purebloods ruling hundreds of subordinates, all loyal to the word of the Creed.'

'With *thousands* of followers the world over,' Arcady added.

Marduk nodded. 'And I am the supreme leader,' he said. 'I will take this society into an all-powerful future. Who are you, Leland, to question your monarch, your religion, the privileged life you lead? You sit here in a position above the eight elders, above the *massu*.'

Leland nodded at Marduk as if he was nodding at a

close friend, as if they were discussing a sport. 'I thank you,' he said. 'But our followers are either blackmailed, greedy or under threat of death. Useful, yes, but not exactly loyal. We are splintered, I feel. Not whole because we have flawed goals. And the *massu*? They are not enough.'

'Each *massu* controls a section of the globe,' Kuthu said. 'We do not need more. The very name means leader or expert in old Akkadian. And they too, have subordinates. Between us, we hold this world in terrible thrall.'

'And yet we shed our own blood,' Masterton said, again softly.

Leland looked down, fixing his eyes on the *Book of Secrets*. 'It divides us. This folly.'

Marduk studied his every movement. 'The Creed unites and fixes us. It is both our mother and our father. It is *my* world and I will sacrifice everything in its name. But this . . .' He waved at the *Book of Secrets*. 'This is our victory. Our revenge for the sins of the past. This is how we destroy the church.'

'It feels theatrical,' Leland said earnestly. 'Dramatic. Honestly, is it really worth it?'

Pure fury flooded Marduk's veins. 'The *Book of Secrets* is *my* revelation,' he grated and found himself lunging forward. There was a blade in his right hand, a wide curved dagger, and it cut through Leland's windpipe as if it was butter. Blood spewed everywhere as Leland tried to scream. The man's eyes were wild but not as wild as Marduk's. White heat overcame him and it was minutes before he returned from the fog of madness to find himself stabbing a bloody, dead and ragged body over and over again. He was soaked in Leland's blood, as were Kuthu and Arcady, his desk and the front cover of the *Book of Secrets*. Masterton had leapt aside and was staring at him as if he'd gone mad.

'He betrayed us,' Marduk spat. 'Tainted blood has no place in my world.'

'*Your* world,' Masterton began.

'The elders never did like him,' Kuthu interrupted, showing no emotion. 'Too vindictive.'

'He was my Archgeneral,' Marduk hissed, attempting to wipe blood from his face but only smearing it to form a bright red mask. After a moment, he stopped trying, thinking the image was quite fitting.

'Does anybody else question our four-thousand-year-old society?' he rumbled, biting his gums to hold onto some semblance of sanity. 'A society that saw crusaders attacking the Holy Land, priests ordering death, torture and burning. That saw Christianity as their greatest enemy and have been attacking it ever since, trying to raze the religion from the Earth. Does anyone else question us, or are more lessons required?'

Both Kuthu and Arcady looked chastised. Masterton said nothing but looked pensive. Marduk walked back to his desk, sat down and opened the *Book of Secrets*. The first sheet was blank. There were no title papers. Marduk saw immediately that he'd have to browse through every page.

'This may take some time,' he said, ignoring the steady seeping of blood across the floorboards and the sharp, metallic stench that filled the air.

'A shame there is no full chapter concerning Jesus Christ, his remains and burial objects,' Arcady said smugly.

'It is entirely disjointed,' Marduk said with some amusement. 'Fragmentary. Bits and pieces added infrequently, just like a scrapbook with countless footnotes. Perhaps it is organised by calendar date.'

'That doesn't help,' Arcady pointed out. 'We don't know when they came by the new information concerning Christ's remains and acted upon it.'

'A good point,' Marduk said. 'And there is no huge rush. Not now.' He grinned. 'We can destroy them at our leisure.'

The Archgenerals grinned with him, even Masterton.

Around them, the huge study lay pooled in darkness; only the great oak rectangle of his desk was picked out by a bright spotlight.

Marduk took some time to savour the moment. He could barely express, even to himself, his feelings of accomplishment, pride and outright rapture. With deliberate slowness, avoiding Leland's repulsive remains, he crossed to a sideboard, reached inside, and pulled out a vintage bottle of cognac worth around £100,000, specially reserved for the finest of occasions. With care, Marduk poured three small glasses.

'To the Amori, who will finally achieve their rightful reward,' he said and raised his glass. 'And to me, the future leader of the world.'

Masterton hesitated. 'Is that right?' he asked. 'It is the Amori's victory, the Amori who will reign.'

'Of course.' Marduk nodded.

'Perhaps we should also toast your daughter,' Masterton went on. 'It is largely due to her efforts that we even have the book.'

'*Her* efforts?' Marduk's eyebrows climbed his forehead. '*Hers?* This is *my* plan. My victory. I have brought the Amori to this point and I am responsible for our victory.'

'I merely meant to recognise her sacrifice,' Masterton said, his face taking on a clever, knowing expression.

Marduk struggled to prevent himself from spitting out a raft of reasons why Nina had failed, why ultimately she had been sacrificed in favour of Marduk, and of course the Amori. In the end, he breathed deeply and held his silence.

They drank together, savouring the flavours, before Marduk turned his attention back to the book. Pages crackled as he turned some and unfolded others, his dark eyes drinking in two millennia of garish secrets.

'Their kingdom is built on a plague pit of crumbling bones,' he said. 'It is only a matter of time until it collapses.

In the past, even with this knowledge, we might never have accomplished total destruction. But today, the media has become a vast, hungry, greedy beast which feeds off sensationalist ruination. Nothing spreads better, or makes more money, than the press-covered downfall of an icon. In this, they are our ally.'

'All through the hideous crusades our people were forced to watch the Christians,' Kuthu said. 'To hope they would wither and expire . . . but they prospered. The Knights Templar debacle was dreadful, the trial of Galileo one of their most infamous and embarrassing moments. How dare he say the Earth is not the centre of the Universe?' Kuthu looked like he wanted to spit but refrained. 'They killed Joan of Arc, and then there were the inquisitions and the witch hunts.'

Arcady reached out a hand to steady her colleague, concerned by his rising indignation, the trembling of his hands.

Marduk glanced up for a moment. 'Calm yourself, my friend. The day of reckoning is close. Retribution is at hand.' He went back to thumbing through the book. 'Most of this is old dross. Fit only for the fire, I think. But as they say – the diamond is in the rough . . .'

Minutes passed that turned into an hour. Marduk digested centuries of clandestine work at a steady pace, stopping occasionally to comment.

As the storm outside diminished, and as he read further Marduk was struck by a mental bolt of lightning. Until now, everything had been moving perfectly. The theft, the escape, the delivery of the book. Already, Marduk was imagining achieving his goal of being the dominant leader of the world and now something else was starting to churn deep inside. A new hatred for the Church, of the Vatican itself, a hatred that was starting to coat the crust of the ancient animosity like fresh blood coagulating over old.

They killed Nina. Yes, *they* killed her with their old secrets, their arrogance, hollow superiority. They were liars, frauds and murderers. *My daughter would be alive if not for the Vatican's egotism.* And now they might be able to utilise something more against the Amori. He reread the passage twice more. The sense of shock made him sit up and wipe his eyes.

His jaw clenched. 'This is not good.'

Kuthu, Masterton and Arcady were instantly attentive. 'The story of Jesus Christ is not as we expected?'

'Oh, I'm not there yet. For now, this is far more important.'

The Archgenerals looked confused. 'More important than proof that Jesus was *not* the son of God?'

'In this moment, at this time – yes. We are part of this goddamned book.' He was losing his cool. 'The Amori . . . are in here.'

'But . . . wasn't that expected?' Arcady leaned forward, her round face creased with confusion, flowing blonde locks falling forwards across her shoulders.

Marduk collected himself, realising he was ranting inarticulately. 'Yes, yes, of course,' he said. 'But I expected to be portrayed as the ancient enemy. Something along the lines of Satan perhaps. But not this. *Even in the secret book the Amori are purposely concealed.*' He read the passage out loud. '*You do not nourish a monster, you starve it and let it become extinct. There are worse monsters abroad than the Amori, I am sure, but right now I cannot imagine one.*'

Marduk took a deep breath. 'Such hatred,' he said. 'Such blind devotion. Why can they not see the real truth . . . that Jesus was a warrior king? I mean, how many times in the Book of Revelation was Jesus portrayed with a double-edged sword protruding from his mouth?'

Arcady clenched her fists. 'Their entire faith is based on

a lie. No faith, no matter how unshakeable, can survive such a revelation.'

Marduk lifted the book. 'Maybe Jacques Heindl felt the same.'

'I don't know that name.' Kuthu frowned.

'In 1888, Jacques Heindl was an archivist and keeper of the book to the then pope. Heindl trained as a doctor, passing every exam before turning to the Church. He writes that the Church regards the Amori as an age-old, long-forgotten enemy. It prefers to bury its head in the sand and pretend we no longer exist, like so many of its past wrongs. So, each successive pope would read of the Amori as a past history – like the Crusades for instance – rather than as an enduring war. Most modern leaders have not heard of the Amori because we choose – or were forced – to operate in the shadows.'

'I still don't see the significance of this Jacques Heindl,' Kuthu said.

'Yes, of course. He writes: "... *the most dangerous enemy the Church has ever known were the Amori. I have left a riddle that points toward their lair, for I cannot reveal it here ...*" And later: "*The Church will not even recognise their existence, let alone pay them a visit ...*"'

'And that is from 1888?' Arcady shook her head. 'The arrogance of it.'

Marduk was inclined to agree, but that wasn't the issue. 'I am afraid we have a serious problem. Jacques Heindl has indeed penned a riddle, a tough but decipherable one. It is: "*Seek the Amori at the altar of the first of the Five Great Churches, at Calvary.*" That alone tells me Heindl knew what he was talking about—'

'But this was 1888,' Masterton pointed out. 'And as you say, the Amori are but an antiquated footnote in these modern times. Who could possibly use the old riddle to find us?'

'An antiquated footnote?' Marduk frowned.

'Yes,' Masterton said. 'Much like your daughter.'

Marduk knew right then that Masterton was shaping up to be a major problem, the proverbial spear in his side. Sooner or later, something was going to have to be done about Masterton. Something that, if he could pull it off, might even be entertaining.

'Any living archivist, of course,' Marduk said. 'All are fully conversant with the entire book. They have to be, as new and old questions and answers are posed.'

'The Amori cannot be tied to the theft,' Kuthu said.

'Of course, but you must think. *Think ahead . . .*' Marduk pressed on. 'The whole point of the plan, and the theft, is to prove *publicly* that the Catholic Church is a fraud. The Amori are emerging from the shadows. As soon as we do, the people will be aware of us, the governments will know and the Church will know. They will track us down because, even as we use this book as proof of their lies, it holds a clue that will lead our enemies to our home.'

'Is the clue that good?' Arcady asked intuitively. 'Much has happened since 1888.'

'Not perfect,' Marduk admitted. 'But it could lead someone in the right direction and straight to our oldest stronghold. We just can't allow that. They can never be allowed to find all the trappings of our heritage, our precious objects of wealth and worship, our *birthplace*. We're too close to victory to risk outright discovery.'

'It's a dilemma. They can't be allowed to find . . .' Arcady couldn't bring herself to finish the sentence, the name of their home.

'Yes, and again I quote the Book of Revelation: "*For this reason in one day her plagues will come, pestilence and mourning and famine, and she will be burned up with fire; for the Lord God who judges her is strong.*" Our origins are clear even in *their* bible, protected and unchanging. But we can never return there.' Marduk hung his head.

'Wait.' Kuthu didn't understand. 'We hold the only existing copy of this book. You're suggesting that one of the still-living archivists may be able to recall the riddle and locate our so-called lair? How many archivists are there?'

'Just two,' Marduk said, reaching for the telephone. 'The current archivist – Sergio Pagano – and the man who served Pope Benedict XVI until 2013 – a man called Mateo DeVille.'

'And what will you do about them?' Arcady asked with a smile.

Marduk answered by picking up a phone, jabbing buttons and almost snarling as his call was answered. 'Hassell?' he asked. 'Is that you?'

'Yeah, sure, what is it?' The leader of Gido's team, the crew who had planned the theft and then retrieved the book from Nina's dying hands, sounded at odds, as if he hated Marduk for what he had done.

'I have another job for you.'

'We're done, bud. We're not colleagues. You burned that bridge when you ordered us to murder your daughter.'

'Would you rather I called Gido?' Marduk ignored the guarded look of challenge Masterton sent him across the table. The older Archgeneral would have to be handled very carefully.

'The boss said one job.' Hassell sounded shaken, as if something fundamental had changed in him. 'We gave you one job.'

'And now I need another. Look, both you and I know your boss will sanction it so why not capitulate right away? I own Gido.'

Hassell was silent for a while. Marduk was about to prompt him when he spoke up in a quiet voice: 'What do you want?'

'You may want your two assassins to hear this,' Marduk began. 'I have a new mission for you.'

Both Kuthu and Arcady smiled as he laid out a plan.

Chapter 16

Mason drove through sheets of rain, leaning forward to squint through the windscreen as the water surged at them out of the darkness. Their headlights picked out random, violent flurries as thick hedgerows and deep ditches flashed by on both sides. The roads to the north of Rome were narrow, tree-lined and twisting. Probably lovely in the warm light of day. But at night, in this storm, they were treacherous.

Mason glanced at the satnav and then towards Sally, who occupied the passenger seat. 'Any luck finding Mr DeVille?'

'Just keep going.' Sally ruffled the paper map in her hands, peering harder before tapping the car's built-in satellite navigation panel. 'Don't slow down.' Her voice quavered with suppressed tension.

'It's not working.' Roxy leaned in from the back seat. 'And neither is my phone. The weather, maybe.'

'Or the cowboy who rented us this piece of crap,' Mason grunted. 'Wait until I see him.'

'It was short notice,' Roxy said. 'And in the middle of the night. I'm surprised we managed to find anyone at all.'

Mason cleared his throat. 'I guess money talks.'

Sally made a non-committal noise. They had scoured the

internet and made several calls before finding a low-key private rental company who would rent them a car so early in the morning. Sally's credit card and the amount she offered had sealed the deal.

'Any luck?' Mason asked again.

'I'm *trying*,' Sally snapped. 'I'm aware of the bloody urgency. And if I weren't, your driving would certainly remind me.'

Mason eased his foot off the accelerator, but Sally shook her head. 'No, keep going. I'm sorry. There's no time to waste.'

'You think Patricia realised that you lied to her?' Roxy asked.

'I don't know,' Mason replied. 'She can't realise we went rogue, so to speak, or she wouldn't have helped us. Telling her that Sally was re-employing us to find her father's great friend seemed the best way around that.'

'The time of night might have given it away,' Roxy said.

'Or maybe it helped,' Mason retorted. 'Made our request more legitimate. Twenty-four-hour client service is what she prides her company on. And . . .' he added, 'she probably wants to keep her best asset.'

'Thanks.' Roxy sniffed. 'But I do have other offers.'

'I didn't mean *you*. I meant *me*.'

'Oh, you think? Really? There's a shocker.'

Mason half-turned, keeping one eye on the road. 'And what the hell's that supposed to mean?'

'Well, where do I start?' Roxy was finding it hard to keep a straight face.

Mason glared at her before turning once more to Sally.

'If you say "any luck" once more, I'm gonna ram this map sideways down your throat.'

'Whoa.' Mason held up both hands before grabbing the steering wheel once more at ten and two. 'Looks like it's the "let's pick on Joe show". I'll just stay quiet.'

Sally's map-reading skills and the intermittent satnav

eventually brought them to a small, white-walled cottage behind a low hedge, one of several such homes along a tree-lined street beyond the northern borders of Rome.

Mason sat motionless for a long minute after he turned off the car, gazing through the rain that drenched the windscreen. The terrible murder of Professor Rusk and the events that followed had left him feeling sceptical, dubious of his own motives.

The book was just one vast explosive secret, according to Sally. They couldn't waste time dealing with the police. Sally was grieving, desperate and in need of support. Mason wondered if he were feeding his own needs when he refused to stop her, to question her, to turn this whole thing over to the authorities. But he had always been an amiable kind of guy, a team player, and perhaps this was a punitive kind of penance.

For Mosul. For Zack Kelly and Harry Lewis. The circumstances of their sudden deaths beat at Mason like demonic wings; they punished him. His seven-man team had been a strong, honest group, reliant on each other, willing to work for each other, but Zack and Harry had died alone.

Roxy spoke into the silence, snatching him back to reality. 'We going in?'

Mason reached for the door handle before even darker thoughts hijacked their current intentions.

Seconds later, they were out in the rain once more, walking through a rusty, creaking gate and up a winding garden path to the cottage's front door. Sally pressed the bell and waited, the three of them unable to take shelter as they waited for signs of activity. It took another two presses before a light went on in the hallway.

Mason stamped his feet. 'Heads up.'

Sally stepped forwards as the door cracked open. 'Hi, are you Mateo DeVille? And *please* tell me you speak English.'

The creased face blinking at them puckered even further

with confusion. Mason imagined DeVille to be in his eighties. He wore an ankle-length white dressing gown and bedsocks. The few strands of hair remaining atop his head were set at different directions of the compass and it was taking quite some time for his eyes to focus.

'Ciao?' he said.

'We need your help,' Sally tried. 'And we need it fast.'

'Non capisco. Ti sei perso?'

Sally narrowed her eyes, taking in the disorientated look but not quite buying it. 'I'm Professor Sally Rusk,' she said. 'My father was Professor Pierce Rusk. He was murdered tonight by thieves who stole the *Book of Secrets* and we need your help.'

Mason watched as the old man's face lost its absent-minded appearance and smoothed into a look of recognition.

'I remember your father,' he said. 'Come in.'

Mason widened his eyes, exchanging a look of respect with Roxy at Sally's intuition.

They entered DeVille's house, shedding water in the hallway, before following the man into his kitchen. It was a modest room dominated by the four-seater table DeVille waved them to. As they sat down and relaxed, he pottered around the kitchen, first turning the heating on and then preparing a percolator of coffee.

'What has happened?' he asked in perfect English. 'I no longer watch the propaganda channels.'

Assuming he meant the news, Mason listened as Sally brought him up to date on recent events. It took far less time than he'd imagined and involved none of the drama. Of course, Mateo DeVille was an archivist and no doubt preferred facts.

'I respected your father. A great man. I often debated with him. He had great skills in that arena too.' DeVille smiled. 'I regularly found myself being cross-examined and wondering more about his morbid craving for controversy than the actual question posed. Anyway . . .' He waved at them as the kettle rumbled.

DeVille whipped it off its stand before boiling point so that he didn't burn the freshly ground coffee beans, and poured. Then he turned and faced them with his hand on top of the percolator. 'What do you know of the Amori and the book?'

Again, Mason listened as Sally explained their position.

'You realise I am an ex-archivist to the Holy See?' DeVille reminded them. 'I serve God, I serve the Church, I serve the Papacy. Servitude brings a kind of nobility.' He bowed his head. 'My responsibility . . . it is to the Church.'

'We're fighting for the very future of the Church,' Sally said.

'Perhaps you are right,' DeVille said. 'An archivist has to be pragmatic. But the secrets I know . . . I wonder if sometimes we delude ourselves – eschewing the everyday over the celestial. I mean, what is more real than the everyday? To the man who lives in the streets . . . the man who protects his children from corruption . . . the woman who fights for her people.'

'The secrets you know,' Roxy echoed. 'Now *that's* a nail-on-the-head moment. Shouldn't you have some kind of security?'

'For a secret book.' DeVille smiled. 'Written in Latin. Stored in a secret archive. In arguably one of the most protected buildings on earth?'

'Nothing and nobody is safe,' Roxy said. 'I can assure you of that.'

'We're not asking you to reveal any secrets,' Sally assured him. 'Just help us track down the Amori. If they're really this ancient enemy come back to destroy the Church, isn't it your duty?'

DeVille slid three coasters before them and placed steaming mugs on top. 'Duty? I see such hideousness abroad in the world right now that it makes me shudder. It makes me weak. Those who should protect us bleed us dry. Those elected to serve us line their own pockets. There is no nobility in leadership anymore. No sense of *duty*. Where have all the trailblazers gone?'

'The world is in a fragile state,' Sally admitted. 'But doesn't that elevate the role of the Church? Shouldn't you just try harder?'

DeVille smiled as he sat down. 'Yes, but I am no longer part of that. When the pope's principal archivist is no longer required, he is put out to grass. But still . . .' He sighed. 'We waste time. Of course, I am honour-bound to keep the secrets of the great book, but I am horrified to learn it has been stolen. As I said, I remember you and I respected your father. I will help in whatever way I can.'

Sally heaved a sigh of relief. 'Thank you.'

'The Amori was a group of evil men and women, the kind with no morals, no sense of humanity. You know the type. The modern world breeds them relentlessly.'

As Mason listened to DeVille, he formed a picture of a paradoxical figure – a man who had embraced the Church and its divine duties only to find that the real world was laced with nightmares he'd prefer to forget.

'The Amori wanted to change the face of the world,' he said. 'And they wanted to change it in their image. The Amori invented all the worst vices and controlled entire governments. Maybe they still do, although I haven't heard their name connected to any machinations in my lifetime. I imagined they were defunct. A man named Jacques Heindl spoke of the Amori in the book many years ago, along with notes on how to find them.'

'What else did he write?' Roxy asked.

'I can't tell you that. But I can tell you that there are three, maybe four, secrets in that book which utterly terrify me. Which could . . . destroy Christianity and cause many wars. Inspire worldwide uprisings. I can't express enough the desperate need to find that book.'

DeVille's face was fraught with worry, his eyes glistening. As he lifted his mug to drink, Mason noticed his hands were shaking.

'But your faith holds steadfast?' Sally asked.

'I devoted myself to the Church long before I learned of its failings,' DeVille said. 'I am loyal to an ideal, a view, a raft of principles. I am part of the family of God and that, my friends, transcends all. I didn't have to believe in God, I *chose* to, and the way God has answered my prayers through all these years proves to me that He exists. Faith is acceptance of the mind to the revelation of God, accessed through free cooperation and divine grace.'

'I'm sorry for asking.' Sally bowed her head slightly before continuing. 'What can you disclose of Jacques Heindl's additions?'

'The passages he added in 1888 and before are not sensitive,' DeVille allowed. 'It is said that Heindl was a contentious figure, quirky but loyal. Once a doctor, he turned to the Church in his hour of need. He had bad knees, so could not genuflect without great pain. Perhaps some saw that as a sign of faithlessness, but I would not. As I said, he was odd, eccentric. He added quotes from the Book of Revelation to embellish his Amori verses and copious footnotes but never explained any of them.' DeVille sighed. 'And now we will never know why.'

'Maybe we will,' Roxy said. 'I assume there's more?'

'Oh yes,' DeVille said with a smile. 'The 1888 passage is quite illuminating.'

Chapter 17

'You recall one passage from a two-thousand-year-old book?' Roxy asked in surprise.

'I was the pope's principal archivist for eight years,' DeVille said. 'I could quote that book front to back and back to front with absolute accuracy. Pope Benedict once said: "*We let ourselves be moulded and transformed by Christ and continually pass from the side of one who destroys to that of one who saves.*" I would like to think that my actions now would make him proud.'

DeVille took a breath and another gulp of coffee before continuing. 'Heindl wrote that he'd penned a riddle which would blaze a trail to the Amori's lair. His wording, not mine. The Church itself wouldn't recognise their existence, let alone pay them a visit.'

'Because acknowledging something exists gives it power,' Sally guessed.

'Perhaps. I believe they saw it as an age-old conflict, long forgotten. Heindl said that each successive pope read about the Amori as an episode in history, like the Crusades, rather than a persistent threat.'

'This riddle,' Mason spoke up. 'Does it mention Calvary at all?'

DeVille nodded. 'It does. The first line goes thus: "*The riddle begins: seek the Amori at the altar of the first of the Five Great Churches, at Calvary.*" In the same passage of writing, he later mentions the Revelation quotes. He writes: "*My life's greatest ailment meant that I could never do this, but five times I overrode the agony to touch the unseen written word.*" You see? What does that even mean? Heindl was a peculiar individual.'

'But sane.' Sally's comment was half-queastion, half-hope.

'As sane as global news reports allow any of us to be,' DeVille said with that world-weary melancholy they already knew to anticipate.

'And the rest of the riddle?' Roxy asked.

'That's it,' DeVille said. 'That line *is* the riddle. Of course, he's sending you to the church at Calvary where there will be another clue to lead you to the second of the Five Great Churches. In his writings, the actual text is so consumed by footnotes it is sometimes difficult to separate one body of writing from the other.'

'It seems . . . thin,' Sally said. 'And worse, we don't know when the Amori are planning to drop their bomb-shell.'

'Every moment counts,' DeVille said, standing. 'But I doubt they would want their secret location revealed to the world at the same time. You should go.'

Feeling dismissed, Mason rose with him. 'I don't get it,' he said. 'What are we supposed to do at this church? What are we looking for?

DeVille blinked at him. 'Perhaps I misspoke,' he said. 'The words "the riddle begins" are part of the riddle, not my addition. And the line "first of the Five Great Churches." means that you will have to follow clues and solve all five riddles to obtain the final answer.'

Sally stared at him hard enough to raise his eyebrows. 'What you're saying then is that Jacques Heindl carved five different clues on five different altars, inscriptions that point the way to the Amori's lair? And by following these clues, one by one, we can find it and prevent the release of the book?'

'Find the Amori, find the book,' DeVille said simply, his eyes sparkling with mischief. Mason drained the last of his coffee. In truth, he had no idea where the great church at Calvary was, but he guessed Sally would take care of that. The only issue now was Mateo DeVille.

'Can you go somewhere until this is over? A friend's house maybe? Even a hotel?'

'You think I am in danger? Well, thank you for caring.'

'I don't want to help bring harm down upon you,' Mason said.

'In that case, I would be in danger whether you came here or not,' DeVille told them. 'My faith is my shield, and I am too old to run away.'

Mason looked to Sally for help. The brunette rose and went to DeVille's side, the blue tips of her hair brushing his shoulder as she leaned in.

'Sir,' she said, 'the Amori were responsible for murdering my father. They have no conscience. Every fibre of my being wants to track them down. I will not stop until they are behind bars, but you . . . you are caught in the middle of this and you are irreplaceable.'

DeVille turned to her with what was almost a fatherly smile just as the blast of an explosion ripped through the kitchen. Mason saw a window shatter, glass scything into the room, and Mateo DeVille jerk backwards, all in the space of half a second. Blood burst from DeVille's shoulder as the old man crashed to the floor.

'Gunshots!' Roxy yelled and slipped out of her seat.

Mason leapt for Sally as a second window exploded.

Chapter 18

Debris littered the floor. A chill wind blasted through the fragmented windows. Mason heard two more gunshots and the clatter of pots and pans as they fell from hooks on the far wall into the sink.

DeVille groaned in agony. 'My . . . shoulder . . .'

Roxy was already sliding across the linoleum floor to his side. Mason grabbed one of Sally's outstretched hands and pulled so that he could shelter her body. Several heart-beats passed in tense silence.

'They're moving,' Roxy said.

It was their cue. Mason, staying low, dashed to the knife rack and grabbed the two largest blades he could reach.

Roxy urged DeVille to crawl as fast as he could out of the kitchen, towards the hallway bisecting the house.

Sally stared at Mason like a deer caught in the headlights, unsure what to do.

'Go,' he urged. 'Get out of the kitchen.'

She started crawling fast. Mason ran and skidded back to the rear wall, boots grating through glass. More than one shard snagged his flesh through his jeans, but he barely noticed. He and Roxy had two wards to keep safe.

He sat with his back to the wall, looking up at the shattered window. Once Sally was clear of the kitchen, a silence fell. He could hear the approach of at least one person.

He waited.

A man whispered outside the window, his voice louder and closer than Mason expected. Mason guessed he spoke into a portable communications system as he clarified that he was entering the house.

Mason tensed.

A boot crunched on the glass-littered windowsill above his head. Then hands appeared, grasping the inner frames. A figure balanced there, checking inside the kitchen.

Mason reached up, grabbed an ankle and jerked the man off-balance.

There was a crunch as the man fell inside, landing spine-first at Mason's feet. Mason lifted the knife and plunged it at the man's heart.

A gloved hand caught Mason's wrist.

The guy was strong. Mason jabbed with the second knife, slicing at his opponent's thigh.

The figure rolled straight into Mason, narrowing his angles, and tried to sit upright, but Mason held him down with brute strength. He recognised at once that the infiltrator was military trained.

A rifle was looped over the man's right shoulder. Mason chopped at the strap with his knife, hoping for a bit of luck. The blade severed a third of the material before a second figure filled the frame above.

'Preston? *Preston*, you okay?' came the urgent whisper.

Mason assumed these were the same guys who'd left the woman to die in cold blood. He knew they wouldn't hesitate to kill him and the others.

The second figure withdrew and then booted in the back door and charged into the kitchen.

Mason dropped one of the knives, grabbed the man's

jacket and threw him so that he fell face first onto his colleague. Mason fell too, upended by the struggling men.

Mason thrust a knife at them, seeing the blade glance off a stab vest but still nick an arm. Mason used that as a distraction to go for the rifle.

A third figure appeared at the window. Mason got the feeling that he was fighting a losing battle. He received an elbow to the nose that made him see stars. Still, his fingers curled around the sturdy rifle strap. His vision cleared.

A face was next to his own, snarling. 'I'm gonna seriously fu—'

Mason smashed him in the nose, breaking it and terminating the verbal threat.

The third figure shouted: 'Ash! Base! Step away!'

Mason jumped up, reached out and tried to pull the third man into the room. If he could tangle them up, then maybe he could gain precious seconds to escape the kitchen.

But they were too many, and they were too strong. The second man who'd entered rose to his knees and lunged from his heels, striking Mason at the waist and driving him into the back wall. Mason hit hard, flinging out a hand at the third man, dropping the knife but hitting flesh.

It didn't help. The third man jumped in and landed safely on two feet. Mason could see his face over the back of his opponent.

Mason delivered two crushing elbow strikes onto his attacker's spine, forcing him to his knees, then stepped away, panting heavily.

'Ash.' The third man, speaking in an American accent, held out a hand. 'Give it to me.'

'Use yours.' Ash's reply was deeply nasal.

'I can't, man. It jammed.'

The man whose nose Mason had broken unhooked his rifle and held it out, still trying to stem the flow of blood. The third man took it. That meant the attacker at Mason's feet must be Base. He jumped up without looking, blocked the other man's aim and struck out at Mason.

The third man sighed. 'Move out of the way, Base.'

'One through each eye, Hassell,' Ash said in a muffled voice. 'And then the old man.'

Base slowed his attack. Mason took advantage, ducking and delivering three hard blows to his kidneys. Base groaned and staggered. Mason stayed behind him, getting as close to Hassell as he could.

Ash struggled to his feet. Mason's options were quickly contracting.

'Stop fighting,' Hassell said.

Mason could only hope he'd given Roxy and the others time to escape. Three lives saved to help make up for the ones he'd lost in Mosul. Still, he held onto Base's jacket, keeping the big man between him and the gun.

'Give me back the gun,' Ash said, reaching out to Hassell. 'I want the shot. And Base, get away from him. We'll take our time.'

Base grinned and jerked free of Mason's grip, almost toppling backwards. Mason rued the loss of the knives but under the circumstances they probably wouldn't have helped. He waited at the back wall of the kitchen as his three opponents moved closer.

'Gun,' Ash growled once more.

Mason saw a flicker at the doorway. *Roxy.* Inwardly, he cursed. She should be far from here by now. Her job was to protect the assets, not return for her colleague.

Maybe she's looking for atonement too.

Mason focused on Hassell, trying not to draw any attention to the figure in the doorway. But then Hassell took three quick steps back.

Mason winced, expecting him to turn the gun on the approaching Roxy, but instead Hassell reversed the gun in his hands and swung its stock like a baseball bat at Ash's face. It hit hard, jerking Ash's head sideways and knocking him unconscious.

Base's mouth fell open in shock even as he started to react, but Hassell was too quick, stepping forward and smashing the butt into Base's nose. Base staggered, only for Hassell to strike twice more on the top of his head, driving him to the floor where he lay unmoving but still breathing.

Mason, spattered with blood, gaped. His mouth worked, but nothing came out. To his right, Roxy stood rooted in shock and uncertainty.

'What?' Hassell said to Mason's stunned and questioning face. 'I'm trying to make the world a better place. I knocked out two cold-blooded, depraved killers who'd murder their own mothers for a goddamn doughnut. I don't work with killers. This was supposed to be a no-kill job. Nina killed Vatican Guards, that professor guy, and now *they* killed the old man . . .' Hassell glanced at Roxy. 'Did they kill him?'

Roxy shook her head.

Hassell held out the gun in his hands. 'Here, take it. I want to help. To make up for what they've done. I'm not part of their team. Did Nina survive?'

Mason accepted the gun. 'You left her to die.'

'No. I told them I'd take care of her, but I fooled them. I fired a bullet into the sofa and led them away. I wanted her to live.'

Mason digested that before saying, 'She died of blood loss.'

Hassell briefly closed his eyes. 'That old bastard, Marduk. His own daughter and he ordered her to be shot.'

Mason continued to take it in, mind racing, then noticed the comms wire running from Hassell's ear. He made a frantic motion towards it.

Hassell cursed before snatching it free and throwing it to the floor where he crushed it under his boot-heel. 'You need to get out of here,' Hassell said.

Mason kept him covered by the barrel of the gun. 'How's DeVille?' he asked Roxy.

'He needs to go to hospital.'

'I didn't kill anyone,' Hassell insisted. 'You have to believe me. My boss assigned a crack team to this madman called Marduk who wanted to rob the Vatican and then later ordered the murder of his own daughter. By the time I knew what I was into it was too late. Please . . .'

Mason studied the two unconscious men on the floor and then Hassell's face. He appeared to be genuine, but then he had just attacked two members of his own team.

'This madman you mention,' he said. 'Did he work for a group called the Amori?'

'Yes,' Hassell said. 'He's their boss. And the only way to retrieve the book is to find *him*.'

'Move,' he said. 'We'll talk about this on the way.'

He couldn't leave Hassell behind. The man might have important inside information regarding the Amori. He might know where their lair was, or where the book had been taken. And they didn't have enough time to discuss it now.

'You have any other trackers or comms on you?' Roxy asked.

'No,' Hassell said. 'I'm clean.'

Roxy came in close and patted him down anyway before nodding.

Mason had a hundred questions but stowed them away and motioned to Roxy. 'Lead on.'

The American filed after her, helping DeVille, with Mason at the back taking one last look around. The kitchen was a mess, the unconscious bodies on the floor not exactly helping. Someone would have called the cops by now.

Mason urged them all to move faster.

The deeper they delved into this mystery, the harder it became to unravel. And the more dangerous it grew. They could hardly count on Patricia and the help of Watchtower now. They'd gone beyond that. Whatever happened from this point on, they were on their own and might not have a job to go back to.

Is it worth it?

Mason had a feeling he was fixing his need for emotional recompense on Sally, using her as a starting point for a healing process that was two years in the making. Still, if he moved forward and helped her at the same time, where was the harm in that? He breathed deeply, balancing emotions, knowing that one false step would bring everything crashing down.

The only way forward was all the way through.

Chapter 19

Hours later, Mason stood with Roxy, Sally and Hassell in a muddy clearing close to a large area of thick woodland. A full moon shone above and, for now, the rain had stopped and the winds died down. It was the quietest part of their night and close to dawn.

Mason ran through the last half hour in his mind. They had dropped Mateo DeVille off at the nearest hospital, leaving the man for the medics to take care of. Then he had run back to the car where Roxy was watching Hassell, and Sally sat fretting in the passenger seat.

'Will he be okay?' Sally had asked.

'He's lost a lot of blood,' Mason had told her for the tenth time. 'But I've seen and treated worse in war and watched them come through without a hitch.'

Hassell had stared at him. 'You were a soldier? I was NYPD.' He had looked momentarily proud before deflating. 'Two years.'

Mason hadn't answered. Instead, he'd driven them to this clearing for a little peace, quiet and privacy. They'd hidden the car as best they could, parking it behind a skip at the far end of the parking area, and then traipsed along a soggy path for almost ten minutes.

Finally, Roxy had stopped, sighed and turned to Hassell. She still carried the rifle he'd handed over and waved it at him. 'Start talking,' she said.

'I came with you of my own free will,' he reminded them. 'I won't run, and you don't need to threaten me to make me talk.'

'Why?' Mason asked simply.

'Because, despite what I'm deeply involved with, you have to believe that I never wanted it to go this far. I no longer trust my boss and I want to . . .' He hesitated, searching for the right word.

'Atone?' Mason asked.

'Yeah, giving you the gun was just the start. By helping you I've signed my own death warrant. Gido will never stop hunting me now. It'll be a matter of honour for him.'

'I know something about atonement,' Mason said. 'Look, can you leave us for a minute?' He spoke directly to Hassell, waited for the man to walk away and then whispered to the others: 'I want to say something first. Sally, before I dropped him off, DeVille spoke. He grabbed me as I pulled him from the back of the car. He was bleeding, gasping, but pulled me towards him and said, "*Remember the words of Jacques Heindl. Five times I overrode the agony to touch the unseen written word. Five*," and then asked me if I knew what he meant.'

Mason pursed his lips. 'Of course, I said, "Yes, it's clear," but to be honest I've seen clearer clouds. Any ideas?'

Sally's expression was elsewhere. 'What? I'm sorry. Men are trying to kill me. I'm trying to process what happened at DeVille's house. I . . . I . . .'

Mason realised he'd shrugged off the effects of the deadly struggle like an unwelcome second skin. Thirteen years in the army had helped him do that. He glanced at Roxy, but there was no way the straight-talking American was about to comfort their client.

Mason walked over to Sally. 'Hey,' he said. 'We focus. We focus on the mission objective. Everything else is driftwood. Do you understand?'

Sally nodded, taking two deep breaths. 'It's driftwood.' She clung to the word. 'Floating past in a storm surge. I get it.'

Roxy was staring at Mason as if she envied him. For a moment, Mason believed he'd received a momentary insight into what troubled her. Was she searching for a gentler side? He could have walked over and tried to extricate a truth – and would no doubt risk injury by doing so – but he let it drop.

Hassell stood looking miserable and uncomfortable, and they needed to debrief him.

Mason took the easy route and beckoned him back to join them. 'So,' he said. 'Spill.'

Hassell looked relieved. 'Okay.' He frowned, clearly wondering where to start.

As he waited, Mason studied him. Hassell had short dark hair, a rough scrub of a beard and black eyes. He carried himself like a man trained to fight and appeared physically fit. There was a haunted weariness in his otherwise youngish appearance and an expression that put Mason in mind of a cornered animal about to bolt.

'Hey,' he said more gently. 'You saved my life, mate. We mean you no harm.'

It was true, to a point. Hassell accepted it and appeared to settle down. 'Name's Luke Hassell,' he said, 'from New York City. Used to be a cop. Now, I'm an . . . an infiltration specialist, or so they tell me. I find the weaknesses in secure buildings and exploit them, everything from Fort Knox to the house next door.' He showed them a pristine set of homemade lockpicks.

As he spoke Hassell paced, boots squelching through the thick ooze. 'My boss, a guy called Gido, was bulldozed into helping this Amori steal the *Book of Secrets*. He pulled together a crack team to work with Nina, Ash and Base – the two assassins, me and one other guy. A comms and IT expert named Mac who masterminded the shutdown of the Vatican's security system. Now, Nina's dead, Ash and Base could be in custody, and Mac will be explaining to Gido how I jumped ship. The Amori will be threatening Gido because they want the old guy dead.'

Mason tried to keep up. 'They wanted Mateo DeVille dead? Why?'

'Didn't explain everything. We're just the hired help, you know? All I do know is what Mac overheard by listening in to some of Marduk's conversations. Mac was like that, you know, always looking for dirt on people, especially influential people. Anyway, it's something about a clue to the Amori's ancient, private sanctuary being mentioned in this book. It's so sacred to them they'll defend it at all costs.'

'This Mac told you that?' Roxy asked.

'Yeah, and Gido.' Hassell hesitated. 'We used to be close.'

'How close?' Mason pressed.

Hassell studied the ground as if deciding how much he was prepared to reveal. 'Back when I was a cop, my girl was murdered. There were no witnesses, no one to point the finger of blame at. I didn't take it well and eventually quit. Gido ran the biggest local gang and helped me track down Chloe's murderers. After that, he gave me a new life. I wouldn't kill or hurt people, so he got me trained in infiltration. Kept me close.'

Mason caught an odd tone in Hassell's last sentence. 'You stopped trusting him before this job?'

'Yeah, but that's another subject, man. I gotta figure that out for myself.'

Mason guessed there was a lot more to Hassell's story, to Hassell's life, than they had time for right now. An ex-cop running with a crime boss whom he'd been *close* to? He tried to pick the clean bones from that rotting carcass. 'Where did you take the book? And who are the Amori? Did you meet any of them?'

'It was a blind drop,' Hassell said. 'There's this guy – Marduk – who leads this secret society called the Amori that's hellbent on destroying the Church. Have been for centuries, apparently. He told us that the Church has many foul secrets and even more deadly enemies. He mentioned the Holy Land, Babylon, the Vatican . . .'

Hassell creased up his face as he tried to remember. 'He mentioned Jesus Christ and secrets that would bring the modern-day Church to its knees. The guy was seriously unhinged and power-hungry. Oh, and Nina, the woman who stole the book . . . she was his *daughter*.'

'You said that he ordered her killed?' Mason asked.

Hassell shook his head, as if repulsed by the memory. 'Yeah. I tried to save her. Sent Ash and Base out of the room and shot the sofa. Hoped someone would get to her in time.'

Mason saw only grief in the American's expression. 'As much as I believe you did it for the right reasons,' he said, 'your decision is gonna come back and haunt you sooner than you think.'

Hassell swallowed hard. 'Don't I know it. But it can get in line.'

'Anything else you can tell us about the blind drop?' Roxy asked.

Hassell shrugged. 'I can tell you everything, but it won't help. We left Nina and took the book, wrapped in a water-proof bag we brought, to a prearranged point. As per instructions we left it and got the hell out of the way.'

'What point?' Mason asked.

'You know the National Gallery of Modern Art? To either side of the entrance there are some landscaped gardens. Well, we left it under a bush.'

'You left the *Vatican Book of Secrets*, a private and extremely hush-hush collection of explosive secrets, under a bloody *bush*?' Mason asked in disbelief.

Hassell nodded. 'Yeah, and got the hell out of there. I'm assuming Marduk had it under surveillance and moved in as soon as we'd gone.'

Mason digested it all, realising that Hassell had told them as much as he knew.

Hassell smiled awkwardly at him. 'Marduk was incredibly guarded. The information he gave us was just flotsam really. There's nothing concrete, just exalted conjecture from a stranger. A bit like scrolling through Facebook . . .' Hassell paused when both Sally and Roxy smiled. 'I'd like to help you find him and get that book back.'

'And Gido?' Mason asked.

'Gido and I are done. I owed him. He saved me after . . . after I stopped wanting to be a cop. He saved my life. Took me under his wing and taught me all he knew. But I wonder.' Hassell looked dejected standing there with mud all over his boots, hair plastered down by the drizzle suffusing the air. 'I wonder if he's been using me all these years.'

'It's not something we have the time to resolve now,' Mason said.

'Hey, of course not. I didn't mean it was.'

'Wait,' Roxy said. 'What are you thinking? Hassell's the enemy.'

Mason turned to her. 'He saved my life,' he told her. 'He didn't have to. Could've killed me and then got to you and Sally. There's a time . . .' He paused to think. 'A time when saving a stranger helps your soul. Smooths over some of those past mistakes. I believe he can help us.'

Hassell scratched his scrubby beard. 'Normally, I'm pretty quiet,' he said. 'You'd barely know I'm there unless you need help getting in and out of places.'

'Don't you have somewhere or someone to go back to?

123

To protect?' Roxy asked, thinking beyond the moment and drilling down to Hassell's basic needs. 'Won't this Gido guy want to hurt someone you love if he knows you betrayed him?'

Hassell suddenly looked very young. 'There's nobody left that I love,' he said. 'Hasn't been for years now. It's just me.'

'Let's be straight,' Mason interjected. 'I don't trust you. But you saved my life.' He started ticking points off on his fingers. 'You know what Marduk looks like. You know Gido, who may well send another team against us if we continue searching for the book. And you tried to save Nina's life. Also, it occurs to me that we may well need an infiltration specialist before we're done.' He looked to Roxy and Sally. 'What do you think?'

Roxy glared. 'Makes sense,' she growled.

Sally broke her silence. 'My strengths lie in research and historical knowledge,' she said. 'I'll leave the strategising to you. But I also think we may have need of his skills.'

Mason held out a hand to Hassell. 'That's it then, mate. You're on board for now. Don't capsize the bloody boat. Got it?'

Hassell nodded. 'Don't be the iceberg. Got it.'

Mason gave the floor to Sally. 'Your turn. Where do we go first?'

Chapter 20

Marduk couldn't help but feel more than a little smug. He'd been waiting for this moment his entire life, waiting to crawl out of the shadows where the Vatican had ruthlessly obscured them. This was *his* time, a beautiful moment of revenge.

'Bring me the number,' he said out loud. 'The phone number.'

It was all ceremony, expected of a monarch. Marduk knew the private phone number of the Apostolic Palace by heart. He might not reach the pope directly, but he would gain the attention of the bishop of Rome and his most trusted cardinals. It was said that each new pope gained the keys of Heaven. Well, Marduk was about to show *this* pope the cataclysmic path to Hell.

The disciple who handed him the mobile phone assured him it was secure. Marduk expected nothing less and dialled a number.

'Yes,' he said to the person who answered. 'Just tell somebody in power that the man who stole your precious book is calling. I'll wait.'

Minutes later there were three loud clicks and a voice in his ear. 'Questo é Cardinal Feroci. Chi é?'

'For ease, shall we speak English? My Italian is not first class. I am Marduk, of the Amori. We have your book.' He kept his opening volley simple.

'What are you talking about?' the cardinal demanded, revealing nothing.

'For years, we have watched you. Stayed in the shadows, waiting for you to fail. But, by promoting fear, using bribery and silent force, you have persisted. I know that your faith is built on ruins. Your religion a fragile spiderweb. I know your deepest fears and soon so shall the world.'

'Look, this is—'

'Be quiet, Cardinal Feroci,' Marduk said. 'Your religion has destroyed too many souls in its endless pursuit of divinity. In its insistence that God is all, and God is everything. Believe me, *God is not everything*. As you will soon learn.' It was delicious to know that he stood on the verge of achieving his dreams. Total power and influence stretched out before him like an endless shining sea. The sense of triumph had recently been curdled by the knowledge that the Vatican had killed his daughter but, rather than detracting from his victory, it served only to push him to more brutal lengths.

'You seek to extort the Church?' the cardinal asked.

'Are you even listening? No, I will destroy *the Church*. The book's secrets will be released whether you scream, threaten or blubber like weak men at a Christian altar. Falling to your knees is not the answer. The Amori will view your triumphant demise and we will be *laughing. Rejoicing.* Finally, the Amori will take their rightful place in this world at the conception of a new Babylon.'

'I have never heard of you,' the cardinal scoffed.

'That is unfortunate. But you *do* know that your book was stolen, don't you? Two Swiss Guards shot? One unfortunate professor killed in the crossfire? Tell me that I am lying.'

There was no response, but Marduk knew he had their attention. Right now, the Amori had them exactly where they wanted them after a two-thousand-year undertaking and it was all because of him.

'You know the Amori too. We have existed since the dawn of sin. You speak of us in your Book of Revelation, where you attacked and destroyed our Babylon, though you never name us.' He took a breath and then intoned: '"*The woman whom you saw is the great city, which reigns over the kings of the earth.*" Through two millennia, you sought to forget us, but all we have been doing is biding our time, building towards our own Babylon and a new world order.'

'*If* anything was stolen from the Vatican,' Cardinal Feroci said, 'rest assured, our police will find the culprits and bring them to justice.'

'Your police?' Marduk sneered. 'Which ones? The ones we own, or the Italian gendarmes who care little for the Vatican? It is the Church who taught us all about infiltration. About leverage and oppressive influence. I find it beautifully fitting that we now use it against you.'

'What are your intentions?'

'Finally, a suitable question.' Marduk could hear the other man moving around as he spoke, cupping the receiver and talking to comrades, whispering vehemently. 'Let us talk, for a moment, like normal people. For countless decades, the Church has been perpetrating a lie. A necessary lie, I understand. You really had no choice.'

Marduk paused to let out a gloating laugh. 'Your Jewish preacher and *religious* leader, the awaited Messiah, the Son of God. You built your entire religion around this Galilean. And when I drip-feed the truth about him through online video and social media platforms to countless millions, your entire religion will collapse.'

'The truth?' Feroci said warily.

'The Amori know exactly what he was. No different

127

from your modern freedom fighter. His weapon of choice was not religion, prayer or God's word but something far deadlier. *Our own history tells us this.*'

'You intend to spread news about this so-called book worldwide?' Cardinal Feroci sounded aghast.

'Of course. We have Latin translators already at work. I will start to destroy Christianity first through teasers that will build my audience. You might not know when they're coming, but each one will make the truth harder to deny until – when I have seen you squirm to my satisfaction – the final truth will crush your false church.'

'You cannot know where He is—' Cardinal Feroci caught himself at the last minute and clammed up, eliciting another crowing laugh from Marduk.

'I will reveal . . . *everything,*' Marduk said with intentional drama.

'You have no idea,' Feroci said softly and carefully. 'No idea of how the thing you speak about was coded. I doubt you are capable of seeing any secret language but your own.'

That gave Marduk pause. Frowning, he considered that maybe he hadn't given the Vatican enough credit and might yet have a fight on his hands to stop them finding the Amori's great sanctum. To hide his surprise, he went on the offensive. 'I will back up all my revelations with *fact*. And then *you,* the Church, will discover what it's really like to be nailed atop a hillside for all to see, your agonies displayed, your lifeblood seeping away as the bloated masses judge you. And that, Cardinal Feroci, is what *I* have devoted my life to seeing.'

Marduk ended the call, more hyped-up than he'd been in his entire life. It was beautiful; it was unavoidable. The book proved that the legend was true – not that he'd been in any doubt, but it was good to see it confirmed by their deadliest enemies. And he didn't let the mention of a code diminish his jubilation. He would deal with that later.

Marduk paced the room, letting the euphoria wash over him. This was devotion, the act of feeling adoration for one's deity. *This* was how it felt. Only *this* deity was the four-thousand-year-old entity known as the Amori. Now, they were a global organisation complete with regional leaders who kept their subjects at their deceitful and secretive work, who looked to their elders to select a leader, who followed the word of the Creed to the letter and worked tirelessly to defeat their eternal enemy – the Church. The Amori had successfully intertwined their poisonous fingers into the fabric of society and, every hour of every day, tugged on the strings of the people they'd turned into marionettes. Marduk couldn't imagine a more formidable and terrifying force abroad in the world.

Of which he was the Monarch.

Marduk finally came back down to earth just over an hour later and returned to his desk, scooping up the telephone to make another call.

'Hello,' he said when the phone was answered. 'Is this Gianluca Gianni?'

'It is,' a deep voice replied. 'Who is this?'

'I'm glad you asked.' Marduk settled back into his plush leather chair, enjoying himself immensely. 'You are Gianluca Gianni, commander of the Swiss Guard of Vatican City. I am Marduk, leader of the Amori. To be blunt, I have ordered the abduction of your wife and daughter and will gut them live on video if you do not follow my orders.'

Marduk waited, letting the horror of that beautiful sentence sink in.

'No.' Gianni's voice creaked as he spoke. '*No!* That's not possible. Who is this? I will . . . I will—'

'I am your new boss. Repeat that to me.'

'I will find you and I will rip your—'

'Have you seen your wife and daughter today? Heard from them?'

'No. I . . . I . . . please, don't do this. It's not possible. Who are—'

Marduk spoke over the man's protests. 'I am now sending you video proof that I am deadly serious.'

Marduk picked up a mobile, found the right file and messaged it across to Gianni. The video was fifty-three seconds long and Marduk waited, gazing into the darkness of his study, enjoying the silence and Gianni's sounds of misery. The first crimson smudge of a new dawn appeared through the eastern window, and he likened it to the birth of a new day for the Amori. The beginning of the longest night for the Church.

'You bastard,' Gianni sobbed, terror radiating through his voice. 'You utter piece of shit. Nobody sane would do this. Please . . . Please let them go—'

'They will come back to you in *melted* pieces if you betray me.'

Gianni went quiet in utter horror.

Marduk took the silence as acquiescence and went on. 'For now they are with us. And if you want them to stay safe you will wait for my call. When I send instructions, you will follow them to the letter.'

Marduk laughed and replaced the phone in its cradle. Gianni was yet another cog in the wheel, waiting to begin his rotation.

His attention turned to the final matter of the moment, requiring one more call.

'Gido?' he asked when the chirping phone was answered. 'Tell me . . . what happened with the old man?'

As expected, the depraved little criminal had a raft of excuses at hand. 'Hassell betrayed me,' he said in one of those recognisable fast-talking New York accents. 'You just wait until I get my hands on that—'

'Old man DeVille still lives,' Marduk said. 'The team that chased my daughter from the archives and forced *you* to murder her are still alive. They spoke with the old man.'

'I didn't give the order to kill Nina,' Gido said.

'Your incompetence caused that. And the arrogance of the Church itself.' Marduk was convinced he spoke the truth. 'You told me that they were the best team. The best of the best, you said. They failed.'

'No plan survives first contact—'

'Oh, shut up. You weary me. We shouldn't have allowed anyone to speak with the old man, as he has the knowledge to unmask us. Your idiot men should have prevented that.'

Gido's breath whistled between his teeth. 'Look,' he said. 'My men – Ash and Base are their names, by the way – they're now rotting in prison for you. For your cause. Mac heard everything that happened at DeVille's through the communications system. It was Hassell. He ruined our victory.'

Marduk frowned. 'Not that I care but you make it sound personal.'

'Personal?' Gido echoed. 'Of course it's personal. I saved Hassell's life. Brought him into the family. I mentored that traitor and will hunt him down and kill him.'

'You wasted your time with him.' Marduk laughed at the other man's indignation.

'Thought I'd squeezed all the cop out of him,' Gido said. 'He was my best. But that'll make vengeance all the sweeter.'

Marduk rolled his eyes. 'Good, that's great for you. But we still have a problem. One that could grow exponentially. On the positive side, this gives you a chance to redeem yourself.'

'Redeem?' Gido sounded resentful. 'Man, we just by-passed security at the *Vatican* for you. Teams in the world capable of that no doubt number in low single digits. And you have the book.'

'Do not throw figures at me,' Marduk said. 'Loose ends mark failure, and you've left several loose ends. I expect you to tie them up forthwith.'

'Tie them up how?'

'They may try to track us, yes? Track down the Amori with information gleaned from the Book. I also have the first clue from the *Book of Secrets*. I expect you to solve it and send people to meet any team that arrives. And then I expect you to murder them with extreme prejudice. They cannot be allowed to decipher all those clues and walk up to our front door. Our private refuge is too important to tarnish, the most important location in all of history. Yes, it draws more attention our way, but if they follow those clues to our door we will be exposed for the first time in millennia. I will not let that happen. And stopping them finding us also means they will not attempt to retrieve the book. Do you understand that?'

'Solve . . . a riddle?'

'Yes, yes, I thought that might throw you. Don't worry, you only need to go to the correct locations. And the first is Calvary . . .' Marduk waited for several seconds before shaking his head. 'Do you even know what Calvary is?'

'I've heard of it,' Gido admitted. 'Is it one of those specialist restaurants in Brooklyn?'

'Calvary,' Marduk said through clenched teeth, 'also known as Golgotha, is a little site outside Jerusalem where Jesus Christ was supposed to have been crucified. Perhaps you've heard of *him*?'

'Ah, yes, I understand. Wait . . . you want me to send a team of mercs to Jerusalem?'

'To Calvary for a start. I'll send you further instructions shortly.'

'I don't know much, but I do know that place is a powder keg. Any kind of spark could set it off.'

'And that's the whole point,' Marduk explained. 'What better place is there to exercise some deniability? Use a variety of mercenaries, all races, all skills. And remove yourself from the deal by several steps. But do it quickly. They might already be on their way to Calvary.'

'And the remit is to kill them all?'

'Kill them all. Do you think you can handle that?'

Marduk replaced the receiver, thinking on the obstacles that life presented even in the midst of one's finest hour. Still, work was done for now. He could rise, order breakfast and watch the new dawn.

The first new dawn of the Amori's greatest triumph.

Nothing could save the Church now.

Chapter 21

Gianluca Gianni battled a churning combination of incapacitating emotions. The phone call had brought him to his knees, the final words making his heart sink and his thoughts catch fire.

'. . . *if you want them to stay that way you will wait for my call. And when I send my instructions, you will follow them to the letter.*'

Gianni, kneeling in his dark apartment, knew that this Marduk would want him to betray the Church. Already, yesterday, two Swiss Guards had given their lives. If Gianni's own family weren't even now in mortal danger would he feel differently about that? But Gianni was their commander, responsible for many other lives. Working towards and being chosen as a Swiss Guard had been a lifetime achievement, seconded only by the birth of his daughter. He'd taken a declaration of loyalty to his sacramental calling. His standing in life formed the crux of his character, a crux from which all his honour, his strength and qualities sprang. Before yesterday, his life was complete.

I was where I was supposed to be.

To serve the successor of Peter – that was the aim. How was he serving if he betrayed his calling? And where was it written that personal feelings intruded where faith was concerned? Family was integral in the transmission of faith. But 'family' didn't only mean a mother or a daughter, Gianni believed. *It refers to the apostolic unit.*

The Swiss Guards had been held in high esteem ever since the infamous 'sack of Rome', in which the honour guard had defended the Pope, many giving their lives. That day had been replete with spiritual marauding – the people rioting and looting, stealing the valuable and the invaluable.

These days, of course, the new 'sack' could be attributed to social media, celebrities and lifestyle gurus. These media-labelled idols and heroes encouraged a culture that responded only to material desires or needs. Their ideals were greedy, and shallow.

With His help and the strength of the Holy Spirit, I will calmly face the trials and impediments of life. He is always at my side. A reassuring, soothing presence. Where are you now, my Lord?

The apartment was cold. It was silent. For so many years it had been quite the opposite. Gemma, his wife, filled it with her warmth and good heart, not to mention dozens of uplifting quotes pinned to noticeboards and fridge doors and mounted in picture frames. Some bordering on risqué perhaps, but that was Gemma – a beautiful mind living a full life with a touch of mischief. Eight years after they met, Aria had come along, filling their lives with a wonder they'd never dreamed possible. Aria, now nine years old, was a livewire with a perfectly balanced moral compass that went way beyond her years. Just last week Aria had saved two bees from exhaustion and held up traffic in two directions to allow a family of ducks to cross the road. The good things that Aria did brought tears to Gianni's eyes on a good day. Now he knelt in a world of hurt, enveloped by a miasma of stress, guilt and nervous anticipation. What would he do when the call came? Would Marduk spare his beautiful family if he complied? How heavy a burden could he truly carry?

And what were poor Gemma and Aria putting up with at this very moment?

Saint Teresa said: 'At the end of our lives we will not be judged for how many things we have done, but for how much love we have put into those things.'

Gianni believed he'd served the Church and the doctrines of his religion with all the devotion in his heart. Leading the Swiss Guard was a confirmation of faith. It had taken just one phone call, and one evil video, to shake the foundations that his life had been built on.

What horrors were to come?

In the dark, Gianni knelt to pray for his family.

Chapter 22

Mason sat in the passenger seat of their car, a brown take-away bag resting on his lap, a polystyrene cup of black coffee in his right hand, a carton of hot fries in the other. A rain-suffused dawn rose beyond the car windows, the whole world seeming wet and damp, the new sun appearing almost mutinous as it challenged the drab, melancholy sky.

Mason was too hungry to speak, having eaten nothing since the previous day. He shovelled fries and then a break-fast wrap into his mouth with barely a pause, washing it all down with the surprisingly agreeable coffee. All he needed now was eight hours' sleep.

'The first clue.' Sally was in full academic mode, showing no signs of fatigue as she ate and talked simultaneously. '"*Seek the Amori at the altar of the first of the Five Great Churches, at Calvary.*" Clearly, there's not a lot to go on. But, thanks to DeVille, we also have Heindl's own words: "*My life's greatest ailment meant that I could never do this, but five times I overrode the agony to touch the unseen written word.*" It's vague but things are always clearer on site.'

'Is that another of your father's sayings?' Roxy asked, one hand on the steering wheel, the other holding a poly-styrene cup.

'Yes, and another good one. When someone dies, you recall only the good that they did, which hopefully is a comfort to the dying. How soon can we get to Jerusalem?'

Her quickfire weaving between subjects threw Mason for a moment. His mind had been focusing on something else. 'Listen, are you okay? You saw your father shot and kil—'

'No, but this is what I have to do. My father's sacrifice can't be in vain.'

'I'll find out.' Hassell was seated alongside Sally in the back, remaining quiet for the most part. He pulled out a smartphone and accessed the internet. 'A little over three hours.'

'Not bad. Can you book a flight for us?'

'Do you have your passports with you?'

'I do,' Mason said, and Roxy also nodded. It was a requirement of the agency that passport ID be carried at all times. The agency insisted on covering all bases, and client protection – as well as a wealthy client's *whim* – was rarely predictable and might include country-hopping.

Sally also produced her passport. 'Never leave it in the hotel room. Another pearl from Dad.'

All eyes turned to Hassell. 'Yeah,' he said quickly. 'I wasn't taking part in the raid, obviously, so my risk was minimal. Nina was supposed to bring the book to us. Gido wanted us ready to return home at the drop of a hat.' He turned back to the phone. 'Give me a few.'

'Calvary,' Mason said as the sun rose higher, brightening his spirits more than their surroundings. 'I know it's the spot where Jesus was crucified, but I'm afraid that's as far as my knowledge goes.'

'Jesus Christ was crucified on the hill at Golgotha, or Calvary, with miscreants to both sides of him,' Sally said. 'An inscription identified him as "Jesus the Nazarene, the King of the Jews". Jesus died around AD 30, his death

138

depicted in the four canonical gospels, the New Testament epistles, and confirmed as an historical event even by non-Christian sources. He was arrested, tried by the Sanhedrin and sentenced by Pontius Pilate to be scourged and crucified. The details are grim. On saying he was thirsty, they offered him vinegar mixed with myrrh. He was stripped down. He died around 3 p.m. His clothes and robes were later divided among soldiers, and his side pierced with a spear to make sure that he was dead.'

'They really hated him,' Roxy said. 'His death pleased them.'

'His death *freed* them,' Sally said, 'from the central figure of a new religion. Or so they thought. Jesus's suffering was named *the Passion*. It relates to salvation and atonement, something we might all connect with.'

Mason didn't move, staring into a wall of grey. Sally's words rang true in the silence that followed, allowing them all time to reflect.

'Calvary was identified a few years later by the mother of Constantine the Great,' Sally went on, 'who had the Church of the Holy Sepulchre built there. It is said to stand close to two of Christianity's most important sites – Calvary and the tomb where Jesus rose again on the third day. That's our destination.'

'The Church of the Holy Sepulchre is one of the Five Great Churches?' Mason asked. 'And leads us to the other four? Any idea which ones they might be?'

'Well, we have no reference for that. Jacques Heindl categorised them for reasons unknown. Perhaps we will discover that too. But, so far, we have been presented with the story of Jesus.'

'Makes sense,' Roxy said. 'He was the central figure of Christianity.'

Mason listened as Sally and Roxy threw suggestions back and forth in an attempt to coax forth an enlightening idea, but his mind had drifted elsewhere. Even as Hassell confirmed that he'd booked the tickets, and Roxy started the car to drive them to the airport, he dwelled upon Sally's earlier words: *salvation* and *atonement*.

Later, sitting next to Roxy on the plane, he was surprised when she leaned over and whispered in his ear.

'So what's your story, Joe Mason? I've heard whispers, for sure, but never really cared before now.'

'Is that your idea of a compliment?'

'About as close as you're ever gonna get.'

'Back in 2018, Mosul was a terrified, lethal city. Car bombs. Snipers. Squads of bandits, some ISIL, some unclear. I earned the blame, nourished it like . . . like . . .' He turned his head away from her, staring out the porthole-style window at floating white clouds and patches of Pacific-like blue. 'It's not something I talk about.'

'I'll tell you mine if you tell me yours.'

Mason looked back at her, at the hair darker than sin, into that hard-lined face that, on occasion, hinted it might be willing to display a softer version of itself. 'Are you flirting with me?'

Roxy chortled. 'If you think that's flirting, you've been out of the game far too long, Mason. I mean, it seems we're both in this for the long run. Putting our asses on the line. I just thought getting to know you better might elevate our chances of survival. Form a deeper bond of trust.'

'You have a point. You go first.'

'No, *you* go first.' Her eyes sparkled.

Mason folded. 'I heard you were a force of nature,' he said. 'I didn't think you'd end up telling me what to do.' He paused. 'I was married before Mosul. Afterwards, after what happened, my wife, Hannah, told me to rant, to get drunk, to unleash all the guilt and bad feelings. But . . . all I felt was this hollow, emotionless void. I went introspective, you know? Didn't share. Didn't care. I forced her away.'

He wondered what he was doing, expressing his deepest regrets out loud, but thought, *Maybe it's time. Maybe the fact that Roxy's mostly a stranger helps. Maybe our sharing combat and a near-death experience helps even more.*

'Most people would unleash,' Roxy said.

'I'm not like that. Nobody ever said I looked like a fighter, a soldier, a bodyguard.' He indicated his blond hair, blue eyes and wiry body. 'I guess I'm different.'

Roxy nodded, studying his physique. 'You got a point, Babyface. If we were ever to get it on, I think I'd break you.'

Mason took that on the chin, consoling himself with the thought that she was trying to put him at ease. 'Hannah and I split. I couldn't talk to her, to anyone. I was a shell, wandering around aimlessly. I don't blame her.'

'And now she has a new man. I remember. Get to the point.'

Mason closed his eyes as memories clashed like broadswords. 'The point,' he said, 'is buried deep. I haven't addressed it except in my mind. Ever.'

'Remember,' Roxy said, 'my mantra . . . don't listen when the Devil's calling. You remember that? But you can grab that bastard by the neck and choke him out. Can you do that?'

Mason was amused despite himself, but still struggled for words. It was like Roxy's devil had hold of both his tongue and his brain, preventing him from stringing a sentence together.

'That day,' he forced out, 'thirteen years in, I'd accepted the army life. My team was my world. Life wasn't complete when we were apart, like my right arm was missing. The downtime between rotations was unreal, like I was walking through a dream. The bond, the camaraderie, the accountability we shared to one another – that was our reality.

That was truth; a real and genuine faith between soldiers.'
He remembered now their mood as they left camp, the
send-ups and witticisms, the camaraderie, the endless
leg-pulling that helped them override the horror of what
might happen every day, every hour.

'It's not just you,' Roxy said. 'Most soldiers feel it.'

'I know. I just wanted you to see where my head was
at. *Is* at. I never really left Mosul, 2018—'

'The ghosts don't let go.'

'Yes, well, there were seven of us, investigating a clump
of rundown homes north of the city. The villagers had
cleared out, or maybe ISIL took them, I don't know. But
there are always sightings of insurgents, you know? Every
day. Several times a day. It's just a staple of everyday life
in Iraq.'

'What happened?' Roxy asked.

'I never saw it,' he murmured low in his throat. 'Never
fu—' He caught himself, swallowing hard and turning away
from her, back to the window. 'Seven homes. Seven men.
We searched them in pairs. There was nothing. No sign,
no indications, no tracks, no smells or footprints. But when
we rechecked, an IED exploded, killing two men in a home
I'd already cleared. Two men . . . died . . . five went home.
And it was my fault. The sound of that explosion . . .' It
struck him hard then, like a mortar blast. The devastating,
reverberating detonation that sent him to the floor. The
swirling smoke, the stench of blood, the sense of dislocation.
The only reality was the earth ground into his face and the
ringing in his ears, the hard-edged pebbles clinging to his
right cheek. He swallowed hard and went on. 'The way we
crept through those buildings in the stifling dark . . . looking
for Zack and Harry. It's as clear now as the day it happened.
I failed and they paid the price.'

'You rechecked them for a reason,' Roxy said. 'They
were just as dangerous the second time you went in.'

'Doesn't change the aftermath,' Mason said. 'Seven men were broken that day. Seven would never be the same.'

'Did you stay in touch?'

'With the survivors? Three kept in touch; we still talk as friends. The fourth? I don't know what happened to him.'

'Your unit fell apart. You lost more than two men that day.'

Mason let out a deep sigh. 'Yeah, I know that.'

'Sorry. Just thinking aloud. Is that why you joined the agency?'

'I don't follow.'

'To help. To armour yourself against the guilt?'

Mason considered that. 'Maybe,' he said. 'I know I let them down and could never run a team again. I wasn't good enough. I failed them, and then I failed to return to my wife, despite being there every day. To numb the guilt, the memories, I help those who need it. I can't stop taking the blame.'

'It was war,' Roxy said. 'You can't guard against bad luck and circumstance. You can't save everyone. A soldier knows that.'

'I didn't want to save everyone,' Mason said. 'Just the two men I failed.'

'So you're helping Sally now, why? To make amends? To do penance? As punishment? How many people do you have to save to heal yourself, Mason?'

He gave her a tight-lipped, humourless smile. 'I don't know. And that's all I can tell you. What do you have for me, Roxy?'

The American sat back in her seat, pursing her lips. 'Later,' she said. 'The plane's descending.'

'Are you kidding? We made a deal.'

'You made a deal. I never put a timeframe on it. I promise we'll talk later but, for now, that church, that riddle and the *Vatican Book of Secrets* are far more important.'

Mason accepted that without comment. His churning stomach also told him that he'd revealed way too much and needed some quiet time, a period in which to assimilate. Whether he'd done right to open up to Roxy was hardly the question now. The words were out and, like a flyaway kite, impossible to retrieve. Maybe vocalising his struggles would highlight their core strengths, making it easier to define and alleviate them.

His internal battle continued as the plane landed in Jerusalem.

Chapter 23

Jerusalem sat between the Mediterranean and the Dead Sea, one of the oldest cities in the world, and central to three key Abrahamic religions – Judaism, Christianity and Islam. A hotbed of conflict, Jerusalem had been destroyed twice, besieged over twenty times, captured and recaptured over forty, and attacked more than fifty.

Mason knew, when you walked into Jerusalem you walked into a barely contained cauldron of seething anger and conflicting beliefs. Some days it was safe, other days not so much – with tourists prohibited from entering its sacred walls when the threat levels were high. Today, there were both security and demonstration alerts, draping the city in a sense of impending peril.

In contrast to Rome, King David's city was dry, although cool and beset by bracing winds, the diffused light glancing off sun-bleached walls of ancient stone and throwing long shadows along its wealth of narrow alleyways. The team, as Mason loosely thought of them, rented a gleaming SUV from the airport courtesy of Sally's credit card, and drove through the busy city.

On the outskirts, the roads they took were uneven and coated with dust, but as they neared their destination and the people-traffic grew heavier, the pavements were of polished cobbles and the roads neat and tidy.

A gathering of stunning architecture complemented the city and filled their vision, but Mason did his best to ignore it and stay focused. He was pleased to see both Roxy and Hassell doing the same.

Which brought the issue of Luke Hassell back to the forefront of his mind.

Deal with the basics, not the drama.

The fundamental truth was that they knew nothing about him, save that he'd engineered a robbery at the Vatican, left a woman – albeit a murderous thief – to die and saved Mason's life by killing two assassins. Mason didn't need a whole lot of experience to know Hassell required careful attention.

It wasn't his actions nor essentially his words that had struck a tolerant chord within Mason, it was more of a gut feeling. Mason had once led one of the most badass crews on the planet, but he'd also led one that understood the union of kinship. An empathic bond had grown through adversity, the kind that only grows between like-minded soldiers willing to die for each other. Since those days, he'd trusted his gut instinct.

Roxy found a parking area not far from the Church of the Holy Sepulchre. Mason, unsure what to look for and what to do when they found it, stared out the window at a cluster of old buildings. 'Are we here?'

Sally opened her door, signalling the affirmative and allowing a cool rush of air to sweep through the car. Mason joined her outside and slipped on a set of mirror sunglasses.

Roxy joined him and shook her head. 'Makes you look like young James Bond.'

Mason pursed his lips, unsure whether she meant *a* young James Bond or *the* young James Bond. Probably the latter since she wasn't exactly known for outstanding compliments.

He ignored her and turned to Sally. 'Let's leave our bags in the car, shall we? Lead on.'

The young woman was already marching away. Mason fell in line, keeping a close eye on their environs. The Amori had the book, and far more resources, but had lost two assassins and a master thief to this mission already. Also, until they revealed the book's shocking secrets to the world, they hadn't gained a single foothold in their fight against the Church.

Another galvanising thought struck him. They might already be a step ahead. Maybe Marduk hadn't seen the Amori reference, or someone else was scanning through the book for him and hadn't noticed. It wasn't concrete, but it was enough to give Mason hope.

Several people glanced at them as they passed by. Mason noted a pair of policemen to the right, leaning against a wall, and people seated on stone benches around a small square. The hollow echoes of their bootsteps rang out in the air, the speed of their passing probably attracting more attention than anything else.

Mason asked Sally to slow down and blend in, pretending to stop and study nearby architecture and point it out to Roxy and Hassell.

'You think Marduk sent men?' Hassell said under his breath.

'You would know that better than me, but he will act fast once he knows, and he might want us out of the way. How extensive is the Amori network?'

'Oh, they're everywhere if Marduk is to be believed. High and low level. They've infiltrated governments, banks.' Hassell shook his head. 'You name it.'

'In that case, and if they've seen that reference in the book, they'll use locals to search this place,' Mason said. 'We could already be too late.'

'Unlikely,' Hassell said. 'From listening to Marduk I

believe he tries to keep the circle of people aware of his business to an absolute minimum. People who know of the Amori, their plans, their goals, and of *him*. For those reasons, he'll stick with Gido and assume that Gido, in his fear of the Amori, will try harder to make amends.'

'Then we should be hyper alert,' Roxy said. 'Make use of the skills that we were . . . taught.'

Mason caught the hesitation but didn't have time to consider what and how Roxy had been taught. Sally was at the end of the street and bearing right, about to disappear from view.

He ran to her side, catching up just as she rounded a corner. He stopped. 'Is that the church?'

'Yes,' Sally said in awe. 'The site where Jesus was crucified and where his empty tomb stands. Such a sacred place draped in turbulent history.'

Mason saw a courtyard facing the church, a single arched entrance to the left of an identical but long since bricked-up doorway, the L-shaped church and its facades dominated by a central belltower. This was Calvary.

'Do you know what's inside?'

'Just beyond that door is a sumptuously decorated stairway that leads up to Calvary. Opposite is the exit, which leads to a covered passage. There are two chapels, each with its own altar, the rock of Calvary – which you can touch. Statues and more chapels. Relics which may have held fragments of the Holy Cross. The Stone of Anointing, where Jesus's body was prepared for burial by Joseph of Arimathea. Want me to continue?'

'I'm good,' Mason said, not able to process the information that quickly.

They crossed the open courtyard together, just four tourists heading for the dark interior. Mason spotted two locals observing them, but could hardly accuse them of anything but people-watching.

Mason was not a religious man, but on crossing the threshold into the Church of the Holy Sepulchre, he felt a shiver of respect pass through his body, no doubt driven by the sheer number of people who venerated this age-old building.

'We can't get distracted by the wealth of religious history inside,' Roxy told them as they followed a group of tourists. 'We're here for one reason. To find the Amori.'

Mason saw the loner speaking in Roxy. She'd worked alone for many years, a detail that no doubt helped her stay focused.

Sally, ahead and enraptured, didn't hear her. 'There's a chapel containing the tomb of Joseph of Arimathea, the chapel where Mary Magdalene met Jesus after his resurrection, and the complex, the prison where Christ was held, although the religions cannot decide if that part is true. The chapel where the true cross was found—'

'Lot of chapels, lot of altars,' Hassell said as they entered the Greek Orthodox chapel, still shuffling along in line with the tourist trail. 'But what are we looking for?'

Mason was thinking the same thing. 'Are you waiting for inspiration to strike, Sally?'

'Clearly, the clue regarding Calvary left by Jacques Heindl was meant to be read in conjunction with another,' she said, her voice pitched low so as not to intrude upon the reverent hush permeating the church. 'And the only other clue, and one also emphasised by the archivist, is *"My life's greatest ailment meant that I could never do this, but five times I overrode the agony to touch the unseen written word."* Now, Mateo DeVille asked us the question: *"what does that even mean?"* I believe he knew exactly what it meant and was testing us. Then, obviously, all hell broke loose.'

'What do you think it means?' Mason asked.

'Heindl had bad knees,' Sally said. 'He was a Vatican

archivist, a priest, a cardinal. And what's the one ritual all men, women and children perform as a sign of worship?'

Mason narrowed his eyes, thinking it through, knowing he'd get there eventually, but Roxy beat him to it.

'They genuflect,' she said. 'Bend the knee.'

'Heindl was unable to genuflect,' Sally said. 'Due to the pain in his knees. But *five times I overrode the agony to touch the unseen written word*, he says. Which, to me, highlights one word in the main clue . . .'

'Altar,' Roxy said.

Mason fought to keep up. 'A priest genuflects before an altar,' he said. 'But you don't have to kneel before every altar, even significant ones like this.' He indicated the golden Altar of Crucifixion as they passed.

'True.' Sally bit her lip, happy to stay in line as she processed her thoughts. 'But churches like this have dozens of altars, both principal and lesser, more obscure. What if . . .' She paused, pondering.

Mason used the hesitation to reassess their surroundings, a thankless task in here. Behind him, Hassell was on constant watch.

'What if Heindl is pointing us towards the lesser, obscure altars?' Sally said. 'Those deemed so insignificant in the Five Great Churches that they sit gathering dust, passed by, mostly ignored by the multitude, their inscriptions mostly *unseen*. Just look around you now. The masses flock to the well-known objects and then move on. Everyone's guilty of it. They take little time to properly explore. We should seek them out.'

'It would make perfect sense to carve his clues on obscure items,' Roxy said. 'For secrecy, longevity, lots of reasons.'

'And what do we do when we find them?' Mason asked.

'Well, we get down on our knees,' Sally said. 'We forage in the dirt. We seek out that which Jacques Heindl left behind. This is the first of the Five Great Churches. This is the first site of the blazed trail that will lead us to the undesirable treasure – the sanctuary of the Amori.'

They found a place to stop and gather without holding up the masses. Sally drew out a guidebook and reeled off names of various chapels and altars. There were many and they needed to check every single one that required genuflection.

First, they explored the Greek Orthodox and then the Catholic chapels. They passed through the rotunda, visiting the golden-roofed aedicula that enclosed the Holy Sepulchre.

They knelt and exposed the low altars to torchlight as inconspicuously as they could, using their mobile phones, cupping most of the strong beam with their hands, occasionally taking photos of an inscription, hopeful queries to which Sally always shook her head.

The best part of an hour later, a dirty, sweating Mason confronted Sally with a developing, thorny issue. 'These altars. Most are centuries old. Heindl lived in the 1800s. How could he have added script to them? Shouldn't we be looking for an altar from that era?'

Sally nodded at him. 'A great theory. A good question. And, principally, you are right. But human ethics must come into play, even here, even at the heart of religion. Put simply, kings of Jordan and the Saudis have paid millions over the centuries in restoration bills, in addition to the many reconstructions undertaken by Byzantines, Arabs, Christians and of course the crusaders. What I'm saying is that money talks. If Heindl, by way of secret Vatican accounts to which the Pope's personal archivist would have access, wanted to leave his mark on some unassuming, humble altar, then it's not beyond the realms of possibility that he could succeed. But hey,' Sally reached out and tousled his hair, 'good conjecture, Babyface.'

Mason stared in surprise, caught off guard and slightly annoyed at being patronised, before reaching up to smooth his hair. On the one hand it was a good sign that Sally was at ease with Roxy's sassy traits and embraced them; on the other, it highlighted a difficulty he'd struggled to overcome his entire life.

Always undervalued and underestimated.

Maybe I'll grow a beard or go bald.

For now, he said nothing and fell to his knees in front of yet another altar.

Chapter 24

Mason had lost track of time, and finally rested on his haunches after another failure. 'Nothing,' he said. 'How many more?'

'Maybe we should split up,' Hassell suggested.

'No offence, but I won't feel entirely satisfied unless I personally examine every altar.' Sally wasn't being bad-mannered, just candid. 'Keep going.'

Mason followed her lead, thankful the church wasn't as crowded as he'd imagined, finding that as they delved deeper, many small interior areas were controlled by different Christian branches, making the contrast in decoration from area to area intriguing and magnificent. Mason could never have imagined such a sprawling, diverse church sat here, with so many different chambers and chapels and altars all dedicated to but one source.

They passed a small chapel, empty of tourists, where several monks were chanting. The high, dark walls, the tenor of their voices and the significance of the church evoked a sense of old dreams, as if they'd passed from the modern world to the ancient. Mason, watching every person and every movement, narrowed his eyes on seeing one of the men who'd been seated outside. He caught Roxy's attention and alerted her to the potential threat, feeling his heart rate rise. The man only followed and studied artefacts, nodding quietly to himself, but Mason noticed how his eyes glanced occasionally across at them.

Sally found another altar and then another. They took turns dropping to the hard floor, trying not to attract the attention of the black-robed priests who appeared to be patrolling the place. They spent so much time in there that, Mason knew, if someone was looking out for them, they would surely have been alerted. On leaving through one arched door, he saw the eyes of a priest fix on them and start to follow. The eyes didn't drop even as Mason let the man know he'd seen him. Feelings of claustrophobic dread started to enfold him as he imagined that they were being watched, evaluated and followed.

Down here, there were no exits. Nowhere to go. Mason alerted Hassell to the fact that he thought they were under surveillance.

In one of the furthest, most obscure niches, in the north transept, Mason dropped once more to his knees and performed a quick inspection of all four sides of a low, dark-stoned, timeworn slab. Amid the dust, grime and old cobwebs he saw a single reedy line of elegant inscription, a line that ran the entire length of the altar.

'I think I've found it,' he said in a voice reflecting his own disbelief. 'There's something here.'

Sally was already on her knees beside him, plucking at his arms to pull him out of the way. 'Let me in.'

Mason rose and nodded at Hassell and Roxy, making sure they knew to keep any nosy onlookers out of the way. It was a dark alcove, and Sally snapped quick photographs, an action that would attract the attention of the priests, but barely a dozen seconds later she was back on her feet.

'Go,' she said.

A few minutes later they were back outside in the full

glare of the winter's sun, the bright skies forcing their sunglasses back on, the cold breeze attacking their bare skin with icy abandon.

'It's perfect,' Sally said. 'Exactly what we were looking for.'

Mason noticed several men staring in their direction, some with unconcealed interest. A closer inspection revealed a startling array of weapons holstered upon the men's belts and tucked into their waistbands. 'I do not like the look of that, and I'm sure we were being followed in there. We need to move.'

'So presuming that we've found the clue,' Hassell said, 'shouldn't we make sure nobody else does?'

Sally stared at him aghast. 'You want to destroy an item of immense historical substance? I would think only a dupe, a dullard or a terrorist would ever think to do so.'

'Yeah, it's not like it's your grandma's urn,' Roxy said. 'That's the friggin' church of the holy whatever right there.'

Sally eyed them both before turning to Mason. 'At least you're normal. Please don't tell me you want to destroy the altar too.'

'I understand why *they* want to, and why a historical researcher like yourself wouldn't. But, humanitarianly, we can't. The religious significance here is off the scale. Look, guys, we need to move. *Now.*'

'The Amori will find it and then destroy it,' Hassell assured them, starting to walk as the group came together and looked at one man, an animated man who glared in Mason's direction with cold eyes. 'To prevent anyone else from finding their millennia-old sanctuary. And when they do . . .' He shook his head. 'You just have to hope they only target the altar.'

Sally looked ready to cry. 'Can't we stop them? They will need to find and destroy every clue in turn, which could be devastating for all the cities involved.'

'We'll already be lucky to get away alive,' Mason said

as the watchers split up and started toward them. 'Listen, these guys are starting to look dangerous. Stick with the back of the crowd if you can. What's the clue?'

His words made Sally focus. She plucked her phone from her jeans pocket and expanded one of the photos. *'Built by the Man of the First Plague, and by the Emperor of Eboracum, this is where the Star was Stolen.'*

Mason nodded. 'Clear as mud then. I'm guessing you've already cracked it and know the location of the second church?'

'Are you kidding?' Sally looked insecure. 'This is gonna take hard work, in which I'm looking forward to immersing myself.'

Mason saw more men join the suspicious group at their backs and started to walk faster. He moved closer to Sally, aiming to protect her at all times. This was quickly turning into a treacherous situation. The figures were spreading out, filling the path behind, blocking it. Their hands were drifting towards their weapons.

'Eight of them now, Joe,' Roxy told him. 'All armed. You got a plan?'

'Yeah, we get the hell out of Jerusalem.'

'Whoa, you do have a knack for stringing a sentence together.'

Mason couldn't hold back a snort of laughter. 'Well, I was a soldier,' he said. 'We eat dictionaries for breakfast.'

'Do you know your way around Jerusalem?' Sally asked as the group following them drew closer.

Mason stared at the narrow stone streets, the high walls and random crowds of people. 'No idea.'

Sally was already pulling Google Maps up on her phone. 'Don't worry. I—'

'Hey,' Hassell told them. 'I can help. This is kinda what I do.'

'I thought you were an *infiltration* expert,' Roxy said.

Hassell raised an eyebrow. 'I am. And I normally plan it all over a month or more, using blueprints and a computer. But *infil* goes hand in hand with *exfil*, right? And what do we have to lose?'

Mason was practically running already. Several followers were gesturing angrily towards him and Roxy, who were at the back of their crew. 'A fair bit actually,' he said. 'But, please, lead the way, mate.'

'You hoping he gets shot first?' Roxy asked loudly as Hassell moved out in front.

Mason urged them to move faster.

Chapter 25

They took off at a sprint, hoping to put some distance between themselves and their hostile pursuers. Mason had already assessed all eight armed men and was reasonably sure that two were trained, maybe ex-military, and the others local thugs. There was no doubt that they were all in the employ of the Amori though, which put them outside the law. They began to shout, to gesture furiously. Two men unzipped their jackets to reach for weapons, apparently not caring that they were in a crowded area. Mason readied himself to turn and confront them as they came closer and closer, worrying that those on the outside could easily flank both him and Roxy. He could hear them panting now, see the hard glinting in their eyes. Four more steps and they'd be upon them.

He skirted the edge of a large group of tourists, slipping sideways between them and a rough wall, making for the top of the sloped street. Hassell was already pulling away ahead.

'Keep up,' he shouted back, darting to the right in front of the tourists.

Mason followed, making sure Sally stayed ahead of him. They entered an even narrower street, little more than an alley. The sweat was just starting to bead along his forehead. A glance back saw the pursuing group being hindered by the tourists, unable to enter the alley through the slow-moving throng.

Good job, Hassell.

So far. The alley stretched before them, heading west. Hassell reached the end and didn't hesitate, dashing northward, passing a tall-spired, grey church on their right, still charging ahead. He shouted at people, most of whom got out of their way. Those who didn't were circumvented, slowing them down.

The sunlit streets were a dusty maze, many bounded by high walls and thick with pedestrians. Mason wondered just how far the Amori were willing to go to protect their refuge and their plan.

The answer came soon enough as Jerusalem's ancient walls echoed to the sound of a gunshot. Ordinarily, Mason assumed the security would be tighter than an ageing actor's facelift, but today the patrols were strangely absent.

They hadn't seen one security guard, soldier or policeman so far.

Coincidence, right?

No, the Amori could orchestrate that. If they had enough men and women secured in the right places, they could orchestrate anything.

Hassell burst out of a junction and slowed. Mason caught up to him in seconds, standing in the centre of the street, surrounded by history. Even now, he could discern the elevated plaza above the western walls, which was the hallowed site of Temple Mount.

Behind them, a short walk away, was the Cenacle, the first Christian church and, supposedly, the site of the Last Supper.

Mason didn't quite know where to turn, not because he was lost in Jerusalem, but because he was momentarily lost in history.

Remembering his training, he pulled Sally closer as harsh voices came from behind.

Hassell took off to the north, threading through street after street in an effort to lose their pursuers. They pushed people out of the way and held their hands up to stop cars in the road. The cars didn't stop but slowed dramatically. Hassell leapt over a bonnet, sliding across to the other side. The vehicle then jerked to a halt, allowing Mason and the others space to sprint around its front end.

'Where are you going?' Roxy asked urgently.

'Trying to lose them,' Hassell returned. 'And then we can double back.'

'You know where we are?'

'Roughly.'

Mason made a face. *Roughly?* Sally's safety couldn't be compromised. But Hassell's plan seemed to be working. Mason no longer heard sounds of pursuit.

They threaded their way through another narrow street, having pulled out enough of a lead to avoid any more gunshots, and were nearing its end. Hassell was steps away. Mason wondered if now was the perfect time to pull out a map and devise a better plan but, with their pursuers presumably still chasing, decided it was too dangerous. Intersections came up quickly, allowing Hassell to thread a winding path through the dust-baked streets. Mason slowed after half a minute to check behind but saw no one chasing them. Roxy was at his side.

'Have we shaken them?' she asked.

'I think so.'

'Awesome. My lungs are on fire.'

Mason noticed that the others were still running and raced off to catch up. He gave a shout. Hassell turned, slowed and nodded. Moments later, they were together again, walking swiftly and trying to catch their breath. Mason stayed at the rear, always alert.

Hassell marched across an intersection ahead, stopped abruptly and threw his hands up in the air. Mason barely had time to feel a rush of trepidation before he reached the American.

A wide, square plaza stood before them, occupied by seven unsavoury-looking men. Mason spotted a pistol in one man's hand, a curved dagger in the grip of another. Carefully, he shoved Sally behind him and gestured at Roxy to move to his right.

'Ready when you are,' he said softly.

Chapter 26

A tension as thick and abrasive as fresh volcanic ash fell upon the scene. Mason readied himself as several men brandished their weapons – everything from short, wickedly curved knives to blood-encrusted machetes and powerful handguns.

Mason also noticed dozens of scared civilians scattered around the perimeter of the square, some ushering away young children, others leaning back to watch, and still others urging the men to pull back, to think again about committing violence within the walls of the old city.

Mason had had his initial doubts about Roxy, but here she stood calmly at his side, a solid ally. To his left, Hassell completed their battle line, an unknown quantity but so far faultless in his contribution to their efforts. Sally stood at the back of their group, clutching her arms in apprehension but not backing away.

A short man wearing smart clothing stepped forwards and signalled the others to stop. He was clean-shaven and carried a thin-bladed weapon in his right hand. He held himself like a man who thought he knew how to fight.

Mason had seen them all over the world – the boxers who practised three hours a week and believed they could own a ring on fight night, the soldiers who'd barely shuffled through training and bragged about their prowess, the hand-to-hand artists who'd reached second Dan black belt – none of them had experienced up-close, do-or-die combat. The kind that made you immensely strong and weak, implausibly courageous and scared all at the same time. The kind that formed bonds which turned colleagues into family. This man glared at Mason, an unspoken threat in his eyes and face, body language announcing that he was preparing to strike. To his left and right, his accomplices fanned out in a line, each man ready to launch an attack.

'Why are you chasing us?' Mason stalled him, hoping that a local police patrol might come by and scare them off.

The well-dressed man closed one eye and squinted at him through the other. 'I am Josef. We want to know what you learned from holy church and if you passed it to anyone else.'

Mason pursed his lips. It was a menacing request delivered by a local in broken English. It might be designed to enlist the help of the other locals gathered around him. It might be all that he'd been told by his superiors. But it was a legitimate request – Josef had to assume they carried mobile phones and other devices with them which they could use to convey information quickly to someone else.

Mason stood under the cold glare of the sun and tried to engineer a getaway. 'We're tourists.' He spread his arms in a non-threatening manner.

As he did so, Roxy leaned in and said, 'Only two guns in view. Two men to the right of Josef, and three men to the left.' She was highlighting their primary targets.

Mason went on, 'We carried nothing away from the church.'

Josef considered that, looking down and scratching marks in the cobbles with the tip of his long blade. The sound was cringeworthy and displayed his naivety. Mason noted men in the crowd who quietly shook their heads at him.

163

'But you *did* find something, yes? What did you find?'

'Maybe you should go look for yourself,' Roxy said.

'You'll live longer if you tell me.'

'Who do you answer to, Josef?' Mason asked, partly stalling and hoping for some unforeseen intervention, partly interested.

'A higher cause.' Josef sniffed.

'Be careful,' a man hissed beside him. 'Remember where you are.'

Mason sensed the animosity between them and guessed it was an enmity overcome at least for the moment by thick wads of cash exchanging hands. He wondered if he could stoke them into turning on each other.

'You work for the Amori, don't you, Josef? Don't they want to *destroy* Christianity?'

Josef looked uncomfortable. 'As I said, I work for an authority concerned with relic smuggling—'

'That's not what you said.'

Josef chipped at the cobbles with the tip of his blade, displaying annoyance. 'Hand over what you stole. I won't ask again.' Now, he raised his sword and brandished it toward them. 'I want information. I will cut it from your hide piece by piece if I have to. In fact,' he licked his lips and grinned appallingly, 'I look forward to it.'

Mason appealed to the men gathered around Josef. 'We have no bags,' he said. 'What could we have stolen?'

Their bags were stored safely back in the car. They carried nothing on their persons other than their mobile phones. Mason challenged Josef with a steely glare.

'You believe that you are on a treasure hunt,' Josef scoffed. 'A *religious* treasure hunt. Searching for some long-lost enemy. I think that you're deranged.'

'And I think that your masters are petrified that they'll be discovered,' Mason said. 'Why else would they send us such a murderous guard of honour?'

'Petrified?' Josef looked as if such a notion had never occurred to him. Of course, he couldn't elaborate. You could hardly defend a society which had wrapped itself in secrecy for thousands of years.

'Scared,' Roxy offered. 'Terrified. Literally shaking in their tighty whities—'

'I know what *petrified* means.' Josef seemed not to be blessed with reasonable common sense or to be able to respond to it. 'Do you want to die here today? I have orders. My men will torture you for information and then kill you.' To his left and right the line of men inched forward as if in anticipation of the bloodshed to come and, when Mason glanced at them, he saw little other than violence and death in their eyes.

'Here?' Roxy asked with doubt in her voice.

'Our cars are close by. This is your last chance. Talk or die,' Josef raised his sword now and Mason saw a small amount of congealed blood spread along the blade. He had used it before then.

'Your masters have the book,' Mason replied. 'They found out that they're *in* it, yeah, but you still have the book. What are your bosses waiting for? Are they so terrified that we'll find them?'

Josef didn't answer, probably because he couldn't. The Amori's ruling body wouldn't apprise minions of their long-term plans. It was also true that twenty-four hours hadn't yet passed since the *Book of Secrets* was stolen. One issue that worried Mason was – would searching for the secret society hasten their terrible revelations?

'Last chance.' Josef took another step forward. 'My superiors *will* win the day, whether it is in Jerusalem or elsewhere.'

Mason studied the plaza's cobbles, lightly brushed with sand. He took in the city's high walls on three sides, enduring and unrecognised monuments to years of strife and bloodshed. He looked to the blue skies that presided

165

without judgement over mankind's greatest and most heinous acts.

Divine intervention?

Not today. He stepped forward, flexing his arms, making himself the centre of attention, and expecting both Roxy and Hassell to target the gunmen.

'Can you use that blade, Josef? Or is it just a tool to scratch your arse with?'

Chapter 27

Josef whipped up his blade, but Mason was already beside him. Roxy and Hassell leapt forwards, trying to keep at least one body between themselves and the gun carriers. The hostiles were prepared for violence and brandished their weapons as they charged.

Mason clamped Josef's arm below the wrist, restricting movement, and delivered a double jab to the man's throat. Josef's eyes bulged. His grip on the blade loosened. Mason sent him to his knees with a blow to the sternum and prepared to finish him off but Josef rallied unexpectedly. The guy was tougher than he appeared. He threw a fist at Mason's stomach and then charged, grabbing Mason at the waist but dropping the sword. Mason pushed back, trying to remain upright and hammered both elbows down onto Josef's back. Josef pushed and fought as if he didn't feel the pain. Mason switched tactics, punching down at an angle into Josef's ribs and kidneys. Josef fell to his knees, gasping, but then rolled to the side, grabbed his sword and slashed out as Mason attacked.

Mason redirected his forward momentum just in time. Even then the sweep of the blade nicked his temple, drawing blood. Mason fell to Josef's right, landing on his back and that was when Josef made his mistake. He rose and tried to bring the blade to bear instead of trying to render Mason unconscious. With time to think, Mason swept his legs in a wide arc, taking Josef's legs out from under him. The Amori soldier fell on his own sword, impaled through the right bicep. Mason leapt up and whirled towards his next opponent.

Who was already swinging a machete.

Mason ducked, weaved and sidestepped, creating a foot of space. The machete-wielder swept his weapon upward, aiming to gut Mason where he stood.

Mason jumped back, saw the sharp blade flash by, and then stepped in. A strong jab to the throat and then the right eye made his opponent yelp and falter. Mason took hold of the arm clutching the weapon, reversed and broke it, all in the blink of an eye.

The man screamed.

Roxy, an untried yet reputable quantity until now, performed a bruising, deadly ballet. Fast on her feet, and trained by the best to target the tenderest places on the human anatomy, she debilitated, hindered and fractured her enemy.

This wasn't standard army training, Mason saw, gauging her progress in brief spells between combat; this was pure hand-to-hand dominance, a fighting force of nature that was as elegant as it was unstoppable. As poised as it was lethal. Also, amidst the chaos, he saw Sally back up against a far wall, her hands at her sides, an expression of cold fear stretched across her face. Sally could not hope to defend herself against this kind of onslaught and possessed information their enemies wanted. Maybe she would run, use her training, if the need arose. Mason hoped so.

Roxy chopped one man down like a felled tree. He hit the cobbles with a spine-crunching slam and would never get up. She broke the next man's arm in two places and, whilst the owner clutched it in an agony, spun and elbow-jabbed his throat and administered three swift strikes – breaking his nose and several teeth, and putting out an eye.

Hassell had immediately confronted one of the gunmen. If Hassell respected the weapon he didn't show it, affording the man no mercy as he employed some dirty street-fighting skills, using knees and elbows to target groin, shins and sternum. Hassell sent the man to his knees with a headbutt, ignored the fountain of blood and followed his opponent to the ground, grappling for the gun.

Which left one loose gunman. Only seconds had passed since the start of the fight, but already the second pistol carrier had his weapon trained on Hassell, the easiest target.

Mason saw the trigger finger tightening, saw the malicious snarl as the man squeezed.

Thinking fast, he grasped hold of Josef's long blade, wrenching it free, and threw it at the shooter. It wasn't a perfect throw by any means, barely slicing the other man's bicep, but it did throw his aim off. The bullet discharged, flew to Hassell's left and thudded into a wall. The shooter yelled and stared at his bleeding arm.

Sally screamed. The bullet had impacted the wall just inches to the right of her head. Stone splinters bit at her flesh. The noise of the collision sent her to her knees with her hands over her ears.

Mason leapt at the shooter and wrenched his gun arm towards the ground. With a vicious twist he broke the wrist and took the gun, leaving the man gasping on his knees.

He glanced around to gauge the situation.

Roxy was matched against a thug, the pair prowling around each other. She had proven herself to be deadly, and he held a military blade in a way that showed he knew how to use it. He lunged forward with the knife, jabbing her shoulder with the point. Roxy jerked away and let the wound bleed, too troubled by the man to risk taking a defensive stance.

Hassell lay underneath his opponent, but had the man's

arms trapped. The two were wrestling for supremacy and Hassell was slowly losing.

Josef had climbed to his feet, still choking from the blows to his throat, reeling from the pain in his arm, and regarded Mason with angry eyes.

All their other opponents had been neutralised.

Mason aimed the gun at those infuriated eyes. 'Call your men off.'

Josef struggled to speak. 'I . . . can't . . .'

Hassell grunted and strained against his assailant. Roxy feinted left and right against hers, but the man didn't lunge, just waited for his chance.

Mason fired at cobbles between Josef's legs. 'Call them off, *now*.'

Josef coughed, terrified, and cleared his throat. This time, his words came easier. 'If I do, they'll kill me. Kill us all. This is win and prosper . . . or die.' He lunged as he spoke the last two words, face set in the stony expression of a gargoyle, fully expecting to lose his life.

Mason didn't want to shoot and kill anybody he didn't have to, so, despite his gun being aimed at Josef's central mass, he spun it and swiped Josef across the forehead as he attacked. Mason backpedalled as Josef's body weight struck him, but managed to stay upright and let the other man slide to the floor.

Josef, bleeding profusely, groaned into the sand-dusted cobbles, 'You should kill me.'

Mason first checked Sally was under no threat and then ran over to help Hassell. Assessing the wrestling match, he located the gun trapped beneath both men, then started kicking the Hassell's opponent in the ribs. Four direct hits took the wind out of him.

Hassell scrambled up, grabbed the gun and nodded. 'Thanks, man.'

Mason flicked his eyes to the weapon. 'Cover them.'

He turned his attention to Roxy. The military-trained thug with the knife watched him whilst keeping Roxy at bay. When Mason sighted the barrel at his face, he held up both hands. 'Don't shoot.'

Mason winced as Roxy stepped in and delivered a thundering kick to the man's groin. 'Asshole,' she hissed as he collapsed to the floor, groaning in a kind of high falsetto only opera singers should be able to achieve.

'You didn't have to do that,' Mason said.

'The bastard reminds me of a past I'd far rather forget. And besides, he called me a bitch.'

Mason dropped it, figuring she had her reasons. He turned to check on Sally, who stood at the back of the square. She gave him a jittery, hurried nod.

He motioned to Hassell. 'Can you find our car?'

'Are you kidding?' Hassell sounded aggrieved. 'It's what—'

Their dialogue was interrupted by a roar of fury. Mason looked up to see a new thug charging towards them, machete held high. His black robes flowed behind him, his heavy boots stomped at the ground. Spittle flew from his lips. Mason had just a few seconds to decide what to do and noticed that both Roxy and Hassell were watching him.

Was this them acknowledging his role as leader? Or were they judging his method of defence?

The training kicked in. Mason stepped in under the machete's swing, dropped a shoulder, and heaved the attacker over his back. The robes slapped him in the face as the man flew high before crashing to the ground. The machete skittered away.

The man let out a surprised grunt as if shocked to find the cobbles so close to his face. There was no pain in his expression though, just fury. His eyes were wild, flitting left and right, and Mason knew he wouldn't stay down long.

'There's a substance other than blood in that one's veins,' Roxy noted matter-of-factly.

Mason agreed but had no time for chit-chat. It didn't matter what kind of manufactured ferocity fuelled a person's system if you found the right place to hit them, and Mason knew several. The escalating problem was how long it was all taking.

Hassell, Roxy and Sally were ready to move. Mason allowed their latest attacker to roll over and then delivered three draining blows as accurately as possible, sapping his strength. Then, with a last glance over at Josef, he backed away towards Hassell.

'Go,' he said.

As one, they turned and ran, the gleaming, dusty streets of Jerusalem flying by under their heels, the ancient walls, buildings and golden minarets standing in judgement – their verdict no doubt harsh. But Mason was convinced that they were doing the right thing. Convinced that helping Sally would not only benefit the world at large, but possibly save Roxy and him from themselves.

They would see this through to the end no matter what. Mason was starting to find a new purpose in this quest and, judging by the way she'd fought, so was Roxy. Who'd have thought that the Amori was the catalyst they needed to start facing reality again, to emerge from under their homemade shield-wall?

Mason raced towards their car, a new purpose quickening his step.

Chapter 28

Marduk worked with a loyal colleague named Ruben, an expert on all things interweb-based. Marduk never pretended to have skills or even interest in cyberspace, but recognised the incredible worldwide coverage it offered. If some young geek in California could get twenty million YouTube views by jumping off a trampoline into a swimming pool, then the Amori could spread their word incalculably, mask their location and identity, and reach the homes of everyone they needed to. The rest would be accomplished through social media platforms and word of mouth.

'It won't delay the revelation too long?' Marduk checked with Ruben.

'Four or five days,' Ruben said. 'But the delay is necessary to grow an audience for the revelation, otherwise we'd be announcing it to a few hundred. Followers need time to find us, to grow curious, to spread the word and just *watch*. And the beauty of YouTube is – the more people watch the more visible they make it. The more they use notifications and ads and Push announcements. If we delay . . . we snag millions.'

'The Church has two billion followers.'

Ruben shifted, uncrossing his legs. Marduk and he were crammed into Ruben's small apartment within the HQ, surrounded by scattered video game boxes, stacks of information printouts and old food cartons. The place stank of stale sweat and fried food. If Marduk didn't need Ruben so badly to spread the word, he'd force-feed him cheeseburgers until he exploded.

'It will multiply exponentially,' Ruben said. 'I will bombard all platforms at once. We will trend day and night. We release the first video, one day later the next, and then a day later the final teaser with a date for the ultimate revelation. I recommend waiting at least a full twenty-four hours and then releasing it between seven and eight p.m. in the countries with the most Christian followers. We will then make sure targeted ads and prompts spread to all other countries at the right times.'

'Devastation.' Marduk smiled grimly. 'An end to the Church and all the power to me.' He blinked and quickly added: 'And to the Amori, of course. We will have our new Babylon.'

'I just need material for the first upload,' Ruben said.

Marduk handed over a thin folder. Inside, Ruben would find photographs of the Vatican Secret Archives, and of the stealing of the *Book of Secrets* taken from Nina's head-cam that Mac had set up, a teaser photo of the Book itself, and several lines of text that Marduk had penned that promised a terrifying and crushing revelation that would destroy the very cradle in which Christianity had been born. It also promised a swift and candid disclosure.

'You must embellish this for the masses,' Marduk said.

'I can do that easily. It will be a professional presentation.'

'I have written it deliberately to draw in the public, the newsmakers and the Vatican alike. To inspire curiosity. Of course, it will bait the Vatican mercilessly . . .' Marduk was forced to stop talking as his face split into a wide grin at his own brilliance. 'It will torment them, harass them, prevent them from sleeping.'

'Perhaps priests and even cardinals will end their lives rather than see our revelation,' Ruben suggested.

'Such a beautiful thought,' Marduk said. 'I will bring you the second video's material shortly. It will include information on how we plan to prove our claims. Many will think we are not telling the truth, but comprehensive evidence will show that they are wrong.'

'Carbon dating of the pages, the ink, that kind of thing?' Ruben asked. 'References to books that may still exist, carvings perhaps? Proof that Jesus was a warrior king, proof of when the Vatican first knew, of how long they've covered up the secret, of their fear that it might one day get out?'

'All of that, and more,' Marduk said. 'The original tomb location is mentioned. Deposits of soil and rock can be matched from that site to dates in the book. Matched independently. We can invite this scrutiny because we know *it is all true*. That alone will give the Pope nightmares.'

Marduk sat back and smiled to himself, so content now that the filth surrounding him no longer mattered. The stench that infested Ruben's room no longer mattered. The day – the day that had been promised for millennia – was coming.

And it would all happen on his watch.

Chapter 29

Leaving the area, Mason and his companions travelled for thirty minutes, finally bringing the car to a stop down a dirt track, high in the hills overlooking Jerusalem, far away from anything that might be classed as a main road.

'Any bad cuts or bruises?' Mason asked, selecting park but leaving the car and air conditioning running.

Both Hassell and Roxy reported nothing major. Sally remained quiet. When Mason turned in his seat, she regarded him under hooded eyes.

'I was so scared,' she said. 'And alone. And it . . . reminded me of my . . . father. Of how he died. What if . . . they'd killed you?' She shuddered, unable to face that reality.

'Hey.' Mason reached out and laid a hand on her shoulder. 'We're all good. Nothing chopped off, lost or broken.'

'Except that guy's balls,' Roxy remembered. 'He's probably still looking for them.'

Sally didn't smile, probably because she didn't share the soldier's sense of camaraderie. In the field, dark humour could help you overcome a darker situation. In adversity, making light of painful subjects helped ease their impact.

'I'm okay,' she said. 'Just let me work. I'll be fine. We have to stop the bad, put an end to it all.'

Mason turned away. A bright afternoon sun slanted

through drifting white clouds, sending monstrous shadows floating across the Mount of Olives to the east. Cars and trucks dotted various twisting highways as people got on with their day, oblivious to the looming threat posed by the Amori. For a moment, Mason was pinned by a memory and propelled back two years to what he'd come to think of as the last good night of his life. He'd been seated at a table along with his entire team, chilling out and shooting the shit as another dangerous day came to a close. Nothing was etched deeper into his memory than these men, their faces and names, their characters and dreams.

It had been their last night together and they ate too much, laughed too much and regaled each other with tall tales of wild antics back home and over-colourful visions of the future. They were a tight unit, each man practically nailed to the others, and, whilst they functioned perfectly during missions, Mason was aware that they were a dysfunctional lot in between.

He was the same. Honed like blades by like-minded men, taught the art of warfare and how to make a swift kill, they were at a loss when it came to such civilian mainstays as social gatherings, supermarket shopping and exercising for fun. The required swift adjustment between war and peace wasn't possible.

Their table was cast in shadows that played over the men's faces, surrounded by trucks heavy with camouflage, some still ticking the heat of the day away. There was a smell of diesel and barbecue cooking, of leather and steel.

'You okay, mate?' Mason recalled Zach Kelly's question as clearly as the letters of his own name.

'Yeah, yeah.' Mason had been forced to shout over the braying laughter of the pack. 'Just a little misunderstanding with Hannah.'

'Why? She catch you pricing up a new Ford Mustang again?' Zach had laughed.

'Funny. That was one time. And no . . . This was more . . . personal.'

'Oh, she'll forgive you, mate.' Zach had clapped him on the back. 'She's one of the best. Just accept it, you might be pretty but you're punching above your weight with Hannah.'

Mason had shaken his head, smiled, let it all wash over him and concocted a suitable riposte. The truth was, Hannah believed his absences from their relationship made him *less* sharp, a notion that unsettled him, preyed on his mind.

Zach had died the following day.

Mason remembered everything in perfect clarity. The mission, the explosion, the aftermath. The mistake that had destroyed his team in more ways than one. The . . .

It was war. It happens. There is no perfect plan for enemy contact. You can only adapt. Suffering is easy, but can you forgive?

'So, the clue we found,' Sally said. '"*Built by the Man of the First Plague, and by the Emperor of Eboracum, this is where the Star was Stolen.*" Any ideas?'

'Wait,' Hassell said. 'This will lead us to the second great church, right? And another clue?'

'Assuming you're still with us?' Roxy tested his conviction.

'Sure.' Hassell nodded. 'I mean, yeah, I have some personal issues to handle now with Gido. He'll definitely be hunting me down now after what he'll see as my betrayal, but that can wait. We're on the same team, right?'

'It's hardly a team,' Mason began, but then stopped. Back there, in the dust and blood of battle, it had felt like the beginning of something. Maybe something bigger than themselves.

Sally's voice snapped him back to reality. 'Keep up. Jacques Heindl left five clues, I think, inscribed upon five different altars. A global trail leading to the lair of the Amori. Only by following this trail can we hope to prevent them from releasing the *Book of Secrets* into the public domain.'

'If only we knew what those secrets were,' Mason said. 'We could evaluate their impact.'

'Only Heindl knew then, and Mateo DeVille now,' Sally said. 'And the Amori, of course. But don't worry, I *can* do this.'

Mason was about to remind her that they weren't worried, that they didn't judge her by her successes, but then realised she needed to prevail for *herself*. Sally saw her wealth and privilege as a hobble and needed to succeed under her own steam.

'Distinct questions,' Sally mused. 'Who was the man of the first plague and who was the emperor at Eboracum? And where was the star stolen? Let's break it down.'

Mason watched her think, sifting through the filing system in her brain as well as dragging information from the notes in her computer cloud or using the internet.

'The worst plague in England was mostly in the fourteenth century, but in London by 1666 they'd lost roughly 15 per cent of the population to the Great Plague, probably over 100,000 souls. The plague peaked in the summer months as rats carried their fleas into city streets filled with rubbish, especially in the poorer areas. King and courtiers left in July for Hampton Court along with the doctors. The Lord Mayor was left to deal with the disease and build the plague pits. Scotland closed its borders, people lost their jobs, quarantines were introduced. But there was no *man* of the plague. Similarly in the 1300s, the Black Death was one of the deadliest diseases known to man through all of history, killing one third to one half of Europeans. It ravaged Europe and then England, but . . . again . . . no one man was credited either positively or negatively.'

'Was the Black Death the first plague?' Roxy asked.

Sally looked unsure and turned back to her laptop. 'Wait,' she said at length. 'The first terrible pandemic occurred in AD 541–549. A contagious plague driven by the bacterium

Yersinia pestis, it tormented Europe and severely affected the Roman Empire, especially its then capital – Constantinople. Some believe that the first pandemic was the deadliest in history.'

'And does it have a person associated with it?' Hassell asked. 'And *why* would it?'

Sally nodded. 'Yes. The plague is named after the Roman emperor of Constantinople who, according to historians of the time, contracted the disease and recovered in 542. It's called the Plague of Justinian.'

'And from where did this one originate?' Roxy asked.

'Asia. Same as all the others. The root-level existing strains of the plague these days are found in China.'

'This Emperor, Justinian,' Mason said. 'I'm guessing he built a number of things?'

'Oh, yes, he ruled from AD 527 to 565 and began the so-called restoration of the Empire. A plan to revive the realm and, more importantly, his building programme produced creations such as the Hagia Sophia.'

'You think the Hagia Sophia is one of the Five Great Churches?' Mason was well aware of the exalted building in Istanbul, one of the most impressive structures ever created.

'Hold your horses,' Sally said. 'Yes, the Hagia Sophia was built by Justinian as the Christian cathedral of Constantinople. The sheer scale and wonder of its design are credited with changing the face and history of architecture. But . . . that's not the whole clue, is it?'

Mason was already kicking himself for speaking up too fast. Sally's reaction made him feel like an over-eager kid in class. 'Of course,' he said. 'I was coming to that.'

Roxy tried to hide a smirk. Mason didn't even bother to look at Hassell, assuming the newcomer would also be amused.

Sally continued, oblivious to the interplay. 'The Emperor of Eboracum,' she mused. 'Now who might that be?'

180

'I know part of the answer,' Hassell said, keeping his voice neutral. 'Eboracum is the old Roman name for the English city of York.'

Sally blinked at him. 'How could you know that?'

'I had friends who lived there. What, you think all us Americans are just pretty faces and airheads?'

'No,' Sally muttered. 'No, I didn't think that at all.' Then she smiled. 'Forgive me, but I've been working with a pretty face and an airhead for the last few days.'

Mason frowned and glanced at Roxy. 'Which one's which?' he asked Sally.

'Let's get back to the riddle, shall we? There's a statue sitting outside York Minster today that has been there since 1998. It commemorates the accession of Constantine the Great as Roman Emperor on this site, after the death of his father in 306.'

'Constantine was made emperor in York in 306,' Mason repeated. 'Well, there's your answer. Whatever church Heindl is leading us to was built by Justinian and Constantine. But, wait, weren't they *both* Roman emperors?'

Sally nodded. 'Separated by two hundred years, give or take. I don't see how both men built the same church.'

'Could it have been destroyed and then rebuilt?' Roxy asked. 'I believe it happened an awful lot back then.'

'Yes, even the Hagia Sophia was rebuilt three times. But that would be hard to cross reference. I believe the third part of the clue is the clincher.'

'"*This is where the star was stolen*"?' Mason said dubiously. 'Isn't that the hardest part?'

'Maybe, but everything centres around Christianity.' Sally frowned and went quiet for a while. Mason leaned back against the headrest, taking a break.

A moment later, Roxy leaned through from the back, mobile phone in hand. 'Patricia again,' she said, showing him the screen. 'Can't keep the agency at bay for ever, Joe.'

181

Mason agreed and cracked the car door open. 'Give us five minutes,' he told Hassell. 'Bit of business to take care of.'

'Sure.'

Outside, he and Roxy walked across to a sparse trio of trees. Their boughs were thin, barren and tall, stretching hundreds of feet above their heads, their entire lengths bathed in lustrous fire from a glowing orange sun.

'If we call in, we're screwed,' Mason said after the phone stopped ringing. 'You know that.'

Roxy turned so that the sun was at her back. 'This is more important.'

Mason slipped sunglasses on and stared down into a valley bristling with brown vegetation. 'You wanna ask Sally to pay us to stay on? It's a bit insensitive.'

Roxy shrugged. 'Hey, I do insensitive better than anyone. I'm the hammer to your pencil. Remember that.'

Mason stared. 'You're my *what*?'

'I'll explain later. Patricia's gonna fire our asses. We're already working rogue. Making it official is only fair to everyone.'

'No more agency?' Mason hesitated. 'What about next week, next month, next year?'

'Are you so comfortable with the agency that you wouldn't miss it?'

Mason stared into her questioning eyes, pondering that. Of course he wasn't comfortable. His break-up with Hannah had proved that, not that he needed proof. Hannah had never put a foot wrong – staying by his side after everything that happened in Mosul – but he'd pushed her away. He'd failed her too.

There was no comfort in sinking so deep that you alienated those who loved you.

'The agency's a lifeline,' he said. 'I don't like it, but the work stops you . . . feeling.'

Roxy nodded. 'Same here. It makes life bearable.'

Mason thought he saw a slight softening of the rigid lines around her eyes and mouth. A brief respite. He said, 'And what's your story? Why do you fight the Devil every day?'

Roxy's face hardened. 'I don't listen to him,' she said. 'Well, I try my best not to listen. The rum helps. Not that there's a drop around here.'

'Yeah, I was thinking your mouth must be as dry at that shrub over there.'

Roxy shielded her eyes, staring into the sun. 'When I was young,' she said, 'it was easy. Every day an adventure where nothing could hurt you. There's a softness to innocence, you know? A cocoon. You knew the bad things were out there, but they could never touch you. Oh, no. Not me. I was gonna grow up to be a nurse, a vet, a world traveller. My mum and dad were proud.'

She tapered off, lost in memory. Mason let her reminisce.

'They recruited me at eighteen, while I was still in college. Naturally, they tantalised and encouraged, drawing me in deeper and deeper until there was no way out. Until I couldn't tell my parents and my friends what I was doing. It started easy, just an office job, but then the training started. And then a mission, just as backup. Easy. That's how these agencies and the Army draw you in. They promise you a world begging for heroes; then they make heroes who are forced to beg for food.'

Mason cleared his throat, moved by her passion. 'Who are "they"?'

'Oh, not the CIA,' Roxy said. 'That'd be too trite. Another government agency. Twelve years they had me and moulded me. Twelve years they turned me into their weapon, a lone wolf who followed orders and didn't ask questions. Dark places, Mason. Dark, lonely and desperate places, all over the world. No trace, no evidence, just a body left on the ground, one more unsolved case.'

'You're telling me that you were an assassin? For the US government? Good God.'

'I got out after twelve years but, by then, I'd forgotten who I was. I could never know who or what *I might have become* if I'd never joined up. That's what bothers me. It's all gone now. The woman I was, and might have been, I will never be. How heartbreaking is that?'

Mason smoothed a hand through his hair. 'I understand.'

'I became a stranger in my own skin. I want to remember my childhood. The dreams I had. The person I *was*. But all I see are old kills, dead bodies and the missions I accepted.'

'You're trying to make a better future?' Mason asked.

'Yeah, something like that. A future where I can face my parents again without guilt, without thinking of them as strangers, as *civilians*. They say do or die for your country. Well, I did both.'

Mason touched her wrist, wanting her attention. 'You deserve a future,' he said.

'I want to believe that, but I took so many. I want to find my way back to that softness of youth. To see what I might have become.'

Mason nodded, seeing how deep and complex her struggles ran, and wondered how he could help. Then he realised he wasn't doing such a great job of looking after himself. 'We're certainly a fine pair,' he said. 'Maybe we were made for each other.'

Roxy arched an eyebrow.

'Nope, I don't mean like that. I realised I wasn't your type when you stated it very clearly to my face. I don't know what I mean really, but maybe we should stick together for a while?'

'Whoa, you got game. You're such a smooth talker.' Roxy laughed.

Mason understood she was moving the conversation on, having revealed all she was prepared to for today. 'The game?' he repeated. 'I was never in it. Too busy overseas. Hannah and I met at spin class.'

Roxy shook her head, wanting to hear no more, and made the call to Patricia.

Three very long minutes later, she made a face at Mason. 'That went well.'

'She's pissed. I don't blame her. Two of her favourite operatives just quit. We really are on our own now.'

Mason turned back towards the car, seeing Sally's head with its two-tone hair framed in the front seat and Hassell's shadow in the back.

'We have those two.'

Roxy grunted. 'Hey, it makes a joke. Hassell is still on probation with me and has demons of his own. Including this Gido guy. Sally . . . It's hard to see who'll she become when this is all over. Her life's changed now.'

'Agreed,' Mason said, walking back to the car. 'So let's see if she's cracked this clue, shall we? The Amori can't be far behind us.'

'You think we're gonna come up against them again?'

'I think this Marduk, and maybe Gido, are desperate to stop us finding their sanctuary. Not the Amori, I might add. They are ready to come out of the shadows. I mean their true, ancestral home. They never anticipated someone might have laid down a trail of clues to their front door. I guess they could flee, move out, but would you want to quit the safe haven you'd occupied for thousands of years? Your real home and all its historical objects? No, I think they'll be anxious to stop us before revealing the big secret.'

'The big secret,' Roxy said. 'I'm truly dreading to hear what it is.'

So was Mason but, as he approached the car, Sally's upbeat greeting drove all that trepidation out of his brain.

'I've found it,' she shouted through the glass. 'And it's not far!'

185

Chapter 30

Gianluca Gianni walked through halls of Hell as he strode through the twisting, polished innards of St Peter's Basilica. When men saluted him, he grunted. When cardinals nodded at him, he grimaced. There was no rest, no peace, no fine moment until he knew his family was safe.

Marduk had given him a simple task for now. Chart the movements of various cardinals, copy down their diaries and itineraries, gauge the emotions inside the sacred dome and its hallowed halls. Marduk wanted to know exactly how the priests were being affected.

Gianni hated himself even as he carried out Marduk's commands to the letter.

The night before, as he sat on the carpet halfway through a bottle of whiskey, Gianni's phone had started to ring. With a leaping heart, Gianni had sent his hand in search of it, plucking it from the floor and jabbing the answer button.

'Hello?' His voice was rasping.

'Dad? Daddy?'

Nothing could ever describe the raw emotion he felt in that instant. It was overwhelming love and desolation. 'Aria? Oh, Aria, are you—'

'There,' Marduk's vile tones cut in. 'There's your proof of life. Both of your women are alive for now. They will continue to be so long as you do as I say.'

'Please,' Gianni breathed. 'Oh, please . . .'

'Did you hear that, little girl?' There was a shuffling sound as Marduk probably turned to look at Aria. 'If your father loves you, he'll save your life. If the bad men start hurting you, that means he doesn't care.'

Gianni squeezed the phone until it hurt. 'I will hunt you down, you depraved psycho.'

'Good. A little audacity is exactly what you need right now. Now, listen . . .'

Marduk's orders had lasted all of three minutes. Reports on the cardinals, on their reactions, on their attitudes and opinions. Marduk had then told him that a video would be released the next day and that Gianni must gauge any and all mood swings.

'And Gianni . . .' Marduk said as he wound up the call.

'Yes?'

'Any talk of seeking the Amori must be derailed. If I smell even the slightest whiff of a Swiss Guard drifting in my direction I will sever your daughter's right ear.'

'I agree,' Gianni managed to grate out.

'Did you hear that, dear?' Marduk again addressed Aria. 'If Uncle Marduk chops your little ear off it's because Daddy doesn't care.'

Gianni could not comprehend the depravity of a man who would address a child that way. The purest mix of hatred, fear and love choked his throat, rendering him speechless.

'Are you still there, Gianni?'

'Y-yes. I will do as you ask.'

'Good. And I will be back in touch soon.'

Gianni had spent the rest of the night in a numb kind of purgatory. They said life could change on a sixpence;

187

well, his had turned on thirty-plus years of life choices. Chance had brought him to this juncture. *How heavy is my burden?*

His faith tried to ground him. Gianni called for His help, for the strength of the Holy Spirit. *God is always at my side.* But Gianni felt none of the reassuring presence. It was a hand reaching to him in the darkness, a hand he could not grasp. This was a trial he faced alone.

Gianni kicked himself for the thought. Of course God was at his side. He could draw on that. But personal sentiment should never shake your faith. Faith was absolute. It was the mortar that held the idea of Family together.

Gianni sat for hours, unable to get past the fear he'd heard in Aria's voice.

Chapter 31

Inside the car, Sally was buzzing. 'Boom!' she said a little uncharacteristically as Mason climbed in, talking faster than an Italian supercar changes gear. 'You think Amori, you think Christianity, right? But not just that. You drill down. You go to the very *heart*. And what's the very heart? It's not a trick question . . . It's Jesus Christ. It's all centred around Jesus, I'm sure.'

Mason enjoyed the car's interior warmth. 'Stands to reason that Jacques Heindl would build a riddle around the hub of his religion. I'm guessing you found the place where the star was stolen?'

Sally nodded. 'Of course, and it links in beautifully. Heindl created a perfect symmetry with this clue. This church, *commissioned* by Constantine the Great soon after his mother visited in AD 325, then destroyed by fire around 529 and *rebuilt* by Justinian, who held to the original vision of the building, has a fourteen-point silver star. It was installed by the Catholics and removed by the Greeks 150 years later. It was replaced soon after that by the Turkish government. The fourteen-point silver star represents the genealogy of Jesus and, essentially, has a small hole in the middle through which you can touch the original stone that Mary lay on when she gave birth to Jesus.'

Sally glanced at them all, waiting with bated breath. 'Don't you see? It's the Church of the Nativity. A basilica built over the very place where Jesus was born. And it's in Bethlehem.'

Mason took that in. 'That's the West Bank.'

'I know. Some say that the stealing of the star was a catalyst for the Crimean War against the Russians. The Holy Land is the breeding ground for religious devotion and fanaticism. You don't get one without the other.'

'Can we talk on the way?' Roxy said. 'Because the Amori ain't gonna be sitting around chilling and talking shit. They're barely a step behind and we *have to* find them to find the book.'

'We should lose the guns,' Hassell said with smart foresight. 'We can't take weapons from Jerusalem to Bethlehem.'

Unwilling to risk a repeat of the Jerusalem street fight, Mason nodded and fastened his seatbelt as Roxy drove. The car wound through a series of sweeping bends.

A phone chimed. Hassell fished the device out of his back pocket. Mason saw his eyes flash when he looked at the screen.

'Problem?' he asked.

'My boss.' Hassell's voice was thick. 'Gido. Keeps calling. Probably calling to bust my balls. Make threats. He's a show-off and enjoys that kind of thing. From the two voicemails I've listened to, I can tell you he's coming for me.'

'Hey, Hassell, I know there's a grey area between Hollywood myth and reality,' Roxy said. 'But I'm pretty sure a good IT guy can trace you on that.' She nodded at his phone. 'You should get rid of it.'

Hassell wound down the window. With a quick flick of the wrist the still-chirping mobile arced outside and landed on the rear bed of a passing truck.

'Are you military trained?' Roxy asked.

'No. The NYPD did a decent job and then I enrolled in a couple of special courses. I can shoot pretty good. I learned the scrappy, nastier stuff *after* I switched sides.'

'And why *did* you switch sides?' Sally asked, breaking off her research for a moment.

Mason, having a huge vested interest in Hassell's answer, didn't move a muscle, trying not to put pressure on the man.

Hassell looked down at his feet. 'That's not something I want to discuss right now.'

Mason accepted it and turned back to Sally. 'Are we allowed to visit Bethlehem?'

'Fifteen-minute drive.' Sally had already checked. 'It's part of the Palestinian authority. There's a border check so get your passports ready. The only issue is the car. Do we know where it was registered?'

Mason reached for the glovebox and the rental agreement. 'Why?'

'Cars registered in Israel aren't insured for driving in Bethlehem. We're okay if it's hired from an eastern Jerusalem car rental company though, which I think it was. Otherwise, we'll have to join a private tour or catch a taxi.'

Mason read through the document, provided in Hebrew, Arabic and English. 'We're good,' he said. 'Just keep going.'

'The quicker we do this the less chance there is of another fight,' Roxy said. 'What else can you tell us about the Church of the Nativity?'

Sally blinked. 'Well, how long do you have to digest seventeen hundred years of history?'

Roxy winced and checked her watch. 'Yeah, about eight minutes to be honest.'

'The grotto contained by the basilica is the supposed birthplace of Jesus. It's the oldest continuously used place of worship in Christianity, the oldest key church in the Holy Land. It's been on the watchlist of most endangered

191

sites for twelve years. Of course, there are several altars of varying importance, and below it lies the grotto itself. The traditional place where Mary laid the newborn Christ in the manger is opposite the Altar of the Magi.'

Sally fell silent as they came to the border. There were tense minutes as they all tried to look like tourists, the guards on edge probably in part due to reports of the Jerusalem street fight.

Eighteen minutes later they had parked up, shrugged on their backpacks and were in sight of the holy church. Mason found his pace slowing out of respect as he approached.

There were other factors too. In particular, the hordes of visitors jostling for position outside the entrance and across Manger Square. Mason and the others stopped to study the lie of the land.

It was late afternoon, almost early evening. A chilly breeze stirred up sand from cracks in the streets, sending it gyrating through a hundred moving legs and then a hundred more. Shouting, laughter and the quieter sound of conversation saturated the air from wall to wall. Mason smelled cooked foods as well as body odour and diesel fumes as they stood unmoving in the street, finally turning their gazes upon Sally.

'Is there a faster way inside?' Mason voiced their thoughts.

'Not a chance.' Sally sighed. 'And we won't have as long to examine the altars as we did at the Holy Sepulchre. But the good news is, it's getting late. The wait shouldn't be much more than an hour.'

Mason made a face but joined a queue composed of everything from single men or women on a religious pilgrimage to entire coach parties, drawn by the religious significance of the area. It occurred to him that they'd be better off being the last group admitted. Fifteen minutes later, and with help from a local, they were two groups in front of the last admissible party.

Mason, Roxy and Hassell scoured Manger Square and the discernible streets for signs of the Amori. A bell tower above them and to the right lit up as darkness encroached, its stone walls a gilded symbol of divided faiths.

They entered the building just as Roxy was starting to complain about how little they'd eaten since their arrival in the Holy Land. Mason had to agree, but they had little choice now but to keep moving forward.

Inside, the church was cramped, the going slow. Soft light illuminated most of the rooms, fixtures, altars and archways. Mason found they were afforded a little extra room and leeway since they were at the back of the crowd. He saw a priest to the side and another at their backs. Sally had already noted the positions of the nearest altars.

The first two were easy to locate and examine without causing too much suspicion, but yielded no clues. As they ventured deeper inside, they paused for a processional mass to pass and witnessed the burning of incense and voices raised in worship on this hallowed ground. The distraction enabled Sally and Roxy to scrutinise two more altars.

They ended up following the procession deeper into the bowels of the church.

Mason found it hard to relate the intense religious experience of the church to the overall racket of the crowd, but kept his focus on the altars.

A priest had already approached Sally, backing off when she demonstrated that she was only using her phone to step safely through the shadows. Mason moved over to distract the same man as Sally stooped to scrutinise yet another altar.

'The Chapel of Saint Joseph?' he asked next, referring to the chapel commemorating the appearance of the angel to Joseph, the guardian of Jesus.

'In the caves,' the priest answered in passable English.

Sally had already explained that there was a network of

caves underneath the church as part of the grotto. 'Thank you,' he said, and turned back to Sally.

The confused smile she gave him told him everything he needed to know. Sally had found something. The next twenty minutes passed sluggishly as they made their way towards the exit.

Mason's excitement built as they left the building behind and stopped to get their bearings under dark, cloudless skies. 'You got it?' he asked as the others grouped around.

Sally tapped on her phone's photo app. 'There is only one inscription,' she said. 'At the base of the altar and confusing to say the least.'

'You sure it's the only one?' Roxy asked.

'Yes, yes, I've scrutinised them all and it's in the right place, same as the first. It's just . . . odd . . .' She trailed off.

Mason frowned at her. 'Tell us.'

'Ibid, 27,' she said.

Mason waited for more but, after a moment, he realised nothing else was coming. 'Is that it?'

'I'm afraid so.'

'But what does it mean?' Roxy asked.

'It's a code,' Sally said. 'Has to be. A code we have to crack. Only I don't have the slightest clue as to how we're going to crack it.'

Mason frowned. 'Couldn't Heindl have just written, go to church A, B and C?'

'Not if he wanted to keep his instructions secret from a very well-represented Amori. But don't despair, I might have an idea.'

Mason smiled at her. 'I hoped you might.'

Chapter 32

In the cooling dark, as the thinning crowds meandered away and the louder visitors dispersed, Hassell grabbed Mason's arm.

'Ah, crap,' he said. 'I know those guys.'

Instantly alert, Mason followed the direction of Hassell's brief nod. Gathered against a stone wall opposite were a dozen men. They were of all shapes, sizes and ethnicities, but they had two things in common.

The callous, remorseless look of those willing to kill, and an unmistakable shared purpose. Every single man stared at Mason and his group.

'When you say you know them . . .' Mason prodded.

'Sorry, I know four men. They're Gido's people. Some proper degenerates. He's sent the worst of the worst in this time, guys.'

'Which means?' Roxy wanted more clarity.

'Meatheads. Not an ethical thought among them. Gido points them in a direction and they kill. No questions asked, no shits given. And, unfortunately, they're real good at their job.'

Mason took a breath. With so much happening it would be easy to make a break for it but it would risk putting hundreds of innocents in danger. Seconds passed. Mason sensed his companions growing more and more anxious.

Waiting for him to make a decision.

When did I take on the burden of leadership?

'We have to hurry,' Sally said. 'There's no time to waste.'

Mason stepped up, as anxious for the unsuspecting tourists and locals as he was for his team and himself. In this situation, you assumed the enemy was hostile, that it was armed and willing to cause collateral damage. You also assumed it was proficient.

Mason turned back towards the church, hoping that Gido's men would think twice about risking a shootout inside the Church of the Nativity and hesitate. He had no intention of returning to the church. He broke into a jog, taking the others with him, and, as he reached the exit door, ran past, sped up and started threading through the crowds. He didn't look back, figuring the wider a gap he created the less chance there was of a shootout in Manger Square.

Roxy was running alongside Mason. He touched her arm. 'The streets.'

Ahead, several side streets branched off the main road. Roxy nodded, reading his mind and yelled for everyone to speed up. Together, they raced across the road. A solid sixty feet separated them from their opponents.

Mason darted up the first street, a narrow alley that stank of decay. Darkness pooled around them like a thick mantle, reasonably reassuring for now. Mason dropped back, letting Roxy take the lead and making sure Sally stayed close. He needn't have bothered. Sally galloped past him at full speed, easily within her comfort zone. At the rear of the group, Mason chanced a look back.

Only one man was visible back there, his shadow outlined against the lighter background. Seconds later, his cohorts appeared, a bunch of stone-faced killers running in silence. Mason counted the seconds between the first man and the following group, an idea springing to mind.

Roxy pounded across a intersecting street and straight

into another alley. It was the prime moment Mason had been waiting for. He exited the current alley, ducked around the side of the wall and waited. Six seconds later the lead pursuer emerged.

Mason lashed out, striking him on the side of the head. The man sprawled forward and face-planted the concrete road. Blood gushed from either his nose or a gash on the head. Mason, conscious that he had only seconds to act, plucked the man's gun from his nerveless fingers and turned back to the alley to unleash three shots.

The bullets flew into the darkness, followed by a scream and a grunt. There was a sound like men falling and a good deal of cursing. Mason knew his time was up. He didn't want to waste any of the bullets and needed to catch up with the others. Stuffing the gun into his waistband he took off, racing into the next alley.

Mason poured on the speed. He caught the last person, Hassell, just as Roxy burst out of the alley's far end into a busy street market. Mason followed fast. A quick glance back told him that their surviving pursuers were still coming. He sprang among the market stalls, weaving and ducking around stands filled with food, condiments, clothes and books. Exotic spices filled the air and there was the low rumble of guitars and beating drums. Following Hassell, he dodged around people and cut through the crowds.

Another look back. Mason saw their pursuers closing slightly, now near enough to start using their guns. But would they here, in this busy place? His thought was answered in less than two seconds when one man raised his gun.

No!

'Go right!' he yelled.

Mason reached out, grabbed one of the wooden poles that supported the nearest stall and pulled. The entire stall collapsed, its shell and merchandise sprawling into the path of their pursuers. He did the same to the next stall, pots and pans, plates and saucers smashing and clanging to the ground, spreading across the market's walkway. As the last stall collapsed, Mason darted in between stands, pushing his way through canvas awnings and coming out along another walkway, still following Hassell.

Behind, they left pandemonium in their wake.

The market erupted with noise, angry voices raised. Mason chased the others along the aisle, keeping up the pace. Roxy reached the other end of the market and slowed. Mason looked back once more.

Three chasers were back there now with more emerging along the aisle. Shoppers jumped out of their way or were pushed aside. One man crashed into another stall, smashing it to pieces. Mason reached the end of the market and, once more, pulled down an entire stall in an effort to suppress the pursuit.

Roxy emerged into a busy street. Mason was a second behind her with the others fanning out. Traffic crept along the road in time to two sets of traffic lights. Roxy took off, crossing the road at speed, weaving in and out of slow-moving cars, and headed towards the far side of the street. The Amori mercs were closing again, looming now so that Mason could see their faces. He ducked and ran behind several cars, making sure he presented no easy target.

But they were close now. Gunshots rang out, bullets peppering cars and the facades of buildings. A shop window shattered. A woman screamed. Roxy, with no time, darted into the first open door she could find.

Mason had a second to see that it was a restaurant. Inside, about a dozen tables sat closely together. Roxy snaked between them, pushing several to the side. Shocked occupants looked up, their eyes wide. Mason slowed just as the first Amori mercenary burst through the door. He grabbed an empty chair, threw it at the man's face. The mercenary's head snapped back and he fell backwards into those cramming in behind him.

'Hey,' Mason called to Hassell. Together, they upended an empty table, hefted it, and then launched it in the same direction as the chair, felling men left and right. They collapsed, they staggered, they cried out in pain. Their guns clattered to the floor. During the act of throwing the table, Mason lost his grip on his own gun. He considered trying to find it but decided the delay would be too risky.

Roxy was gone, along with Sally. Mason raced after them, exiting the restaurant through a kitchen swing door and then a fire exit at the back. They ran back out into the night with a far bigger gap between them and their opponents. Mason walked to the front of their group, looking for any sanctuary that might offer them a fighting chance.

'Come on,' he said. Hassell and Roxy followed him towards the dark and deadly byways of Bethlehem.

Chapter 33

Mason kept hold of Sally's wrist as they dashed away from the wrecked street and pursued the deepest shadows. Old stone buildings stood highlighted against the darker skies on both sides, their windows shining. Mason's boots pounded the concrete, seeking a refuge.

Roxy's yell split the night. 'Look left! Right there.'

Mason saw it. A hotel, part of a long, uninterrupted row of buildings, sat just a minute or so ahead. A hotel should generally offer multiple exits, both at ground level and higher. Mason determined that it was worth the risk.

They raced across the road and reached the front doors just as shouts went up from behind. Mason yanked open the door and looked inside the lobby. 'Out, out!' he yelled at a handful of startled, milling guests. 'Get out through the back.' He made the shape of a gun with his hand and fingers. 'Gunmen!'

A typical slice of humanity: some people looked terrified and ran in fear, others retreated in caution, and another retaliated with profanity.

Pushing into the lobby, he yelled at them again.

Roxy noticed one of the uniformed staff behind the front desk reaching for a phone. She burst into motion, crossing the tiled lobby and vaulting the wooden counter in a matter of seconds. All the staff retreated as Roxy urged them to run for a back entrance.

Hassell sprinted towards an unhappy and tired-looking security guard who'd been seated close to the foot of a winding staircase at the right side of the lobby.

It was their actions more than their words that made enough of an impact to swiftly clear the lobby. Mason followed Roxy, taking the easier route behind the front desk. Sally ran alongside him.

Hassell shouted at the security guard to hand over his weapons but was offered only a Taser before the man fled. He looked a little nonplussed as he too ran for the front desk.

Men burst through the front, slamming the twin doors back so hard the glass shattered in its frames. They held handguns and knives in open view; one man came in bouncing a grenade gently up and down in the palm of his right hand.

Hassell dived behind the front desk.

The men opened fire, bullets smashing into the thick wood and breaking the higher panels behind. Key fobs, drinking glasses and framed pictures were hit and sent flying. Broken shards rained down on Mason's back as he knelt in the space between the front desk and the rear wall.

'What's the plan?' Roxy yelled.

Mason looked up. Hassell brandished his Taser. Both Mason and Roxy rolled their eyes at him. Crawling fast, they made their way to the far end of the desk, their knees and hands cut by splinters of wood and glass.

Mason tried to sweep the way clear with his hands, but jerked back as several sharp fragments jabbed his flesh. Within seconds, they reached the end of the counter.

Bullets destroyed its curved edge in front of Mason's eyes. The steady crunch of their attackers' boots advancing through the lobby made a low, menacing counterpoint to the raucous sound of gunfire.

Mason saw a closed door to their left and just four feet

of open space between them and the foot of the curving staircase. One person might make it up with the element of surprise, but the attempt would surely make them all easy targets. They were running out of time.

Mason heard some men reloading as others continued the onslaught. They were organised, disciplined and relentless. Mason swung around to look at Roxy and Hassell.

'Surprise attack or risk the stairs,' he said. 'Either way, it's somebody's death warrant.'

'Always figured I'd go out fighting,' Roxy said. 'I say we attack.'

Hassell nodded his agreement.

Sally looked terrified. Mason took an extra few seconds to grasp her shoulders with both hands. 'Stay here. In all the confusion, try to open that door and slip away. If we don't make it . . . contact Cardinal Vallini.'

With that, he collected himself and prepared to dash around the end of the desk into whatever lead-riddled hell awaited. A lull in the assault should come as the attackers converged warily on the counter. That was the time to act. That was—

A moment of sheer disbelief froze his thoughts.

He could only stare as a tall, older man stepped out of a back room. The man wore a chef's hat and a white apron, and held a battered AK-47 in his scarred and steady hands. The gun clattered with that characteristic bark Mason remembered so well, taking him back to old enemy engagements. Bullets riddled the lobby, driving the attackers to their knees.

The chef waved at Mason. 'Come on! Hurry!'

Hearing an English accent and seeing the face of an older man made Mason feel unaccountably trusting. Of course, the AK could just as easily have been trained on him, but it wasn't. It was taking a toll on their enemy.

'Move,' the man cried, firing with one hand and waving at the stairs with the other.

'Can't we go the way you came?' Roxy yelled at him.

'It's just the kitchen and they're coming in the back door too.'

Mason exploded from behind the ravaged desk like a sprinter out of his blocks. Looking neither left nor right, he ran for the stairs and took them two at a time, climbing to relative safety. When he was clear, he stopped and crouched, looking back down.

Roxy was three stairs behind him, Sally a step further back. Hassell was still clearing the lobby. Mason got a snapshot of their attackers, guns in hand, kneeling or sprawling in a clutter of debris as the AK-47 laid waste to everything more than two feet above their heads.

The gun's owner sidestepped towards the stairs, still firing, following in Hassell's footsteps.

Mason counted two more attackers lying dead, which left eight. He turned away from the lobby as Hassell approached, and then their saviour pounded past to his left. 'You waiting for an invitation?'

They hurried up to the first-floor landing, pausing as the machine-gun-toting chef spun to face them. Mason didn't know what to make of the now crooked chef's hat and the food-spattered apron. The man facing him was slim but strong-looking, with a craggy face, twinkling eyes and grey sideburns tipping a lustrous head of black hair. Mason put him between late forties and early fifties.

'I don't know why you helped us but I'm grateful for it.' An even but inquisitive opening, he thought.

'I'm Quaid.' The man nodded. 'Follow me.'

Mason and the others followed him in silence. They could hear their attackers picking themselves up off the lobby floor downstairs and faint screams coming from outside. Hard words were exchanged below.

The man reached the far end of the corridor and then, to Mason's surprise, produced a key card and entered a room. Roxy held the door open, peering inside.

'Hurry!' he shouted back at them. 'We won't have long.'

Mason battled with himself, presented with a stranger and a room that could be a kill box. They should keep moving upward. On the other hand, the guy did have access to weapons which, right now, were just as essential to their survival as making headway.

'Two minutes,' he said. 'Go.'

Roxy pushed inside first, staying alert. Sally followed and then Hassell. Mason brought up the rear, watching the far end of the corridor for movement.

Quaid was standing in front of an uncurtained window, highlighted by the stark streetlamp just outside. 'This is my room.'

Roxy reeled off their names as introduction before asking: 'You got any more Kalashnikovs lying around?'

'As a matter of fact.' Quaid pointed at the wardrobe. 'Check inside.'

Roxy strode to the double doors, slid them open, and turned her nose up at the assorted shirts, jackets and jeans hanging there. She fell to her knees, found a wooden crate under a pile of dirty pants and dragged it out, fixing Quaid with a dangerous glare.

'Don't worry,' he said. 'The pants are camouflage.'

Roxy finished hauling the crate out, leaving them looking at an oblong, pale wooden casket the length of a rifle. Judging by the way Roxy was panting, Mason assumed it was fully loaded.

'Whoa,' Roxy said. 'Fortune is finally on our side, and it brought us to you.'

'About time,' Mason muttered. 'It's been all bad luck so far.'

'Open it,' Quaid said. 'We need to take as much stock as we can carry.'

Mason cocked an eyebrow. 'Stock? Who the hell are you?' He wasn't asking the guy's name.

'Middleman. Buyer. Procurer of exotic goods,' Quaid explained, and then, seeing their faces, stressed: '*Legal and useful goods*. Well, maybe a little under the radar, but nothing dangerous. The AKs are just for protection.'

'An Englishman selling shady goods in Bethlehem,' Hassell commented. 'Sounds like a long story.'

'Kind of,' Quaid said. 'And we don't have time for it right now.'

'Quickly then.' Roxy prised off the lid of the crate with a screwdriver she found on a low shelf. 'Why did you help us?'

'You mean – why'd I save your lives?' Quaid smiled. 'Hey, when you get to my age you start to run out of friends. And I'm ex-British army, left because I'd had enough of bureaucrats telling me what to do. I help and procure now. I saw those armed mercs chasing you guys and couldn't just let them murder you defenceless. I'm not built that way. Plus, the bastards would've shot up my kitchen.'

Mason crossed to the window and studied the street below. Groups of people milled across the road from the hotel doors, probably residents. Looking further afield he noted the approach of police cars and ambulances.

'We have to move,' he said. 'Please talk sense. Make us trust you in the next thirty seconds.'

Quaid let out a deep breath, looking uncertain for the first time. 'A tall order. Well, as I said, I'm ex-army, ex-officer. Valuable connections all around the world. Using them to help those who otherwise might get trampled underfoot. Those whose voices can't be heard. Disillusioned with leadership, I decided to make a difference at ground level.'

'Here?' Sally asked. Until now, Mason had thought she'd regressed, driven silent by the violence she wasn't used to or prepared for.

'Here, for now,' Quaid said. 'I travel wherever I need to. I really do have great connections.'

Mason turned his attention to Roxy, who had removed the lid. An eye-opening amount of diverse content nestled inside the crate – from Levi jeans and leather belts to sparkling timepieces, tins of food, can openers and plush children's toys, to packets of oats, electric toothbrushes and die-cast model cars. Mason shook his head, wondering.

'Dig to the bottom,' Quaid said.

'Dare I?' Roxy raised an eyebrow. 'I'd best not find any sleazy magazines, Quaid.'

'You won't. There're two handguns. A Glock and a Colt M1911. And spare mags. Bring it all.'

Hassell had already found a pile of large, multi-coloured backpacks on another shelf, some plain and some decorated with well-known branding. The American handed out three unadorned bags to Mason, Sally and Quaid before slipping spare magazines into a light-blue *Frozen* rucksack for Roxy. The raven-haired American was too busy to notice as she grabbed the Colt.

They exchanged their own small backpacks for Quaid's larger ones, which could conceal more weapons and ammo.

'Is that it?' Mason took the Glock.

'Do you trust me?' Quaid asked, waving the AK.

Mason motioned everyone towards the door. 'Let's see, shall we?'

Chapter 34

'I help locals on both sides of the Gaza Strip,' Quaid said as they headed for the door. 'It makes me a permanent target. But, hell, I still sleep better.'

Mason nodded, focusing on the door. Roxy took hold of the handle, but then paused. 'Wait, this is a hotel, right? And your chef's whites. You work here?'

'They let me live here for . . . a few free favours.' Quaid shrugged. 'Works both ways. And I enjoy cooking. Is that a crime?'

Roxy gave a soft laugh and turned her attention back to the door. 'For me, that depends on how well you cook jambalaya.'

'Orange chicken,' Quaid whispered. 'That's my speciality.'

Mason was first into the corridor, training his Glock towards the lobby end. Seeing no discernible movement, he frowned. 'Nothing,' he said. 'No movement. I don't like it. They could be lying in wait.' Seeing no other option, he carefully motioned the others into the hall and nodded at a set of double doors to their right. 'Staircase,' he said and stepped towards it.

Muted, sporadic gunfire rang out from the street. Mason frowned and headed back into the hotel room. 'I don't like the sound of that.'

Crossing to the window, he took in the scene in front of the hotel. As he'd feared, a large contingent of police officers had arrived, confronted the gunmen and were being assaulted by automatic weapons. The sizeable group of law enforcement meant they received the gunmen's full attention. Several cops were taking cover behind their hastily evacuated vehicles whilst at least one body lay on the road.

Mason took it all in with a heavy heart. 'Though seeing the police is uplifting,' he said, 'they're facing trained, well-armed soldiers that we brought here. We have to lead them away.'

Returning to the corridor, he dashed for the lobby stairs, Glock held ready. Roxy hissed at his back, questioning his sanity, but Mason felt compelled to do this. Reaching the top step, he leaned down and fired twice, sending two bullets into the carpeted stairwell and attracting the attention of those below. When a shooter looked up, Mason lingered until he cried out in alarm.

Then, he ran.

Roxy entered the far stairwell as Mason caught them up, and took the concrete steps two at a time. Only Mason and Quaid were still in the corridor when the lift doors dinged.

He'd half-expected their adversaries to risk using the lift instead of the stairs, and spun, crouching, waiting to see who emerged.

The first was a thickset, bald man toting an Uzi. Mason shot him through the chest. Quaid tagged a second adversary through the shoulder. The rest fired through the open lift doors without showing their faces.

Mason urged Quaid into the stairwell. 'Go.'

Following a step behind, he chased Quaid into the cold stairwell, their footsteps echoing up and down the plain concrete shaft. Roxy was ten risers above, making good progress. Mason knew he'd done all he could to prevent these animals annihilating the cops, and urged Quaid on.

The lower stairwell doors burst open.

Mason spun and fired, aiming low. Four men crashed through, sprawling for cover. Bullets ricocheted off the hard floor. Mason backed up the stairs as Gido's men returned fire.

Roxy reached the top of the stairwell and shouted about finding a fire exit. Mason heard her strike the steel bar and crack it open.

Quaid covered him as he climbed higher, getting a quick, gratifying glimpse of Hassell looking out for Sally as they ran through the fire exit that Roxy had left open. The team were working well together, affording Mason a brief but satisfying sense of purpose. They were organised, adept and focused.

Quaid fired four more shots as Mason ascended the final stairs.

He burst out through the fire door and into the exposed darkness of night. Trusting that Roxy had already assessed the most judicious escape route, Mason followed.

Up here, atop a roof overlooking the benighted city of Bethlehem, the light breeze contained a heady cocktail of perfumes and a featherlike dusting of desert sand. The clamour of the city rose in a swell, too many noises to differentiate. Eight steps to the right, the edge of the roof fell away to the concrete streets below. Further away to his left, another narrow lip did the same.

Ahead, an uneven, pitted, snaking line of roofs led to the east.

Mason ran, crossing the hotel roof at an ever-increasing pace. Quaid was to his right, the others several steps ahead.

Scattered debris threatened to trip them, but they kept a careful eye on the ground. Mason's right boot slipped in a pile of dust, but he caught himself before falling headlong into what looked oddly like a stack of old car parts. Roxy slowed as she approached the eastern end of the hotel.

Mason caught up. The gap between buildings was tiny, a barely there smudge of darkness. They jumped, landed on the next roof, and picked up speed.

As they hurried along, Mason nodded at Quaid. 'You have an escape plan? Hard to believe an ex-army officer wouldn't have something up his sleeve.'

'*This* is it,' Quaid said. 'It's why the room was opposite the stairwell doors.'

Mason grunted and looked back. So far so good. He leapt over the tiny gap between buildings with the others as they spread out across the rooftops.

Quaid shouted out: 'Contact!'

Mason ducked, still running. A bullet flew way over his head. He turned, spotted three men crouched outside the fire-exit door, and squeezed his trigger three times. The shots weren't accurate, but they did send the men diving to the ground. Mason took stock of their own position.

Four roofs from the end of the row.

Roxy was turning, seeing the opportunity to lay down an uninterrupted hail of covering fire if they each took turns. Mason rose and ran whilst Roxy fired four shots before Quaid took over. They dashed across two more rooftops, closing in on the far end.

'They have radios,' Mason noticed and shouted out. 'Be careful what's waiting below.'

Roxy didn't acknowledge the call, but he knew she'd have taken it on board. They'd been through enough together during the last few days to earn each other's respect.

Behind, their enemies were advancing, crab-walking at speed. Mason counted only five pursuers and figured the others had stayed behind to occupy the police. Quaid was keeping them contained.

Roxy reached the last roof and dashed across. When she reached the edge, she cursed.

Mason caught up with her and winced. 'Doesn't look good.'

Roxy gave him a gritty stare. 'Ya think?'

The roof ended in a vertical stone face which dropped over fifty feet to the street below. Their only way down was a rickety metal staircase which clung to the wall, so old its railings had mostly crumbled away and had clearly been left to rot. Roxy hesitated to step out onto the top landing, which would also leave them exposed.

Quaid laid a hand on her shoulder and stepped past, putting a boot onto the square metal platform to test its stability. 'Good as new,' he said a little too quickly. 'We can't go back, so follow me, and keep an eye out below.'

Mason took over from Quaid to keep the enemy at bay. He didn't have to look at Roxy to know she didn't like it. He wasn't exactly wild about the plan either. But there was only one way off this roof.

And Quaid was already on it.

Chapter 35

Quaid started down. Mason tried to block out the grinding, tortured sound of old nuts and bolts, but found it hard to ignore the rickety twisting of metal as first Sally and then Hassell stepped out from the roof onto the top landing. Quaid was already a dozen steps down, his boots clanking on the metal risers.

The fire escape switched back three times on its way to the ground. Roxy stepped out as Mason laid down covering fire back the way they'd come. Even then, one of Gido's men fired back wildly. Roxy ducked and Mason's bullets hit only fresh air.

An air conditioning unit to his left clanged as bullets struck its metal grilles.

Roxy slithered down the first few steps. Mason found himself rolling blindly onto the top deck of the staircase, knowing it didn't have any railings, and desperate not to roll too far.

His judgement was sound. He came to a stop facing the stairs, but realised he was going to have to slide down head-first.

The bare structure was being riddled with bullets, some of them skimming past only inches above. As Roxy slithered to the fifth and then sixth step, Mason heard their pursuers shouting into handheld radios.

Mason didn't have time to swing his body around, so launched himself down the narrow flight of stairs. Head first, and with gravity lending a hand, he glided down the first few steps but then got stuck, the metal stair edges painful. Just past the halfway point he had to pocket the Glock to grab the structure itself and pivot onto his side to help pull his body down.

He reached the first switchback. Mason used the extra space created by the metal landing to swivel and half stand. The lack of rail protection along the fire escape's side was head-spinning, the exposed edge leading only to a deadly void and the ill-lit street below, which was intermittently swept by the lurid red-and-blue flashing lights of dozens of police cars.

Roxy tripped on a step, managed to catch herself and kept going.

Both Sally and Hassell were moving well, catching up to Quaid as he approached the second switchback.

Back on his feet, Mason pounded down the steps, forced to keep one eye on the landing above and one hand on the wall to keep his bearings. Just as he passed beneath it, the structure's open mesh design affording him a perfect view, Gido's men appeared above. Mason grabbed his gun and leaned out to fire three times, keeping them at bay.

Quaid hit the third switchback and ran for the final flight. Roxy added her own bullets to Mason's, providing him precious moments in which to speed up. Hassell herded Sally along as safely and rapidly as he could.

Quaid whistled and pulled up, boots skidding across mesh. 'If I were you,' he yelled. 'I'd duck.'

What that meant, Mason didn't know, but he took the man at his word and fell to his knees. His right shin grazed the edge of a riser, sending a painful jolt to his brain. As his face came close to the mesh floor, he saw the scene on the ground below and understood Quaid's warning.

Two men had automatic rifles trained on the fire escape. Malicious grins creased their faces as they opened fire and sprayed bullets across the entire structure.

Mason gritted his teeth, rolled himself into a ball, and held on. Roxy yelled at the top of her lungs, voicing her anger, her powerlessness and her strength.

Bullets reverberated against the metal edifice, puncturing and ricocheting left and right. A torrent of lead struck the stone wall, tearing at mortar and creating mushroom clouds of dust and cement which plumed out and upwards.

Mason stayed calm and small. He tried to fit the barrel of his Glock into one of the mesh holes, at first finding the gap too tight but, with a bit of grinding, managed to force it through. Three squeezes of the trigger banished the grins from the faces of those below and sent them stumbling for cover.

But they didn't cease firing.

Bullets passed close to Hassell, and one smashed metal shards from a support in front of Quaid's face, making him bellow in shock. Echoing from nearby came more gunshots as those men who'd stayed behind to occupy the police kept up a barrage of fire.

Mason was forced to switch magazines, cursing the timing and the valuable seconds it took.

The big stone wall took a heavy pounding. A row of windows stretching across the building's outer face also exploded inward, the shooters delighting in their mayhem.

Mason and the others were showered in razor-like fragments as shards of glass fell from the frames, raining towards the ground, shattering across the fire escape.

Between volleys of gunfire, Mason heard the men still on the roof cheering, yelling for more. Those below didn't disappoint. They reloaded with expert speed and continued their onslaught. Mason saw now why those above hadn't ventured onto the fire escape.

Mason wondered fleetingly how the cops were doing outside the hotel. Driven back . . . or worse? But more would be coming, including the Army.

He angled the Glock some more, trying to fix his targets, but, in a change of tactics, the shooters unleashed a flurry of bullets, focusing on one of the iron girders that held the staircase to the wall, destroying the bolts and the stone it was moored to. When the assembly disintegrated, they gave a cheer and the whole structure shifted. Mason held tight, feeling suddenly light-headed.

'Move,' he shouted. 'Get moving, *move!*'

The shooters focused on the next fixing, obliterating the stone holding it in place. The fire escape lurched another metre away from the wall.

Mason clambered to his feet, staggering lower and lower as the staircase dipped towards the ground, which was still twenty feet distant. He aimed the Glock as best he could in the circumstances, his erratic shots annoying the men below rather than worrying them.

The five-strong crew above were also still active. Perhaps they'd communicated with their colleagues via radio, but the fact that the ground-fire was now far more focused meant that they could fully concentrate their fire on their prey.

Mason, beset by multiple enemies at all angles, knew that forward momentum was their only choice. The metal stairs leaned away from the wall, the joints groaning and splitting, the angle increasing and making their descent more perilous. The men above leaned out precariously in their efforts to put a bullet in him.

In front, Quaid was halfway down the final flight, approaching the ground, focusing machine-gun fire to his left. A volley rattled from the barrel, just as the entire staircase twisted.

Mason stumbled, weaving. He fell to his knees as a bullet

215

passed close to his right shoulder and grabbed a metal riser to stop himself from falling over the edge.

Unable to maintain its precarious stability, the fire escape broke from its moorings, skewing away from the wall.

Mason held on as the entire structure tipped. Still, he progressed downward, sensing that the closer to the ground he was, the lesser his injuries might be.

The fire escape twisted into mid-air and gathered speed as it collapsed. Mason fell about fifteen feet, the others less, as it hit the street.

Something smashed him across the head, making him see stars, but he held onto the Glock. His left arm stabbed with pain, and his face slammed mesh hard enough to leave an imprint in his flesh. The fire escape came down in one piece, rather than collapsing in on itself, which was what probably saved their lives.

Mason's vision cleared. The first thing he saw, since he was lying on his back, was the men now stranded on the roof above. One appeared to have fallen, and was sprawled lifelessly at the foot of the building's outer wall, lying amid broken glass and heaps of mortar.

'Are you okay?' Roxy yelled at him.

Mason was fighting for equilibrium, attempting to get a bearing on the ground-level shooters. They too, it seemed, had been impeded when the structure gave way.

Driven back by the collapse and by Quaid's bullets, they'd either darted or jumped back into the main street, escaping the destruction.

Mason focused on them as they climbed to their knees and scrabbled around for dropped weapons.

It was now or never.

'*Look out!*' Roxy cried.

As he sat in the ruined mass of the metal stairs, trying to focus, a grinding sound made him look back at the wall. Roxy's warning shout then rang in his ears.

Where the metal supports had been attached to the wall, a portion of the remaining concrete was shearing away, plunging to the ground in a deadly mass. Lethal chunks of cracked stone smashed down six feet in front of him, sending a cloud of dust and multiple concrete missiles his way. One struck his forehead with so much force it made him see stars and laid him on his back once more.

Blinking, Mason knew he had to force himself to get moving. First, he crawled and then staggered clear of raining rubble, invigorated by a rush of adrenalin but feeling sick to his stomach from the blow to the head. The blurs to his right assured him the others had escaped the resulting explosion as heaps of stone struck the ground with a noise like thunder.

Even then, flying debris shot past their moving figures. Mason was struck again, this time in the spine by what felt like a boulder.

He collapsed, finding himself once more on the ground, with an up-close view of the dirty street.

To his right, Roxy was on her feet. She'd leapt clear of the falling fire escape at the last minute before rolling, and had only been interrupted in her forward momentum by the need to help Sally when Hassell yelled furiously about a badly hurt ankle.

Hassell was crawling, face screwed up in pain. Beyond him, Quaid was groaning, holding the AK and studying the edge of the roof above, checking for at least one shooter who might be an imminent threat.

Mason struggled to his feet as Roxy took off at speed, singling out the two shooters who had caused all this destruction. They'd been enjoying themselves. Now, with the raven-haired righter of wrongs bearing down on them, their grins slipped away.

Mason stared in awe, bent and wracked with pain, as Roxy, covered in and surrounded by rock dust, bleeding from numerous cuts, still with the *Frozen* backpack strapped over her shoulders and the black Colt handgun held firm, tackled them head on.

'Look out!' Her voice rang out.

As she'd no doubt hoped, they hesitated. One fired a shot whilst glancing over his shoulder. The other looked up, then back at her and squeezed his trigger. Roxy fought for her life, doing the unexpected. She dived headlong, hit the floor and shot twice without aiming. The bullets flew wide but the men both ducked. Still, they were able to train their weapons on her. Roxy stared death in the face. Even with her training Mason could see they'd get their shots off first. But then, in a split second, rubble struck from above, medium-sized chunks that hit their shoulders and drove them to the ground. Roxy squeezed her trigger twice and hit them both at centre mass.

The aggressors fell dead.

Roxy lowered the Colt and heaved several long breaths. Mason hobbled over to her, an assortment of bruises, cuts and scrapes hindering his progress but not stopping it. Hassell couldn't walk and was holding his ankle, grimacing in pain. Sally and Quaid were slowly approaching. Mason and Roxy took an extra minute to sweep the area and the roof above as best they could to establish there were no further threats. It wasn't a perfect assessment, but it was the best they could do.

When Quaid reached them, he bowed, clearly in pain. 'You're welcome.'

Roxy grunted in surprise. 'Yeah, man, thanks for everything. Since we met you, we've been shot at, chased across the roofs of Bethlehem, forced to climb down a condemned fire escape and then hang on as it fell off the side of a building.'

'To be fair,' Quaid said, 'you were being shot at before I met you.'

Roxy laughed. Hassell struggled to his feet, gasping, and put a hand on her shoulder for balance, still unable to subject his ankle to any kind of weight. 'And don't think I wasn't aware of the *Frozen* backpack,' she warned him.

'I've never seen anyone wear it better,' he said.

Mason threw a glance at the building. 'We should get the hell away from here,' he said as sirens split the night and flashing lights painted the surrounding buildings lurid blues and reds. 'If the police catch us, our search is over.'

He sent a concerned look at Sally as they walked, worried the danger and death that pursued them might be weighing on her mind. 'Are you okay?'

'Honestly, I don't know.' She seemed determined to keep pace, making sure she wouldn't be the one to let them down. 'I still need to prove all this, to *stop* what the Amori are doing. Everything else is driftwood right now, as you said. I can sift through it later.'

'It's a good, immediate coping method.'

'Understood. I think the urgency of our situation helps. Now, where are we going? Because this new line of riddle needs solving, and we have to escape Bethlehem.'

Mason saw her point. 'We're screwed,' he said. 'The airport will be on lockdown. The roads blocked.'

'Diversity is what you need,' Hassell said. 'And exactly what I bring to the mix.'

'And I can help,' Quaid said, looking back with some regret. 'At least for now. I guess I'm homeless too.'

Mason studied the pair and then looked at Roxy, who shrugged as if to say, 'Let them get on with it.' She was probably right. What did they have to lose? So far, this journey had mostly been about winging it. Learning, planning and researching on the hoof. And how else were they going to escape the Holy Land?

'What did you have in mind?'

Chapter 36

Marduk shook with anticipation. His fingers trembled, his jaw worked ceaselessly. He paced the length of his office time and time again. The hour was almost upon him.

Ruben had prepared a barbed package that would shake the Vatican and garner interested parties at the same time. A short teaser, promising to reveal Jesus' true heritage, prove that Christianity was based upon a lie and offer the facts to prove it all, would whet many appetites and cause quite a stir, Ruben had assured him. It was just the right way to start. Plotted and planned to perfection, it would first release on YouTube and other video channels to little attention until Ruben rolled out his trending packet, an array of advertisements, hashtags, clickbait headlines and popular ID tags that would propel it into the public eye. The Amori's global network would also bring a heavy influence to bear here, helping the video trend, accumulate millions of views, by switching it to the best algorithms, by making popular influencers aware of it and offering money for exposure, and propelling it into the digital spotlight. By the time the second video released in a day or so with the added publicity offered by big social media platforms, the promised news would have gone global, perking the interest of believers and non-believers every-where.

And then, the third release would melt mainframes from sea to shining sea.

Marduk imagined his every dream soon to be fulfilled alongside the Amori's lifelong vision. The Book of Revelation spewed its rhetoric about the destruction of Babylon in long, repulsive paragraphs. The Amori would seek to reverse all that, to show the Church how mistaken it was about the so-called city of sin. Marduk now distracted himself by bringing up a new live feed. Fifteen fun-filled minutes would do it. The feed came from two cameras mounted on the ceiling of an interrogation room. At that moment, three Hoods were terrorising Gianluca Gianni's little family and filming a new proof-of-life record for their puppet commander of the Swiss Guard. Marduk laughed out loud at the scenes, wishing that he had the time to take part.

The tallest Hood was scraping a knife across the wife's throat. The blade was dulled by congealed blood which she could no doubt smell and would make her wonder to whom it might belong. The daughter cried and begged and curled her legs up, whimpering as the shortest Hood approached with a taser in his hand.

Marduk watched with a wide grin, imagining how Gianni would feel when, later tonight, the edited video would drop into his personal Messenger account. In all fairness, Gianni was being instrumental in muddying the waters for the Vatican, offering arguments that shouldn't exist to slow them down. The machinery that ground the Vatican's gears was slow at best. Gianni was making every step forward a laborious task, rallying those who believed the Amori were mere legend, letting their protests be heard, laying obstacles both mental and physical before those who might act sooner. His task would become harder the moment the first video released.

221

Feeling good, Marduk was then beset by an unexpected obstacle. Its name was Masterton, and the senile old man seemed to be obsessed by the way Marduk had ordered the murder of his own daughter. To Marduk it was routine, a sacrifice made to further the cause. To Masterton, it seemed personal. Every time Marduk saw Masterton, he was aware of that accusing stare, the hooded eyes, the unspoken criticisms. It was becoming clearer by the day that Masterton could become more than the annoying fly he currently was. Already, his relentless words of condemnation were making people quietly question Marduk's state of mind.

It wasn't right. Marduk was worried. He looked up then as Ruben entered the room without knocking. He was early, but Marduk didn't care. The tech clutched a laptop in his right hand.

'Is it ready?'

'Just needs someone to press Enter.'

'That will be me. Have you changed anything?'

'Nothing fundamental since you saw it last. I've just tweaked the presentation, the Amori branded intro, the professional appearance. It's vital.'

'And you're certain we can't be tracked?'

'I employ irregular and disproportionate security algorithms that will bounce between thousands of different servers from one side of the world to the next. We're secure.'

Marduk took it at face value. 'And the content?' He'd written it – he should know – but he loved it so much he just wanted to hear it from Ruben's lips one more time.

'A quick drone shot of the Vatican, of the image of Jesus Christ, and then our hook – "*For two thousand years you have been fed a lie.*" Hashtags then blitz the screen, things like "false prophet", "son of Joseph", that kind of thing. Then the words "Proof is Coming", and a countdown begins. A voiceover will reiterate the information as our picture closes in on the image and then the face of Jesus nailed to a cross. We end with an earnest message – "Witness the collapse of Christianity".'

'And that's enough?'

'For the first release, yes. The social media channels, influencers, newspapers and internet crazies out there will add all the authenticity we need. And, of course, the second video will slay them.'

Marduk liked Ruben's choice of the word 'slay'. It was what he would have used in relation to the Church. 'I can't wait for the Vatican to see it,' he said. 'This torment, this provocation will both enrage and terrify them because they know every word is true.'

'Think we'll get a suicide?' Ruben asked.

'I hope so. But I believe the time has come, has it not?'

Ruben opened the laptop. 'It all starts at the press of a button,' he said.

Chapter 37

Mason was provided with an ambiguous glimpse into the world of expert in- and exfiltration, and some of the devices and machinations required to operate at a cutting-edge level.

Hassell came into his own, though still only able to hobble for a short distance. Only time worked against him. That was it. The authorities – the police, the Army and the forensics people – didn't bother him. It was Sally's insistence that everything happened immediately, that if they dawdled even an hour too long then the Amori might win and potentially release their devastating secret, that high risk was worth any amount of progress. It was the time constraint.

Quaid was able to source them transport in a food truck going to the coast and, specifically, a place called Ashdod. He paid the driver, who helped hide them under rugs smelling of mould and animal droppings. He furnished Hassell with numerous burner phones, a new laptop and even an ankle support bandage. Sally reminded them that they wouldn't achieve internet access until they found somewhere with a good Bluetooth signal that they could artificially boost.

Between them, Hassell stamped out a plan and Quaid added manpower.

Once the truck was clear of Bethlehem, Quaid, sitting up front, banged on the wooden panel dividing the cabin from its rear compartment, signalling that they could shrug off the reeking covers.

Two more slaps would warn them to revisit the unsavoury hiding place.

Sally sniffed her clothes and screwed up her face as she roamed free in the back of the bouncing truck. 'Stay away,' she told the others. 'You stink.'

'I think that's your perfume,' Roxy grumbled.

Mason held onto a support rail. 'All that matters is it fooled the roadblock. They took a look, pinched their noses and waved us on.'

'I think the fact that they recognised the driver *and* Quaid helped,' Hassell said. 'Truck's local. It's all about the fine details, guys.'

'Don't you have phone calls to make?' Roxy grunted. 'Y'know, before you launch into a victory song, or something?'

Hassell got the message and opened one of Quaid's burner phones. It was an outmoded flip-cover device which, after the AK, was the second old-school tool Mason had seen Quaid using. He wondered idly if the guy distrusted new technology as the top-heavy truck jounced between ruts in the road, forcing him to hold on two-handed and wish for a quick journey. That was never going to happen; Ashdod lay an hour's drive to the west.

Around them, in secured crates, stood an assortment of food supplies destined for some cargo ship that would leave Ashdod for Egypt in the not-too-distant future. Not that they wanted to go to Egypt, but Hassell was contriving a way to get them aboard a vessel – *any* vessel – that would see them clear of Israel. The real trick wasn't getting them on board – it was keeping them safe during their journey and allowing them to furtively slip away from the ship after it docked.

'I've found a ship that leaves forty minutes after we're due to arrive,' Hassell told them at one point, brightening Sally's mien. 'The next step is . . . a container.'

Mason frowned and Sally coughed, but neither complained. It would have been good to take a nap now or even shovel down a few energy bars, but the rock and sway of the truck discouraged all attempts at movement, and Hassell was sitting with his ankle elevated to help reduce any swelling.

After thirty minutes on the go, Mason was reminded that he hadn't eaten for as long as he could remember by a deep rumbling in the pit of his stomach. It wasn't just hunger; it was energy depletion, which could become an issue. He made a point of clouting the wooden divide and demanding they grab some food, but Quaid said they'd have to hold on until they reached the port.

Sally passed the time by giving the latest riddle some preliminary analysis. '*Ibid, 27,*' she reminded them, voice warbling in time to the motions of the truck. 'Any ideas?'

'For a code it's a bit short,' Mason said.

'That's true. However, I do have a theory. The *Book of Secrets* is written in Latin. The word *ibidem* means "the same place". I assume you all recognise the word *ibid*?'

Roxy nodded sagely and Mason bobbed his head up and down. 'Not really,' he said.

Sally's eyes widened involuntarily. 'Oh, well, I'm sorry. The Latin link is why I felt so sure back at the altar that this is the correct clue.'

'And the fact that it was the *only* clue also helped,' Roxy said.

'That too, yes. *Ibid* is a contraction of *ibidem*. It's most used for footnoting in scholarly manuscripts. The author uses the word *ibid* instead of repeating a reference.' Sally looked at them expectantly.

'You've lost me,' Mason admitted. 'You're saying Jacques Heindl left a footnote for the next clue?'

'Exactly. The inscription is a clever code that ensures you must have the *Book of Secrets* to hand to crack it. You see, others might have stumbled across the inscriptions down the years. And, for whatever reason, others may have tried to chase down the clues. But, at this point, you'd be done.'

'Without the book,' Mason said.

'Without the book,' Sally repeated.

'But we don't have the book,' Roxy reminded them.

'Yes, well, that's unfortunate. I believe *Ibid, 27* refers to a footnote in the *Book of Secrets.*' Sally smiled proudly at them.

Mason held tight as the truck hit a pothole. 'Can we be sure? I mean, are footnotes that important?'

'Are you kidding?' Sally sounded upset. 'Footnotes were developed around the seventeenth century and made it possible to combine a scholarly narrative with intellectual investigations. They were devised to counter scepticism about historical tales by adding points of relative fact. Historically speaking, footnotes are one of the most important tools in our arsenal.'

Mason held up a hand in defeat. 'Okay then. But that does leave us a problem.'

'Maybe,' Sally said. 'Maybe not.' She looked at Quaid. 'Do you have one of those phones?'

Quaid threw her a device. Sally spent some time making calls. Twenty minutes passed and then another twenty. The phone's battery died. Sally raised her eyebrows but said nothing, deeply involved in her task, her face sheened with sweat and creased in concentration. Mason wanted to ask what she was doing but didn't think he should interrupt. Finally, a look of excitement transformed her features.

'Hello,' she said. '*Hello?*'

Someone gave an affirmative on the other end of the line. Sally grasped her phone tighter. 'This is Sally Rusk again. Yes . . . again, sorry. Do you remember telling us that you knew that *book* inside out, that you could quote it front to back and back to front with absolute accuracy? Now, Mr DeVille, can I test that declaration?'

Mason listened as Sally asked Mateo DeVille to scour his memory in search of a footnote labelled number 27. It was a grand theory and made sense. Adding some kind of code that related back to the book was a masterstroke and took away any chance that the Amori sanctuary might be discovered accidentally through Heindl's riddles.

The truck bounced on, testing the strength of their bones. It was as they rode a long straight hill, breathing easily for the first time in half an hour, that Sally repeated a new line of text gleaned from DeVille's memory.

'"*His Sacré Coeur, the Perpetual Adoration of His Last and First Rite*",' she said. '*Sacré Coeur* means *Sacred Heart* in French. The second line is vaguer.'

'Maybe Heindl initially thought this clue too easy,' Mason suggested. 'And came up with the code as an added layer of security.'

'Maybe,' Sally said. 'But it's not *that* easy.'

Mason took the much-needed short break to rest his bruised and aching limbs and to think about what Roxy had revealed to him on that hill near Jerusalem; how she was struggling to face a future without guilt, trying to regain the person she'd been before being put to work for a clandestine agency. He also needed to consider what they should do about Hassell and Quaid.

Neither were strictly part of the team, but both boasted valuable skills. The Amori were in the ascendant and now wasn't the time to break ties with potentially effective allies. Mason guessed Roxy felt the same since she wasn't complaining about either man.

When they arrived at the port, Hassell made two more calls whilst Quaid's friend and driver started about his business. After first finding a forklift, the man offloaded his cargo at a slow pace, giving his stowaways time to work. Mason, Roxy and Sally stayed out of sight in the back, not willing to risk detection even to eat.

Hassell hobbled away from the area, finding darkness and a Bluetooth signal with which to work. Quaid joined him. The clock ticked down.

They missed the first boat that Hassell had targeted, but quickly found a second scheduled to leave in only thirty minutes.

Mason finally exited the truck on Hassell's signal into a cold and blustery evening. The skies were a pitch-black vault, any illumination offered by moon and stars hidden by cloud as the team took lungfuls of fresh air for the first time in almost two hours.

Hassell identified several containers to which they could gain access, and then devised a convoluted route across the dock. He flitted between containers, buildings and machinery, avoiding detection as he refined the route. It would take long minutes and none of them wanted to be seen, let alone identified. Finally, he had a course.

'Get a move on,' he greeted them on returning to the truck. 'And follow my lead. This is gonna take pinpoint synchronisation.'

Sally was the first to approach him, moving faster than any of them. 'Lead the way,' she said. 'We don't have all night.'

Hassell limped to the edge of a container and peered around. Mason, behind him, stared over his shoulder at ten feet of open ground that stood before the ship's boarding bridge, a rickety-looking metal meshwork walkway.

'Steady,' Hassell said.

'We've got twenty-seven minutes,' Sally said. 'And we have to hide too.'

Hassell nodded, bent down and massaged his ankle.

Mason tapped him on the shoulder. 'Let me go first, mate. Quaid, can you support him?'

Quaid nodded. Mason slipped to the front position. Aboard ship, about a dozen crew members walked the decks, securing cargo and checking the vessel's general readiness. Mason saw no easy access. 'We go in twos,' he said. 'Stay low, move fast. Wait for your chance.'

'And hope time doesn't run out,' Roxy added helpfully.

Mason watched along with Sally. The crewmen came and went. Another man strolled along the dock and then onboard via the bridge. Mason saw a chance in his wake.

'Now.'

Together, he and Sally raced across the open ground. They stayed almost in a crouch, eyes darting left and right. A sailor wandered into their eyeline, strolling across an upper deck.

Mason dropped to his stomach, waiting. His heart beat against the concrete. The second the sailor vanished he rose and ran again. As he neared the bridge a man wearing a white hat came out of a conning tower door and took a look across the dock.

Mason collapsed on purpose, hugging the floor. Sally fell across his back, ungainly but necessary due to the urgency. There was a shout that made Mason's heart leap. Cautiously, he raised his head but the man with the white hat was still there and staring at something in the middle distance with earnest concentration.

Mason crawled onto the bridge and felt it sway. The walkway's mesh sides rattled. He held his breath, exposed and desperate. They couldn't get caught now.

'Go,' Sally said. 'Hurry. There's another one coming.'

Mason crawled faster, reached the end of the bridge and rolled onto the deck. The new sailor was quite a way off, his face barely discernible in the dark. Together, he and Sally melted away among the containers.

That would be Quaid's and Hassell's cue to proceed.

Nerve-wracking minutes passed as the clock ticked down. Mason saw they had seven minutes to go before the ship was due to cast off. Soon, someone would come to draw the bridge in and then they were well and truly screwed.

Only Roxy was left on the dock. Mason peered around the side of a container, watching her progress. Roxy's raven hair, black eyes and dark clothing blended perfectly with her surroundings. She stepped out, crossed the open space and stepped onto the bridge just as the man who'd come to wind it in appeared.

Shocked, the two stared at each other.

Roxy acted first, jumping forward and grabbing him around the neck. The man fought back, swiping at her with arms and elbows but it was all just useless flailing against someone of Roxy's skills. She looped her arm around his throat, slipped behind him and squeezed until she'd choked him unconscious. She didn't let him fall to the deck, but threw his body over her shoulder and headed straight for their container.

'He's coming with us?' Hassell asked.

'He's coming with us.'

Chapter 38

Alexandria, Egypt, provided the perfect place to lie low while Sally attempted to decipher the third riddle. By late afternoon they had paid the unfortunate sailor an extortionate amount of money to stay quiet, exited the container, evaded the Alexandrian port authorities and found a suitable hotel on the seedier side of town.

Mason felt a sense of grandeur on entering Alexandria. Founded by Alexander the Great and subdued by Cleopatra, the city had a long history, a complex tapestry of famous names. Dazzling alongside the Mediterranean, it was once home to the Great Library and the immense Pharos Lighthouse. More recently, it had become a sprawling Bohemian tourist attraction, home to a happy proliferation of artists. Here, in what Mason saw as the heart of Egypt, ancient history lay in heaps, communicating a profound sense of days gone by as well as the vibrant modern world. Mason saw the age-old meeting the contemporary at every mismatching street corner.

He didn't have to take a whiff of his armpits, catch a glimpse of his reflection in a passing window or feel the pangs of hunger to know they'd been on the go – and on the run – for days with no real chance to rest or eat. All they had with them were their backpacks.

Entering the cool but tiny lobby of the hotel, Quaid touched Sally's shoulder. 'Do you have any cash?' he asked.

Roxy made a point of studying the front desk. 'I don't think they sell Dinky Toys here, bud.'

'Funny,' Quaid said, 'because I'm older than you, right? Well, just—'

'Nothing to do with your age, it's because I've seen your flip phone and your AK.' Roxy shrugged.

'Old-school.' Quaid nodded. 'Yes, I understand. But there's a good reason behind that.'

Mason had already leaned close to Sally's ear while the others engaged in banter. 'Don't worry,' he said. 'Quaid's trying to tell you not to use your credit cards, which can easily be traced. Even withdrawing cash from a machine will give away our position. I suggest we make a large cash withdrawal when we're about to leave town.'

'What we paid the sailor is most of what I had, but there's a little left,' Sally said. She was looking more and more anxious by the minute, desperate to get started on solving the clue that might lead them to the next leg of their journey. Inside the container, every lost second had wound her tighter and tighter. Mason had seen it straining her face, hunching her shoulders.

'We can always pool cash,' he said, knowing Roxy and he had their wallets and that Quaid – being the man he appeared to be – would hardly have left everything behind without bringing along a substantial wad.

Roxy and Quaid continued their repartee as the desk clerk appeared. Sally stepped forwards and asked for five rooms, which weren't available. She was offered three and took them. Mason asked where the best nearby place to eat was.

Ten minutes later, they were stretched out in Sally and Roxy's room, taking the weight off their aching limbs. Mason sat on the floor with his back to a wall as Roxy headed for the shower. Sally took the bed, sitting upright.

233

Quaid handed her the laptop and sat down to watch her work. Hassell positioned himself at the net-covered window to study the street.

Sally cracked her fingers. 'Finally.'

Mason breathed deeply, relaxing as Sally got to work, staring into space and taking some time to think about precisely nothing.

Ten minutes later, Roxy reappeared wrapped in a towel and searching for a hairdryer, which the room didn't have. Mason found himself studying the old scars on her legs and arms, the way they blended together like a fine lattice-work.

'Ya jealous?' Roxy had caught him staring.

He was about to apologise but then, what did he have to apologise for? He wasn't being lewd, and he hardly believed Roxy was self-conscious.

'Quite a collection,' he said.

'I hate them,' Roxy said, turning away. 'They remind me of the person I was.' She disappeared back into the bath-room.

Mason kicked himself, understanding her discontent. Trying to find the person you once were must be hard enough without a permanent reminder tattooed onto your body. He was grateful when Quaid spoke up and steered him away from the problem.

'I don't trust modern tech,' he told them, still watching Sally work on her laptop. 'Yeah, I can get it. But give me old-school any day. It doesn't reflect my age.'

'Never said it did,' Hassell said. 'You're not even close to old, man.'

'Nope. Fifty-one and I'd take you in a race any day. Providing it's a short one.' Quaid laughed. 'Hand-to-hand too. You don't lose that level of training.'

'You mentioned that you're an ex-army officer?' Mason said.

Quaid nodded. 'Twenty-five years in,' he said. 'Four of them at high level. I quit eight years ago.'

'You quit?' Mason was surprised. 'I guess that's another long story.'

'And you'd be right. Basically, I got sick of sending people into harm's way to suit political agendas.' Quaid shrugged. 'Did it too many times. Lost too many good men and women to whim, greed and corruption. The people you were fighting on Monday became friends on Wednesday and were back on the kill-list by Sunday. It's . . . akin to walking in molasses. By the time you've made it to one side of the sticky pond, you have to fight all the way back to the other.'

'The people we trust to lead us don't understand us,' Hassell murmured.

Mason studied Sally as the room fell into silence, trying to gauge her progress without interrupting. All that he could see was that she was working fast, fingers flying across her keyboard. In the end, he couldn't tell how she was doing and didn't want to interrupt, so ordered a wide range of food through room service.

He showered and by the time he returned, Hassell and Quaid were laying the hot and cold fare and bottles of water in a mouth-watering row along the bottom of the bed.

Mason didn't speak again until he'd finished eating and the sustenance was firing renewed energy through his system. He poured strong black coffee from a steaming cafetière and sat at the foot of the bed alongside Roxy, sipping from the cup and feeling sated, rejuvenated and content for the first time in days.

'I am sorry,' he said under his breath at one point. 'About the scars.'

'Thanks,' she said. 'Like I mentioned, new memories made will help shield me from old ones. I just gotta keep moving forward.'

Mason pursed his lips. 'Amen to that idea,' he said. 'All we need now are a few drinks to toast it.'

'You mean like *cheers*.' Roxy affected a bad English accent. '*Cheers, pal, let's drink on it.*'

Mason regarded her as if she'd grown a third eye. 'Have you gone mad?'

Roxy rubbed her eyes tiredly. 'Yeah, maybe a little.'

Quaid fell to a crouch beside them, rummaging in his backpack. 'Speaking of alcohol,' he said.

'Do not tell me you brought some,' Mason said.

'That's what I do.' Quaid grinned. 'I *procure* things. Like this . . .' He pulled a dark bottle from his backpack with the enthusiasm of a magician pulling a rabbit from a hat.

'I bet it's matured,' Roxy murmured, smiling.

'Of course. Thirty years old and single malt. Fancy a drop?'

Mason finished the last dregs of coffee and held out his cup. 'I'll take more than a drop, mate.'

Night fell outside and, as Sally worked, the others sipped at the strong liquor, passing stories that Mason guessed were heavily censored. Even Sally took a moment away from her laptop to savour two mouthfuls of whisky before continuing to tap at keys with one hand and use a fork to spear food with the other.

Mason was wondering if they should call it a night and retire for a few hours of much-needed sleep when Sally broke a comfortable silence.

'The Amori have released their first video and are surely becoming desperate,' she said. 'We know they're holding off releasing the actual secrets until their sanctuary is safe. We know that finding Marduk is the key. Everything they've accomplished depends on the *Book of Secrets* and how they leak the revelations. *Everything*. And that's millennia of expectation, of frustration and strife. If Marduk messes this up, he'll be remembered as the worst leader in their history rather than the man who achieved their goals. He's treading a fine line.'

'Any idea what the secret, or secrets, might be?' Quaid asked, having been brought up to speed earlier.

'Something centring around Jesus Christ,' Sally said. 'At least, *one* of them is. The video kind of intimates that Jesus isn't the son of God, that the Church has purposely lied to its flock for centuries. It must be a terrible secret to expect that it will destroy the Church.'

Quaid whistled. 'I'm not a religious man, but I can't imagine a secret that would hit with such an impact.'

'Mateo DeVille, the ex-pope's archivist, told us that the book holds three, maybe four, secrets that utterly terrify him. That could destroy Christianity and cause many wars. My father died trying to protect it. The Amori should at least pay for that, but there's no doubt in my mind that the secrets they seek could change the world as we know it.'

'In any case,' Roxy spoke up. 'We're on their hit list now. No future for us.'

'Only because we're bothering them,' Hassell said begrudgingly as they all watched the video play. 'I worked for Gido and his criminal empire and then betrayed them. That goes beyond the Amori and the book. Where the hell do I go from here?'

'I doubt they'll ever stop hunting us,' Mason said. 'To finish this, we must finish them. And we can't go to the authorities because we have no idea who's sleeping with the enemy.' This was another reason he'd decided to keep Quaid in their team. If they couldn't travel using their passports, then having a man along with the means to navigate the darker byways of the world might prove useful.

'And we quit the agency,' Roxy reminded Mason. 'Which leaves us exactly where?'

Sally looked up. 'You did? Then I'm guessing they wanted to ditch me?'

'Something like that,' Mason said. 'Watchtower can't be associated with the mayhem we've caused.'

'Well, to hell with them. We're doing the right thing here. And I have some good news.'

Mason snapped out of a yawn and glanced at her. 'You've cracked it?'

'I've cracked it.'

Chapter 39

Sally rubbed her eyes and the back of her neck before she continued, wilting before their eyes. Hassell handed her a cup of strong black coffee which she sipped as she talked.

'Let's break it down. *"His Sacré Coeur, the Perpetual Adoration of His Last and First Rite."* The real revelatory word here is the first: *His*. There are many examples of the sacred heart around the world but Heindl used *His,* not *The*. A subtle difference but an important one. The *Sacred Heart* itself is one of the Catholic Church's most famous holy symbols. The heart of Jesus Christ represents God's boundless love for mankind – the long-suffering love and compassion that Christ bore for humanity.'

'Catholic devotion the world over,' Mason said.

'There is a church in Paris called Sacré-Coeur, located at the summit of Montmartre, the highest point in the city. The riddle draws our perspective towards it through the first line. The Sacré-Coeur is actually dedicated to the Sacred Heart of Jesus and broke ground just a few years before Heindl included it.'

'Perfect,' Roxy said. 'He probably visited during its construction.'

'Very possibly, as an emissary of the pope, which would have made his job easier. But it's the second half of the riddle that ties it all in. The phrase *perpetual adoration* is mostly used in a precise sense. It specifies that the adoration is *physically* perpetual, interrupted only for a short time or in uncontrollable circumstances. Most devotees unite in adoration for many hours.'

'Adoration of what?' Roxy asked. 'God?'

'No. They come together to complete hours of worship before the usually exposed Most Blessed Sacrament by day and by night, throughout the week. Sacré-Coeur has maintained a perpetual adoration of the Holy Eucharist since 1885.'

Hassell held up a hand. 'Not meaning to be a dick,' he said. 'But what is the Blessed Sacrament? And the Holy Eucharist too for that matter?'

'The Holy Eucharist is the Communion.' Sally paused. 'The Christian rite introduced by Jesus Christ. During the Last Supper he gave out bread and wine, referring to the bread as "my body" and the wine as "the new covenant in my blood". They ate and drank as commanded so that Christians for evermore could take the Communion and remember Christ's sacrifice on the cross.'

'Go on,' Mason said.

'The Blessed Sacrament is the altar bread and wine itself.'

'So, to be clear,' Hassell said. 'This church in Paris has upheld this adoration for more than a century?'

'Since before it was officially open. Before it was consecrated, yes. Which brings us to the final part of the riddle. "*His Last and First rite.*"'

'An allusion to the Last Supper?' Mason wondered. 'Or something that happened on the cross?'

'He was crucified beside two robbers,' Sally said. 'But any act of forgiveness he may have undertaken would not have been a first and last rite. I mean, we're talking the Son of God here. We're looking for something he performed for the *first* and *last* time . . .' She glanced around the room, gauging the reaction.

'You already mentioned it,' Roxy said. 'Bread and wine at the Last Supper.'

Sally's voice snapped Mason out of his contemplation. 'It all points us to the Sacré-Coeur, the Roman Catholic basilica in Paris. Even though there are many churches bearing the name Sacré-Coeur, this is the only one that has upheld the adoration.'

After a moment's silence, Hassell stepped forward. 'Clearly, all normal means of transport are out of the question. I can arrange passage between Alexandria and Paris, but it won't be pretty.'

With that, he fished out the burner phone Quaid had given him and asked to borrow Sally's laptop.

Quaid laid his AK on the bed and asked for the other weapons and ammo to take inventory. 'We will need more,' he said thoughtfully. 'And they'll be easier to procure right here rather than in Paris. I can arrange something.' He made for the door.

'Need a bodyguard?' Roxy asked, not without a little irony.

'I'm better on my own.'

It was late. Mason let them go to work, eventually wandering off to find his own room. He fell onto the bed fully clothed and slept fitfully until dawn when an incessant thumping sound dragged him from oblivion.

'Roxy?' he called out blearily.

'Hey, Babyface. How'd you know it was me?'

'It's your annoying knock.'

'Just be glad I ain't dragging you out of bed in your underwear. I still owe you for that.'

Mason raised his head and scanned the room, heaving a sigh of relief to see that it was empty before remembering he'd fallen asleep still dressed. 'Do you hold a grudge?'

'No, but I'll sure as hell get you back for it one day.'

Mason smiled, climbed off the bed and opened the door to find the raven-haired woman leaning against the wall opposite, holding a croissant in one hand and a paper cup in the other. She allowed his hopes to rise for several seconds before sipping from the cup and taking a bite from the pastry. Mason felt deflated.

'Don't worry, there's some waiting for you in Sally's room. Quaid brought them back this morning.'

'He's been out all night?' They started along the carpeted corridor.

'Appears so. Hassell hasn't stopped working either. Together, we're applying enormous effort to this mission.'

Mason thought he detected a negative note in her comment. 'You think we're overreacting? That Sally's going over the top in response to the death of her father?'

'Well . . . you've clearly considered it.'

'Maybe.' Mason paused outside Sally's door and fixed Roxy with an earnest look. 'Listen, the last thing I want to do is drag you through the coals against your will. Nobody will think less of you if you back out.'

'Do *you* think these secrets could change the world?'

'The evidence says yes. I mean, look where the Vatican stored the book. In a guarded vault *inside* a secret vault. Only one pope and archivist allowed to examine it at a time over two thousand years. That's pretty bloody clandestine by any measure. And then we spoke to Mateo DeVille, who backed everything up.'

'And the Amori?'

'They've proven they're a serious threat and well connected. That they want to scandalise and demonise the Church. Plus, if the secrets the book holds weren't so devastating, why would they be so intent on stopping us from reaching them? But religion isn't my motivation here, it's pure human decency. The Amori are just an enemy, like ISIS, like the Taliban, a force for evil. If good men and women don't stand against them, they win.'

Roxy nodded, accepting his words. Mason knocked, then

entered Sally's room when Hassell opened the door. Quaid was standing by the window and turned to look at them.

'All I could acquire at short notice.' He nodded at the bed. 'An old friend drives a taxi these days, but still has access to basic weaponry. The Sig Sauer is popular and the Glock, but there was no time to secure rifles.'

Mason considered the stash remarkable and said so. Two Sigs and three Glocks lay atop the embroidered duvet with additional magazines at the side. Mason noted that the guns were well used, dirty and chipped along their outer shells.

Hassell stooped to choose a Sig. 'I've been working a bit outside my usual purview,' he said. 'The infrastructure around here is based largely on taxis and seagoing vessels. I tried bartering for a small boat before realising the weather, season and inclement seas would probably kill us, so ended up hiring a chopper.'

'As much as I'm happy to avoid another sea voyage,' Roxy complained, 'how the hell did you manage that?'

Mason remembered all too well the swaying container after the hour in the smelly truck. 'It kept us in front,' he said. 'By a thread, but a thread was enough. How fast is this chopper?'

Hassell made a face. 'It's rented, slow, but faster than a boat and much safer. At least . . . it should be if it makes it the whole way. We'll find somewhere to land in Italy, since that's as far as the pilot's willing to take us.'

'That sounds . . . great,' Sally said shortly. 'The quicker the better.'

Hassell shrugged. 'Quaid found us a pilot who doesn't check passports. I found us the helicopter at a local rental firm. Chopper rental companies are as common as seashells around seaports.'

'Do you have any contacts in Italy that might then help us along to Paris?' Mason asked.

Quaid scratched his head, looking extremely dubious. 'I might have an old friend I can call on.'

243

'Please,' Sally said. 'We can't afford to fall behind the Amori.'

'Another old friend.' Roxy smiled.

'You should see my Friends Reunited page.'

'Is that still a thing?' Roxy pursed her lips. 'Social media moved on over a decade ago, I think.'

'Yeah, I don't have a Friends Reunited page,' Quaid admitted. 'Nor any page. But I do have a phonebook.' He tapped his head. 'And a world of goodwill.'

'Are we ready?' Sally's voice was strained with anxiety as they lingered. 'When will the chopper be available?'

'Right now,' Hassell said, scooping magazines to add to his rucksack.

Mason shouldered his own. 'Then let's move.'

Chapter 40

Behind them, the sweep of office blocks, cranes, jetties and palm trees that defined Alexandria's busy port fell away into the distance. The water beneath was calm, as smooth as glass.

The chopper skimmed the waves at first before lifting gradually into the sky. Mason saw small craft bobbing on the waters below and signs of a strong breeze and was glad of Hassell's foresight in picking a helicopter rather than a boat.

The Bell aircraft was old, so old in fact Mason could hear its nuts and bolts and rivets fighting to stay put. His tattered and fraying seat didn't have a spot that hadn't been patched and when even the pilot's face remained ashen after take-off, his knuckles tight on the controls, confidence levels weren't running high. If this was supposed to be safer than taking a boat, he hated to think what the boat would have been like. Mason braced himself to endure several painful, distressing hours.

'The GPS isn't working,' their pilot shouted after a minute. 'Any of you guys have a smartphone?'

'It's north-west from the fort,' Hassell said and then shrugged in apology. 'No, I don't have GPS on my phone.'

'Worry not.' Quaid produced a new supply of phones from his rucksack. 'I got more.'

'To be fair,' the pilot said, 'this old bird only has a range of five to seven hundred kilometres. Italy's roughly two thousand. We're gonna hug the coast to Tunisia, then fly across the short stretch of water to Sicily, refuelling where we can. Buckle in.'

The sun was approaching its zenith, making the rippling waves glitter with a light too bright for the naked eye. Mason donned his sunglasses and checked the new phones Quaid had bought them, passing one to each member of the team and noting that they had four spares. In addition, Quaid had packed bottled water and pre-packed sandwiches along with European maps, a spare battery for their laptop, gum and even sun cream.

Mason whistled at the haul with appreciation. 'Some forward thinking here, mate. I never would have thought of two-way radios.'

Quaid shrugged. 'Figured it wouldn't hurt. Packing light's not always packing *right*.'

Mason dug deeper, finding a grey baseball cap which he slipped on to ward off the sun before offering the bag to Roxy. 'Take a look. Maybe you'll find one to match your backpack.'

The helicopter bounced amidst air currents, battered left and right and groaning so hard in protest that the blue waters below began to look inviting. The pilot made a beeline for some unseen coast. There was little traffic to be seen across the seemingly endless expanse of blue sparkling waters below, and a sense of solitude up in the skies that Mason enjoyed at first.

As the hours passed, though, he became bored. There wasn't a lot of chatter between the team, a consequence of their wild flight so far, which left them to their own thoughts.

Quaid handed out sandwiches after a while, along with bottles of water, before revealing his *coup de grâce* – a box of fresh apple pies.

'Made locally,' he told them. 'Best you'll ever taste.'

With a destination in mind, Sally appeared once more at ease, although with each passing mile she scanned the horizon harder as if hoping for a sight of their destination.

Hassell directed the chopper north and then west towards Italy as the sky darkened. His strategy seemed to be that if you pointed your nose at a landmass, then sooner or later you were bound to hit it. Mason had grown accustomed to snatching anything from ten minutes' to eight hours' sleep in most situations, an ability that leaned heavily upon the amount of trust you had in your teammates. Sitting there, surrounded by people he'd only recently met, he thought it through.

Roxy was no longer an enigma. The rum-soaked, hard-hitting loose cannon was battling to be better, just like everyone else who didn't suffer from a narcissistic personality disorder. Being good at your job didn't offer a whole lot of comfort if its requirements destroyed the person you were.

Mason's battle wasn't quite the same. Two years after Mosul, he still didn't trust himself. Protecting affluent civilians worried about their wellbeing hadn't worked so far, but that didn't mean he should just walk away.

Thinking of trust and the need to have it in the people around you, Sally was reliable but didn't have the instincts and training of a soldier. Quaid on the other hand *did,* but they'd only just met him. And Hassell?

What did they know about Luke Hassell?

Only that he'd worked for the enemy and that he'd quit being a cop to become a criminal. That he knew this New York gang leader Gido well. And that he'd been involved in the theft of the *Book of Secrets.*

He saved your life too.

Mason caught the glitter of eyes watching him in the dark. It was Roxy, and even without speaking he knew they were thinking the same thing. In the next second, the burner phone in his pocket vibrated. Mason checked, not surprised to see a message from Roxy.

You first. I'll keep watch.

A sign of a great partner was an ability to anticipate what each other was thinking. Maybe they had the beginnings of a team here. The very thought made Mason take a mental step back, signalling that he was far from ready for that prospect.

Switching mindsets, he combed through memories of recent events, recalling Sally's opinions of the Amori and the dangers any revelation of the *Book of Secrets* might pose.

Then he dozed for a while as the helicopter ploughed on towards Italy.

Chapter 41

On passing over Calabria, a region of southern Italy, and identifying a quiet village, their pilot deposited them in a field of stubble on the outskirts. It seemed their first course of action should be to scan the news outlets to get an idea of where they stood and, perhaps, where the authorities were in their investigation into the Vatican theft.

They shouldered their backpacks. On finding a small café, they crowded inside and hooked up to its WiFi signal as Quaid ordered coffees and pastries. The ex-army officer then gave them an uncertain, speculative look before taking his own food and drink outside so that he could make a few private phone calls and work on the next leg of their journey.

Sally tapped her laptop screen. 'Four emails to my private address, and even more to my father's. When they weren't able to contact me by phone, they resorted to this.' She shook her head.

'Who did?' Mason asked.

'The Vatican, no doubt encouraged by the cops. Of course, it's not a surprise. They must have a lot of questions.' She paused, then added, 'For all of us.'

Roxy was scouring the news channels. 'It's been three

nights since the Vatican attack,' she said. 'And no shock to see conflicting reports. Ignoring the rags, it appears they found Nina's body and linked her to the theft. They also believe a broader criminal ring were involved, maybe even a mastermind. Your father is mentioned.' She glanced up at Sally. 'In a minor context, along with the murdered Swiss Guards. Interestingly, *we* aren't.'

'Because they don't know how deeply we're involved,' Mason said. 'And it sounds like they gleaned very little from the apartment where we found Nina. Anything else on the theft or the perpetrators?'

Roxy shook her head. 'Nah. They'd never name a stolen item. It's all very vague and is probably culled from a general memo released to the press.'

'Then we don't know what the Vatican knows.' Mason nodded. 'I wonder if the Amori are baiting them over the *Book of Secrets* and when they'll release it to the public?'

Hassell inclined his head at that. 'From what I know of them, and Marduk, I'd say baiting's a distinct possibility. He strikes me as the kind of guy who wants a grand stage from which to sing his own praises, and a captive audience on which to work. Also, he's a highly disturbed psycho.'

'And the Church might be compounding the problem by insisting fanatical groups like the Amori don't exist,' Sally said. 'They've done it before, denying that secret societies pose any danger whatsoever. It may be that they're not burying their heads in the sand, it's more that acknowledging something gives it power. But if they don't acknowledge *this* problem, everything will go bad very quickly. There's a chance that if we weren't following this trail, threatening to reveal their ancient sanctuary to the world, the secrets would already be out.'

'It's that important to them?' Mason asked.

'I think so. I think it's vital that they keep it hidden. Imagine the attention if its location was revealed. The leverage it would offer. The coverage it would get. Imagine the exposure.'

'But they want to come out of the shadows,' Roxy said. 'Don't they?'

'On their terms,' Sally said. 'No one else's. And surely not with the threat of losing their ancient sanctuary hanging over their head.'

Mason was pleased to see an absence of mugshots in the papers, but not naïve enough to think the police wouldn't be looking for them.

'In other news,' Sally said without a hint of irony, 'there's been some trouble in the Middle East.'

The clashes in Jerusalem and Bethlehem warranted only a tiny panel of allotted space in the well-known newspaper, most of the page being taken up by sponsored ads and a melodramatic headline above the main story concerning a soap star and a footballer. The news wasn't real anymore, Mason reflected, just a lurid jumble of clickbait and fakery designed to make money.

He skimmed over it, noting that the Middle Eastern authorities had released some shaky, distorted video of the events, all of which focused on the shooters rather than those who had been trying to escape. Mason read it with a sense of relief and quiet surprise.

Of course, in the same way that the Vatican were drip-feeding vapid details, the Israelis were probably glossing over pertinent facts whilst conducting a quiet but intense investigation. Hopefully, that investigation would lead them straight to the Amori's front door, but he doubted it.

Sally pushed the laptop away and sat back, rubbing tired eyes. 'But where does all this leave us? Thousands of miles from Paris. My head is spinning, my stomach unsettled, my legs as stable as the sea in a storm. The lead we have on the Amori is evaporating as we sit here. It's a long way from Southern Italy to France.'

Mason searched his brain for any way he could help, but short of hiring a fast boat and trying to make the south of France in half the time, it just wasn't possible.

The café door opened, and Quaid poked his head through. 'People,' he said. 'I've found us a fast way to France.'

Chapter 42

Roxy shielded her sunglass-covered eyes as she studied the windswept skies.

'I see something,' she said. 'Is that her?'

Mason squinted hard but all he could see was a distant black speck that could very well be a bird gliding in. Quaid was standing on tiptoes and craning his neck as if that might help. Both Sally and Hassell were sitting on a nearby rock with their socks in their hands, complaining about the cold and the fresh blisters on their feet.

Quaid sighed. 'She's late.'

'Is that normal?' Roxy asked.

Quaid gave her a vague look. 'Well, yeah, to be honest.'

Mason kept his eye on the ever-growing speck. It had taken them almost three hours of walking to find a small private airfield belonging to a wealthy friend of a friend of Quaid's which had been agreed upon as a meeting point for the ex-officer and yet another old friend.

This one was an American woman named Anya who worked in Italy as a freelance pilot just for the thrill of it, since she'd sold a well-known condiment concern for undisclosed millions just a few years ago. Quaid and Anya went 'way back'.

Apparently.

Now, Mason saw that the object approaching was indeed a plane, a Cessna Turbo Stationair: a fast and versatile six-passenger land-or-float plane. It could land anywhere from a dirt strip to the vast ocean and sported all the latest avionics. Mason walked clear of the makeshift runway as the white aircraft levelled off to touch down.

It bounced once and then a second time before the pilot eased off the throttle and coasted to a stop. Quaid gazed up through the cockpit window at the indistinct face staring back at him. 'Shit, she's pissed off.'

Mason raised an eyebrow. 'I thought you two were *old friends*.'

'We are. But that doesn't mean she won't throw me out of the plane.'

Unsure what to make of that and intrigued to find out, Mason followed the others around the side. A moment later the door cracked open.

A woman filled the gap, standing with her hands on her hips, glaring down at Quaid. 'And where the hell have you been?' She worked as she grouched, lowering a thin steel ladder to the ground. 'Come on, you guys. I thought you were in a hurry.'

Sally leapt forward, climbing before Anya had stopped speaking.

Mason studied the woman as he waited in line. Anya, still with her steely glare fixed on Quaid, had short blonde hair, fine cheekbones, full red lips, and the lithe figure of a person who spent a lot of time looking after herself. An astute glint glowed from her blue eyes, a gold Rolex from her wrist, and twin diamond bracelets from her ankles. She also carried a military knife holstered at the waist of her denim shorts, despite the cool weather, which left Mason with all sorts of questions.

Still, he climbed aboard the plane and took his seat whilst

Anya retrieved the ladder and sealed the door. With a last glare in Quaid's direction – that was studiously ignored as he found something overwhelmingly interesting to study outside the window – she returned to the cockpit and taxied the plane around.

'I filed a flight path to Paris as you asked,' she said. 'Don't worry. Private landing field and all that. Should be through in a matter of minutes.'

Sally thanked her before Mason could open his mouth. Anya told them to buckle up and sit back and then they were speeding down the dirt strip, the plane feeling far less smooth now that they were inside.

'Are you *aiming* for those ruts?' Quaid asked at one point.

Mason winced, fearing for the man. Anya turned around, still speeding towards a looming mountain, and fixed him with an even more intense glare. 'Don't like it? There's the door.'

She guided the plane to take-off speed before lifting them gracefully into the air. Mason hadn't always flown well in small planes, but it wasn't something you made everyone aware of. Not back in the Army. Now, he gripped the seat's leather armrests and stared ahead, wondering if there might be a mini bar and consoling himself with the fact that the plane was considerably better than the helicopter.

Roxy beat him to it. Even as the plane climbed, she unbuckled and opened a compartment in the front bulkhead. Anya turned as Roxy grabbed an armful of miniatures.

'You see any bourbon there,' the blonde said, 'throw it in my direction.'

Mason exchanged a worried glance with Quaid as Roxy laughed and left Anya with a generous supply before making her way back to her seat. She threw Mason three miniature whiskeys, extricated half a dozen Captain Morgans for herself, and looked at Sally and Hassell.

255

'Take the edge off?'

Sally took one, but Hassell told them he'd rather stay clear-headed and sank into his seat, eyes far away. Mason wondered if this was a good time to talk to the New Yorker, to get a feel for where his head was at. Hassell's priority was not the *Book of Secrets* – and Mason didn't blame him for that, knowing a little of what he was going through – but any amount of distraction or complacency now could get them killed.

As he deliberated, Anya levelled the plane off, knocked it into autopilot and unbuckled her seatbelt. Mason sensed a volcano about to erupt.

'Been a while, Quaid,' she said loud enough to grab his full attention.

'Thanks for coming to get us,' Quaid said weakly.

Anya knelt in one of the front seats, arms draped over the headrest. 'So, where've you been?' Her voice was dangerously even and soft. 'For the last four years?'

Roxy knocked back a miniature and watched Quaid closely. Mason averted his eyes, feeling a little embarrassment.

Quaid took a deep breath, but Anya couldn't help herself, bursting out with another barbed observation. 'And how the hell can anyone have thick black hair and light grey sideburns? Have you started dyeing it now? And which bit?'

Quaid sat forward. 'I had to get out,' he said. 'You know that.'

'Of the *Army*,' Anya allowed. 'I remember what you told me. I'm assuming we're all friends here, so I'll hold nothing back. Quaid here found a higher calling, a—'

'I've only just *met* them—'

'Close enough. Quaid here found a higher calling. Got pissed at the Army, the background politics, the endless agendas. He got sick of sending soldiers into harm's way, to start skirmishes in the interest of good old *England* so that fat old pricks could prosper. Sound right so far?'

Roxy looked like all she needed was a bag of popcorn. Mason started to move to a back seat but then thought better of it, not wanting to become the object of Anya's ire.

'Walking away like that was the hardest decision of my life,' Quaid protested. 'I—'

'Are we talking about the Army?' Anya snapped. 'Or me?' The timbre of her voice rose on the last word.

'Damn it,' Quaid breathed. 'I decided to go it alone. I used reliable contacts all over the world to send vital goods to desperate people. *My* contacts. People *I* supported and developed and befriended over twenty-five years of service. I eked out a living. Didn't charge much above cost. All to compensate for the mistakes I was forced to make as an officer. I worked twenty-four-seven. Didn't sleep or mess about. I had a useful network of friends, and I could do some good with that.'

Anya pursed her lips as the plane flew through a bank of wispy white clouds. 'And I helped you,' she said. 'Remember?'

'I put you in danger,' Quaid mumbled.

'Are you saying you left to protect me?'

Even Roxy winced as Quaid sought the correct answer. 'The truth is . . . we became too close.' He sighed. 'Every day I would wake thinking of you instead of my new goals. Every night the dreams became worse. I didn't think you'd let me go so . . .' Another sigh. 'I walked away.'

Anya studied his face, no doubt gauging the sincerity of his admission. Mason, having only just met her, had no idea how she would react and hoped it wouldn't put them in danger.

'Fool,' she vented eventually, standing up. 'I moved on after the first week. Got myself a pool boy, a car detailer and a window cleaner for those long days and nights. Turned out pretty well, to be honest.'

She turned away and returned to the cockpit, dismissing

257

Quaid. Mason tried to ignore the emotions struggling for control in the man's face. Roxy knocked back another tiny bottle of rum.

'How long till we land?' she asked nobody in particular.

Sally was tapping away at her laptop, oblivious to everything around her. 'Just over an hour to go.'

The Cessna motored north and then west without issue, transporting them safely through the clouds. Quaid retained his seat, watching Anya's back through the open cockpit door and no doubt aware that she didn't turn around once.

The door might be open, but it was most certainly blocked.

Anya gave them twenty minutes' warning before landing, but Mason could already see several famous landmarks through the window. In review, he didn't think their twelve-hour journey from Egypt to Paris had taken overly long, but the proof of that assumption lay 40,000 feet below.

If the Amori beat them to Sacré-Coeur, their desperate, breakneck mission was over. The secret society would deface the altar in any way possible, thus making it impossible for anyone to ever find their lair.

Then the Amori would be free to circulate the book.

Even now, they were racing towards potential disaster.

Mason took a deep breath as the plane came in to land.

Chapter 43

Marduk prepared himself for the most delicious, enjoyable phone call he would ever make, perhaps even the greatest moment of his life. The culmination of the Amori's lifelong mission and *he* was the man chosen to deliver the killing blow to the Vatican. *Well,* he amended mentally. *The first of several killing blows.*

He would make them pay for killing his daughter.

A vibrant energy hummed through his body, like a superior lifeblood, filling every part of him from his fingertips to his toes with vigour. Barely able to remain seated, he snaked his right arm towards the phone, but then saw his mobile phone screen start to flash.

Even now, they seek to deter my greater purpose.

Marduk snatched the device from the table and placed it to his ear. 'What is it? I'm busy. Are they dead?'

'It's Gido.'

'Yes, yes, I know who it is. What do you want?'

'They escaped. Still don't know how. The men think they had inside help.'

Marduk allowed himself a few silent moments of utter fury, of white-hot, blinding rage, before whetting his mind once more and pointing it at the problem. 'This is unacceptable. I thought you were supposed to be the best. Did you somehow manage to stumble across the next clue?'

'Sure.' Gido was as blithe as he was obtuse, so obtuse in fact that Marduk began to wonder if he was being played. Surely no gang leader could be this thick-headed.

'Then let's hear it. I need every clue delivered the moment you find it. Only then can I direct you onward.'

'Ibid, 27,' Gido said.

Marduk hesitated. 'Is that it?'

'Yeah, that's it.'

Marduk frowned hard into the middle distance. Of course, he should never have expected the answers to Heindl's clues to come easy. This was the code that Feroci had mentioned in passing. But there *was* something here. Somehow, the clue had to lead back to the book, that much was obvious. In this case, the clue itself had been contracted. And wasn't *ibid* in itself an abbreviation?

'Let me get back to you,' he said.

Furious at the interruption to his plans, Marduk contacted the two foremost academics in the Amori ranks. Men named Shippon and Chequer. Soon, he knew all about endnotes and bibliography citations, about scholarly references used to refer to the source cited in the indicated note. One of the men, Shippon, was currently perusing the *Book of Secrets* and did Marduk the service of examining footnote number 27.

'"*His Sacré Coeur, the Perpetual Adoration of His Last and First Rite,*"' Shippon said.

'How many footnotes are there in this book?' Marduk asked.

'Thousands.'

'Bring it to me now.'

Without thanking the man, Marduk wrote the phrase down and studied it for a long while before calling Gido back.

'I've spent my whole life immersed in their vain religion,' Marduk told him, 'and the story of their Christ. I can tell your men to travel to Paris and visit the Sacré-Coeur. Do not fail me again, Gido. The moment of *our* revelation is almost upon us.'

'Why wait?' Gido said. 'My old mom used to say – if there's something on your chest, cough it up. And it's not like I'm being paid for this damn job.'

Marduk held the phone away from his face, studying it as if it might have caught fire or been possessed by a demon. 'Do you know how many ways I could have you killed? Have you lost your mind?'

'Years ago, yeah.'

Marduk tried to see beyond this man's bonehead attitude to the greater good. 'The revelation, ravenously desired by the Amori for two thousand years, must come as flawlessly as it comes crushingly. Our sanctuary must be preserved. Do you understand?'

'Yeah, you don't want assholes stealing your thunder.'

'Time is of the essence,' Marduk snarled. 'Send your men to Paris to watch out for Joe Mason and the others. Find the next clue. *Do not* let them find it first.' He kept it as simple as possible. 'And Gido?'

'Yeah?'

'Get yourself to Rome.'

'Rome? Me? But isn't that where you—'

'Shut up. Just come to Rome with a selection of your best men and call me when you arrive. And do not fail me again, Gido. The consequences will rip you apart.'

A minute later, he was free. The office was dark, the atmosphere much lighter and the rain once more lashing against the windows.

Mason is headed for Paris and the fourth clue.

No matter. He was still two clues removed from locating the Amori's secret refuge and, although he didn't know it,

261

even further adrift from the place where Marduk and his disciples now lived. But that didn't allay the niggling fear at the back of Marduk's mind.

Mason had proved that he was good enough to succeed.

There was one more precaution he could put in place. Marduk had European contacts too. With another swift and direct call, he put as many men as were available in place to watch Sacré-Coeur, wishing he could trust them enough to send them inside. But this network comprised the homeless, doormen and taxi drivers, men and women paid to be the secret eyes of a city. Marduk and the Amori were tapped into every network in Europe and many in America.

Finally, he let out a pent-up breath, reached out a hand for the phone and lifted the handset from its cradle before putting it to his ear. Every movement, every moment, was savoured. This was *his* moment. Against the surging counterpoint of the torrential downpour outside, he pressed each backlit number in turn and listened to the whirring mechanisms as the call went through.

'This is Cardinal Feroci,' a voice he recognised answered.

'I hoped that it would be you again,' Marduk said.

'Who is this?'

'Oh, don't pretend that you do not know. Unless you're trying to trace the call, which is understandable but futile and a little disrespectful. I am Marduk, Monarch of the Amori.' His mouth split into a proud grin as he said it. 'You know me. Soon, *everyone* will know me.'

'You stole from the Vatican.'

'Oh, from those dusty old vaults? From your hermetically sealed coffins? Who cares? It is the great revelation that the world will remember.'

'The Christian spirit cannot be broken. The only truth is that Jesus Christ is a revelation of God in the flesh. You cannot threaten a conviction founded in everlasting belief.'

Marduk paused for a moment, wondering. 'One pope, one archivist,' he mused aloud. 'That is all that knows what is in the book. Tell me, Feroci, do you even *know* how badly I can hurt the Church?'

'I thought you were *the Amori*.'

Marduk was surprised to hear the somewhat feisty reply. Maybe Feroci was more than the puppet he appeared. 'You want to hear me say it?' he asked. 'To utter the blasphemy that will demolish two thousand years of adoration? I have it right here.'

Marduk let his eyes flick to the right, where the open *Book of Secrets* took up a good portion of the room on his desk. 'It's five or six inches thick, wrapped in a frayed crimson jacket. Its cover bears the Vatican's coat of arms. The edges are crumpled, the pages tatty. Not uniform, just messy. There is no title and there does not need to be. The pages within tell all.' He paused and then said, 'Don't they?'

Feroci sighed. 'If what you're saying is true, then explain this – why would the Vatican keep such a dangerous volume?'

'A question with more than one answer, *arrogance* being the one that immediately springs to mind. *Complacency*, another. But mostly it is – *necessity*. You couldn't destroy the book because it's not the only proof. *You found the body, didn't you?*'

Feroci's silence gave Marduk licence to embellish. 'And there's not a force or emotion on Earth that would make the Church dispose of it properly, is there? Even though it's not everything you hoped it would be.'

Marduk licked his lips, relishing the delicious silence for a moment before continuing. 'Jesus Christ was not adulated, was not worshipped in the universally accepted manner claimed by the Church. He was not the Son of God. The great religious leader. Jesus Christ was *entirely* . . . something else.'

Cardinal Feroci was audibly agitated, his breathing heavy.

Marduk wondered if he was taping the call and regretting it. That would be delightful. Maybe the Swiss Guard and the Vatican City Police were listening in.

Marduk turned the screws. 'Jesus Christ was a warrior, a legendary king. A leader of armies. Yes, a hero, but a hero who carried a sword and a shield. Back in the old days, in the Dark Ages, in the world of savages and peasants, do you think they venerated priests and religious saviours? No, most fell in behind strong warriors. Men or women who could protect them, their families and their villages. They *worshipped*, trusted and followed the alpha warrior, because he could *save* them with men-at-arms, with brawn, an aptitude for violence and diplomacy, with a blood-stained sword and a pockmarked shield.'

'Jesus Christ is the saviour of mankind,' Feroci managed.

'Not the saviour of mankind. He was its *greatest warrior*.'

Feroci was panting as if he'd just completed a marathon, as if fury and brimstone were coursing through his veins. 'There is no precedent, no proof . . . How can you possibly believe this . . . this *desecration*?'

'And therein sits the second great lie,' Marduk said smugly. 'Do you really think I would go this far without proof? Search your soul, Feroci. Where's *your* proof? The remnants of a cross? A shroud? A few tall tales? The Bible?' Marduk laughed. 'We have our own bible. We call it the Creed. Do you recognise this text and the smouldering core to which it refers? *"For all the nations have drunk of the wine of the passion of her immorality, and the kings of the earth have committed acts of immorality with her, and the merchants of the earth have become rich by the wealth of her sensuality."'*

Marduk waited, the sinful verses of the Book of Revelation running through his mind, all the hateful references, as Feroci debated how he should answer.

'Revelation 18:3,' Feroci finally said.

'Is that it? Your Book of Revelation seeks to destroy that which we created with its hateful prejudice.'

'I don't understand your reference to a "smouldering core". And what did you create?'

'A once-great city now sunk beneath the sand. One that shall rise again. One that shall breathe again. Old Babylon.'

Chapter 44

'*Old* Babylon? I don't—'

Marduk bit though the cardinal's confusion. 'Stay on topic, Feroci. The second great lie, remember? Do you know what it is?'

'I do not have to listen to this.'

'And yet you will because you know that I have your book. That I hold your future in my hands. You have watched the short video example we uploaded and there is more to come in a few minutes. The second great lie the Church told is that the body of Jesus was—'

A sudden commotion filled the airwaves, the sound of Cardinal Feroci snapping at aides and law enforcement officials to stand down, to hang up, to stop listening. That act, as much as any other, told Marduk that Feroci knew all about the desperate magnitude of the Church's crisis and that they were terrified.

Minutes passed. Marduk allowed Feroci the time to settle himself, knowing the coming exposure would hit him that much harder.

'Your fabrications may intrigue the faithless,' Feroci said. 'Amuse the agnostics. But they will never—'

'Oh, shut up.' Marduk had heard enough of the cardinal's

waffle. 'The body of Jesus Christ was recovered long ago. Yet another secret that cannot be revealed. You couldn't destroy it, so you stored it and preserved it somewhere with top-secret classification. Never to be seen by ordinary eyes.'

'That's an absurd accu—'

'Backed by *fact*. The *Book of Secrets* tells all. Will you deny it so easily when the disreputable rags have access to it? When your shame drowns you? When the great infrastructure shudders? Will you produce the body then? *Can you?* Was it left in the same state that it was found?'

'Historical fact will corroborate Christianity's statement of belief.'

'Historical fact *proves* that the majority, the uneducated, poor people of the time, respected and followed strong warriors. Security was the only god they needed, the strength of a powerful leader. Historical fact will *prove* that the body of Jesus Christ was discovered in a grand tomb, surrounded by the paraphernalia of war. All manner of items and scripts filled this warrior's resting place. But, by then, your Bible was prevalent, and you had already painted him as a religious redeemer who had risen from the dead. You couldn't exactly change your minds.' Marduk laughed. 'And so the lies were sown, the secret buried, the evidence ignored.'

'You cannot stay hidden for ever,' Feroci hissed. 'And when we find you . . .'

It was a good point, and gave Marduk a slight jolt. It also made him wonder about the capabilities of Joe Mason. 'And how's that investigation going?' Marduk snorted, wanting to say more but holding onto the secret knowledge that Gianluca Gianni, the commander of the Swiss Guard, was working for the Amori in return for the lives of his wife and daughter.

'But listen,' he went on. 'The day is almost upon us. The final revelation is imminent. One more day perhaps? Two?'

Marduk laughed, imagining his adversary's discontent but revealing nothing of Joe Mason's quest. He had no intention of giving the cardinal any hope. 'You will have to wait upon the whim of your new masters.'

Feroci emitted a strained grunt. 'We are patient. God is eternal. You do not seem to be able to grasp that faith is not tangible. Those called have no choice but to see the light. You cannot simply abolish something untouchable.'

'Let's see, shall we? You think you know us? You think you know the Babylon that was identified and destroyed in the Book of Revelation? Think on this: *that* Babylon was a city of seven hills. It was Babel. Victorinus, around AD 280, wrote about "the great overthrow of Babylon" which, in reality, didn't happen until centuries later. What great state was actually overthrown at *that* time, I wonder . . .' Marduk allowed a moment to play on Feroci's fears. 'The mystery religions of Babylon paganised Christianity and were the source of religious rites upheld by the Church.'

'The mystery religions were cast out.'

'Exactly. But to where? You know where, don't you?'

'Rome,' Feroci said, his voice a mere whisper.

'The Babylon of Revelation *was Rome.* The very place your church chose to build its Vatican. Revelation 18:24,' Marduk said. '". . . *in her was found the blood of prophets and of saints . . .*" Does that sound like a description of a sinful Babylon to you? Or some other, more venerated capital like Rome? You people know nothing of the ancient city, of history, of the Amori.'

'I know that you are mad.'

'Ah, is that because I don't share your beliefs? Maybe two thousand years of your festering lies have tipped us over the edge. But the next thousand will be *ours*.'

'Reveal your proof. We are not afraid of you.' With that, Cardinal Feroci hung up on Marduk.

If the act had been designed to show defiance or scepticism, or to enrage Marduk, it paid off. The Amori leader slammed the handset into the cradle three and then four times, smashing the plastic and sending shards to every corner of the room. Livid, he threw the device to the floor, rose and paced to the window overlooking the vast, shining city.

In the distance, the grand dome of the Basilica of St Peter shone, the bastion of the great Church.

It was time for another lesson in leadership. Marduk picked up his mobile phone and dialled a number. The call was answered quickly.

'Yes?'

'Is that you, Masterton? Good. Come to my office. I have something I'd like to explain to you.'

Marduk sat down, wreathed in a delicious cocoon of simmering rage. Masterton had already proved to be the outspoken one, the fool who questioned Marduk's motives and even his commitment. Masterton had questioned Marduk's state of mind, his reasoning when Nina had been brutally murdered by the Church.

Marduk wanted to set that line of query straight.

The knock came. Masterton entered. Marduk rose to meet him, allowing the man to enjoy radiating that supercilious smile one last time. He shivered inside as the rage and the passion began to grow. The passion inside him was the glowing future of the Amori, everything they could become.

'You have an explanation?' Masterton began, questioning, his tone that of a man comfortable in his skin, in his position, in his superiority.

Marduk pinned him with hooded eyes. 'You think Nina is dead, don't you?'

Masterton frowned in confusion. 'Your daughter? Yes, and it was you who ordered her shot in cold blood.'

'Nina is not dead.'

Masterton swallowed several times and then leaned

269

forward. 'I saw her body. In the crime scene photographs. They were the ultimate proof of your failure.'

'No,' Marduk grated. 'Nina is not dead. She is alive, in the Amori pantheon. In our history. In our souls; souls that look four thousand years into the past. Nina will never die because she is a hero. Her sacrifice was a beautiful and necessary feat.'

Masterton's face fell. 'You are crazier than I thought. Already, I have put the word about that you are not fit for this office. Already, they question you. Already—'

Marduk put an end to his spiel. The razor-sharp knife in his hand ripped across Masterton's abdomen, cutting deep. Masterton's mouth opened in shock, his eyes blinked rapidly and then he was just standing there, trying to hold his stomach together as Marduk laughed.

As Marduk danced from foot to foot before him. 'I am the rightful monarch of the Amori. *Me*. Nobody will dethrone me. Nobody will question me. Not you. Not *anyone*.'

He stepped away, grinning, as Masterton's entrails slithered onto the floor. It was a splendid sight, a deserved and pleasing spectacle. Marduk recalled passages in the Amori bible, called the Creed, where murder could be interpreted as justifiable when taken in the right context.

What better context could there be than a challenge to his leadership?

Just then, there came a knock at the door. Marduk gave Ruben leave to enter and once more experienced a delicious shiver of anticipation. Ruben carried his laptop and a sly grin.

'Would you like me to return later?'

Marduk noted the hungry glint in Ruben's eyes as he watched Masterton die, the desire of a dormant killer. Perhaps that was something they could explore together. Later.

'I am ready to upload the second piece,' Ruben said, turning away from the mess that was Masterton and taking a seat at Marduk's desk. He placed his laptop carefully on the polished surface.

Marduk placed himself directly behind the man. 'You followed my instructions?'

'To the letter. We got through all the methods of proof and how it will be published. The influential scholars of society who will test our claim. And we begin to hint at an incredible new truth – a revelation – surrounding Jesus Christ and his body. His remains.'

'And the first video has captured their imagination?'

'Of many,' Ruben said a little warily. 'The viewership is growing. Subscriptions are doubling by the hour, especially as the hour of the second release grows near. Many are aware that history is about to change.'

'I want more,' Marduk said. 'More followers. More drama. More coverage. This beautiful torment is already bringing the Vatican to its knees. I want it crushed.'

'I could embellish . . .' Ruben began uncertainly.

'No, release the second video and make sure it reaches every dark and dirty corner of social media. We will turn up the heat significantly with the third.'

Marduk watched as Ruben readied the upload. Seconds later, his index finger hovered over the 'enter' button. 'Now?'

'One moment,' Marduk breathed deeply, turned and studied the shining Christian dome in the distance. His enemy had lit up the night sky one too many times. 'Now,' he said.

Ruben smashed the button and emitted a nasty laugh. 'Enjoy, world,' he whispered.

Marduk, in a slice of irony, found himself trapped in the same inexorable dilemma as the Church had been for centuries. They couldn't obliterate history. The old sanctuary, which Mason and his team were hunting, could reveal where the Amori now resided; but, for ancient and important reasons, it couldn't be defaced or destroyed. It shouldn't be touched.

Shouldn't.

How's that for absurdity? For irony? Marduk tried to smile at the contrary nature of fate, but the rain-soaked window only reflected a nauseating grimace. Fortune wasn't arbitrary, it was squeezed from hard work, intelligence and guile.

Marduk looked within himself, at all that he had accomplished, and found a place from where he could start to fashion a smile. Building on that, he considered when might be the best time to call a press conference.

Once Mason was taken care of.

Chapter 45

Gianluca Gianni wept, caught in excruciating circumstances. He was a proud man, a strong man and a man of faith but there were fewer trials harder to face than being forced to watch the torment of your own family.

Marduk's latest proof-of-life exercise included his wife and daughter being subjected to Marduk's wrath. There were no obvious bruises, no cuts and no blood shed. But the mental trauma would last a lifetime.

Gianni cried for them, sitting alone at home. An uneaten meal lay on the floor to his right, a bottle of cheap alcohol to his left. No matter how hard he tried, he couldn't stop seeing his daughter's face.

Aria, I am so sorry.

He believed there was a safe place in the arms of the Saviour. He placed faith and hope in God. But life was precarious, a hard truth he'd been taught since the very beginning. *Life is precarious.* Gianni had built his life on the rock-solid foundation of the Word of God. Tonight, those foundations were being tested to their fullest extent.

Perhaps God was the only true, safe place but surely *family* should come a close second. The knowledge beat at him with serrated wings. On the physical plane, at least, family was exalted. Gianni's faith kept him grounded, kept him sane. One issue was that he couldn't talk to anyone about his suffering. Another was that he was betraying the very cornerstone of his existence. The people he'd known and served for years. But his position was utterly indefensible.

Gianni watched the TV screen, having inserted a flash drive into one of its sockets. His wife and daughter were tied to chairs inside a prison-like room with no windows. They were blindfolded and gagged. A man who'd already introduced himself as Marduk prowled around them, front and back, jabbing a taser at them, letting them hear the electric spark that snapped between its electrodes. Gianni watched his family flinch, cry . . . and then scream.

Marduk pressed the taser to his wife's cheek and then paused, looking directly up at the camera. An evil, sly smirk crossed his face as he moved over to Aria.

Gianni closed his eyes but was unable to unhear the muffled scream. A small television played in the background, tuned to a news channel that clearly displayed the time and date on screen. This had happened just a few hours ago whilst Gianni had been working frantically for Marduk. As Gianni furthered the madman's plans within the Vatican, the madman harmed that which he most loved.

Gianni watched as the entire eighteen-minute video played out. The only thing he could be thankful for was that Marduk hadn't sunk to even ghastlier depths, although Gianni dreaded to think of the future.

Marduk ended his presentation with a few words. The footage cut quickly from the prison room to an office setting, to Marduk sitting comfortably, a tumbler full of spirit in one hand, a white handkerchief in the other. On closer inspection Gianni saw that the handkerchief was wrapped around Marduk's open palm.

'The good news, my dear Gianni, is that your involvement is almost over. I need you to keep them working against each other for a few more days. I do love your descriptions of the in-fighting and even the disbelief. The indecision in many annoys me, but I am sure that's just normal human behaviour. Anyway, do you want the bad news?'

Marduk paused even though this wasn't a live conversation. He knew the distress it would cause Gianni.

'This is your wife's blood,' Marduk turned his hand so that his knuckles pointed toward the camera. Fresh crimson had soaked through the white material.

Gianni's heart fell through the floor.

'This woman, this Gemma, she chose to scream and shout when I removed her gag. I was forced to shut her up.' Marduk shrugged. 'It wasn't without some pleasure.'

The screen faded to black. Gianni's head fell and he reached for the bottle. Tomorrow, he would try as hard as today. Tomorrow, he would fight for his family by manipulating the Church.

His two most loved commitments forced to war with each other.

The alternative was unthinkable.

Chapter 46

Sacré-Coeur stood atop Montmartre, the highest point of the city of Paris, built of white travertine stone and symbolic of nationalist themes. A three-arched portico was embellished with equestrian statues of the saints Joan of Arc and King Louis IX, above which the grand dome rose and offered a spectacular 360-degree view of Paris, where the clusters of stone and winding streets that had become famous monuments of history sprawled all the way to the stunning Eiffel Tower, the Arc de Triomphe and the Musée d'Orsay. A whole map of illustrious times gone by in one expansive view that caught the eye in every direction.

Standing amid the crowd flowing around the foot of an extensive staircase that led up to the bronze front doors of Sacré-Coeur, Mason drifted into the shadows cast by nearby trees. No matter where he turned, hundreds of people filled his field of vision. The Amori's men could be scattered among the vast acres, watching out for them.

Mason's ears were filled with passing chatter, with jingling chimes from a nearby carousel, with booming music from an unknown direction and excess yelling from aggressive street vendors trying to force their goods on nervy tourists.

Most importantly, Mason saw a worrying number of

French gendarmes. No telling if they'd been alerted by the Swiss Guard, the Vatican City Police, the Italian Carabinieri or darker, shadier forces. Even if it was a response to some other security threat, their presence meant that walking straight through the front door was out of the question.

'Nothing's easy,' Roxy sighed at his side, having also spotted the impediment. 'It's probably for the best though.'

Mason understood the vague comment: they'd be forced to employ a certain craftiness in evading detection rather than trusting to sheer luck. Before, they'd been ahead of the Amori. Now . . . they weren't so sure. The last time they'd seen the Amori had been two nights ago in Israel, thousands of miles distant. The Amori knew exactly where Mason was headed and would have put their entire network on high alert. Getting into the basilica unnoticed was out of the question unless . . .

'Fall back,' he said.

'New plan?' Hassell asked.

'Yeah, *yours*.'

Walking away, and with Hassell still limping slightly, they regrouped under the overhanging branches of a large tree. Mason, worried by the passage of time, deferred to Hassell's intention to concoct a swift plan. Roxy and Quaid kept an eye out for anyone taking an interest in them.

'The situation calls for a sudden, loud distraction,' Hassell told them. 'Nothing aggressive. We don't want to shut the place down. But it has to be enough to grab their attention.'

Sally straightened her backpack. 'Please,' she said. 'Just make it quick.'

'Give me an hour,' Hassell said, walking away.

Mason made a non-committal gesture at Roxy, who returned a supportive smile. Mason was struck by Roxy's different demeanour in the field; all her struggles faded away and she became positive, purposeful and compelling. It was what she needed. New encounters created firm bandages that covered old, open wounds.

They turned towards Sacré-Coeur and studied the flow of the crowd heading up the steps, the position of the authorities. They bought and then donned hats and coats and fixed sunglasses to their faces, fake veneers that wouldn't make them conspicuous in the crisp, cold but sunny winter's day.

With time to kill and preferring to remain relatively well concealed, they searched out a ropey café on a quiet backstreet. They ordered drinks and spent the entire hour listening to Quaid elevating the merits of the endangered manual gearbox over the new-fangled, paddle-shift semi autos.

Mason eventually got drawn in after listening for fifteen minutes, unable to help himself. 'Dinosaur waffle,' he said. 'You'd rather spend a full second or so changing gear and waiting for the right engine note, rather than making a couple of shifts in the blink of an eye?'

Quaid paused with his cup halfway to his mouth. 'It's a skill.'

'So was manual TV channel changing, but look what happened to that when they released the remote.'

Mason tuned Quaid out, joining Roxy in a sombre examination of their surroundings. It didn't help. He found himself counting down the minutes and grew frustrated when sixty became sixty-five and then seventy.

'You think he's okay?' Roxy asked. 'Gido will have instructed his goons to be on the lookout for him.'

Mason rubbed his forehead. 'I've been thinking the same thing. I should have gone with him.'

'No, *one* of us should have gone with him. Didn't have to be you.'

Taking on too much responsibility will leave only a burned-out shell of you. Mason recalled his ex-wife Hannah's words when she'd recognised what he was going through.

'Yeah,' he said aloud. 'You're right.'

'Who's staying outside?' Sally asked.

Mason shook his head. 'What do you mean?'

'I mean, who's staying outside and looking after the backpacks? They'll check for weapons and stuff at the doors.'

Aware that he should have considered that, Mason addressed it now. 'Hassell,' he said. 'He can stay out of sight and use one of the two-way radios to keep us apprised. *And* stay clear of Gido's men.'

Roxy almost leapt out of her seat when her mobile rang. 'You're late.'

Mason watched her listen for thirty seconds, not enjoying the range of emotions creasing her face: everything from surprise to disbelief to suspicion. 'Where's the car?' she asked at one point, and 'You think that'll work?' at another; but, by then, Hassell was gone.

'Hurry.' She rose so quickly the collection of empty mugs on their table rattled. 'We gotta move.'

Mason struggled to keep up as Roxy slammed through the café's exit door and marched out into the cold day. Quaid and Sally rushed after them. Roxy ran until she saw the ninety steps leading up to Sacré-Coeur.

Mason fought through the thick, milling crowd to catch up. 'What the hell is going on, Rox?'

Hassell was rushing at them as fast as his bruised ankle would allow. Mason only recognised him when he smiled. 'Hey!'

A commotion broke out on the steps behind him.

Mason's eyes widened as more than a dozen people came together, shouting. Placards appeared from nowhere. People donned masks. A chant went up, high and rhythmic. Six or seven more people joined the group from higher up the steps.

Hassell jumped onto the grassy hill beside the staircase. Mason and the others, seeing the blockage twenty feet above, followed suit. The chanting voices joined and rose in volume, attracting massive attention. Their freshly painted signs jabbed furiously at the air above their heads.

'We should move quickly,' Hassell said as they joined him. 'I was forced to use a contact known to Gido.'

'What the hell is this?' Roxy asked, falling in alongside the American.

'A pop-up distraction.' Hassell grinned.

Mason caught up, striding upward. 'A flash mob?'

'A flash mob?' Roxy blurted. 'What they gonna do next? Start singing *The Greatest Showman*?'

'A flash *protest*,' Hassell corrected them. 'You know the French. Always ready to be part of an angry uprising. Flash protests are all the rage these days. Mostly, I guess, because they can't be prevented.'

Mason liked the unconventional means by which Hassell had created the distraction. 'And what happens when they all get arrested?'

'Flash protesters melt away as quickly as they appear,' Hassell said. 'Ten minutes and they're out.'

'Hence the hurry.' Quaid appeared on their far left, climbing the hill with his head down. 'Don't look right.'

They were passing the main contingent of police who, to a man, were facing the protesters. Mason cast a quick glance around. Nobody was taking any interest in them. 'Good job,' he said.

'Thanks, but this only works for a few minutes.'

Taking the cue, Mason sped up. Together, they came to the top of Montmartre and faced the triple bronze doors.

'This truly is a church dedicated to the heart of Jesus Christ,' Sally said as they approached. 'Depictions of the Last Supper, the multiplication of the loaves, the conversion of Mary Magdalene and more adorn the doors. Sculptured upon the triple-arch peristyle we're about to enter are three scenes that proclaim, justify and validate the action of the Sacred Heart; namely Moses bringing forth water from the rock, the soldier piercing Jesus's side after his death, and the apostle Saint Thomas touching the wounds of the risen Christ.'

'Any idea where the altar might be?' Roxy asked.

Sally didn't answer. Mason followed her indoors through the opening and then into the central nave, a vast, high-domed space supported by four great pillars, which inspired a sense of awe and a desire to pause and absorb.

The ceiling above the altar exhibited one of the largest mosaics in the world, beneath which was a huge pipe organ, recognised as a national monument. Moving on, the Chapel of the Blessed Virgin displayed nine beautiful stained-glass windows above and opposite a large statue of Saint Peter on a marble base.

Mason nudged Sally as they passed. 'Saint Peter,' he said.

'Yes, it's a reproduction of the statue in Vatican City,' she said, then hesitated. 'You think it could be a marker of sorts?'

Mason shrugged. 'Jacques Heindl lived, worked and slept in the Vatican. He was here when this church broke ground. What better marker could there be?'

Sally didn't look convinced, but nodded along a line of wooden pews to where an openwork bronze-chased gate stood closed before an impressive chancel housing a white marble altar. The floor was a carpet of many-hued marble tiles: white and dark-blue curlicues against a light-blue background with antique red and African yellow motifs.

The great altar, made of Carrara marble, stood beyond, watched over by Our Lady of Peace, a prodigious statue of the Virgin Mary with Jesus on her knees, holding an olive branch.

Mason was able to see it all in great detail, just seconds before a bustling coach party crammed into the chapel and took up every square inch of space.

'You're kidding me,' Roxy growled. 'Now how're we supposed to get close?'

Mason backed away. 'We'll come back later,' he proposed.

'We got lucky in Jerusalem and even Bethlehem,' Sally said. 'Can't win them all. And, still, there's the chapels of Saint Benedict, Saint John the Baptist and many others to inspect for altars.'

Mason updated Hassell by two-way radio and followed Sally into the various chapels lining the interior walls of Sacré-Coeur. For some time, they toured the niches and corners, doing their best to hide Sally's movements as she bent to examine each and every altar, waiting their turn as the crowds ebbed and flowed.

Time marched by. Hassell informed them that the sun was sinking outside and the temperature falling. No one had said finding the altar would be easy, but Mason was seriously starting to wonder if they needed to find a place to hide when the doors closed tonight. Roxy was quick to tell Hassell that it was toasty warm inside the basilica and she was thinking about shedding some layers.

It wasn't, and *she* wasn't, Mason knew. The temperature within the sacred white walls was way south of cool, kept manageable only by the mass of warm human bodies crowded within. They had completed their tour of the outer chapels, all but one, and were becoming somewhat desperate, wondering if they'd perhaps missed something as they approached the Chapel of the Blessed Virgin once again, when Sally stopped dead and bit her lip.

'I should have realised,' she said. 'This could easily be the place.'

Mason stared at the guide map in her hands. 'The Chapel of the Physicians,' he said. 'What makes you—'

'Jacques Heindl,' she said, '*was* a physician. He studied to be a doctor before turning to the Church, remember?'

Without waiting for an answer, she rushed into the niche

and dropped to her knees beside a low guardrail. Mason, Roxy and Quaid crowded behind her, trying to block access to the more intimate chapel.

Mason's heart was in his mouth. Would they find that Gido's men had already been here and defaced the altar? Gido was new to this chase and had come a long way to get started. The only positive alternative idea he could cling to was that the basilica's inhabitants surely kept archival records more plentiful than those listed on the internet and would have some notation describing the altar's text. The issue then would be how to access any archives.

But by now Sally was swift and practised at her job, and, after some serious scrubbing and grousing, finally rose to her feet.

'Done,' she said and returned their expectant stares with a grin. 'It's not great, but we got it.'

Mason cheered on the inside before radioing Hassell and telling him they were on their way. A brief study of the crowd discovered it weaving towards the exit in search of evening activities and restaurants, but also revealed two stern expressions turned their way.

When Mason met the eyes of the suspect men, they turned away and pretended to study nearby marble pillars, but two other figures now started to work their way against the crowd.

'Mercs don't fit,' Roxy said, also seeing them. 'They assume this brutal appearance that makes them stand out.'

'They have the exit covered,' Quaid said. 'Which means . . .'

'They're outside too,' Mason finished. 'This is the Amori. I'll warn Hassell.'

Sally shrank away. 'You mean we're trapped?'

'Maybe,' Mason said. 'Is there another way out? I don't want to have to fight our way out of here.'

Sally gawped. 'Considering where we are, neither do I. Listen, I might be able to find us a different way out.'

Quaid joined the shifting crowd as it undulated by, joined seconds later by the others. Sally pulled out her phone and googled Sacré-Coeur so that she could better study the building's blueprint. Standing once more in front of the main chancel, shoulder to shoulder with cheerful tourists, she took a moment to log into the cloud account holding her father's notes, and started flicking between screens.

'He studied Sacré-Coeur too?' Mason asked.

'Of course. It's one of the most important basilicas in Europe.'

'And what are you hoping to find?' Roxy asked.

'A secret,' Sally said. 'Any secret. A secret to save our lives.'

Chapter 47

'There.' Sally jabbed at her phone. 'I think.'

Mason peered over her shoulder. 'What?'

'The crypt. It's also a tourist haven. If we can reach the crypt we can get outside without being spotted. Accessed *outside* the basilica, at the bottom of the staircase where we started off, it houses tombs, monuments, statues and the foundation stone of the basilica. Many side chapels too.'

'The point?' Roxy kept a surreptitious eye on the mercenaries searching the crowd.

'The point is that it can be accessed from *in here*, though it's a little-known fact. My father was granted access eight years ago, which meant he could travel quickly between the crypt and the church.'

'Makes sense.' Mason nodded. 'The priests wouldn't want to be forced to use the outside steps five times a day. Where's the entrance?'

'East wing, beside the chapel of Saint Margaret Mary. There's a corridor. The access should be there behind a door marked *Private*.'

'Your father was extremely thorough,' Mason said.

'You have no idea.' Sally spoke in a long-suffering

whisper. She led the way, moving with the crowd. Mason risked a quick glance behind but saw only a bobbing sea of people.

Reaching the east wing, Sally turned north. Quaid and Roxy flanked her. Mason brought up the rear, firing glances like barbs to all sides. Roxy was on the two-way to Hassell, instructing him to verify if the crypt exit harboured any threat, as Sally vanished from sight.

Mason's heart leapt before he realised she'd ducked into the aforementioned corridor. Roxy went next. Quaid glanced back at Mason before following.

A couple of tourists wearing beige jackets and beige hats and with matching binoculars hanging from their necks barged in front of Mason and then decided it was a great idea to put on the brakes. He didn't slow, but used his elbows to jab them out of the way.

As he reached the right turn, he saw the others ahead of him, having ducked under a red rope to gain access to a dark, wood-panelled hallway.

Sally stood facing a closed door, and gave it a gentle knock.

Mason assumed that was in case anyone was inside. Before joining her, he took the chance to scan the basilica once more, trying to identify their enemies in the crowd, and was unsurprised to see them following, catching up.

A face leapt out at him.

Lean and carved from bad choices, the face didn't belong here. Mason saw the cold eyes lock onto his, a grim smile creep across the face, and realised he'd been staring too long.

Cursing, he spun towards Sally. '*Move!*'

She twisted the handle, but the door didn't budge.

Roxy pushed her aside, lifted a boot and kicked out at the lock. Three kicks splintered it, the sound of cracking wood loud even in the noisy church.

The door sagged inward.

Roxy shouldered it all the way open. Mason was behind them, urging them inside. Roxy entered first, followed by Sally.

Mason pushed Quaid in and then tried to close the broken door, succeeding only in dragging its shattered frame noisily across the stone floor. He looked around for something to drag in front of it, saw a pile of boxes half full of cleaning supplies and shoved them against the inside.

'That's not gonna hold them for long,' he said.

'Are you kidding?' Roxy asked, looking around. 'This is a *storeroom*.'

Mason saw brooms and mops, cardboard boxes, tools and coats organised in neat rows against all four walls. The room was tiny, barely large enough to fit all four of them inside. Mason guessed they had about half a minute.

'Are we in the right place?'

Sally gave him an annoyed look and swept the mops aside to reveal another old door beneath the draping of coats and hats, this one equipped with an old bronze handle and no lock. One downwards thrust of the handle cracked it open. Sally hit the light switch to the right side of the door.

Roxy leapt through the opening first. Mason got a quick glimpse of a steep stone stairwell and rough walls, before Sally filled the gap and then Quaid. The small room emptied.

Mason waited his turn. When it came, he took four steps across the room, hoping their luck would hold out; but before he could slip away, the outer door shuddered under a solid blow and then flew back hard against its hinges.

The cold-faced man stood there, grinning, and this close, Mason saw the network of old and new scars covering both his cheeks. The guy was a solid unit, broad-shouldered with thick, well-muscled arms and an easy way of holding himself. Mason saw training in that stance, and braced himself.

'Mason, isn't it?' the guy growled. 'Yeah, we checked you out after Bethlehem, your careers. Mason and Banks and some washed-up officer called Quaid. And then there's Luke Hassell. Where is he?'

Mason braced for an attack, but became aware that Quaid was hovering just out of sight at the top of the stairwell. It was a crucial moment and required a pivotal decision. Did he send Quaid away to safeguard the others' escape, or enlist his aid in the inevitable fight to the death that was about to happen?

'Go,' Mason said after several seconds. 'I can handle this.'

Self-belief flooded him with energy. The merc forced his bulk through the door with an effort, grinning around the tiny room. 'Name's Pascal,' he said. 'I think I'll kill you by sticking that mop down your throat.'

Mason believed he'd certainly try, and prepared an attack, but before he could strike, Pascal held up a hand.

'Hassell,' he said. 'You shouldn't defend that asshole. Got his girl killed and crawled to Gido for help. Gido picked him outta the gutter, saved his ass.'

Mason sought to give Roxy and the others time to escape and answered, 'Hassell was a cop.'

'Rookie kid back then. Gido taught him everything he knows. You can't trust Hassell, man. He'll cut your legs out from under you.'

Still speaking the last word, Pascal attacked.

Mason blocked. The sound of his striking fists and rustling jacket was amplified by the small room, the violence seemingly increased because neither man uttered a sound as they fought.

Mason parried a right and then a left, struck back with an elbow, and found himself unbalanced by a cardboard box. The right-hand wall was close enough to catch his fall and he rebounded off it. He ducked under Pascal's swing and drove two jabs into his ribcage.

Pascal barely flinched. He slammed an elbow onto

Mason's exposed neck. Mason surged up, his skull catching the tip of his opponent's chin, staggering him. Pascal raised an arm.

Mason threw punch after punch, each a short, devastating blow aimed at a vulnerable area, pursuing the advantage.

Pascal backed off, coming up against the damaged door. As Mason delivered a solid overhead blow, Pascal fell to his knees, changing the flow of the battle. Mason adjusted.

Pascal thrust up from his knees, a tin of paint clutched in one hand, and swung it at Mason's chin. The can caught him a solid blow, making him see dark motes for a second. By the time he recovered, Pascal was raining blows at him.

A fist smashed against his left cheek, another glanced off his forehead.

Mason covered up and kicked out, landing a satisfying blow against the other man's knee which brought him up short and made him gasp.

Mason struck again, elbows and uppercuts bringing the most success in the limited space. He paced back and forth, a boxer in a tiny ring, using the skills he'd learned from an early age and taking the punishment expected.

He got in close, stifling Pascal's attempt at an offensive, then punched and headbutted the man, drawing streams of blood.

When Pascal fell to his knees, Mason grabbed a paint-spattered steel rod and lashed it down at the man's head. The nearby wall made it impossible to utilise his full strength, but Pascal yelled out in pain and collapsed to the floor.

Mason upended the rod so that its tip pointed downwards and slammed it into Pascal's stomach, ribs and chest.

Pascal squirmed, his face creased in agony, but then managed to catch the rod as Mason raised it for the fourth time.

Pascal kicked out.

Pain exploded in Mason's shins. He sprang back, but Pascal dived across the floor in pursuit.

The mercenary hooked the handle of another tin and swung both at Mason, finishing by throwing them up at his face.

Mason retreated, still holding the steel extension rod.

'Not bad for a British grunt who got his men killed,' Pascal breathed.

Mason went still as an emotional bolt impaled him, electrifying his synapses and giving his mind full focus.

When Pascal rose, Mason was ready, jabbing twice, stiffened fingers spearing into the soft flesh of the man's throat.

As Pascal choked, Mason threw a devastating full-strength punch which smashed the other man's eye socket. Pascal was strong and resilient and kept coming, but Mason saw it all as if he were viewing the battle from above, anticipating the attacks with ease.

He deflected and returned strikes before Pascal could blink, barely moving his feet, drawing on experience and training, as well as years of combat in the ring and, later, in the Army.

It all came flooding back.

Mason was immovable. Combat had never been graceful or dignified. It was a tooth-and-nail melee, a grunting, spitting, grasping, blood-smeared fight for life after which one man would never breathe air nor feel the sun on his face ever again. Mason was determined not to be that man.

But most of all, as Pascal retaliated, resisted and strove to break him, Mason realised that this was him at his best, that he'd been holding back during this mission and every other event since Mosul. He knew that failure today was not an option.

This unavoidable confrontation in this tiny room had laid it all bare: the struggle and the restraint. He'd moved forwards even as he'd laid it on the line to help Sally escape, to give Roxy and Quaid time to escort her out, to prevent any pursuit.

After one final uppercut, Pascal collapsed unmoving before him. Mason stepped over the prone figure, grabbed the edge of the fractured door and shoved it closed, finishing with a shoulder barge that inserted it back into its frame. Clearly, Pascal hadn't told anyone where he was going, and his accomplices hadn't discovered the storeroom yet.

He considered searching the storeroom for rope to tie Pascal's hands but decided taking the time wouldn't be as productive as getting the hell out of there.

Seconds later, he exited the room and pounded down a narrow stone staircase, feeling a sudden chill as he ventured deeper underground. The steps were hollowed in the middle though years of use, the walls dusty and uneven as if they'd been carved out with a blunt shovel.

He couldn't hear anything from above or below, the abrupt silence disconcerting.

Thirty steps flew by. Mason nursed wounds as he ran – a pain in his right shin, several scrapes on his face, a bruised rib. By the time he reached the end, any adrenalin acquired by his victory had been depleted.

Mason spotted Quaid's face lurking in the shadows, holding up a two-way radio.

'Roxy and Sally are hidden outside with Hassell. I waited to see who emerged in case I needed to slow them down.'

Mason nodded appreciatively. 'It's all clear out there?'

'So far. But hurry.'

Mason followed the man through a door, then threaded between the sturdy columns that supported the crypt and the basilica above. The exit was clear ahead, framing a rectangle of darkness revealing full night had fallen. Mason saw Roxy, Sally and Hassell as he emerged.

Hassell. The mercenary, Pascal, had thrown up a dubious question about the New Yorker.

Hassell handed him his backpack as he approached. Unable to see each other's faces, the five of them carried their emotions intimately and guardedly as they melted away into the deeper darkness.

Chapter 48

Mason decided to take charge as they drove the fast saloon car Hassell had rented through the heart of a busy Paris, seeking a place where they could sit in safety and mull over the new clue.

Sally's excited voice filled the car as she revealed what she'd found inscribed upon the altar in the Chapel of the Physicians. '*Ibid, 111.*'

'Oh, no,' Roxy groaned. 'Not another one.'

'Same code,' Sally said. 'Uncrackable without the book. This is Heindl's extra safeguard. It's perfect.'

'And requires another call to Mateo DeVille,' Mason said. 'And the hope that he can help crack the code.'

'He came through last time.' Sally placed the call, spoke to DeVille still in his hospital bed, and left him to ruminate over the new code. When Mason stared at her questioningly, Sally could only spread her arms.

'I don't know,' she said. '*He* doesn't know. It might take some time.'

Mason, conscious of the lost time and the presence of the Amori shooters, but also conscious that DeVille was trying to trawl through years of memory, gritted his teeth and sat back.

* * *

Roxy, in the driver's seat, made her way to the tenth district, close to Gare Du Nord, where ample parking and a seedy night-time neighbourhood indicated they'd be left to their own devices whilst also hopefully being shielded from the Amori's hired marauders.

Still, Mason was conscious of their enemy breathing down their necks. Only minutes had separated them at Sacré-Coeur. Where would the fourth clue lead them?

Whilst they waited, Mason twisted in the passenger seat, eyeing the cramped passengers in the back, and then, deliberately, Hassell. 'The guy I fought,' he said, 'called himself Pascal. Friend of yours?'

Hassell looked surprised. 'Haven't needed or wanted a friend in seven years,' he said with a faraway look in his eyes. 'Don't talk about it much.'

'We know that,' Mason said. 'But silence isn't always a sign of reliability.'

Hassell blinked. 'I see. What did he tell you?'

Mason chose his words carefully. 'Said you were a real dodgy bastard.'

Hassell's eyebrows raced upwards as Roxy laughed. Mason had wanted to put Hassell at ease, believing he was a good man with a cruel past. 'We need trust between us,' he said. 'All of us. That's the way a good team works.'

'Team?' Hassell repeated. 'That's a new one on me. I'm used to a judgemental, deceitful environment where your co-workers smile at your face and stab you in the back.'

'Clock's ticking,' Mason said into a profound silence.

'*I know*,' Sally snapped.

Roxy threw the car around a tight corner. 'Approaching the station.'

Mason studied Hassell. 'You stopped being a cop to become a criminal. I'm not asking for the gruelling details, mate, just a rational explanation.'

Agitated, Hassell struggled to remain calm. 'Got offered

a better deal,' he said eventually, looking away. 'Gido's a persuasive guy.'

Mason saw the conflict in the American. 'Okay, let's talk about Gido. Who the hell is he?'

'A gangster, a conman, something I should have taken into account. A dark-web figure who commands huge respect throughout the underworld. Practically a criminal legend. I mean, even the Amori knew of him. They came to *him*. I helped . . . cement him as a global criminal figurehead.'

Mason sensed that Hassell was holding back on the details for a reason. 'So you befriended a criminal. It happens.'

'They were dark days. The days leading up to Gido, I mean. Three years of living hell. What did Pascal tell you?'

Mason had been wondering if a quick revelation of Pascal's words would jolt the truth from Hassell. It occurred to him now that Hassell might never have discussed the worst of his past aloud before.

'We're here,' Roxy said, pulling into a parking area and reversing the car into a spot between two vehicles whose windows were obscured by heavy condensation. 'Where we at with DeVille, Sal?'

'He's still working on it,' Sally said tightly.

Roxy let out a pent-up breath. 'I'll keep the car running.'

Mason didn't look across at the architecturally striking station to their left. 'Pascal said you got your girl killed. His exact words.'

Hassell lashed out, not at Mason but at the back of Roxy's seat, striking the leather with long-repressed aggression. 'The *fucker*,' he hissed. 'That bastard.'

Mason gave him a moment, turning to Sally. 'The Amori will be working on the same clue by now.'

'Don't you think I know that? Bloody hell, Mason. Give DeVille some breathing space.'

'Gare du Nord,' Roxy said, her voice light as if trying to alleviate the tension. 'Always wanted to see it.'

'It's a train station,' Quaid said. 'Looks like every other train station.'

'It's associated with *The Bourne Identity*,' Roxy said. 'And one of my heroes.'

'Robert Ludlum?' Quaid asked, impressed.

'Matt Damon.'

'Interesting,' Sally said out of nowhere just then. Mason turned to her expectantly. 'What is?'

'DeVille left me a voicemail. Listen: "*Consecrated Ground of Nazareth, where Military was Crowned, and the Relic of Thorns preserved.*" That's as close as he can remember.'

Quaid frowned. '"Military was Crowned"? Is that *French* military, I wonder?'

Sally was already sliding her laptop out of her backpack and plugging it into one of the car's USB connections. '"*Where Military was Crowned, and the Relic of Thorns preserved*",' she said. 'It's awkward. Military is crowned in churches all around the world. St Paul's. St Dunstan's. The list is endless.'

'But France,' Quaid pushed. 'What of France?'

Sally slapped the edge of her laptop. 'Same,' she blurted. 'They have churches and generals too.'

Mason hadn't seen Sally this upset since the death of her father. 'Take a breather,' he said. 'You can only work so hard before you stop being productive. Now, Hassell, have you stopped punching that seat?'

He spoke lightly, eliciting the ghost of a smile from the younger man.

'I guess I was a decent guy trying to make it in a callous world,' Hassell said. 'Gido's world is not for the merciful. Luckily, I excelled at the one thing he needed – figuring out how to gain access to almost anywhere. I pissed off a lot of people in a lot of places.'

'Understood,' Mason said. 'But you still haven't answered my question.'

'How did I go from being a cop to working for Gido? I won't talk about that right now. I can't. Suffice to say that Gido pulled me out of the gutter, put me to work and helped me get revenge. I'm done talking. It's not my forte. If you don't like it, I can get out right here.'

Hassell cracked his door open, letting a waft of cold air inside. Mason didn't stop him right away, recalling how Hassell had saved his life and how he'd acted since.

Hassell climbed out, slammed the door behind him and walked away, a forlorn figure with both hands thrust deep into his pockets.

'You know he has a good heart,' Roxy said quietly. 'You've seen it.'

Mason cursed, at odds with himself, then opened his own door and strode after Hassell. 'Wait,' he said. 'I get it. God knows, we're the last people on earth qualified to advise anyone on getting past adversity. I'll respect your privacy if you want to stay but I had to ask the question. I need to be able to trust everyone on this team.'

Hassell sighed deeply, turned and shook his head. 'I don't know. I'm on my own now. Cut loose. I haven't been this alone since . . .' He paused. '*Ever*. I've *never* been this alone. I sure as hell can't go back to New York.'

'Then help us to help Sally,' Mason said. 'I didn't mean to push you away.'

Hassell hesitated, unsure.

Roxy's voice pealed out. 'Hey, you two, we all need to strip off. Right here and now.'

Hassell smiled despite himself. 'How can I refuse a request like that?'

Roxy climbed out of the car. 'Our enemy knows what we were wearing, and we don't wanna give them the slightest edge.'

Mason nodded. Roxy dragged their backpacks out and handed them over. Quaid joined them in about four feet of space behind the car, before black railings, where they quickly stripped off jeans, jackets and shirts to help change their appearance.

Knocking elbows and hips, they were careful to keep their eyes averted but, even then, when they were done, Roxy gave Quaid an appreciative nod. 'Nice abs, man.'

'Cheers. Was thinking about grating a block of cheese on yours.'

Roxy punched him. Mason jumped back into the car with its warm interior and agitated occupant.

'Where have you been?' Sally snapped. 'I've figured it out.'

'What? When? I mean, crap, well done.'

More doors opened, admitting Roxy, Hassell and Quaid.

Sally waited until they were settled. 'Why don't I get a change of clothes?' she asked.

'You do, just as soon as you're done,' Mason said. 'I thought it best not to disturb you.'

'Listen,' Sally said. 'I'll change later. Roxy – start driving. Head south for now and get your foot down. The Amori can't be far behind us. The second video went live tonight.'

Mason put a hand on her shoulder. 'Is it bad?'

'More Amori rhetoric promising world change,' Sally said. 'On a larger scale and with a growing audience. There's one more teaser and then the full reveal.'

Roxy sighed. 'We're running on borrowed time.'

She gunned the engine, rolled out of the parking area and joined the main road. She changed gear quickly, using the paddle-shifts and letting the engine do the work, which prompted Mason to send Quaid a smug look.

Before the two men could get back into their unfinished argument, Sally made them aware of her findings in an unstoppable rush of enthusiasm.

'It's the last part of the clue that bears the fruit. I mean, "*consecrated Ground of Nazareth*" and "*where Military was Crowned*" are generic references at best. But the relic of thorns was preserved at only one hallowed location and, when you have that, the rest of the clue falls into place.'

'What's a relic of thorns?' Quaid asked.

'It's the entwined crown of thorns that was placed on Jesus Christ's head when he carried the cross through the streets. It's an object of *the Passion*, employed by his gaolers to both mock and hurt him. Since around AD 400 a relic considered by many to be *the* Crown of Thorns has been kept in Notre-Dame Cathedral, which is where Jacques Heindl would have assumed it would stay. The crown was moved to the Louvre in April 2019 after a fire.'

Mason leaned over and punched the cathedral's address into the satnav to make Roxy's job easier. 'That's an eight-minute drive,' he said, mildly surprised. 'We'd better make ready.'

'How do the other clues support your theory?' Quaid asked.

'Notre-Dame was consecrated to the Virgin Mary, a woman of Nazareth and mother of Jesus. And in December of 1804, one of the best-known military leaders of all time was crowned emperor there.'

'Napoleon?' Quaid guessed.

'Spot on. Yes, Napoleon Bonaparte, successful in the French Revolution and the Revolutionary Wars. And of course, the Napoleonic Wars, during which France dominated most of Europe.'

'"*Where Military was Crowned*",' Quaid intoned. 'Has a kind of proud finality about it. I have to agree.'

Sally blinked and gave Quaid a surprised look as if the thought of someone doubting her hypotheses hadn't occurred. She sat back and closed the laptop, taking a deep breath. 'I just hope we make it before the Amori.'

She flinched as Mason rammed a fresh magazine into his handgun.

'We're prepared to school them if we don't,' he said.

Chapter 49

Having not expected to enter the field of combat again so soon, Mason rolled his shoulders and hips, trying to assess the stinging aches and pains that afflicted his body, finally deciding on a handful of painkillers and a nip of brandy from one of Quaid's handy hipflasks to wash them down.

They faced a murky quagmire of decision. Notre-Dame was the fourth of the Five Great Churches. If and when they found the next clue – which should be soon – they would arrive at a momentous crossroads, from which they could choose to proceed with targets pinned to their backs, or shed a load of responsibility.

Mason felt better now than at any time in the last two years. Maybe it was due to the way they'd outpaced and outdone their enemy, made headway as they tried to save souls and lives, instilling in him more purpose and a deeper motivation. He wasn't failing – he was winning with a new team.

Until tonight, or until tomorrow. What then?

Roxy's focused voice cut through his deliberations. 'Three minutes. Find me a place to park.'

Quaid jumped on it, and soon they were sitting in the ticking car, staring through drizzle-misted windows into a darkness replete with the gilt-edge atmosphere of a Parisian night.

Facing the main road, they could see and hear crowds of tourists hurrying along, lone couples strolling arm in arm despite the light rain, their faces so close they might have been fused together, a knitted romance of rich colour, ornate edifice and resounding history which imbued the City of Lights with the pride of a grand nation. Mason paused with three fingers on the door handle.

'There're cops everywhere.'

Notre-Dame, closed to the public after the April 2019 fire, nevertheless stood besieged by tourists either taking in the imposing site or recording its image in digital splendour. Mason could see at least three groups of gendarmes as they climbed out of the car to make their way across the busy road.

'Another problem,' Sally told them. 'Is that Notre-Dame is closed. We might not even get inside.'

Mason frowned. 'You're kidding? We might not even *get* the clue?'

'Unless you can find a way in,' Sally said gloomily. 'No.'

Mason studied the crowds, the police, the sheer press of humanity in the area. Getting *anywhere* unseen was going to be a challenge but any chance of gaining access to Notre-Dame's interior probably lay with Luke Hassell.

'West facade.' Sally made her way to the left. 'Over forty metres wide with four Gothic buttresses and three portico entrances. The west rose window sits above the Virgin's Balcony and the north and south tower. The—'

'Please save the history lesson for later.' Mason had slowed and was staring across the vast square bordering the cathedral's secured entrance in the west facade. 'I'm counting over a dozen cops but no Amori. Which raises the thorny issue—'

'That they could already be inside,' Roxy finished.

Mason eyed the cathedral's daunting edifice. 'Unfortunately, yeah.'

'Or somewhere in that crowd,' Quaid added.

Mason watched the cops, wondering how far the Amori's reach extended.

'If they've beaten us into the cathedral, it's all lost,' Sally fretted. 'They'll deface the altar at the very minimum.'

In battle, before Mosul, Mason had always enjoyed a clear-headed talent for quick thinking. It returned now and spurred him into action.

'Hassell, Sally,' he said, 'your job is to find the clue. The rest of you, come with me.'

Angling to the right, he sped up, hurrying across the square. Sally was right – they were out of time. They'd come this far against the clock, storming their way across countries. Now the headway they'd gained was lost, leaving them a window of minutes before ghostly chimes of doom echoed around the great, spoiled cathedral's immense church bells.

'Hey!' he shouted. 'Quaid. Move!'

A policeman looked idly at them. His friend glanced over and frowned. Mason shouted again. A face popped out of the crowd, hard eyes looking his way. It was followed by another. Mason saw Hassell and Sally passing them to the right. Mason bellowed for a third time, diverting their attention. One of the mercs locked onto him and yelled, giving Mason the distraction and warning he needed.

Clenching his fists, he turned to Roxy and Quaid. 'Run.'

'Run?' Roxy gawped. 'That's your plan? *Run?*'

Quaid looked equally offended and mumbled something about *contacts*, but Mason took that moment to turn and cut through the crowd. The mercs started after him, at least eight of them, aided by the gendarmes.

Mason's last sight of Sally was of her blue-tipped hair passing through the crowd in the direction of Notre-Dame's three entry arches. He hoped that Hassell could find a way to infiltrate the enormous church, but at the same time worried that the Amori mercenaries might already be inside.

'Meet in an hour, our old place.' He'd taken the two-way out of his pocket to pass the message along to his team. 'Our old place' was the pastry shop in the backstreets around Sacré-Coeur. When the last word was spoken, he broke into a sprint, giving the seated tourists something to stare at other than the cathedral. He ducked around a raised statue and ran towards a row of buildings.

Roxy and Quaid spread out to left and right, taking slightly different directions.

Mason ran hard, glancing around once when a chunk of space opened before him, smiling grimly to see the dozen-strong mob giving chase. It might not be the entire Amori contingent, but it would thin them out and slow them down.

Giving Sally and Hassell a chance.

Sally Rusk skirted a group of people gathered before a black railing underneath Notre-Dame's daunting frontage, to find the railings were fastened in the middle by an iron padlock. No doubt the arched doors would be similarly locked. Sally had no idea how extensive the fire of 2019 had been, other than the collapse of its iconic lead-clad central spire, but the secured railings sent a clear message.

'Won't most of the interior items have been removed?' Hassell asked as he scouted the cathedral infiltration points.

'Things like the Crown of Thorns, the Blessed Sacrament, statues and other relics were saved by people who made a human chain on the night of the fire, rescuing the works and transporting them to the Louvre. Heavier items still remain. While we can't be certain our altar remains inside, intact, we can't risk not checking.'

'Won't there be workers inside?' Hassell asked.

'It's way past normal working hours,' Sally said. 'But I really hope not.'

Sally saw one of the reasons Mason had sent Hassell with her then as he produced a pristine set of homemade lockpicks. When she questioned him with a glance, he shrugged. 'Never leave home without them.'

She covered him as he worked on the padlock, shielding him from the view of several passers-by, still trying to come to terms with the recent rapid changes to her tedious but fulfilling new life. Since returning to help her father – after realising that living as a runaway wasn't working – she'd managed to get a clear glimpse of the future. She didn't have to embrace wealth to enjoy life but, if she worked hard, maybe she could accept it and find a way to help those less fortunate. Working for her father was a necessary centring hardship on the road to acceptance. Of course, with the death of her father, where did her future lie now?

Hassell pocketed the padlock and opened the gates. Sally tried to cover him but could hardly hide the lone figure walking right up to the front door. Fortunately, only a few feet separated the railings from the entrance. Seconds passed as Hassell picked the second lock.

Sally waited, noticing the Amori mercenaries chase Mason and the others across the square. Many people stood watching, their attention focused on the commotion rather than what she and Hassell were doing.

Hassell turned and gave her a thumbs-up seconds later.

Sally took a deep breath to steady her nerves, pushed through the gate and ran to the nearest door.

Hassell pushed it open, oblivious, Sally thought, to the beautiful wrought-iron strap hinges and arabesques that adorned it. He beckoned to her after carefully assessing the inside.

Sally bit her lip as she ventured over the threshold, trying not to be overwhelmed by the humble emotions the grand space generated on sighting both its interior majesty and fire-damaged remains. The empty nave opened out grandly before her, the view interrupted by several scaffolding towers that marched up and down the north and south aisles and ambulatories. A few piles of debris still littered the floor, either from the fire or from recent refurbishment work.

Hassell paused and let Sally lead the way. 'There are, or were, over twenty altars,' she said quietly. 'Let's get started.'

'Softly,' he said. 'And slowly. I can't see anyone, but that doesn't mean they're not in here.'

They used their mobile phone flashlight apps to help negotiate the nave. The air was light and cold, and smelled of must and something old, like charred coals in a long-forgotten attic. An aura of despair lay inside the old cathedral, a sense of something once splendid that had been ravaged, spoiled by mischance, witlessness and negligence.

Sally breathed lightly, not because of the dust but because she preferred not to inhale the almost palpable anguish.

The main altar and the Trinity chapel revealed nothing. The third and fourth chapels were hard to negotiate, staining their clothes with dirt. Their boots, despite treading softly, still echoed between walls.

Sally checked another chapel's altar and then another. She stopped to check her watch. 'Forty minutes since we came in,' she said. 'I'm a bit surprised—'

The door through which they'd entered creaked, the sound a whipcrack through the overwhelming silence.

Hassell dragged her to the ground. 'Quiet. Turn your torch off.'

In deep shadow, crouched behind a pillar beneath one of the spectacular rose windows, Sally peered down the length of the nave, trying to make out the faces of the two men who'd snuck in. Whoever they were, they hadn't spotted Sally or Hassell. Maybe they were tourists taking advantage of the unlocked doors.

Seconds later, she knew that was the wishful thinking of a professor's naïve assistant.

Hassell had already pulled out his gun. 'Where to?'

Sally tried to focus. 'Beside the vestry there's an unnamed chapel.' She pointed south. 'We'll try that next.'

'Slowly.' Hassell drew the word out as he crept away, staying low and shielding his movements behind wide pillars, shallow steps and a small pile of rubble. Sally crawled steadily, feeling her way and clearing any debris before putting her hands and knees down, and moving three times slower than her brain wanted to.

The mercenaries approached down the main aisle, guns raised, aiming torches left and right for signs of life. Sally and Hassell passed thirty feet in front of them, shrouded by darkness, and stole into the unnamed chapel.

Hassell turned. 'All yours.'

Sally wiped the sweat from her face.

Chapter 50

Mason darted through the crowd, getting a feel for his environment and the heavy press of people in the square. The night skies deepened above, illuminated only by a sparse scattering of stars and a cold, creamy half-moon hanging over the horizon, visible between buildings.

Running along an east-facing wall, he turned left and headed for a pedestrian bridge over the Seine. The low railings protecting each side allowed a harsh blast of cold air to sweep up from the roiling river and sting his face. Mason flinched but didn't slow.

At least three men were chasing him, one of them a gendarme. A siren-less police car approached along the main road ahead, vivid blue lights flashing. Mason cut to the left as soon as he could, running in front of a car before sliding across the bonnet of another.

Shouts went up from behind. The police car increased speed, closing the gap. Mason whirled as he ran. The cops were lagging behind, the two mercenaries just twenty feet away. He couldn't fire his weapon unless the chase became life-threatening – the gunshots would incite a wave of fear that might sweep through Paris.

He dashed up one side street and then tore up another.

It was a risky strategy. He had no map, and no idea which streets met adjoining junctions or might lead to deadly cul-de-sacs.

At the junction of another street, he stopped with his back to a wall and waited.

Peering around the corner he saw the mercenaries separate, one taking his route, the other a parallel one. He decided to wait.

The cold breeze stirred rubbish around his boots and whistled through a crack in a nearby window, but he focused on the approaching steps of his adversary.

A thin, rectangular slice of darkness and stars presided above as he stepped out into the running mercenary's path and swung an elbow. The blow, combined with the man's speed, was crushing, knocking him backwards and onto his spine, blood gushing from a broken nose.

Mason left him gurgling and dashed away along the street, finding another intersection and trusting to luck. Pausing at a blind corner, he took a quick glance around and came face to face with a second mercenary. The guy had a phone to his ear and was speaking quietly. The phone fell and his eyes widened as Mason sprang at him. A solid jab and cross sent him floundering against the wall where the back of his head cracked against the stonework. The merc's gaze flew left and right as if expecting backup. Mason jumped in quickly, aware that anything other than one-on-one was going to get him shot or killed or captured. The merc defended well at first, but Mason's well-timed, well-practised punches began to take a toll. Plus, the back of the man's head was bleeding from making contact with the wall. The merc fell to his knees where Mason kneed him in the face, rendering him unconscious.

Quickly, he scanned the street. Where were his colleagues?

Mason set off once more, approaching a new fork in the street. This one emptied him out somewhere along Rue

Lagrange, opposite a patisserie protected by a ring of crowded tables where people ate cake and drank coffee and hot chocolate, and eyed the stranger who sprinted past.

Ignoring the stares and an embarrassing whistle, he turned a corner past a Japanese restaurant and hit the Rue du Fouarre at full pelt. Irritation filled him when he saw the reflection of a police car cruising slowly to his left. One of the cops was staring, almost leaning out of his window. Mason kept walking, gazing to his right. Once the car passed, he saw its rear lights blaze red before it suddenly stopped.

Without hesitation, he cut through the nearest door, finding himself inside a restaurant with tables packed close together. Mason weaved among them, reaching the far wall before figures burst into the eatery, yelling at him to stop. The kitchen door was right in front of him. Mason barged through, sending a youth balancing four full plates crashing to the ground. Quickly, he spied the back door.

The cops would come quick and would soon call for reinforcements but then Mason reminded himself that they worked for the Amori. Maybe there were no others. He emerged into a back alley dotted with skips full of rubbish, the stench of rotting food thick in the air, and took off at full speed. The sweat flew from his forehead now, and his heart hammered.

'We *will* shoot you,' a voice yelled. Any normal policeman wouldn't have said it and even if he had, Mason wouldn't have believed the threat. But these were the Amori.

He slowed, turned, threw his hands up in the air. The cops started to run. Mason then darted into an alley. A short stone staircase greeted him. Mason took the steps in twos and threes, almost falling twice. At the bottom he had a choice and turned right, noting that the cops weren't in sight.

More running. Mason was forced to slow. Darkness filled

most of the alleys before him, a night-choked network of narrow streets. It looked like a blessing but, again, one wrong move could spell disaster. He moved and checked for pursuers by the dim glare of streetlamps, heart pounding, ready to break into a sprint at the merest sign of trouble.

A siren split the air.

Mason ducked behind a rubbish bin, saw the lurid lights painting walls several hundred feet away and waited. Soon, they were gone, letting the darkness seep back into the streets. Mason broke into a jog, spying a busier street ahead.

Along here, red-and-white-canopied restaurants were fully packed, their windows hidden by lines of people waiting in line for a table, which gave Mason the perfect opportunity to walk into their midst, choose a random street and vanish.

Sally crawled around the low altar, creeping on her hands and knees through black carbonised dust and followed Hassell's instructions to daub a little of it on her face to help merge with the shadows. *It can't hurt,* he said, but it didn't exactly make her feel any safer. Silence was their only ally, the features of the cathedral hiding the approach of the Amori's foot soldiers.

Sally cupped the light of her phone, allowing only the barest sliver of a beam to escape. The faint glow illuminated bare rectangles of stone to each side of the pitted altar. Another failure made Sally's heart pound even harder.

Hassell made a gesture, asking where to go next. Sally directed him further to the south, desperate to move fast but forced to creep steadily along in the dark. The minutes ticked by quickly.

Past the vestry, one agonising metre at a time, it took an age to reach the Norman chapel, and again they came up negative. Sally's fists were clenched with the stress of being discovered, her teeth gritted so hard they ached. They froze as footsteps passed several feet behind them, approaching the main chapel they'd already discounted.

The sound of their enemies making furtive progress was unnerving in an eerie way, worse because the noise came from behind and they couldn't risk the movement of turning around. Sally waited with her head down, willing the footsteps to pass.

Eventually, they did. Hassell patted her right heel to get her moving. Sally crawled cautiously away, ignoring the worsening pain in her scraped palms and scratched knees, willing this nightmare journey of stealth to end.

She wasn't cut out to work amid an overarching threat, among men with guns and ill intentions. But if this was how she earned respect, she would crawl through the dirt all night long.

A profound silence bore down from the vast, arched spaces above as Sally and Hassell moved into the south transept and under the unending watch of its rose window. Time slowed to minutes measured in single steps. Another archway appeared ahead and the entrance to another chapel. Sally crept into it and swept the subdued light of her phone across the altar.

The words leapt out at her.

'*Its Plundered Artefacts, a Unique Church of Gold, the Apostle and the Winged Lion.*'

The fifth and final clue. And, thankfully, not written in code.

A sharp voice rang through the heavy silence. 'You see that light, Conway?'

Hassell shrouded it with his body, rolling next to her and holding his breath, so close Sally could feel his heart hammering.

'Came through that entrance over there, Chalk,' a merc answered.

'Yeah, maybe the cathedral rats are using torches these days.'

Sally rebuked herself but there was no time for criticism. Hassell was holding one of the handguns Quaid had given them. She was low enough to the floor to smell the rot of seared things.

She listened to the sound of approaching boots . . . the steady shuffle of two enemies creeping closer and closer.

'Gun,' Hassell whispered at her. 'Take your gun out.'

The words horrified her. The thought of firing a pistol, of sending a bullet ripping through another's body, was terrifying.

She froze, unable to think, and when she gritted her teeth and forced movement her hands shook so badly that they couldn't undo the straps on her backpack.

Hassell swore softly as the boots approached their hiding place.

'Time to ride or die, assholes,' the one called Chalk said. His voice had a distinctive gravelly quality.

Hassell rose up, showing his face, faint but visible in the dark church from the light entering through the rose window above his head. Conway whistled low and harsh.

'That you, Hassell?' The man's gun steadied on his chest. 'You seriously need your head checking, man.'

'Conway.' Hassell nodded. 'Chalk. How's it going?'

Sally struggled to decide. Mason and Roxy would know what to do, but she was clueless in these situations. Finally, right or wrong, she forced herself to her feet, keeping her hands out of sight below the altar. She saw two armed men clad in black, their machine guns pointed at Hassell. Her appearance made both men's eyes flick in her direction.

'Don't move,' Chalk said.

Conway was broad and muscular, a gym rat with a firearm, she thought. Chalk was wiry and sported a thin moustache plus a gold brace over his teeth that looked uncomfortable. Both men gave the impression that they knew how to handle themselves and faced Hassell with practised ease.

She stopped herself from putting her hands up with an effort. Conway waved his gun at Hassell. 'You pissed Gido off, man. The dude that hired us ripped him *two* new assholes, which was passed down the line. You pissed us all off.'

Hassell shrugged. 'The dude that hired us is seriously unhinged. Ordered us to kill his daughter. Wants to destabilise the whole world. We've never worked for anyone so seriously extreme.'

'So you betray Gido? Fall in with the enemy?'

Sally noted that the guns didn't waver an inch. She also noticed that Hassell was holding his pistol low, unseen. Around them the old cathedral shifted and creaked. A bird flapped in the rafters, sending a trickle of debris raining down to the floor. A shimmer of artificial light played across their enemy's faces, transposing them between light and dark.

'Maybe Gido betrayed *me*,' Hassell said.

Conway shrugged. 'Maybe. He's the boss. But he loved you, man. He saved you. Trained you.'

But Hassell had leaned forward. '*Maybe?*'

'I don't know your past, but Gido always said he'd gotten something over on you. Never said what. But he still *wants* you. Told us, told everyone: if you see Hassell, make sure he knows he still has a home here. Make sure he's invited back.' Conway shook his head. 'If it was up to me, I'd shoot you both in the goddamn face.'

'And then you'd never find what you're looking for,' Sally whispered, surprising herself.

Conway's weapon drifted towards her. 'What did you say?'

But Hassell was frowning, holding onto the lip of the altar with one hand as if unsteady on his feet. 'Gido wants me *back*? Why? To make it easier to kill me? I have questions about the night Chloe died.'

'Your girlfriend? So that's what this is all about? But you were a cop then. Didn't you *investigate*?' Conway made a mockery of the last word.

'Gido wants me back,' Hassell said again and, to Sally, it sounded like he was considering it. She wasn't sure she blamed him. The family that had kept him safe and nurtured him all these years was throwing him a new lifeline.

'Just walk away,' Conway said. 'With us. Back to your old life. Back to the city. No repercussions. Gido ordered it. This is your chance of redemption straight from the horse's mouth.'

'And . . . my new comrades?' Hassell glanced at Sally.

'Oh, they gotta die. All of them. We'll start by putting this one down. They *really* pissed people off. People with power and influence, you know? You gonna shoot her, Chalk?'

'Be better if I use the knife,' Chalk growled, pulling a wicked serrated blade from a leather sheath attached to his belt. 'And much more fun.'

He leered. Sally's legs went weak with fear. Hassell stared at the two men as if making the biggest decision of his life but the options were clear, balanced and laid out before him. All he had to do was take the first step.

He turned to Sally. 'I'm sorry,' he said.

'Wait,' she blurted. 'Wait, *why*? You want answers but you also know the Amori can't be allowed to win.' She wanted to say more, to speak more clearly, but sheer terror choked the words in her throat.

'I have to find out why Chloe died,' he said. 'It's my life's purpose. And I can do it better inside Gido's organisation.'

He stepped away. Sally clung to the side of the altar, begging him with her eyes. White-hot terror ran the length of her body as she looked back at Conway and Chalk. The mercenaries were smirking at her. Conway shot a glance at Chalk.

'Get on with it.'

Chalk shouldered his weapon, raising the knife as he advanced, letting Sally get a good look at its deadly, glinting edge.

Hassell continued to retreat from her and wouldn't meet her eyes. There was a desperate moment when everything was suspended in time. Sally couldn't stop trembling as she stared into the eyes of the man who was coming to kill her.

'Please . . .' she said.

Hassell turned away.

'Don't worry, love.' Chalk grinned. 'You won't live to remember the agony.'

Hassell raised his gun in one swift movement and pulled his trigger. Bullets hit Conway's centre mass and sent him flying backwards.

Chalk dropped his knife, brought up his own weapon and returned fire.

Sally realised she was still gawping at Hassell, still holding her gun at her side and trying to come to grips with the idea of firing it.

Chalk's bullet ripped through Hassell's jacket, its momentum throwing Hassell's aim off, but Hassell kept firing, sending two bullets into Chalk, the first puncturing his neck, the second his cheek. Chalk collapsed an instant later as Hassell put a hand to his own shoulder.

'Did they get you?' Sally managed.

'No. Snagged my jacket, grazed my skin. Nothing more than a tramline. You okay?'

Sally wobbled, dropped the gun and then scooped it up off the floor. 'I'm so sorry,' she said. 'I . . . never held a gun before, let alone . . .'

'*I'm* sorry. I had to fool you into believing I'd switch sides,' he said. 'It lowered their guard.'

'You just shot two friends. Are you okay?'

'Friends? They were two killers, bullies that I tried to avoid. The world's a better place without them, believe me.'

Sally's muscles were starting to feel like they belonged to her again. New thoughts squeezed the debilitating terror from her brain like water from a wet rag. 'Who's Chloe?'

Hassell hung his head. 'Long story for another day. There could be more of them inside. At the very least, the sound of gunshots will alert them.'

Sally saw the indecision in him, a pure need to uncover the truth about what had happened to Chloe, the raw pull of Gido's offer to return to the fold. It had rocked Hassell, forced him to make the toughest of choices, and revealed to her that, in his heart, he was a good man who was now trying to make the right decisions.

Not a criminal. More than an ex-policeman.

Sally nodded as Hassell led her away from the dead bodies, approaching a side door, and only then remembered the clue she'd found.

'Hurry,' she said as the urgency of their quest once more crashed through her mind. 'I found the final clue.'

Chapter 51

Mason saw the hour was up and suppressed a feeling of rising apprehension when Sally and Hassell rounded the corner leading to the café's front door. Roxy, Quaid and he were skulking in a dark alley opposite.

'Hey,' Roxy hissed dramatically under her breath. 'Over here.'

'Do you have it?' Quaid asked as Sally approached.

'Yeah. *"Its Plundered Artefacts, a Unique Church of Gold, the Apostle and the Winged Lion."*'

'"Church of Gold"?' Quaid repeated speculatively. 'Interesting . . .'

Mason focused on Sally. 'Are you okay? Any problems?'

'Nothing Hassell couldn't handle,' Sally said quickly. 'Do you have my laptop? I really need to consult the Rusk Notes.'

'Car's parked over there.' Roxy jerked a thumb to the right. 'I brought it over. And I've been wanting to ask – why do you always call them the Rusk Notes?'

Sally bit her lip as if considering her response. Mason set off along the ill-lit, sodden street, keeping an eye out for police patrols.

'Rebellion,' Sally said finally. 'I got sick of saying "my father". Makes it more impersonal.'

Roxy nodded in appreciation. Mason considered asking what happened back in Notre-Dame, but they'd reached their car. The next leg of their journey superseded all else and he didn't want Sally distracted from her work.

Roxy turned the key, firing up the engine. 'Where to?' she asked. 'On second thoughts, I know exactly where I'm going.'

Mason wasn't sure and said so. Roxy fixed him with an indignant glare. 'Pizza,' she said. 'The freakin' Amori can wait until I'm stuffed with Pepsi and pepperoni.'

Mason couldn't remember the last time they'd eaten. His stomach rolled like a cement mixer at high speed. Also, they could munch while Sally worked.

Roxy drove them to the nearest takeaway, parked up and returned fifteen minutes later fully loaded. She deposited pizza boxes in their laps and cardboard cups in their hands and drove under a motley bunch of sad-looking trees that overhung the rear of the pizza shop.

Mason's mouth watered as the heavenly smells filled the car. 'Take a break, Sally. You deserve it.'

'No need to stop work,' she said, tapping away with one hand and holding a droopy pizza slice in the other. 'And no time to waste. Failure won't do tonight.'

Mason hadn't known her long but was already aware that her work ethic was how she made up for being born into privilege. Her words, not his. Already, he admired how she'd pledged to use her position to help those struggling to help themselves.

Eating, sitting back and contemplating nothing but the roof of the car, he found himself remembering how this all began. How Patricia had called him in, asked him to find Roxy Banks. And then the flight to Rome. He'd been struggling, introspective and listless, alive only at the boxing gym. He'd lost his way, unable to accept that war happened, that men died in unforeseeable, cowardly acts and that failure was not the end product of loss.

You only fail when you quit, not when you lose.

Hannah, his wife, had moved on. The other guys who survived that day had moved on. But Mason was trapped questioning his command abilities, his decision-making processes, and had been flogging himself ever since.

First, helping Sally and trying to avenge her father had occupied his thoughts and actions, giving him purpose. Then, hunting the Amori for a plethora of healthy reasons had almost given him the capacity to forgive past mistakes, creating a new drive and purpose and maybe even a fresh start at life.

It was an odd turnaround and one he couldn't accept right now. If *he* didn't mourn his dead friends, who would? He wouldn't betray their memory. He *wanted* to hold onto the guilt, to feel the claws of responsibility digging so deep he'd never be able to prise them free.

Roxy polished off her pizza first and sat back, satiated. Mason watched her in the rear-view through tired eyes.

'What's up, Babyface?' she asked.

Mason took an involuntary look at himself and wondered for the thousandth time how, after everything life had thrown at him in the past and through recent days, he managed to look so damn fresh. Like there'd never been a single care or a hurdle to overcome.

'Don't worry.' Roxy chortled. 'Action becomes you.'

Mason held up two fingers.

Roxy smiled. 'One good thing,' she said, and added under her breath, 'they'll always underestimate you.'

The way she spoke, Mason assumed she was trying to express a compliment. He accepted it for what it was worth and moved on. 'How are *you* doing?'

'Me? The quiet assassin?' She didn't explain herself to the others. 'Making the most of a new life. Always building that shield.' She produced a beer from a jacket pocket and tried to uncap the bottle with her fingers. 'Damn, why are

Euro bottles so hard to crack? Shoulda bought an opener too.'

'I don't see the bad person you think you are,' Mason said.

'*Were*,' Roxy corrected. '*Were*.'

Mason nodded. 'All right. Hope I can help.'

'Help? It'll take years to build strong walls, and minutes to destroy them. This isn't a battle that ever goes away.' She pushed persistently at the sharp bottle top with her thumb, becoming more frustrated by the second.

'I know. It's a self-imposed limbo built to protect others.'

Roxy stared for a moment before nodding. 'Exactly. That's exactly what it is.' She seemed to be aware of Quaid and Hassell for the first time. 'You guys know what we mean, right? I can see it. See it in your faces. Are we all so broken?'

The ensuing silence grew uncomfortable, so Mason filled it with a distraction. 'Hey, Sally, how's the hunt coming?'

'Ongoing,' she said. 'Listening to you made me think how far we've come. From the Vatican, I mean. We started off trying to catch the woman who murdered my father and here we are, trying to save the world.'

'I wouldn't go that far,' Quaid said.

'Oh, okay, Christianity then. The fact is, we've made ourselves enough of a thorn – or spear – in the Amori's side that they're seriously worried, and murderously intent on destroying the line of discovery leading to their safe haven. But more than that – we're on the *last clue*.'

Excited, Sally tapped harder and faster at her computer, reviewing the Rusk Notes, certain specialist websites and her father's online writings. Mason took a long look at the ragtag crew he found himself running with, a crew brought together by necessity and chance, and through adversity.

Maybe the search for the *Book of Secrets* was a kind of deliverance.

Hell, it's a start.

Roxy opened her door, gathered the used pizza boxes and went to deposit them in a nearby bin. Mason could see that the unopened beer bottle was still in her hand and, when she returned, that her thumb was bleeding.

'You think that's a sign?' He nodded at her bloody hand clutching the bottle.

She nodded. 'Sure. A sign that Euro beers are evil, and all rum is righteous. I need to get my ass to a liquor store.'

'Not tonight,' Mason said. 'We need your head in the game, not in a bottle.'

'I'll drive,' Hassell said quickly. 'Sorry, I'm conscious that Gido's men can't be far behind and the Amori will have discovered that clue by now. And as we know, the century-old thread we're following is fragile at best.'

Roxy changed places with the New Yorker, settling in beside Quaid, the back seat becoming no less cramped. Mason suppressed the urge to ask Sally for another update.

A fresh drizzle coated their windscreen, droplets sparkling, refracted by streetlights. A gust of wind rocked the car and the sign above the pizza shop's door, rattling it to and fro on creaky hinges. Hassell pulled out of their parking space and glanced at Roxy in the rear-view.

'Which way?'

'Wait,' Sally's voice interrupted. 'I think I've got something.'

Roxy sighed. 'You sure do pick your moments, Sal.'

'"*Its Plundered Artefacts, a Unique Church of Gold, the Apostle and the Winged Lion.*" I guess the phrase *plundered artefacts* can mean plundered *by* or *from* the Church. Similarly, a church of gold can be interpreted a hundred different ways. But that one word *unique* is as telling as it gets.' She paused for breath.

'Drive,' Roxy instructed Hassell. 'We can listen as we search.'

'Which way?'

'In the direction of rum.' She sent Mason a vexing grin.

'Another time,' he said.

Sally pointed at her screen. 'My father wrote whole essays on the fundamental differences between old churches. He thought it a significant and influential indicator of the time. He postulated that local tradition and regional diversity were far more important to the history of religion than your ornate, prestigious and sublime Byzantine buildings that dominated the landscapes on which they were built. Religious affiliation doesn't make better buildings, he often said. And a building constructed by one religious group may later be altered to suit the purposes of another. A fine example of that is Hagia Sophia, repurposed many times.'

She paused for a moment, then shook her head. 'I digress. What I'm trying to say is that my father's notes are copious and detailed, incorporating years of study and research. We couldn't ask for more. A *unique* church is hard to find.'

'Okay,' Quaid acknowledged. 'And the last line?'

'Clinches it,' Sally said. 'The apostle and the winged lion. It's obvious.'

Mason winced as Roxy, still jabbing at her beer, opened another wound on her thumb. His face dropped when she reached into her waistband for her handgun and aimed it at the bottle.

'Hey—' he began.

Roxy slammed the gun's barrel against the sharp metal corrugations, sending the bright red top spinning from the rear into the front of the car. Sally eyed it with surprise before continuing. Roxy grinned as Mason shook his head.

'At the very top of the gable stands a statue of the apostle St Mark, surrounded by angels. Underneath is a winged lion, the symbol both *of the Saint and of*—'

'Venice?' Quaid ventured.

'The very same. We already know that many of its precious artefacts and relics were plundered from Constantinople, and by the crusaders in the thirteenth century, all engineered by a man named Enrico Dandolo. It was he who sent the Four Horses of St Mark to Venice, where they continue to adorn St Mark's Basilica, arguably its most famous sculpture.'

'It's hardly made of gold,' Quaid said.

'The basilica's design is influenced hugely by the Hagia Sophia itself. Its gold mosaics, which now cover almost the entire upper part, took hundreds of years to finish. But that is not why it's called the Church of Gold. That label came in the eleventh century when its opulent appearance and gold mosaics, representing Venetian prosperity and influence, earned it the nickname *Chiesa d'Oro*, meaning, literally, Church of Gold.'

'Got it,' Quaid said.

'Not only that,' Sally went on. 'Historians state that its elements of Venetian Renaissance art, its air of Oriental exoticism and its being the product of a multitude of Italian workers made it utterly *unique*.'

'And in Venice,' Roxy pointed out glumly. 'Do you know how far Venice is?'

'A ten-hour drive,' Hassell said, punching the city into the satnav as he drove. 'Faster if I put my foot down.'

The car they'd rented on Sally's dime was a powerful cruiser, an Alfa Romeo Giulia Quadrifoglio, in dark blue. Sleek and muscular, with a big engine and a comfortable leather and Alcantara interior, it was billed as a four-seater but, even with someone perched in the centre of the rear seat, the Italian sports saloon could make an overnight blast across Europe without breaking a sweat.

'Go,' Sally said, waving vaguely at the windscreen and the darkened city outside. 'Go, go, go.'

Mason settled back in his seat, listening as Sally reviewed

more of her father's notes out loud, consolidating her facts, and watching Roxy suck blood from her thumb.

It was going to be a long night.

Chapter 52

The shifting sky turned from an impenetrable well of black ink to a grey-swathed vault to crimson ribbons as it tracked their journey east.

They stopped only to fill up with petrol, grab an early breakfast and two trays full of coffee in a crisp, silent dawn and then visit the last rest stop before reaching Venice. Still, it was late morning before the signs of the A4 Autostrada announced the nearness of their destination.

Venice had always retained an air of mystery for Mason. Built on a cluster of a hundred and eighteen small islands, separated by canals and linked by more than four hundred bridges, some as impressive as the city itself, the islands all sit in the shallow enclosed bay known as the Venetian Lagoon. An enchanting city that weaves an intoxicating spell, by turns wistful and romantic and then a centre of activity, with gondoliers singing to their passengers and stylish cafés plying their trade, it offers the dream-inspiring Campanile and Bridge of Sighs as well as the opportunity to find locals sipping their vino in understated cafés and restaurants prior to sauntering around the Gallerie dell' Accademia.

Quaid, behind the steering wheel, followed signs to St

Mark's Square and was soon snarled up in a splayed tail of traffic jams.

Mason proposed that they should park up and leave the car near an easy escape route, and Sally soon reported that the Tronchetto, an enormous garage built on an artificial island, offered the best prospect from where they currently were, trapped in traffic.

Quaid found it. Sally paid the daily rate for special VIP parking near the exit and then located the No. 2 vaporetto, a water bus which would take them indirectly to their destination.

Mason shouldered his backpack and its rich assortment of contents, including their guns, which, despite the risk, were better stored out of sight of passers-by and local security forces. He approached the swaying craft. This was still a quiet season for Venice – as it had been in all the other tourist locations they'd visited – but it remained lively.

The volume of people would have made it impossible to sit together, so instead they opted for a much more expensive water taxi and a direct route to the great church. Again, Sally handed over money as the rest of the team settled down for the short journey.

Saint Mark's Square was a geometrically paved oasis amid a dense cluster of buildings that seemed drawn to its fame, like fans attracted to the aura of a superstar.

Mason slowed his pace to take it all in as glorious, centuries-old landmarks caught his eye – the Campanile, or bell tower, standing over 300 feet in a piazza which, during tidal peaks and storm surges, was quick to flood . . . the ornate library, the clocktower and more Gothic architecture than he had the time to appreciate.

Sally was staring too, turning a slow 360, as happy as Mason had seen her in the short time he'd known her. She wasn't alone in her delight though; hundreds of visitors stared up at the grand monuments in open-mouthed wonder, and still more saw the sculptures, columns, great arches and marble decorations only through a lens, moving from sight to sight without ever snapping the image with their bare eyes.

An undulating sweep of conversation surrounded them.

Roxy, on the other hand, was watching the crowd for signs of hostility whilst Hassell was using his eyes and Google Maps to determine the best escape routes.

Quaid scratched his greying sideburns and studied a map the size of a Sunday newspaper, trying to fine-tune his bearings.

Mason remembered why they were here, took Sally by the elbow and started towards the basilica. Closing in, he saw the replicas of the four horses presiding over the basilica like sentinels, and then shielded his face as an icy gale tore through the square, laden with rain, and the hum of nearby conversation died away as people huddled together or zipped up jackets and coats.

The midday sun dipped behind a black cloud which quickly ate up the day's warmth. Roxy, untroubled by the rain, tapped Mason's shoulder.

'We're clear,' she said. 'Could be the Amori's day off.'

Mason smiled despite the danger, the burdens and the bitter cold. He smiled because Roxy was heat on a winter's day; because that was her nature despite her issues; and because she brought the fire, the attitude and the insolence every single day. Mason doubted she realised that yet. That time would come.

Sally approached the central and largest of the five great arches of the basilica, joining a slow-moving tourist party progressing through the doors. Inside, the main portal led across the porch and under the stunning Arch of Paradise.

At this point Sally turned to Mason. 'We need to get on with the job and stop bloody sightseeing.'

Mason nodded, facing an entrance that led deeper into the church with a set of stairs to each side.

Quaid shook his map, using both hands. 'Stairs lead to the Museo Marciano. Houses the original gilded copper horses, Gobelin tapestries and other stuff. No mention of an altar.'

They crossed a spectacular floor made of marble inlays. Quaid again rustled his map. 'Chapels left and right,' he said. 'Might as well get on with it.'

Ignoring the golden mosaics and sublime religious art, they negotiated knots of people and joined human traffic jams to get closer to the basilica's many chapels.

They used each other and unwitting visitors to mask their actions, slipping over ropes and around barriers to examine altars of varying widths, sizes and states of repair.

The basilica filled as the weather took a turn for the worse, the rain pounding down on the church's roof and hammering at the stained-glass windows. Mason and Hassell were forced to forge a path whilst Roxy patrolled for any signs of the Amori.

Mason wished there were a logic to discovering Jacques Heindl's clues, a definitive narrative, but he guessed the randomness was part of the secret, and the reason they'd remained hidden from the Amori for so long. You could hardly second-guess a Vatican archivist who foretold the rise of Christianity's worst enemy by centuries.

'Until now,' Mason said as they jostled for space before another altar, 'each of the great churches has had an obvious connection to Jesus. I don't see that here.'

Sally nodded. 'Of course. I should have mentioned. It is the great treasure of this basilica.' She motioned her head upward. 'The mosaics.'

Mason followed her gesture but could discern only vague figures, clouds and symbols inlaid in the gleaming arches.

Sally explained: 'A sizeable and thorough cycle of the life of Christ covers much of the upper areas. The Ascension, the Pentecost, the miracles. The infant Christ, the Apostles and the life of the Virgin Mary.'

Sally stooped to check behind another altar, rising triumphantly in less than half a minute. 'This could be it.' She beckoned them over.

Mason leaned towards her, careful not to create too much of a spectacle. 'What does it say?'

Sally's forehead creased into a frown. 'But . . .' She dropped back to the floor, disappearing. Mason returned to his previous spot, bemused. Thirty seconds later Sally reappeared, rubbing her aching knees and stretching her back. 'It's too short,' she said. 'Doesn't fit with the others. We're done with the north side. Move across to the south.'

Easier said than done. Mason led the way across the central aisle forming the backbone of the building's Greek cross shape, trying his best not to barge anyone out of the way.

The crowd was now a mix of those who'd entered before the rain and those who'd entered after, the first group wearing jackets, jeans and sunglasses, the second with soaked overcoats, wet hair and shivering bodies.

Mason found the Cappella di San Clemente and got to work.

Twelve minutes later, at the end of their exhaustive circuit, Sally pulled them to one side and sighed. 'There is no fifth clue,' she said. 'It's not here.'

Mason felt a knot in his stomach. 'It *has* to be,' he said. 'It's the last bloody clue. Without it, we're at a dead end.'

Roxy frowned. 'How about upstairs?'

'No altars up there,' Quaid said. 'Could it have been removed?'

'The altar? Yes, of course.' Sally nodded. 'That's a point. Can we search for items removed from the basilica? Maybe it was put into storage.'

Mason felt deflated. Several dispirited minutes passed as Sally trawled through online records. Their faces were masked in suspicion and increasingly troubled. Quaid voiced his doubts about the veracity of information on the internet and Sally was forced to agree with him.

'They have no obligation to list artefacts,' she said. 'Not on a public forum like this. We need the proper museum archives.'

Mason thought about the time that would take. 'Are you sure?' he asked. 'I thought you'd hit the jackpot a little while ago, back in the other section.'

Sally groaned. 'Me too. But the text was too short to hold clues so I dismissed it.'

Mason inclined his head. 'Run it by me.'

Roxy pulled a face as if to question his sanity, but Sally spoke quickly and briefly. 'Revelation 17 and 18.'

Mason waited for the rest of it. When nothing came, he said, 'Go on.'

'That's it. That's everything. See what I mean?'

'Easy enough to review,' Quaid said. 'I'd eat my hat if there isn't a bookshop around here that sells a copy of the Bible.'

'Or we could just look online,' Hassell said, whipping out his phone.

Quaid looked suspicious. 'Whatever that thing tells you,' he murmured, 'we should double-check it later.'

Mason agreed, but watched as Hassell pulled up a webpage. Mason took the time to scour the faces to all sides, searching for any sign of the Amori.

'Can we speed this up?' he said. 'It's worrying me that the Amori could turn up at any moment.'

Sally read aloud over his shoulder. '*She has become a dwelling place of demons, a prison of every unclean spirit, and a prison of every unclean and hateful bird.*'

A pause and then another verse: '*For this reason in one day her plagues will come, pestilence and mourning and famine, and she will be burned up with fire; for the Lord God who judges her is strong.*'

330

One more pause as she took a deep breath. '*The woman whom you saw is the great city, which reigns over the kings of the earth.*'

Mason, listening hard, was none the wiser. 'I don't fully understand, but it seems Revelation chapters 17 to 18 describes the destruction of a great city.'

'You'd be right in your thinking,' Sally said. 'These passages of Revelation are damning, describing the city of the prostitute and the beast. Quite clearly here: "*with her the kings of the earth committed adultery, and the inhabitants of the earth were intoxicated with the wine of her adulteries.*" It describes the great abomination, sends out a warning that people should flee her oncoming judgement at once, describes the wretchedness of those who prosper under her evil sway, and then portrays her destruction. It is vicious, furious and final.'

'Which great city?' Roxy wondered. 'Atlantis? Was Atlantis ever in the Bible? What other great cities have been destroyed?'

'It's the great city whose ruins now lie in Iraq,' Sally said. 'In view of one of Saddam Hussein's old palaces. It's referencing Babylon.'

Mason cleared his throat. 'Does anything still remain of the city?'

'It makes a kind of sense,' Sally went on. 'The Rusk Notes explain that the Amori *founded* that city. That they invented most of its sins. What better place to hide the signs of their beginnings, their journey, and then celebrate a final victory? I need to think . . .' She glanced around and motioned towards a door. 'Can we leave?'

Mason nodded distractedly, trying to knit together the modern concept of the Amori that existed in his mind with an ancient cult hanging out in an old, dusty, enormous, ruined city. Something didn't quite compute.

Perhaps the fog would clear when they got outside.

Chapter 53

Struck by a raging blast of frigid, ice-flecked air, Mason almost turned and ducked back inside the basilica for shelter. The wind sought to rip his jacket to shreds, the rain to drown him. Mason turned away from the onslaught to zip up.

'We should go back to the car,' he yelled, his words torn away by snapping winds.

Audible or not, his words made themselves understood, and the group hurried away with the lofty bell tower to their left, the square brick shaft and pyramidal spire one of the most identifiable symbols of the city.

Mason wiped rain from his eyes and studied the length and breadth of Saint Mark's Square. He spotted them waiting in the downpour, their hair plastered to their heads, their leather jackets glistening, their faces so obscured by the rain as to appear almost liquescent.

'Bollocks,' he swore.

Without making any attempt to conceal themselves, nine mercenaries including Pascal waited in a dour-looking group, watching the front portals of the basilica, eighteen eyes that now locked onto Mason and the others. For long, tense seconds, the opposing sides faced each other, separated by just a hundred feet, cloaked by the storm and battered by high winds.

Mason was busy assessing the square for exits and assumed Roxy was doing the same, but it was Hassell who spoke first.

'The piazzetta,' he said, nodding at the wide thorough-fare leading past the Biblioteca to the nearest waterway. 'Just go left.'

Mason's body wanted to move, and swayed initially in that direction, but something held him back. Several tough choices existed for a soldier faced with unavoidable combat. You either went big, you went noisy, you went still or you used stealth. Whichever way, you were all in and it was relentless. To the end. Backing down was never an option.

Mason knew he had three good fighters on his team. Quaid was an unknown, though he had proved capable so far. Sally was an untrained civilian. Nine mercenaries faced them and, whilst some would undoubtedly be prima donnas with little more than gym- and steroid-enhanced muscle, others would be serious military badasses. Add hundreds of tourists to the mix, and Hassell's clear-cut escape plan became foggy.

Don't back down. Atone. Make good. Don't put these people in danger – save them.

The familiar litany brought no clarity, so he improvised. 'Go,' he shouted and then, as they started off, ran in a completely different direction.

Straight at the mercs.

Surprised, they gawped for several seconds. Mason himself was shocked to see Roxy at his side. She hadn't missed a beat.

'You know me that well?' he asked.

'Been saving your ass for the best part of a week.'

There were several ripostes to that, but Mason had no time for them. The mercs, bewildered, were separating, some reaching for weapons, others bracing for a fight.

Mason and Roxy struck, throwing punches and kicks, and pushing one man into another. They broke through their enemy's lines, momentum taking them beyond the group, and then turned back for more.

Mason felt bone and flesh impact his knuckles as punches landed. Spurred on by adrenalin, he ignored a solid blow that should have staggered him.

Sheets of rain swept past them, the blustering wind just another contestant in the melee. Their scuffling boots kicked water as high as their chests, sending up fountains of spray in the midst of battle.

Mason didn't expect to win here; he expected to perplex, complicate matters and buy time.

A merc collapsed. Ice flecks stabbed at Mason's face. Roxy dislodged someone's kneecap and then took an elbow to the right cheek and was momentarily stunned. Mason felled the man who'd tagged her.

The mercenary group was starting to group together, to gel. It was time . . .

Mason yelled his intention to Roxy and cut loose, spinning and almost colliding with a camera-happy tourist before increasing speed.

Other sounds intruded now: the warning shouts that filled the square; the astonished cries of alarmed visitors as they watched the fracas; the hoarse barking of someone calling the police. Shocked faces were everywhere, skimming past his field of vision like a distorted kaleidoscope.

A quick check revealed Roxy breaking free, following a few steps behind, skirting a souvenir cart and using it as a barrier as she broke for the piazzetta.

Halfway along it, Sally, Hassell and Quaid were waiting. Mason waved frantically at them to get moving.

The route ahead, the wide piazzetta and the waterway at its far end, was a blurred landscape filled with curtains of rain, with fast-moving people and huddled groups, with those lined up waiting to cram inside the library, and with those departing the area to look for water taxis. It was a mess, a foot-traveller's nightmare.

But Mason could make the best of it.

Behind, eight of the nine mercs had regrouped, shrugged off their confusion and were giving chase. Mason, pleased that Roxy had disabled one of them, raced through the rain and tried to pull away.

Ahead, the flowing basin of water made it seem that he and Roxy were running headlong towards the wide sea with nowhere else to go. The twin columns of San Marco and San Teodoro only served to focus their eyes and added to the unsettling illusion.

Hassell cut left, slipping for a shocked heartbeat on the slick paving, but recovered well. Sally went with him. Quaid took a moment to slow, unshoulder his backpack and pull out a Glock.

He threw it to Mason.

Great intuition. Seeing that both Mason and Roxy would struggle to arm themselves at speed, Quaid had solved the problem in a single stroke.

Mason thrust the gun deep inside a jacket pocket, hiding it from sight whilst retaining easy access. They caught up to Quaid and ran east alongside the Doge's Palace, picking their way through the crowd.

'Did it work?' Quaid asked.

Mason didn't know and didn't answer. Roxy came up with the classic 'It didn't *not* work' and kept running, now close to the edge of the basin to skirt the worst of the crowd.

'If only they knew we didn't find anything,' Quaid said.

'We found plenty.' Mason saw the Ponte della Paglia ahead, the ornate white bridge which crossed the first canal he'd seen so far, and slowed, frustrated at the size of the crowd occupying it.

'Time to fire a bullet in the air,' Roxy remarked.

Mason's face screwed up. 'No way,' he said. 'Too dangerous. We'll only use gunfire as a last resort.'

Sally and Hassell forged a path across the bridge, barging men and women aside. Quaid caught up fast, ignoring the angry looks and raised voices. Mason and Roxy flew across the bridge behind them, catching a glimpse of the narrow, green-watered Rio di Palazzo and Bridge of Sighs to the left, as everything was pounded by the rain.

The sky was darkening by the minute, clouds the colour of obsidian casting their shadows further. Ahead, Sally and Hassell were already angling towards a berth of water taxis.

A gasp from behind surprised Mason. Looking back, he saw Roxy tackled by a fleet adversary who'd outpaced the rest of his crew by at least thirty feet.

Roxy hit the ground and rolled, her jacket taking the brunt of the initial impact and her backpack arresting the roll.

The man who'd tackled her flew past her, scraping along the glossy flagstones and sending up an impressive bow wave of water on both sides. Mason waited for him to stop moving, kicked him unceremoniously in the side of the head, then reached down to help Roxy.

'Move.' She was already up and giving the man a vicious look as she passed, kicking out as he reached for her. Passers-by stared in shock and horror as they backed away.

Mason and Roxy took off at speed as their pursuers slowed to negotiate the snarl of pedestrians along the white bridge.

Hassell pounded to the front of a water-taxi queue, pushed a man aside and jumped in. Harsh words were exchanged with the pilot, who wasn't allowed to leave his craft for any reason, but the production of Hassell's Sig Sauer soon swayed the argument.

Hassell prepared the boat to leave as Quaid and Sally jumped on. Mason and Roxy were ten feet behind.

'Go, go!' Mason cried.

Hassell gunned the throttle. The boat lifted at the front as its engine roared and its propeller churned.

It pulled away from its berth, gathering speed. Mason and Roxy ran alongside before jumping aboard as it peeled out into the wide water basin, landing heavily but securely inside the craft but making it rock alarmingly.

Mason sat up.

The top pick of immediate choices was simple – put bullets in all the available water taxis sitting bobbing in their berths. Many men he'd known wouldn't think twice about doing it, but the unwanted attention and mayhem it would cause made him grit his teeth.

Hassell steered the boat out into the water, blasted by rain, ice and high winds, and then back towards the concrete shore as a ferry loomed ahead.

Already, the mercs were commandeering another boat.

Mason pointed. 'There,' he said. 'We can lose them among the canals.'

Chapter 54

The boat zipped into the mouth of a narrow canal, the towering concrete walls on both sides focusing Mason's vision on the channel ahead. Hassell slammed across the choppy waves, blinded by torrential rain and sleet.

Water sluiced down the sides of the buildings, gushing towards them. Mason made his way to the stern and crouched down, looking for signs of pursuit.

It came fast. A boat sliced into the canal behind them but, going way too fast, slammed into a wall and rebounded at an angle that sent it crashing into the other wall. A man almost fell overboard but managed to grab a rope and was soon hauled back in.

Mason regarded the whole scene, his face grim. 'Faster,' he shouted back at Hassell. 'They can't drive for shit but they really want to introduce us to a watery grave.'

Hassell gave it everything, making the engine groan and the stern sway. They flew under the Bridge of Sighs, stained white walls to the left and right marked by rows of window openings.

Two gondolas ambled ahead, their gondoliers pushing economically at their single oars. Hassell squeezed the water-craft past to their right, nudging the wall with the prow, scraping the veneer and smashing a window. Mason gritted his teeth.

Another bridge emerged from the mists of rain ahead, this one thick with umbrella-touting visitors and camera-happy tourists. Hassell steered the boat back into the centre of the canal and zipped under it, shedding and spraying water to both sides.

Mason guessed they'd pulled out a decent lead by now, but was worried a police boat might turn up before they made a proper escape.

As one more bridge came into view Sally called out and waved her phone. 'Junction ahead,' she shouted. 'Just after the bridge.'

Mason checked backwards. The downpour veiled his view of the chasing boat, but not enough, since the lack of vision went both ways.

'Take the right canal,' Sally said, using her thumb and forefinger to expand the map on her phone. 'It branches off after a minute or so.'

Hassell waved an acknowledgement. Mason held on. He'd been second-guessing himself about the feasibility of using the canals, knowing that some were shallow and others contained bridges too low for a water taxi to pass under, but the season and the rain and the general bad weather were on their side for now.

The boat turned at speed, careering into the tributary canal, just clipping the side of a gondola and setting it rocking from side to side. A wave of water smashed against the towering side walls.

Hassell opened the throttle once more and gunned the boat harder, sending Quaid and Sally slipping across the slick deck and onto their knees. Mason held onto a bronze grab handle, his knuckles white with strain.

'Guys!' Hassell called.

Mason watched behind as the mercenary pilot threw his

own boat around the bend in their wake, the vessel a faint, ghostly shape, and wiped water from his eyes.

'Hey!' Hassell's shout was louder still. 'What the—'

Mason whirled at an accompanying shout from Roxy, cursing when he saw a blue and white police boat bobbing in the centre of the channel ahead. Four men stood in its cabin wearing the uniform and hats of the Venice Police Force.

Hassell turned. 'What to do?'

Roxy clenched her fists. 'Ram 'em!'

Mason winced, flicking furiously through the options, which were few. But one slim chance did present itself . . .

'Full speed,' he yelled at Hassell. 'And try to pass them.'

The boat lurched ahead, motor booming. A surge of water, displaced by the craft, broke across the sheer walls to their right. Mason held on as both boats closed rapidly and then, holding his gun well out of sight, fired a shot into a nearby wall.

'Get out of here!' He leapt to his feet as the startled cops reacted. 'They're trying to kill us!'

The vessels came close, too close, and then the water taxi swept past the police boat, taking a chunk out of its back end, and sending them into an erratic weave until Hassell managed to regain control through deceleration.

The cops stared between them and their pursuers, but it was clear who were the aggressors in this chase.

Mason kept his eyes on the confrontation as Hassell fought to right their boat.

The cops leaned out, shouting at the oncoming mercenaries. They produced guns of their own, waving them threateningly. The police pilot sought to fully block the channel but wasn't quick enough.

The mercenaries smashed into the side of the police boat, rebounded into a concrete wall and kept going. The pinball effect continued as both boats' sterns also crashed together, the sound of screeching, splintered wood like a tortured

340

scream up and down the canal, but then the mercenary craft was free.

Mason couldn't believe what he saw next.

A small, pineapple-shaped object looped out of a mercenary's fist, flew up into the air and fell into the police boat.

There was a terrible moment of unbearable expectation in which Mason closed his eyes, distraught, before a deep and devastating explosion rocked the waterway. The police boat shattered in all directions, shards and chunks of wood, glass and fibreglass blasting up and outward. A percussive boom surged down the canal, resounding between high walls.

Mason fell into the bottom of the boat. Hassell momentarily lost control, grabbing for the wheel as their bow rammed a building.

By the time Mason raised his head, the pursuing boat was tearing through churning water straight at them. Mason didn't have to warn Hassell. The American had already opened the throttle. Wreckage rained down over the canal, everything from slivers of wood to chunks of engine metal.

Mason checked upwards in case anything heavy was about to crush him and was taken aback by the sight of a breathtaking blizzard of jagged wreckage tumbling through the air above, outlined against the grey sky and shot through by millions of silver rain droplets.

Another heavy swell chopped at the boat, demanding his attention. The mercs were almost upon them as Hassell propelled their boat forward, cutting through the middle of the canal.

Both vessels swept across the water, separated by mere seconds. Mason was close enough to see the malice that shone from the pursuing pilot's eyes. Debris continued to smash down and float around them.

'Left!' Sally shouted out.

Mason saw another intersection. Hassell threw their boat to the left, surging around a tight corner, followed closely by their enemies, who didn't lose an inch of water. Almost touching, the boats increased speed along the new, wider canal.

Rocking to the side, twisting and weaving, the boats cut through choppy waters as each pilot sought to gain an advantage.

Mason held on and watched the mercs, not surprised when one of them reached out around the cabin's window frame, gun in hand, and squeezed off three shots.

Untroubled, Mason took out his own Glock and fired back. With an enormous target to aim at he chose the windshield, destroying it with two shots. The pilot was forced to slacken his speed, the boat dropping back. Mason fired twice more, aiming for the pilot but missing.

When the mag ran out, he dropped his backpack onto the deck and rummaged inside for a fresh one.

Hassell propelled the boat around bends and along straight stretches of water. When he took a corner at speed and then let the boat just accelerate forwards Mason knew they'd hit a much larger channel. He felt it too.

Strong and ceaseless gusts of wind and rain raged atop the waves. Mason saw buildings lining both banks, canopied restaurants, shops and water-taxi berths in yellows and reds and blues, and then shifted his perspective to what lay ahead.

The Rialto.

Even he recognised Venice's most famous bridge on sight. Which also meant this was the Grand Canal, one of Venice's major water corridors. The Rialto was a single-span stone bridge with two sloping ramps leading up to a central portico.

Mason saw it was packed, the side arches lined by crowds gazing up and down the canal. Clearly, if they'd heard the grenade, it hadn't worried them.

Hassell guided the speeding boat in and out of traffic, flashing under the elaborate Rialto and around a long, sweeping bend to the left. The chasing boat crept closer, taking risks. Hassell hugged the inner bank, covering as little distance as possible.

'Is there a plan?' Roxy shouted at Sally. 'To all this?'

'Of course. We're heading back, on a roundabout route, to the Tronchetto.'

Mason frowned, in two minds about the benefits of returning to their vehicle with the mercs at their heels. On the other hand . . .

'The ferryboat harbour,' he said, remembering it from when they'd caught the water taxi. 'Take us in there.'

Hassell grinned back, his face feral and dripping water at the wheel, as if he'd read Mason's mind. Roxy checked her gun and changed the mag. Quaid peered through the downpour to try to get a glimpse of the upcoming terminal as the mercs' boat rumbled closer.

The terminal emerged on the left, a lengthy generic dock for ferryboats backed by a parking garage. Mason counted five boats boarding at five separate berths. They could hear the mercenaries' craft at full speed now, the engine roaring, even the shouts of men. Hassell drove between the third and fourth ferries at speed, passing out of sight seconds after their pursuers rounded the first.

The craft jolted the side of the ferry, just below its lowest row of open windows. Quaid grabbed the bottom lip of a window and hauled himself up. Sally took hold of another, boosted by Roxy's hand. Hassell ran for a third. Mason leapt for a gap and fell to the floor of the ferry in an ungainly heap.

Roxy's boots landed surefootedly next to his head. 'You okay?'

He grabbed her outstretched hand and was about to pull himself to his feet when a grim face appeared at the window

343

he'd just jumped through. Without thinking, he punched it. Roxy hammered the next merc who appeared. Mason punched his assailant again and heard the man fall away, shouting in pain. But it didn't end there. More mercs appeared at more windows. The fight came quickly to the attention of the boarding passengers. Screams lit the air. Mason jumped up but didn't run. The mercs were at a severe disadvantage only when they were outside the windows. Mason smashed another and felt blood gush across his aching, closed fingers. One merc almost made it through, his body squirming across the window sill, but Roxy leapt toward him, hooked him under the shoulders and threw him back outside. Seconds later, there was a resounding splash.

The ferryboat was filling up from the dock by the second and should have been the perfect cover, but Quaid, Hassell and Sally were forced to drive against the flow as they fought to reach dockside. Mason saw that they needed time, but then the entire scenario changed.

A merc appeared, a gun clutched in one hand. On seeing Mason, he fired it. The bullet skimmed past Mason's skull, and hit the roof, and then the passengers started screaming. Mason grabbed the merc's wrist and broke it, sending the gun clattering to the floor and scuttling away between dozens of shoes.

It was now or never.

Acting instantly, he and Roxy sprinted away from the side of the ferry, chasing Quaid and the others, seconds before the civilian mass erupted into panic. Those who had heard the gunshot tried to run; those who hadn't became flustered and unsure which way to turn. Mason grabbed hold of Quaid and shouted at him to get moving. They pushed forcefully through the crowd, seconds ahead of the main confusion and just in front of a spreading wildfire of panic. Seconds later, they disembarked onto relatively solid ground and risked a quick look back.

The ferry rolled with the weight of frightened passengers. Many were scurrying off the deck and along the dock. The sheer mass of flustered bodies eliminated any chance of the mercenaries continuing their pursuit.

Sally ran for the parking garage. The rain pelted down, bouncing off the concrete, whipped and thrashed by errant high winds. Restless grey skies roiled above.

Mason ducked under the shelter offered by the multi-storey garage and stopped for a second, soaked through, trying to take stock of all that had happened.

Quaid beckoned at him. 'Hurry. They won't stop coming.'

That was what Mason was afraid of.

Chapter 55

Hours later, forced to pay for a hotel room in which to take refuge and shed their waterlogged clothing, they huddled close to the room's grungy radiator and unwound as best they could. With boxes of food arrayed on the bed, open bottles and steaming coffee, they processed everything they'd discovered in St Mark's Basilica earlier that day.

'Revelation 17 to 18 describes the destruction of Babylon,' Sally said a little despondently. 'Any ideas? I mean, is this another code? A secret language? Should we consult De-Ville?' She plucked out her phone.

'No, wait, I knew there was something,' Hassell said. 'When you recited some of those verses earlier, I *knew* I'd heard at least one of them before. And, trust me, the streets I grew up in didn't have forces of spiritual goodness watching over them, and I've never read the Bible.'

'You recognised the verses?' Roxy asked.

'Some of them. And it wasn't until we were on the Grand Canal that I made the connection. It was Marduk. The Amori boss recited them like prayers during our first meeting.'

'Everything points to the Amori having a refuge in Babylon,' Quaid said, sitting with his back to the foot of the bed. 'It's right there in Jacques Heindl's clue. Revelation 17 to 18 is a damning description of ancient Babylon.'

'It fits with what we know of their history,' Sally said. 'But a modern-day headquarters? It's just not possible.'

'The passages show how Christians of the time reacted towards a rival group, even if it was just a clique that might not even have bothered them. They sought to paint Babylon in the worst possible light.' Quaid spoke softly. 'And succeeded.'

'But the reality is,' Mason broke in, 'that Babylon was destroyed years ago.'

'One hundred and thirty-odd years ago, it still existed,' Quaid pointed out. 'When Heindl created the clues.'

'True,' Mason conceded. 'But since then we've had the Iraq War, the Iraq–ISIL war and many others. And I'm pretty sure I remember the Americans building Camp Alpha on a substantial part of the ruins, to widespread condemnation. Surely someone would have stumbled across the Amori stronghold.'

'Or seen people passing in and out,' Quaid said. 'And if *not*, then how the hell are we going to find it?'

Sally threw up her hands and paced the length of the room. 'It doesn't matter *how*,' she said. 'We just have to get it done. We find Marduk, we find the book. We find their refuge, we stop these new revelations that are being teased. These bastards killed my father. They stole the book. They're . . . *evil*. You said it yourself.' She glared at Hassell. 'Their leader ordered the murder of his own daughter. Anarchy matters to them.' Her voice rose as she spoke. 'Heindl risked everything to leave these clues behind and we found them. *Us*. You think he did it for a laugh? Or maybe he did it—'

Mason stopped her with a look before putting his arms around her. 'We've been with you from the beginning,' he said. 'And we're with you till the end. If anyone can find the Amori, I believe it's you.'

'Agreed.' Roxy stood beside him. 'We push through adversity to find security. That's what we do.'

Mason had a feeling she was uniting personal goals with team objectives, perhaps deliberately. He pulled away from Sally. 'What next?'

'This.' Hassell had scooped up the TV remote and aimed it at the small, scarred black box hanging on the wall opposite the bed. Switching it on, he flicked to a twenty-four-hour news channel.

Twenty minutes later they were aware that the Vatican and the Swiss Guard were still being resistant to what they called 'conspiracy theories' and, most importantly, nothing had openly materialised regarding the *Book of Secrets*. In fact, news coverage concerning the Amori situation was scarce; it was barely touched upon. Mason didn't have to point out how far their tentacles of influence reached and wondered how much the coverage would change once they revealed their devastating secret.

'What next?' Mason asked again. Sensing the despondent mood, he decided to take charge, thinking action would occupy minds and drive attention away from the Babylon-sized elephant in the room.

'You two.' He nodded at Hassell and Quaid. 'This is where you come in really useful. What can you do?'

'Italy to Babylon?' Quaid's eyes were wide. 'Full pack and gear. Armed. Kitted out. Ready to rock the moment we land. I can do that.'

'And I can help.' Hassell locked heads with Quaid, the pair fishing out their phones and searching for contacts, maps and routes.

'We need *proper* gear,' Roxy was quick to inform them. 'Five handguns and a bag of ammo isn't gonna cut it.'

Quaid nodded.

Mason turned back to Sally. 'We've got the practical part

348

covered,' he said. 'It's up to you to find a way through the theoretical to something substantial. Can you do that?'

Sally let out a huge sigh. 'Do I have a choice?'

Expecting to find the Amori's lair and the *Book of Secrets* somewhere around the ruins of ancient Babylon, the team made sure they were fully prepared.

Quaid used a contact in Verona to assemble a pack of weapons, body armour, boots and provisions. The man – named Lacuna – also sent a good, ear-based comms system, field glasses, topographical maps, the latest insurgent updates and other goodies by fast car, which arrived only minutes before they were set to leave the hotel. Quaid handed out new backpacks whilst shouldering a pair himself.

Hassell had arranged two flights – the first a private plane to take them directly to Turkey, the second a helicopter to fly them in low over Iraq's hills and mountains to their destination. It was notoriously difficult to get into Iraq even under normal circumstances, but Hassell's contact assured him he'd located a pilot with the right mix of crazy skills.

All the while, Sally worked with a sense of urgency.

Roxy watched and, during a lull, whispered to Mason, 'Are we really going to Iraq?'

'Believe me, it's the last place I *ever* want to go.'

'It's a haunted place.'

'Populated by the ghosts of good friends, good soldiers, who never truly die . . . We keep them right here.' Mason touched his chest. 'They only pass when their memories fade. I won't let that happen for Zach and Harry.'

Roxy touched his hand. 'I'll help you, Joe. We'll finish this thing together.'

Chapter 56

Mason enjoyed watching and listening to Quaid work as the small private jet winged its way towards Turkey. On the phone to his contacts, he found it easy to switch from being one of the boys, shooting the shit and cursing for kicks, to a more cultured, laid-back conversationalist or an angry, order-barking ex-officer – whatever was required by the situation.

The change was entertaining, and informative. Clearly, Quaid possessed clever manipulative skills useful in his line of work and was now using them to help people in need without having to answer to rigid, grey-haired bosses with personal agendas.

Mason saw the reason Quaid had quit the Army right there in a snapshot and could only admire the way he extracted information.

Early evening turned to full night as the fast jet outran the storm. Mason catnapped as Quaid spoke first to an ex-SAS buddy, a Yorkshireman working for the US government. This man put him in touch with another infamous ex-army officer who'd run teams out of every war-torn hellhole on the planet, who knew a computer hacker with dirt on a CIA bigwig.

The CIA key player, pulled out of an early afternoon date with his four-iron, put Quaid in touch with his best undercover expert – a man who went by the code name Incite. Quaid played the game, banking goodwill and promising favours in return, which, Mason presumed, he was in a good position to grant. Incite was the hardest man to get hold of but, an hour before touchdown in Turkey, Quaid's phone rang.

The men went through a kind of coded narrative, speaking about football players, certain goals scored, club managers and future prospects before Quaid relaxed and properly identified himself.

Incite spoke quickly and Quaid listened, asking only a couple of questions. Three minutes later, he had ended the call and turned to face Mason, tapping his mobile thoughtfully against the side of his head.

'Incite is an undercover agent, working behind enemy lines, advising on military tactics whilst working alongside US Delta Force soldiers to provide political and professional support. He's worked Kandahar against al-Q'aeda, the mountain ranges against the Taliban, you name it. Incite's speciality is full infiltration undercover work. This guy is what we called *hard routine* – no fire, hot food or drink, takes turns with two other men sleeping in three-hour stints in shallow trenches covered by webbing.'

Quaid turned reflective. 'He's lost count of the days, the months.' He shook his head. 'Anyway . . . as you can imagine, my goal was to collect real in-situ info, something that only those who've breathed, tramped and spat out Iraqi dust day and night for years can give you.'

'Incite sounds like the real deal,' Roxy said.

'He is. And *those* are the people we put our faith in. Now, if you recall, the Americans built Camp Alpha on a section of Babylon's ruins, close to the famous Ishtar Gate. Of course, there was the usual flap of international condemnation at their decision, but some took the time to look deeper, to understand why. Building close to Babylon *saved* more ancient history than it destroyed. You only have to look at other precious ancient ruins damaged by the insurgents, thousands of years of culture demolished by a band of thugs and cowards with guns.'

'And perhaps the Americans were looking for something,' Sally said. 'Or protecting something?'

'The military policy being so stiff and uninformative, and manipulated by those with hidden agendas, ensures we'll never know – but always there are rumours.'

'Wait.' Mason thought he saw where Quaid was going with this. 'You're not saying *those with hidden agendas* manipulated the positioning of Camp Alpha?'

Quaid gave an elaborate shrug. 'Who can say? But *why* position the camp atop ancient Babylon? Iraq's a pretty big place, after all. What better way is there to covertly protect a sacred refuge in the middle of a war zone? When the Iraq war kicked off in 2003, they built Camp Alpha within weeks and kept it open for over a year.'

Mason whistled. 'Sounds like someone really wanted comprehensive protection in that area for a limited amount of time.'

Quaid clicked his fingers. 'Exactly. But that's not enough for me. I quizzed Incite on field reports, boots-on-the-ground awareness. Soldiers gossip as much as any primary-school-parent clique, and men like Incite listen and report.'

Mason cast back to his time in Iraq, before Mosul, when sleep had been fleeting and conversation bold, unruly and free. He guessed a trained informer would have had his pick of juicy material, although nothing traitorous. Of course, one man's throwaway information was another man's treasure trove of intelligence.

'It all comes back to one standout memory, at least for Incite,' Quaid went on. 'The Ishtar Gate – one of Babylon's most famous landmarks. It was covered in a shiny blue glaze of semi-precious stone, built by King Nebuchadnezzar II and stolen by German archaeologists in the 1930s and, it has to be said, was—'

'Never heard of it,' Hassell said.

Sally blinked at him and couldn't help herself. 'Really? Well, let me put it this way. The Ishtar Gate was considered one of the original seven wonders of the world before the Lighthouse at Alexandria replaced it in the third century BC. It was *that* important.'

Hassell looked suitably rebuked and sat back.

Quaid saw the chance to continue. 'Several news reports conveyed that the remains of the Ishtar Gate were damaged by US troops during the construction of Camp Alpha. It remains the main contentious issue for UNESCO, archae-ologists and reporters the world over. But, whilst other landmarks *were* scratched or broken, Incite recalls that the Ishtar Gate was off limits. Nobody ever went near it.'

'Because of its historical significance?' Sally asked.

'That was the official line, yes. Nobody thought to ques-tion it and, to be perfectly honest, 99 per cent of soldiers didn't notice or care. But Incite's job *is* to notice the unusual and the abnormal. The useless information that man has in his head beggars belief.'

'The Ishtar Gate,' Sally mused. 'It's a good place to start. Well done, Paul.'

Quaid nodded. 'That's what I do, and it's the most I can offer.'

Mason noticed the use of Quaid's first name, an inter-esting sign that the team was cementing. In truth, he was surprised that Sally knew it before he did, but they had only met recently and events were fast moving.

'My own research confirms that we're on the right track,' Sally said. 'The Amori founded Babylon as a small town along the Euphrates River four thousand years ago, its first mention being on a stone tablet dated to that period. From that to the largest city in the world and then destruction is a hard pill to swallow. The Amori will savour every facet of this revenge. I did discover one other item of interest though.'

As she paused, the pilot called out that they were beginning their descent into Turkey, bound for an eastern airfield. Mason checked the window to view a rocky landscape below.

Sally went on: 'The Freemasons' organisation, which, unlike the Amori, is a recognised and notable part of society, considers Babylon to be its birthplace.'

Mason frowned. 'Really?'

'Yeah, really. Could be a coincidence, could be something more sinister. Roots tangled within roots. I don't have time to shake that particular tree right now.'

Mason nodded as the plane touched down and taxied along the bumpy runway. As it slowed, he caught sight of their next transport through a side window.

'Black, sleek and deadly.' He smiled. 'You got us an Apache.'

Quaid turned. 'Flown by an Army Air Corps pilot, no less. Though Joint Helicopter Command will know little of it. He's an—'

'Old friend?' Roxy interrupted with a smile.

'Something like that. I dated his wife for a while.'

Roxy grimaced just as Quaid added, '*Before* they got together,' to which Roxy murmured something about Quaid having more lady friends around the world than Casanova. Sally then regaled them with a tale about Casanova and the famous Ponte della Paglia, one of the bridges they'd raced across in Venice.

Mason watched it all go round with a satisfied ease, pleased that this rough, ragtag crew was starting to gel.

The plane turned 180 degrees and deposited them beside the black Apache. Five minutes later, with their packs stowed, they lifted off in a very different craft to the plane; a raw and strident machine that exuded aggression.

Mason held on as they rose from the ground, Sally biting her lips until they turned white whilst the others admired the unfolding view.

Early morning blossomed and later their attention was caught by jagged mountains bathing in the midday sun. The blessed weather was such a transformation that Mason sat back and took it easy for an hour, letting the roar of the aircraft prompt memories he hadn't faced in years.

There was no absolution for him in returning to Iraq, only a conflagration of evils that flared up like unexorcised demons, spitting their venom with a deep-rooted anger. Mason expected the demons to give him no quarter and was not surprised. All he could do was to survive this day and face the next as best he could. It was a way of life.

On the last good day of my life I will love, I will hold; I will fight, and I will die.
Remember that I sacrificed my freedom, so that you could have yours.

The poem of a dead soldier, echoing in the hearts of dead soldiers the world over. Unknown to most but held dearly in Mason's heart. Zack Kelly had written it a month before the IED killed him. Mason felt a knot form in his heart and tried to push it aside.

I'm sorry. My fault. My watch. My blame. You will never be forgotten.

It was an introspective, silent crew that crossed the border into Iraq across a craggy mountain range, before turning south beyond Mosul on a winding route towards Baghdad. The chopper, whilst military, carried no markings that could be attributed to any one country and was generic enough to the casual observer to pass unidentified. The situation in Iraq was uncertain and liable to deteriorate quickly, and there was always the likelihood of being fired on from the ground. The Apache did have self-defence equipment, but Mason's heart was in his mouth as they flew over the hostile landscape. The team fuelled up on food and drink before arriving at their destination.

The pilot departed after depositing them on rocky ground, handing Quaid a sat-phone and telling him to shout when they needed extraction. He couldn't promise when and where that might happen, but at least the offer was there.

Mason paused under a vast, open sky that stretched between ragged horizons. They stood atop a rock formation amid clusters of boulders, strewn stone and gravel, studying a forbidding, inhospitable landscape that offered an arid welcome. Mason gazed across a valley floor, taking in the environment, sweating slightly and reaching for his sunglasses.

'The remains of Camp Alpha.' Quaid swept a hand to the west.

'We're against the clock,' Sally said. 'What's next?'

'We get a move on,' Quaid said before promptly sitting down, shrugging his smaller pack from around his shoulders and depositing it on the ground. Mason watched him un-buckle the straps and pull out a small black object as well as a rectangular plastic box which he passed to Hassell.

'You think the Amori will be waiting for us?' Roxy asked, shielding her eyes.

'In their lair? Their inner sanctum?' Mason said. 'Heindl's led us to their Hotel California. The one place they would never leave.'

'Then how do we get in?'

'Are you kidding? We have Luke Hassell, infiltration specialist. Paul Quaid, procurer extraordinaire. And Sally Rusk, historical genius. What more do we need?'

Sally didn't look convinced. Roxy was eyeing him and looking offended. 'You never mentioned me.'

'Didn't I? Well then, we also have Roxy Banks, the best rum taster outside the Caribbean.'

He was about to elaborate when Quaid pressed a button on the plastic box. A small black drone hummed as it rose into the air. Quaid took out a tablet, already mated to the machine, and received the feed within seconds, a feed that recorded everything the drone saw.

'Let's see what we're up against, shall we?'

Chapter 57

'That is not good,' Quaid said. 'Are we too late?'

Mason viewed the tablet's screen with alarm, leaning in for a clearer view. 'Are they really . . . ?'

Roxy was also trying to fathom the footage. 'I can't believe what I'm seeing.'

Quaid tapped the screen. 'Don't blame the tools. Mavic Pro drone with CMOS sensor that offers the best video quality. Those guys really are packing explosives into the Ishtar Gate.'

Mason closed his eyes briefly in disbelief. In warfare, he guessed, there were no rules, and the Amori were very much at war.

Mason forced the issue aside for a moment. 'And the GPR?'

Quaid had mentioned that attached to the base of the drone was a Ground Penetrating Radar transmitter. Again, they could watch the data returned in real time via the tablet. Quaid had also made it clear that he was in no way responsible for the new-fangled tech and had no clue what to do if anything went wrong. The drone had been given to him by an old friend.

'The tech's rudimentary,' he'd said. 'But this is a rough-arsed crew. Should suit you all.'

Roxy had laughed as Mason nodded his head in agreement. Hassell wasn't quite sure of the jargon but got the drift. Sally was the only one to furnish Quaid with a slightly miffed look.

Mason had handled GPR before in countless operations. 'I don't know the exact terminology,' he said. 'But it fires electromagnetic energy at the ground. When changes *below* ground are detected, like a *cave* for instance, some of that electromagnetic energy is reflected back to the surface and registers on our screen.' Staying low, he looked out over the ruins.

The drone hung in the still air many hundreds of feet above the soldiers' heads. The squad were too busy to spot it as yet, removing packages from the back of a beaten-up old truck and carrying them up the old processional way – a twisting, steep cobbled street leading to the Ishtar Gate – so that they could deposit them inside and around the old relic. Mason recognised none of the faces, so assumed this was a different squad of mercenaries to the one they'd encountered earlier.

The Ishtar Gate itself was little more than an arched mound these days, topped by Iraq's ubiquitous rugged landscape. All around the gate and stretching for miles, Mason saw low excavated mounds and unearthed walls in uniform lines, and the crumbled ruins of ancient structures. A blast of desert dirt struck him in the face.

Mason coughed. 'Two-edged sword,' he said. 'We don't want those soldiers anywhere near so that we can get inside, but if they leave . . .'

'Boom,' Roxy said. 'And have you thought about the other issue? Like – where the hell are the Amori?'

'This is the Amori,' Sally said. 'Don't you see? They've decided to cover their arses before the great revelation. By finding the final clue, they know *we* have the knowledge to find this place. But burying it . . .' She shook her head. 'That's extreme even for them.'

Mason nodded. 'They're clearing out whatever remains,' he said. 'And destroying what they can't take with them.'

'Heindl led us here and now we're out of time. This is the end of the road.' Sally shifted her position in the rocks and looked at Quaid. 'Isn't it?'

'What am I looking for?'

Mason helped him make sense of the screen. 'The reflected wave pattern identifies anomalies,' he said. 'It's pretty uniform there.' He traced the display with his finger. 'But *here* . . . see how the array is reversed? That's a void.'

Sally's head snapped towards him. 'A void? Are you positive?'

'Going by the small amount of training we had years ago, then yes. It's a void. This equipment isn't powerful enough to survey it with any accuracy though.'

'Then we have to get down there.' Sally bit her bottom lip. 'Fast.'

Mason met Hassell's eyes. 'Sally's right,' he said. 'We have to explore that void *before* the soldiers leave.'

'Another conundrum,' Quaid grumbled. 'And how come they're always either just ahead of us or just behind us?'

'Isn't that obvious?' Sally pointed out. 'We're all on the same quest, but we're learning as we go. The mercs always report their findings back to the Amori and wait for new instructions before travelling. Neither they nor we can expect to get too far in front following the trail of clues. But,' she stressed, 'they've always known how this could end and sought to stop us along the way before resorting to such extreme measures.'

'They wouldn't destroy it unless there was no other choice,' Roxy said.

'Which means . . .' Mason said slowly, 'something big's down there that can't be removed. Something that might even lead us to their *new* home.'

'That's my take, at least,' Sally said.

'A couple of hours' lead would have worked just fine,' Quaid complained.

'You can't be sure of that,' Roxy said. 'Maybe they've been watching the area and we'd now be *inside* the cave, trussed up and waiting for the explosion.'

'Or late,' Mason said. 'Looking at a pile of rubble and a smoking hole.'

Quaid held his hands in the air. 'Okay, okay. I get the point. So what's next?'

Mason was intrigued to see how everyone looked to Hassell. Was this part of a new group dynamic? To his credit, the New Yorker took it in his stride, answering quickly. 'Hey, you've hit me with another infil problem and again I'll tell you there's no time. No chance to plan. Only one way in, one way out. Big enemy presence.'

'A distraction?' Roxy asked.

'Not only a distraction,' Hassell said. 'That won't work properly. There's at least a dozen of them, more counting the drivers and whoever's working inside the cave.'

'So . . . a *big* distraction,' Roxy said.

'You have something in mind?' Hassell caught her speculative tone.

'Yeah, I do,' she said. 'Me.'

Mason gawped. 'You? What are you talking about?'

'Aren't I a big distraction?' Roxy pouted.

Mason dodged the loaded question, worried that no simple answer was correct. 'I'm assuming you have a plan.'

'With me, it's fluid,' Roxy admitted, rising and stretching her muscles. 'I'll wing it. Don't worry, something usually comes to me.'

'Usually?' Mason briefly closed his eyes. 'You can't just wander into their camp.'

'Relax.' Roxy drew the word out. 'Come get me when you're done.'

Mason wanted to say more, to *do* more. If she'd been

under his command, he'd have ordered her to stand down. But Roxy answered to no one.

Quaid started to follow but then thought better of it. Mason quelled unexpected feelings of fear, anxiety and warmth. This wouldn't go easy for the raven-haired woman.

She craved the experiences, Mason thought. Each new event, good or bad, was another scarred shield between her future and her past. A way of moving on.

If she survived.

Mason sought to back her as best he could. 'Over there.' He indicated the ridgeline. 'We can get above the gate if we're fast.'

'We'll have to be.' Quaid stared after Roxy with concern. 'She's gonna need us.'

Mason led the way, scrabbling over the rocky terrain in a wide loop, staying just under the line of the ridge to avoid detection. The sun beat down and an errant, robust breeze blew, swirling up mini dust-storms and hammering grit at their faces. Mason moved fast, leaving the others behind, unable to stop worrying about Roxy – a big turnaround since they'd first met in that airport hotel room.

Looping around the site of the Ishtar Gate and the soldiers' trucks, they slowed when a hostile yell rang out, announcing Roxy's detection. Mason raised his head slightly so that he could peer into the basin below. What he saw made his heart lurch.

Eight of the twelve soldiers were hurrying to confront her, their rifles raised. Roxy's hands were in the air. The remaining four soldiers were observing, their backs to the gate. As Mason watched, two more men emerged from the archway, clearly wondering what the hell was going on. Mason clenched his fists and covered the last hundred yards to the top of the gate.

Their destination lay twelve feet straight down.

They hugged the ground, conscious of the men below.

Mason accepted the Bluetooth-powered comms system that Quaid handed him and prodded a bud firmly into his right ear.

He watched as the soldiers gathered around Roxy and started yelling orders, waving the barrels of their guns in her face. Roxy spoke, her words lost under more yelling.

After a moment, another man appeared from the cave below, stretching his back and wiping his brow before taking a good look at proceedings. This man made a careful, guarded appraisal of the ridgeline overlooking the gate, as suspicious as a cornered snake.

Mason pressed his face and body against the ground, waiting.

Eventually, a voice rang out, thick and guttural, speaking in a language Mason didn't understand. The voice then said in passable English: 'They are idiots but don't worry. I tell them you don't speak our language.'

Mason counted to five and then raised his head. The new guy was approaching the pack circling Roxy, who were covering her with their weapons but had backed off several steps. The four men below had advanced too so that they were closer to Roxy than to the gate.

Now or never.

'You two stay here,' he ordered Hassell and Quaid. 'If Roxy needs you, do something.'

He grabbed Sally's hand, ignored the aggrieved and bewildered looks on the faces of the two men, and made ready. The simple facts were that they stood more chance of success if just two of them entered the cave, and Roxy stood more chance of survival if someone watched over her.

Mason crawled in silence to the lip above the cave, grabbed a sturdy boulder and slipped over the edge, lowering himself down. At full length, he let go, falling the remaining six feet or so to the ground and landing quietly before falling flat.

The Ishtar Gate now stood before him, nothing more than an irregular arch filled with gloom. Mason was coiled and ready to attack if an enemy presented itself, but nobody materialised out of the dark innards. A scuffling sound made him look up.

Sally was hanging off the ridgeline in a carbon copy of his own descent.

Mason scrambled up, trusting to luck that one of the soldiers didn't turn around at that point, and supported her as she landed. Without delay, he pushed her inside the cave towards the waiting, welcome, encompassing shadows.

Sally nodded. 'Good. Now we can find out what is really going on here.'

Mason drew his weapon, knowing that any shot fired would start a war, but forced to trust in his team. Sally switched on a torch she'd drawn from her pack, cupped the light and swung it around the cave.

'The Ishtar Gate,' she said. 'I was hoping for more.'

Incomparable to the photos he'd seen, the once wonder of the world was little more than a wide, decrepit arch, compressed by time, despoiled and looted by a succession of ignorant, uncaring powers, the faded shadow of an ancient glory which now presented only crumbled blocks, ravaged walls and a sense of sadness.

Sally shone her light towards the back of the cave. 'Tunnel,' she said.

Mason moved fast, conscious not only of Roxy's dilemma but of the explosives *and* of the Amori's ultimate objectives. Soon, they were enveloped by the tunnel's constricted walls, cocooned in its silence and removed from the world outside.

Mason saw three packages arranged against each wall, wires trailing to a central point which was, currently, unoccupied.

'They're still wiring,' he whispered. 'They haven't brought in the detonator yet. We have some time.'

How much time he couldn't say. That depended on Roxy, Quaid and Hassell.

'Will they . . . shoot her?' Sally fretted.

'Not straightaway. They'll want information first. Luckily, they're not the mercs who've been on our tail, because they'd almost certainly recognise her. But they won't waste time.'

Sally winced at his last sentence. 'I hope she'll slow them down. She's superb.'

Mason agreed, but urged her on.

Sally, in front, then stopped so abruptly that Mason walked into her, striking his face against the back of her skull. When she tottered, gasping, he saw the hole at her feet and reached out to steady her, head ringing from their collision.

At that moment a crackle and flurry of words made him stiffen in shock. He'd almost forgotten about the comms earbud.

'You . . . found . . . yet?' The reception was a mix of crackles and stunted words. '. . . out here . . .'

'Say again,' Mason returned. 'The cave and tunnel are causing issues.'

'What . . . you found? It's stable . . . out here . . .'

'A hole,' Mason said. 'There's a black hole in the ground. We may lose you.'

Sally looked around at him. 'We're going in?'

'We're going in.'

Chapter 58

Never in a thousand years would Luke Hassell have imagined himself positioned on a desert ridge, sighting a semi-automatic machine gun on a bunch of irate soldiers in the Iraqi desert.

The source of their anger, Roxy Banks, stood calmly in their midst, hands in the air. The leader of the soldiers – a man they'd overheard being called Hamoud – had quietened them and was now addressing Roxy.

The man at Hassell's side kept up a running commentary. 'Don't like this . . . We should be in different positions for better angles if this goes to shit . . . Even the bloody driver's joining in now . . . I'm calling Mason.'

Hassell maintained concentration, purging everything else from his mind. There was no Gido in this moment, no complex debate over trust and betrayal. There was only Roxy, her safety, and the intentions of the enemy soldiers.

Quaid contacted Mason. Hassell heard it all through the comms. When Quaid turned to him, Hassell said, 'We've got Roxy's back. It's all on us now.'

One soldier stepped forwards and forced Roxy to her knees. Hamoud berated the man and dragged her back to her feet, waving, smiling and backing away.

Hassell interpreted his hand signals as cajoling, soothing

and passive. He wanted information, and he wanted it painlessly. Of course, that wouldn't stop him shooting Roxy in the head once she'd coughed up.

Roxy smiled, swayed and stood in a relaxed manner, putting them at their ease. As the minutes ticked by, Hassell saw more than half the gun barrels lowered. A little later they were all pointing at the floor. Everyone watched Roxy.

Several minutes ticked by.

Mason illuminated and then jumped into the rough hole, falling six feet. The opening was crude, irregular and clearly man-made. He crouched, waited for Sally and then started along another tunnel, this one barely five feet high.

The fear of the crushing weight inches above their heads was nothing compared to the knowledge that several high explosives waited to be primed up there, explosives that would permanently block their exit. Mason nodded encouragingly as Sally let out a long, pent-up breath and turned worried eyes upon him.

'We're doing fine,' he said.

He moved as fast as conditions allowed, his forehead striking glancing blows off low rocks, his shoulders jabbed by the rough walls. It was hard going; the air was choked with dust. The scraping sound of their boots echoed back and forth, but they were alone down here, ignoring all discomforts as they raced against the clock.

'Shit,' Mason cursed out loud as the tunnel ended and a wash of stale air met his face. In the light of his torch, the walls retreated left and right, and the low ceiling vanished into an unknowable void above.

'What is it?' Sally pushed past. 'Whoa, a cavern.'

Mason made sweeping motions with his hand, painting the cavern with the torch's stark glow, adding his own light to Sally's. He whistled. 'Is this it? The void?'

'I think so.' Sally illuminated a sloping path ahead, made

of old flagstones, that meandered through the cavern. Rows of stepped ledges formed the eastern wall, all empty, whilst a wide semi-circular space to the west might have held tables, chairs, beds or altars.

Niches and arched alcoves – these too clearly man-made – and several raised daises made up another wall; and a row of narrow openings stood at the furthest edge of their torches' light.

'One thing,' Mason said. 'It's empty, though obviously it's been cleared out recently.' He pointed at cigarette butts, some still smoking, and bits of rubbish on the floor.

'We failed.' Sally's voice was tight with frustration. 'We did everything right. Followed Heindl's clues to the letter. How can this be?' She shook her head and sat on a rock, sobbing with frustration. Mason fought his own mix of exasperation and weariness and went over to her.

'Iraq's unstable,' Mason said. 'Because of the war, the dictator, the crazy, twisted groups who want to rule it. But one fact can't be ignored, Sally – *this* was the Amori's lair. Refuge. Sanctuary. Whatever the hell they called it, we're here. Right where they don't want us to be. But why? The whole place is empty.'

Sally considered his words, biting her lip, and soon came to the same conclusion. 'Because, as we thought, there's something here they don't want us to see. It's why they're about to blow the place to kingdom come.' She looked up, drying her eyes. 'Let's get to work.'

Her words, sobering and galvanising, spurred them into action.

They split up, Sally taking the eastern side and Mason the west. Almost immediately, Mason discovered that the cavern wasn't as empty as they'd first thought.

Three old silver plates were stacked in one of the wall niches. Dusty, chipped and dated, they were nevertheless relatively modern, certainly not ancient.

Mason blew the dust off to reveal a strange symbol emblazoned in their centre. With no time to call Sally over he took a quick photo with his phone and moved on. The floor was smooth, easy to negotiate. The air was thick with heat; swirling, timeless particles drifted in the light of his torch.

The scuttle of an unseen animal cut through the silence, but didn't come again. Mason found two stone statues in the lee of another ledge, both portraying a hooded man carrying a sword and a staff.

Was this how the Amori saw themselves? Hidden benefactors with the power to kill or heal? Was this how they perceived their birthright?

Mason snapped another photo and moved on.

Sally worked quickly across the other side of the cavern until she was standing before an enormous, slanting rock face that dwarfed her. The sight actually gave Mason chills, because if that sloping rock fell it would instantly crush her to death. There were no other sounds apart from their breathing. The silence stretched like brittle elastic, threatening to be broken any minute by the sound of a terrible explosion.

And Roxy, Mason thought. *She won't last long.*

Approaching the back end of the cave, he illuminated a rock carving and a symbol which had been cut into the stone. *The same symbol I saw on the plates.* The rock face was vast and formed most of the rear structural wall.

Several photos later he turned and called out. 'Hey, you ready?'

There was no answer. Mason probed the far shadows with his torch to no avail. Where the hell was she?

'Sally?' he shouted a bit louder.

Silence and shadow swallowed his voice. Mason felt a shiver run the length of his spine. Stepping across the main path he approached the western wall. Finally, his torch illuminated a figure, a figure that stood with its back to him.

'Are you okay?'

Sweating, spooked despite himself, Mason approached the figure. As he came close it turned, and he saw the white face, the desperate eyes, the clenched teeth.

'Sally?'

'We fucked up,' she said, and the surprise of the profanity on her lips pulled him up short.

'What?'

'It's been there all along. We followed the clues from place to place, the Five Great Churches, right? We went from city to city and altar to altar, following Heindl's path across countries. And they tried to stop us – the Amori – knowing that they couldn't remove this . . .' She waved a hand at the colossal rock. 'This sacred text. It must have hurt them badly to make the decision to bury this old sanctuary beneath tonnes of rock, but I guess once we'd found the fifth clue, they had no choice.'

That very thought galvanised Mason. 'You're not making any sense.'

'Like I said, it's been there all along. The clue. The clue to the Amori's new refuge. Why didn't I see it?'

Mason resisted an urge to shake her. 'Tell me.'

Sally breathed long and deep, drawing in the stifling air and stale dust motes. 'It's all about the Revelation quotes. When Hassell met Marduk, he recited verses from the book of Revelation. And we went through them recently when we uncovered the last clue: *Revelation 17–18*. Look here, read this.'

Mason slipped past her to see that an elegant line of text had been etched deeply into the wall. Mason guessed this had been a place of worship on seeing the rectangular indentation that bordered the text – the grooves of a missing altar, perhaps, or a pedestal.

'"*In her was found the blood of prophets and of saints*",' he read aloud. '"*The New Babylon.*" Sorry, I'm none the wiser.'

'There's always been a theory,' Sally said. 'And my father researched this briefly but found no clear proof. A theory that the Babylon of the Bible was in fact *Rome*. Revelation stated that Babylon sat on seven hills, but the Iraqi city sits on a *plain*. Rome lies at the heart of seven hills. Revelation mentions a *sea* port, yet this place is beside the Euphrates river. In Revelation it states: "*That great city, which reigneth over the kings of the earth*", and that, my friend, is in the present tense because, in John's day, that city was *currently* reigning over the kings of the earth. It could only be Rome. And this verse, 18:24, states: "*In her was found the blood of prophets and of saints.*" A line that couldn't possibly refer to wicked old Babylon, but *could* refer to—'

'Rome.' Mason stated flatly. '*Rome*. Are you kidding?'

Sally bit her bottom lip. 'The Amori constantly refer to the phrases from Revelation that mention Babylon. Do you see? It's a corruption of Revelation in the same way that Revelation corrupted Babylon. A kind of depraved vengeance.' She shook her head. 'It makes sense. Well, to the Amori at least.'

'Their own private secret?' Mason asked. 'And Rome is the New Babylon?'

'To be clear.' Sally touched his arm. '*This is Babylon*. This is their primary refuge. When they were forced to move, what better place to set up shop was there than the home of their greatest enemy, a place that even the Bible alludes to as the new Babylon?'

'And placing them near enough to the Vatican to watch it fall,' Mason said. 'Shall we get the hell out of here?'

Sally looked left and right. 'Of course. After making the impossible decision to destroy this place, and *this*,' she waved at the inscription, 'probably their most sacred altar – the only thing holding the Amori back now is Roxy bloody Banks.'

He ran back towards the entrance to the cavern, Sally at his heels. He grabbed the irregular rock wall, climbed back up and emerged through the rough hole. He hauled Sally up in his wake and raced along the low tunnel, at first seeing a faint glow ahead and then the jagged cave entrance, filled with light.

He reached the exit archway, stopped as a thought struck him, and checked the explosives he'd seen earlier. In horror, he saw that wires had been inserted into a central detonator whilst they'd been below. A black box with a blinking blue light on top that told him remote detonation could occur at any moment. The sight made his heart clench.

Mason hesitated to remove the wires, conscious that there might be a failsafe. Any tampering could set it off. They needed to disable the remote device first.

Mason touched the comms system in his ear. 'Where are we?'

'Mason, thank God. They're hurting her.'

'Does the leader have the remote trigger for the explosives?'

'Yeah, yeah. I tried, but couldn't make contact. He threw a pack of C4 at Roxy and keeps brushing his thumb over the detonator, threatening to . . . to . . .'

Mason raised his gun. 'Take the bastard's head off.'

Chapter 59

The rugged landscape around Babylon's ancient Ishtar Gate exploded with gunfire.

Mason ordered Sally to take cover, dashed out of the cave and put bullets into the spines of the two men standing in front of him. As they collapsed, they afforded him a clear view of the scene beyond.

Soldiers were gathered around Roxy, giving her a wide berth and covering her whilst Hamoud carried out an interrogation. Except this wasn't an interrogation. It was sick pleasure.

Roxy stood close to a pack of C4 which had been thrown at her feet. The leering, grinning leader practically salivated whilst pretending to press the remote detonator. He laughed and fired shots at Roxy's boots, making her dance to his tune. His soldiers were enjoying it almost as much as he was.

But it was Hamoud's own gunfire that gave Mason, Hassell and Quaid precious extra seconds. Nobody had turned around when Mason killed the two men. Nobody reacted now when Hassell picked off the driver standing twenty feet away from the main group. Nobody moved for stunned seconds when Quaid put a bullet through the back of Hamoud's head.

Mason emerged at full speed as Hamoud fell forward, dead before he knew what hit him, the black box skidding free of nerveless fingers. It clattered over stones to stop next to one of Roxy's boots, along with the handgun he'd been using to terrorise her. Roxy dropped to the ground. Mason sprayed automatic fire into the circle of men, getting a good, even spread. Bullets riddled the ten-man ring.

Quaid and Hassell jumped to their feet and opened fire. Hassell advanced down the steep slope, treading carefully but concentrating on thinning out the vile herd that surrounded Roxy. Quaid stayed high to get a better view of the scene. Their enemies weren't just lying down to die. Some twisted in agony, shot through their shoulders or chests. Some collapsed instantly dead. But others dropped to their knees and fired back.

Mason and Hassell had done some fair damage with their surprise attack, but nine men were still active. Mason was forced to drop to the ground behind a boulder as two men targeted him.

Which left Roxy unprotected and fully in their sights.

Even as bullets smashed into the rock Mason crouched behind, he made ready to return fire, knowing he had to keep the shooters occupied. Hassell had gone to ground too. Quaid was out of his line of sight. Seconds crept by. Mason gritted his teeth and risked a quick glance toward Roxy.

His heart froze. Roxy was lying on her back, arms up, as a man stood over her, gun pointed downward. His lips were twisted into a snarl, his shoulder dripping blood. A second attacker crawled toward her from the left, leaving gory tracks on the ground in his wake, a crimson-stained blade clutched in his left hand.

Mason, risking everything, rolled out into the open and fired. The bullet sailed past the shooter's head but made him pause, look up and send Mason a grim smile even as his finger tightened on the trigger.

Roxy cried out, facing certain death. Just then, there was a high-pitched whirring sound, and skimming through the air at high speed came Quaid's Mavic drone. The small aircraft smashed into the back of the shooter's head, shattering on impact and sending the man staggering away. Mason clenched a fist in triumph but was forced back behind his boulder by bullets. Even then, he followed the action with nerves on fire.

Roxy swivelled and rolled, getting under the stumbling shooter. She reached out and grabbed his gun, spattered by blood streaming from fresh cuts across his forehead. His face was above hers, eyes wide in surprise as she aimed his own gun at him and fired. As he collapsed dead, she sat up and targeted the wounded, crawling man.

He was gone.

He lunged at her from a blind spot to the left, the knife slashing down her bicep. Roxy bellowed in pain. She pinned the man's knife between her legs, gripping tightly, and grabbed him by the throat.

'That hurt,' she said and put two bullets in him.

Hassell rose again, firing wildly. Mason used the diversion to join the attack. He saw men twist and fall, screaming in pain; he saw blood fountain in the air and splash the arid ground. He saw worse as the bullets took their toll, ripping flesh and bone apart in a non-stop stream. Quaid joined the onslaught from higher up a slope, still clutching the Mavic controller in one hand. After a while, Mason quit firing to identify which enemy soldiers remained alive.

Just three.

The surprise attack and the stunning, unstoppable, high-velocity salvo had almost annihilated the Amori's men.

Mason ran toward Roxy in a crouch, laying down heavy cover fire to keep the remaining three soldiers pinned in their hiding places. Hassell and Quaid followed his lead, firing short bursts at the rocks above the soldiers' heads.

'Call the chopper,' he whispered into the comms as he approached Roxy and held out a hand. 'You okay?'

'You came,' she said. 'And I thought you'd convinced yourself that you couldn't save your friends.'

'I guess I was wrong. New scar?'

She winced as she rolled the shoulder where the knife had split her skin. 'I'm greedy that way.'

He hit the ground next to her, lying on his stomach, and fired a covering shot, struck by the realisation that he'd just thundered from an underground cavern, climbed a six-foot-deep hole, run along a tunnel and raced out of a cave to confront more than a dozen armed soldiers to save the life of a beleaguered colleague. But more than that – a friend. A fellow soldier.

Unlike the two men in Mosul, he'd saved her life.

Events had transpired differently. Until now, Mason had put himself in a self-imposed limbo from which he couldn't hurt others. He'd driven his wife and friends away and changed his life because he didn't trust himself to do anything other than fail.

Professor Rusk's death had given him renewed motivation, a compulsion to help Sally, but it was this intense moment, *right here*, that truly and clearly showed him that *he* wasn't to blame. He hadn't got his teammates killed.

War happens. Forgive yourself. The future is yours. You can either let it beat you into submission, or you can stand up and fight.

Roxy was smiling right into his eyes. 'Friends we've lost live on in our hearts, Mason. I call that eternity. Those who die live in our memories. We are who we are because of how they helped us.'

Mason pulled himself to his knees, holding out a hand to Roxy, who saw it and raised an eyebrow, about to slap it aside before understanding it was a sign of friendship, of solidarity.

She reached out, grabbed it and hauled herself to her feet.

At that moment, cries rang out from the remaining three soldiers, still pinned behind their rocks. At first, Mason thought they'd been shot, but then saw them rise, hands raised. They were shouting, gesticulating wildly. Grim smiles filled their faces.

Mason frowned and nudged Roxy. 'What the hell are—'

'What's that guy holding?' Roxy shielded her eyes with her hand.

Pure fear struck Mason like forked lightning. *They have a backup device,* and one of the guys was brandishing it like a trophy.

Sally! She had taken cover by the Ishtar Gate. Dread flooded his body. Mason aimed at the man's head but, through the sights, saw his thumb press the detonator button. A deep rumble shook the ground. He staggered. Roxy again fell to her knees.

An ear-splitting blast splintered his senses. Tonnes of shattered rock exploded skyward. The ground swelled. Boulders flew in a terrible outpouring, a stream of pulverised stone surging from the cave mouth and erupting through cracks all along the valley floor.

Mason fought to stay upright as a flow of destruction gushed along twenty feet to his right, a deadly stream emitted by the cave. A boulder tumbled past his shoulder at high speed. Seeing another flurry of rubble heading his way, he hauled Roxy away and staggered to his left, desperate to get out of the way. A rock clipped his ankle, the impact sending him sprawling. Pain swelled from the joint. Roxy threw herself over him. Mason, facing the cave, saw the torrent of rock racing towards them, a deadly avalanche of stone that billowed dust and shook the earth. It filled his vision, travelling so fast he could never hope to get clear. Roxy's weight was heavy on his back.

The surge began to slow rapidly. Mason closed his eyes as it struck, but it was only a small trickle of stones that fell over them. The deluge of boulders and dust had stopped just a few feet away.

As the sound of the explosion diminished, Quaid and Hassell shot the three surviving soldiers, then ran to join Mason and Roxy.

Mason couldn't keep his balance. He fell, hit the ground hard, but managed to roll onto his back and then sit upright. 'Sally!' he yelled.

She was fine, standing among rocks above and to the right of the cave itself; a place to which she'd fled to take cover after Mason left her to save Roxy.

She waved urgently and started towards them. Mason took a deep breath. This was not good.

Sally reached him a minute later. 'What are you waiting for? *Move*. They released the third video a few hours ago. Don't you get it? *We have to get to Rome*.'

Mason held out a hand. Roxy pulled him to his feet. Mason took a moment to lay a hand on her shoulder to catch her attention.

'Are you okay?' he asked. 'After . . . after that?'

'You mean when they fired at my boots and threatened to blow me up? No, that one's gonna stay with me for a while.'

'I'm sorry. We returned too late.'

'I don't blame you. I blame those idiots. We all do the best we can.' Roxy smiled and turned away, ending the conversation.

'Chopper's on its way,' Quaid said.

'It's nine-thirty a.m. in Rome right now,' Sally said. 'Marduk has made it clear to the world that he'll release the full revelation tonight. When will he get the most attention?'

Hassell shrugged. 'Early evening maybe. But there's no telling what Marduk will do. He's batshit crazy.'

'Which gives us about eight hours tops,' Quaid said.

The sound of the helicopter approaching was a balm to their fraught nerves. Sally raced off to meet it first, climbing the ridge at a dangerous pace.

'Where to?' the pilot asked when Mason reached it.

'Rome,' he said with more certainty in his voice than he could ever remember. 'We're ending this in Rome.'

The pilot's mouth fell open. 'I can't do that,' he said. 'Too far. Rome's more than 3,000 kilometres from here. But I *can* get you back to that airfield.'

They climbed aboard and braced for lift-off, vision spoiled and hearts agonised by the sight of thick clouds obscuring the landscape. Mason could barely see the cave mouth that led to the cavern, the last vestige of the Amori's Babylon, but it was clear that the whole arch had collapsed. What had it taken to order the destruction of their legacy, their ancient refuge?

A madman, or a man following a millennia-old, warped concept of blind worship?

Either way, with that one act Marduk had cleared the way for an even more terrible deed – the publication of the Vatican's worst secrets. Nothing could stop them now.

Unless we find them first.

Mason sat back, deciding it was best to distract himself with other thoughts. Better thoughts.

One thought.

In all his agonising, in all his conflict and need and desire to atone, not once had he considered that Roxy Banks, the rum-soaked loose cannon from across the pond, would be the one to help him find a spark of peace.

How had that happened?

Chapter 60

In the spotlight, in the thick of it, Gianluca Gianni tried not to crumble.

The devastating day was here, the last hours counting down. Gianni had been called to attend a meeting of cardinals following the Amori's and Marduk's third and final YouTube and social media teaser video before what the madman called 'the final revelation'.

'*And Gianni*,' Marduk had breathed earlier, a fallen demon whispering in his ear. '*You will give your finest performance today. You will dial their anxieties all the way to ten.*'

Gianni rose from his seat now, face twitching, brain blasted by the latest horrendous proof-of-life clip Marduk had sent him earlier. It was all he could do to keep his legs from giving way.

'I wish to point out,' he said, 'that everything is hearsay. They have no proof. How can they? The Church is too big to fail.'

'No.' Cardinal Vallini shot up from his seat, resisting Gianni. 'It's the other way around, I'm afraid. The Church is too big *not* to fail.'

There were thirty of them, seated around an empty

table in a windowless room deep in the recesses of the basilica. The meeting had been hastily called and not everyone chose to attend. Gianni fought to save the lives of his wife and daughter.

'This so-called Amori.' Gianni spoke with a catch in his voice. 'Who here believes they could actually bring Christianity to its knees?'

He watched the men squirm, saw their expressions of discomfort and suppressed a terrible sadness. Vallini again challenged him.

'Remember, John the Baptist captured the true essence of Christian living when he wrote: "*He must increase, but I must decrease.*" We must measure success by the degree Christ shares in our life. His love will grow but the Church *can* diminish.'

Gianni stayed standing, refusing to give in. As he spoke, as he baited their apprehensions, visions of his wife's torture ran through his head: of her waterboarding and sleep deprivation. Of a wonderful spirit giving up. Of that beautiful, animated woman uttering the words '*Please kill me*' into Marduk's evil, leering face.

Gianni had never felt such agony. 'This revelation,' he said, turning the screws as Marduk demanded. 'That Christ was a warrior king, a leader of men, yes, but not in the way the Bible dictates, is really so irrefutably detailed in the *Book of Secrets*? And Marduk can date the text? Even the ink? How can he prove that it is *genuine*?' he already knew the answer.

'By analysing and comparing the writing of more recent Popes,' a cardinal said glumly. 'That book can be tied inexorably to the Vatican, I'm afraid, and all its surprises too.'

'Including the date when they found Christ's body and all its . . . warrior trappings,' Gianni said.

The cardinal was so upset by that image, he couldn't

even answer. Gianni had sown the seeds once more, wrapping the debate in misery and confusion. Exhausted, he took his seat. The overwhelming fact was that the hour of Marduk's reveal was nigh, and Gianni had no clear indication as to what the madman would do to his family afterwards.

'I've done everything you asked of me,' he'd said earlier.

'Not yet. I haven't seen a suicide. I want you to turn the screws. To make them writhe in their indecision. I want . . . *civil war*.'

'I can't possibly—'

'But you will. Make the believers harangue the non-believers until their voices break. You can do that, can't you, Gianni?'

'I want my wife and daughter back.'

'And that will happen. But in one piece or many? I leave the choice to you.'

Gianni was a man of action, a take-charge leader of men. He wanted – *needed* – to act. Sitting helplessly like this and actively working against his own people, against his God, tore his heart and soul apart. He breathed deeply now as the wall clock ticked ever closer to their hour of doom.

Chapter 61

Sally used the long plane journey to dig extensively into her research, face increasingly lined with anxiety as the hours passed.

In the end, the team hadn't required specialist help to learn Marduk's plans. Teasers were all over the news. Every paper. Every social media outlet. Hassell even found a trending hashtag, a phrase designed to highlight Marduk's forthcoming announcement and reach infinitely more people.

#bringdownthechurch was spreading across the world, both on- and offline, garnering awareness from all corners. Every hour, every minute, its evil tendrils crawled further into the system.

'It's why he's broadcasting at nine p.m.,' Sally had guessed. 'The longer he drags it out, the more people will hear about it and tune in.'

The closer they got to Rome the faster the minutes sped by. Sally sweated and muttered and rubbed her tired eyes. Quaid tried to help. They spent what felt like hours poring over endless documents, newspaper reports and deeds old and new but found no references to the Amori.

'I can't admit defeat,' Sally almost cried at one point. 'After everything we've been through, I just can't.'

'Trust in yourself,' Mason said. 'Trust in the team. Has anyone got any ideas?' It was getting close to the last gasp, and these were desperate times. Six hours before Marduk's upload rapidly reduced to five and then just over four. For Mason, it passed in the blink of an eye.

'The *Vatican Book of Secrets*,' Quaid had said, leafing through a newspaper he'd found on the plane. 'What horrors might it contain that convinced Jacques Heindl to leave a trail of clues, to force the Church to secure it in the deepest archive and to make the Amori believe they could weaken Christian faith? And, for that reason, why hasn't a pope ordered it destroyed before now?'

'All we know is that it's something earth-shattering centred around Jesus,' Sally said. 'And that we have about four hours to end this. The problem is *finding* Marduk and the Amori. We don't have a single lead, nothing to go on. If Rome is New Babylon, where's its palace?'

They'd been throwing these questions at the same dilemma for hours. Quaid finally dropped the newspaper. 'Look, there are ways to find people. Old ways. I can contact my mate from—'

'We know,' Mason said. 'But how long's that gonna take?'

'Not sure,' Quaid admitted. 'Information like that, from the street, could take hours.'

'It won't work,' Hassell said, his fast-talking style breaking over them. 'And breaking heads is out of the question.' He stared at Roxy. 'Because we don't know whose to break. Laptop trickery won't work either, because this isn't a historical puzzle. And the old ways?' He made a sad face at Quaid. 'Aren't close to being fast enough. But there may be another option . . . if we're good enough.'

'What?' Mason bit hard.

'This is a cutting-edge problem, and the only chance we have of solving it in time is by using modern, cutting-edge tools. Marduk's using technology to spread the word, so let's hop on board that train. You see, *Gido* was summoned to Rome by Marduk himself, according to a message left on my phone before I threw it away. Gido's failure to capture us prompted Marduk to punish him by bringing him here. I'm sure, even if Gido refused to capitulate, Marduk would have made sure he came by force. Do you see? We don't have to find the Amori, or search for Marduk, or call on taxi drivers and streetwalkers. We don't have to seek the dusty relics of ancient Babylon. We just have to locate Gido because Marduk won't allow him to stray too far.'

Mason was impressed. 'Now *that's* an alternative solution. And you think you can do it?'

'Well, that depends on Quaid. You see, as I've mentioned before, Gido was calling me day and night. It's tirade after tirade and promises of a horrible death. So far, I haven't returned his call. But . . .' He paused and glanced at Quaid.

The British ex-army officer nodded slowly. 'You want to trace the call?'

'For sure. He'll answer in a shot. Do you know anyone good enough to jump on the call and trace it back?'

'And hope Gido's in the same place as Marduk?' Sally asked dubiously.

'It's three and a half hours to the reveal,' Hassell said. 'It's Marduk's big moment. He'll want Gido to see it happen. And like I said, after his failures, Marduk will have him on a short leash.'

Quaid jumped to his feet and started making calls, pacing up and down the cabin. As he worked, Mason addressed a prickly issue that had been stabbing at his mind for a while. 'Didn't this Gido guy save your life?'

Hassell sighed. 'Look, it's a long story but my girl, Chloe, was murdered by some lowlifes, a revenge attack for a gang-banger I helped put in prison. I got home one day . . .' He swallowed, his mouth dry. 'She was nearly gone . . . didn't last long. The last thing she ever said to me . . .' He swallowed hard again before carrying on. '"*If I die*," she said. "*Promise me you won't die inside.*"'

Hassell stared up at the ceiling, collecting himself before carrying on. 'I didn't listen to her. Didn't understand. Quit the Department. Spent three years alone, crawling through life. Gido found me and saved me. I was twenty-three. He took me under his wing, taught me how to infiltrate. Gave me a new life. But I still had morals,' Hassell said stiffly. 'And I never forgot that Chloe had morals too. She wouldn't want me working the wrong side of the law. But Gido . . . he raised me out of the *dirt* at the bottom of a very dark well. Anyway, I told him I'd only do the single jobs. No partners. No groups. For her. For Chloe. I worked alone except, at the beginning, with Gido. We took out a lot of criminals, man.'

'Criminals?' Mason echoed.

'Yeah. Gido liked to neutralise his competition. That was his thing and one of the reasons the cops stayed off his back. They fed Gido, or he fed them. Either way, the opposition got taken out.'

'What does this have to do with the Amori?' Sally pushed. 'Clock's ticking.'

Hassell nodded. 'Yeah, yeah. I'll be quick. Four years I worked for Gido, few questions asked. But the big problem ate away at my gut, inflamed by the passing years.'

'Did Gido recruit you specifically to take out his rivals?' Roxy said.

'Exactly. Did Gido engineer Chloe's death to get me? If that's true I'm only tarnishing Chloe's memory by working for him.'

'So why did you stay?' Mason asked.

'I wasn't certain. And I wanted to stay inside Gido's organisation, a trusted man, in case I needed to avenge Chloe's death. But it's also why I switched sides so easily when the chance came.'

'I'm assuming he helped you locate the men who killed Chloe?' Quaid asked.

'Oh, yeah. We did that. And after . . . you don't feel any better. Nothing changes. How can you ever be happy again? The guilt . . . it eats you alive, man.'

Mason's watch showed 7.00 p.m.

Quaid closed his flip phone with a clunk. 'We're on,' he said enthusiastically. 'An old mate of mine at SIS, that's the British Secret Intelligence Service, is owed a favour. He's got someone who can hop onto any signal leaving this plane and trace it to its destination. It helps that they know a little of how desperate our mission is. You just have to keep Gido talking for more than two minutes.'

Hassell scowled. 'Not a problem.'

'And, assuming that works, its journey's end.' Sally stared at them. 'Marduk and the *Book of Secrets* will be there.'

'And an army,' Roxy said gloomily. 'Protecting it.'

A desperate darkness hung over Rome, leaching all joy from the night, shot through with icy hail, a bone-chilling cold and high winds that shredded, wrenched and plucked at every concrete sinew of the great city.

Mason and the others descended into that darkness. Their private plane had landed at a small airstrip just a half hour ago. It was now just after 6.00 p.m. and they were here. In Rome, in sight of the Vatican, with a terrible knowledge spurring them on and with less than three hours to Marduk's broadcast.

A taxi took them into the heart of Rome, to a nondescript parking area where they gathered and started to make ready for their assault. Mason was aware of the passage of time, of the need to strike hard and strike fast. They prepared quickly, drawing guns from backpacks and securing them close to hand, going over the plan one last time. Mason's heart pounded as he faced the others, ready to move out.

'Believe you can do this,' he said. 'And you will.'

As they nodded, he heard it. A slight scraping noise – the crunch of a boot stepping on gravel. He spun and shouted a warning. Roxy went for her gun and drew it quickly. '*Fermare!*' The warning shout, in Italian, gave him pause. His fingers were inches from his own gun. He assessed their chances. Black-clad men confronted them, rifles held to their shoulders and trained on Mason and the others. More ran into the parking area, spreading out. Only Roxy held a weapon with any chance of using it. Sally and Quaid stood gaping at the newcomers. Hassell was behind Roxy but would have to move to arm himself. The Italians were clearly military, dressed in uniform and moving in sync.

Mason made no sudden movements. Eight men closed in. Mason made a point of glaring into Quaid's eyes.

'This is your protection? Your contact gave us up.'

Quaid looked ready to protest, but at that moment a ninth man appeared and walked towards them, carrying a handgun loosely in one hand. Mason studied the broad-shouldered, powerful man, taking in the piercing eyes and haggard expression. He saw pain, commitment and duty warring in that face.

'You are Mason?' he asked in English. 'Miss Rusk.' He nodded at Sally. 'I am Gianluca Gianni, Commander of the Swiss Guard. Do not move. I'd rather not kill you.'

Mason stayed put, keeping his options open, cursing himself for relying so heavily on Quaid. 'We're not the enemy,' he said. 'And we don't have time for this. The bloody clock is ticking.'

'You assumed we wouldn't be looking for you? All this time, you are the trio that vanished on the night of the great theft. I knew the moment you used your passports at the airfield. For now, you are being treated as a passive threat, secondary targets. And, Miss Rusk, I am sorry about your father. I know Cardinal Vallini considered him a great man.' Gianni half bowed.

'Listen,' Sally said. 'We have been pursuing the book, chasing down clues from here to Jerusalem and back. The Amori stole it, and now we know where it is. But . . . we have less than two hours to stop Marduk.'

Something dark and haunted moved in Gianni's eyes. 'Marduk? My objective is to detain and question you. A reason to get away from—' he paused. 'I do not need to hear this.'

'Yes,' Sally urged, stepping forward and increasing the tension in the trigger fingers of Gianni's men. 'Yes, you do—'

'How did you find us?' Quaid put in.

'We are the Swiss Guard,' Gianni answered as if that explained all. 'This is our city. We oversee everything in the Vatican and much in Rome and saw you the moment you stepped off the plane.'

Mason was tempted to mention they hadn't seen the Vatican robbery coming and had failed to catch the perpetrators on the night that started all this, but held back. Sally's protests had given him an idea.

'We're allies,' he said. 'We want what you want. And I'm guessing you know why. The only way to stop the reveal is to find the book. Find the Amori.' He watched Gianni's face as he talked. 'Please, Commander. We tracked the book all this way. We tracked *them* – the Amori. *We've got them.* But, at nine p.m., the whole world changes.'

Gianni opened his mouth then hesitated as if torn between impossible choices. Mason saw the uncertainty and wondered why. 'Help us.'

'You are five civilians,' he said finally. 'What can you possibly have done?'

'Not civilians,' Mason said. 'Army. CIA. Infil, exfil specialist. Historian.' The titles weren't precise, but they were enough to make Gianni's mouth drop. 'The Amori want to destroy everything you stand for. Don't let them.'

Sally stepped in at that point, giving Gianni a potted version of their quest. Mason felt more than a little short-changed to hear everything they'd done boiled down to an essential paragraph. The time constraint bore down on him like a mountain. It was 7.48 p.m.

'The Amori are in Rome?' Gianni asked, admitting with that question that he knew exactly what was going on and that the Swiss Guard didn't know their city as well as they'd believed. He also now understood that the *Book of Secrets* had never left and hung his head. 'My fault.'

'Commander, they were well-versed, well-funded and used one of the best crews in the world to steal that book,' Mason said. 'It took months if not years of planning. Us?' He nodded at Sally and Roxy. 'We were in the wrong place at the wrong time. But we can help you now. We can take you to them.'

'Take me to them?' Gianni repeated, face changed by a glimmer of hope. 'Both of them?'

Mason frowned, confused. As he started to ask a question, Gianni stepped forward, grabbed his shoulder and propelled him away. Mason saw his men's faces as he allowed himself to be manoeuvred, each man regarding his neighbour in surprise and speculation.

Gianni whispered hoarsely, 'They took my family. My wife and daughter. All this time, they told me if I didn't . . . *muddy* the search, I'd never see them alive again. This Marduk is pure evil. A monster.'

Mason fought hard to find the right words. 'The worst kind. I'm so sorry.'

'Marduk told me my family were *with them*. And you say you know where *they* are?'

Mason nodded. 'Yes. I realise you don't know us. I realise you can't trust us. But, even putting your family aside, you *know* what damage that book can do. You have eight soldiers and us. We're running out of time.'

'Soldiers?' Gianni repeated. 'Yes. We are trained in secret through a harsh programme. Hostage rescue. Counter-terrorism. That is the purview of the Swiss Guard.'

'You're worried about how failure affects your family. Believe me, I get it. But there's no guarantee Marduk won't hurt them once he's got everything he wants.'

'I do not need to be reminded of *that*.' Gianni spat the words loudly, drawing more attention from his men. 'My career is over. I have tried to find them but these Amori, they have set every asset against me. I can only look to save my wife and daughter.' He studied Roxy, Hassell and Quaid in speculation. 'You say you've all been trained?'

'In hell,' Mason assured him.

'Good,' Gianni said. 'Because I've a feeling that's where we're going.'

Chapter 62

Mason studied the high-rise residential building that soared eleven floors up into the tempestuous night. The brightly lit edifice drifted closer by the second, an unremarkable concrete tower with nice views across the city. Mason wasn't surprised that it belonged to the Amori – such secrecy and anonymity would be paramount to their continued existence here right under the nose of the Catholic Church. In shadow, they could watch, plot and scheme.

It was 8.30 p.m. Only thirty minutes to the broadcast.

Mason readied himself as the building filled his vision.

It would be a two-pronged attack. The Swiss Guard were assaulting the building both at ground level and from above, using two helicopters, for speed and so as to mount a two-pronged attack. Mason was in the first alongside Gianni, Roxy and Hassell. Quaid was in the second chopper with a number of Guardsmen, whilst more of Gianni's men gathered on the ground below, crouched near the building's entrance and waiting for the signal.

Mason held on as the chopper, buffeted by high winds, coasted down towards the building's roof.

Someone threw open the side doors, admitting an onslaught of cold air. Ropes unfurled and slithered through the dark night before slapping hard against the roof below. The first men climbed out, rappelling quickly down the thick ropes.

Mason glanced over his shoulder. 'Good luck.' He held out a hand.

Roxy slapped it hard. 'Don't be a dick. We're gonna get through this together, Babyface.'

Mason nodded and then it was his turn. The rope twisted in his hands, tugged by high winds. Mason held tight, descending thirty feet to a flat roof before running to a large vent, behind which the team were grouping.

Those already on the roof waited for the rest to deploy. In less than three minutes all eleven men and Roxy were massed and ready to move.

'My lead.' Gianni ran to a roof access door, crouched before it and fixed a small pack of explosives to both hinges and the lock. Backing away, he shielded his face and waited for the fuse to expire.

A sharp detonation sent the door crashing outward. Two men ran to the opening. Gianni and Mason followed.

'This building belongs to the Amori,' Gianni reminded them over a shared comms system. 'As you can see, it's set up to look like a normal housing block. The plans my men obtained from the municipal offices show that the top three floors are all penthouse, followed by a gym and then an unspecified level. Next floor down – meeting rooms.'

Or so the plans alleged. Nothing was certain. Mason had only had a brief glimpse, but they all assumed the Amori's domain was both indeterminate and perilous. As the lead men reached the damaged door, that belief was realised.

Six armed men leapt out of the opening. With guns already trained they opened fire, driving the Swiss Guard back. One Guard fell, killed where he stood, struck before he could react.

Mason dived to the floor and rolled, finding an air-conditioning unit to shelter behind. Bright muzzle flashes lit up the rooftop as both sides laid down a stream of gunfire.

Mason fired from behind the unit, bullets strafing the access doorframe and hitting at least one man. Fire was returned and he ducked back into cover. Bullets glanced off metal and brick.

'On my word,' Gianni said over the comms. 'One . . . two . . . three!'

As one, the whole team stepped out and fired. Mason was with them, knowing that speed and ruthlessness offered their best chance over an inferior force.

Three Amori soldiers twisted and died, collapsing to the ground. Those who were left returned fire. Mason saw a Guardsman hiss and clap a hand over a shoulder where a bullet luckily parted only a millimetre of skin, and another man struck in a Kevlar vest stagger backward.

Right to the edge of the roof.

Falling back, arms flapping, he tried to save himself, but the momentum was too strong. The impetus of the bullet propelled him backward. The roof's lip came too soon, and he stepped off into an utter pit of blackness, eleven storeys high, and would have fallen if one of his comrades had not dived towards him, grabbed his bulletproof vest and jerked him back. Even so, both men lay hanging over the edge, unable to move.

A bullet struck perilously close to them.

Mason took out the man who fired it, leaving just two armed opponents. The Swiss Guard rushed the access door, their weapons switched to fully automatic, nullifying their opponents. Mason was behind Roxy as they leapt through the door and pelted down the roof access's rough iron staircase.

'Keep up,' Roxy breathed.

'Not a problem.' Mason's boots rang off the steps.

Halfway down the roof access stairs was a switchback. More armed men appeared below, shooting up and confirming Mason's suspicion that the earlier force of men had been little more than lambs to the slaughter, a delaying tactic.

Gianni thought the same and ordered his lead men to use stun grenades, stupefying their attackers with loud bangs before running down, zip-tying their arms and legs then forging onward.

The second part of the metal staircase was negotiated in seconds and then the team paused to regroup at the main stairwell door that opened onto the building's highest floor.

The penthouse.

'Go,' Gianni said.

The team pushed through the door, finding themselves inside an open-plan, floor-length, spartan room that held a massive oak desk behind which a plush leather chair stood askew as if someone had vacated at speed, an array of expensive Persian rugs littering the floor. Floor-to-ceiling windows gave the room's occupant a grand view of the city including, Mason noticed, St Peter's Basilica to the north. He pointed it out to the other members of his team. Roxy and Quaid were the only ones to respond with a nod. Hassell appeared distant and didn't look up and Sally was being protected by two Swiss Guards.

The far wall was an oak-panelled masterpiece, draped with two tapestries depicting Babylon in its heyday, all shining towers, hanging gardens and fine palaces.

Had Marduk spent his years dreaming and plotting right here? It seemed likely.

The Guard fanned out and searched the room for enemies and traps, finding nothing. Part of Gianni's plan had been to breach the top floor three minutes before the ground, thus forcing those trying to escape downwards before they realised they had to go back up. Mason had liked the tactic.

They grouped by the penthouse's exit door and returned to the stairwell, dropping another floor.

Yet another oddly sparse, enormous room greeted them; this one populated by a king-sized bed and several wardrobes. The next floor was of a similar pattern, and then they were ready to breach what they believed to be the meeting rooms.

Mason ducked through a door, rifle balanced against his shoulder, moving into a small entrance room with a semi-circular front desk. As he moved deeper into the room, a sharp crackle and then a tense voice rattled in his earpiece.

'We have them trapped in the stairwell,' the leader of the ground assault team stated. 'Lots of them. Herding them up to you.'

It was 8.40 p.m.

Mason didn't like it. Something didn't add up. If Marduk was broadcasting in twenty minutes, where was the set-up, the equipment, the cameras?

The whole team stopped and turned around. Gianni sent two men to scour the empty floor and then two more back up to recheck the floors they'd already checked in the desperate hope that they would find his family.

'Dario, Milo,' he said. 'Please do your best.'

Mason paced back out into the stairwell and glanced eight flights down the concrete chute.

He could hear them ascending. Boots clanging on the risers, harsh voices echoing up the stairwell. Mason waited as the Guard lined the handrail around him, all standing just out of sight of those below.

Gianni liaised with the lower group, agreeing on a twenty-second volley from each team whilst the other took cover under the stairwell's overhang to prevent any crossfire. They would creep towards each other and trap their enemy in an inescapable pincer.

The minutes ticked by.

Mason waited as the lower team engaged first. The Amori's men retaliated, the sound of their guns revealing intense firepower.

Twenty-five seconds later, Mason leaned out and sent a spray of bullets raking across the lower stairs, catching at least one enemy in the elbow, and sending many more diving for cover. They hadn't been looking up, hadn't been expecting an aerial attack.

Mason ducked to safety as their time to fire expired. Every man crept down five steps. Twenty-five seconds later, Mason leaned out again and strafed the concrete shaft. This time he had a clear view of the Amori's men: the soldiers or mercenaries crouched against the outer handrail in a line that descended perhaps nine risers, protecting figures wearing civilian clothes who waited on the inside, their backs to the concrete wall.

Mason touched Gianni. 'You see Marduk?'

The man's grim visage spoke louder than any words. Mason felt a moment's relief, knowing they'd located the Amori's leader. The mercs were becoming increasingly desperate, some even leaning out over the handrail and firing up and down the shaft, hoping to thin out the unknown force set against them.

Mason fired and then descended, following the same pattern time and time again as they closed the gap, triggering the trap to end the Amori in their own stairwell – an ignominious finish to an enigmatic reign.

Bullets flew up and down the shaft, pitting walls and ricocheting off iron supports and shattering windows.

Mason shot a man who was balancing over the wrong side of the handrail, sending him plummeting several storeys. Roxy wounded another in the shoulder and made him lose his grip. Quaid and Hassell did their part, working well with the Swiss Guard. Sally remained sheltered at the top of the descending group.

'Anyone able to ID those guys standing against the wall?' Hassell asked through the comms at one point. 'Describe them?'

Negative replies came back.

'It's *eight forty-five*.' Sally's desperate voice filled the comms. 'Please hurry.'

The Swiss Guard lost no more men as they herded their enemy between the jaws of one great, serrated trap. The mercs knew what was happening, taking deadly risks to prevent it, but the force arrayed against them was too determined and too well organised.

Mason sweated. His lips were dry. After headlong chases, thousands of miles of travel, crawling around dusty old tombs, altars and glorious old churches, it all came down to this: the ingenuity of one leader whose wife and daughter were in mortal danger. Abducting Gianni's family might just have been the Amori's greatest mistake.

One of the moments Gianni had been waiting for finally arrived. He'd been reluctant to use stun grenades here until the gap narrowed, worrying that one wayward throw could impair his own men below. Now, as the space between the upper and lower teams reduced to just four flights with the increasingly fraught Amori in between, he gave the signal.

A trio of small black objects clattered among the legs of the mercenaries.

Mason ducked back, jamming his hands over his ears. Warning cries were drowned out by three dull thuds. Mason waited a moment before looking up.

'Ya coming?' Roxy was staring at him as if he'd finished last in a race. 'Or taking a break?'

Sally's tense voice rattled through the comms. '*It's eight-fifty*.'

They pounded down the stars. The lower team pounded upward. On the fifth floor they merged, lowered their guns and leapt at the dazed mercenaries, bearing them to the

398

ground. Mason cursed when he realised that whoever the mercs had been protecting had escaped.

Gianni indicated the only open door. 'We chase them down,' he said. 'This is the gym level. Keep your wits about you. They've nowhere else to go.'

Mason stepped up to give chase. Raising his gun, he ran through the door first. There was a burst of gunfire. Something smashed into him with deadly force, knocking him off his feet.

He collapsed to the ground, knowing he'd been shot.

Chapter 63

Mason lurched back against a plaster wall, gouging out a man-sized chunk of masonry, and collapsed to the floor. His chest throbbed. For a moment, everything was searing agony, confusion, and bright light.

Seconds later, breathing deeply, gasping, he realised that Roxy's face was hanging in the air above him, a round balloon framed by midnight-black hair. He fixed onto eyes the colour of polished jet.

'Hey, hey, you in there? Joe? Hey, c'mon pretty boy, stop being an ass.'

Mason glanced down, thanking Gianni and fortune for the bulletproof vest which had stopped the bullet.

Roxy held out a hand. 'Did your life flash before your eyes?'

'No, just your face,' Mason gasped.

'Lucky bastard.'

'You're kidding. I thought the Devil really was calling.'

'He was, but only for the guy dumb enough to shoot you.'

Mason let her pull him up and rested for a moment, leaning against the damaged wall. The man who'd ambushed him was dead, lying in a spreading pool of blood to Mason's right. Quaid, Hassell and Sally were nearby, studying him with expressions of concern.

Ahead, the Swiss Guard darted forwards, took cover and then ran again, ducking into and around makeshift shelter. The gym was well equipped, offering multiple but unusual items to hide behind. Rows of cross-trainers, exercise bikes and elliptical rowers stood before a boxing ring and then a good-sized swimming pool at the far end.

Mason's breathing evened out. Roxy handed him his gun. Hassell appeared to his right. 'You okay?'

'Yeah, let's move.'

They joined the attack. Mason saw half a dozen scurrying figures wearing flak jackets and carrying firearms twenty feet ahead being pursued by the Swiss Guard. Beyond them, he made out at least five other people who appeared to be unarmed, all wearing civilian clothing.

'Gido,' Hassell gestured towards the non-combatants. 'He's here.'

'Marduk?' Mason asked.

'Maybe. I think I recognise him,' Hassell said, still gazing ahead. 'Tall guy to the right.'

It wasn't the best report Mason had ever heard. And . . . oddly, it didn't make sense. Why would Marduk be here, now? Shouldn't the executioner be preparing to drop the guillotine onto the Church's collective neck?

He closed the gap to twenty feet, no longer a straggler, and lent his experience to the attack, taking responsibility for several men. His chest still burned, but the pain didn't impair his abilities. He didn't have time for pain. The runners didn't look back.

They passed two open steam rooms to the left, both billowing forth a hazy mist that reduced visibility, and the full-size boxing ring. The Swiss Guards attacked the remainder of the mercs in the room and around the boxing ring, and, in a flurry of gunfire, shot them dead.

Gianni pressed forwards and then slowed. A row of windows established the room's far wall. Mason made sure he stayed beside him.

'Put your hands up!' Gianni shouted, closing in.

The remaining three anonymous civilians, Marduk and the man Hassell had identified as Gido stopped before the windows and slowly turned. They had nowhere else to run to. Beside them lay the swimming pool and now Mason noticed a small room to their right, maybe a shower room, since he could see changing cubicles through the open door. He slowed and studied the survivors.

'You don't want to be threatening us,' Marduk said threateningly. 'After all, we've got some very valuable things belonging to at least one of you.'

'My family,' Gianni said tightly, aiming his gun at the oldest man in the room.

The man shrugged. 'Shoot me and they die,' he said, then grinned and raised his voice. 'Bring them out.'

Two mercenaries emerged from the shower room just then, pushing two wheelchairs to which were tied a gagged woman and a child.

Gianni gasped. The females were unmarked, but crying, their hair matted to their foreheads, teeth bared in pain and hatred.

'Let them go,' he snarled at the older man.

'Again, you talk like a fool. Let *me* go.'

'But,' Hassell muttered, 'that's not Marduk. The man I saw was older, his face more drawn. They look similar, but . . .'

'It's a stooge?' Sally gasped.

It was 8.55 p.m.

'Let them *go*,' Gianni repeated, furiously.

'Marduk's not here,' Hassell said. Mason felt as if ice had been poured over his body. He stared at Hassell in disbelief.

'What?'

'*We have won!*' the older man snarled. 'Soon, Marduk will destroy the Church and, I, Kingu, will happily die to let that happen. And now you will watch your family die. If any of you move, we will shoot you.'

The mercs pushed the wheelchairs toward the pool. Gianni screamed in distress, about to run to save them when the older man held up a hand. 'I said, do not move.'

The mercenaries stopped at the edge of the pool and levelled guns at his wife's and daughter's heads.

'Please . . . no.' Gianni pleaded first with the mercs and then turned to his men. 'Stand down.'

'You see, the Amori always win,' Kingu went on. 'We hold all the cards. You,' he pointed at Gianni, 'are little more than a puppet.'

Mason watched Kingu, the mercenaries and Gido. Sally, behind him, whispered that they were out of time. But what could they do? Roxy inched towards the pool.

'Stop,' Kingu saw her. 'You were warned.'

One of the mercs pistol-whipped Gianni's wife across the back of the head. A scream flew from her lungs. Gianni cringed and then held out a hand. 'No, no, *please* let them go. They did nothing to you.'

'They exist to serve us, to die, to breed when we want them to. If they survive today they will become stock. You will never see them again.'

Kingu held Gianni's eyes, a faint smile playing across his lips. He knew the agony Gianni felt, knew the deadly tight-rope he walked between acting and delay. Sally fretted at Mason's back as the whole team rocked between wanting to save Gianni's family and prevent the broadcast that would change the world. Bare minutes remained. The Amori, even now, outnumbered and outgunned, held the balance of power.

Mason couldn't choose, couldn't sign the death warrant of another person. And neither could Roxy. They'd both witnessed it before. Kingu held dominion over them, dragging it out for as long as he could.

In the end, tied and bleeding but still listening, it was Gianni's wife who broke the deadlock. Whether it was the last few days of torture, the breaking of her spirit or the sheer will to live that made her act, Mason never knew.

But she jammed her heels into the floor, pushed hard and, still tied to the wheelchair, toppled forward into the pool.

The room exploded into action. Gianni sprinted forward like an Olympic champion out of the blocks. Swiss Guards lifted their guns and fired. The merc covering Gianni's daughter pulled his trigger, but half a second too late, as two bullets shattered his skull and sent his body flying backwards. His shots went high. Several more bullets ploughed into Kingu, propelling him into the windows with a resounding crack. Blood splashed from his torso across the tall window.

Gianni leapt into the swimming pool, followed by two Swiss Guards. The merc who'd pistol-whipped Gianni's wife fell in a haze of blood and bullets.

As the gunfire ceased, a terrible silence descended, broken only by grunting and splashing from the pool. Gianni and his men didn't surface. Mason and Roxy ran forward. Blurred shapes occupied the bottom of the pool, trying to wrestle with the submerged wheelchair. Bubbles of air streamed toward the surface. Another Swiss Guard jumped in. Mason saw Gianni grab hold of the chair's arm and frantically start to pull. A Guard swam underneath, struggling to stand. The third man got underneath too but they were quickly running out of air.

Gianni's wife wasn't moving.

As Mason prepared to jump in and help, another two Guards leapt into the pool. Endless, terrible seconds of struggle followed as the five Guards managed to manhandle the chair to the surface. Mason, Roxy and Quaid lay down and grabbed the chair to help haul it to the side. Gianni's daughter was crying, tears streaming down her face, gasping for help. Sally ran to her and shouted for a knife to cut her free.

Mason fell backward with the effort as the wheelchair lifted over the pool's edge. Water sluiced all around. A Swiss Guard helped right it and then started administering aid to the motionless woman. Gianni struggled to pull himself out of the water, his strength spent. His eyes flitted to his daughter and then his wife.

'Is . . . is she . . . ?'

The Swiss Guard closed his eyes. 'I'm so sorry. She's—'

But then Gianni's wife swallowed a great gulp of air. Her eyes flew open, her chest heaved. She coughed and coughed and struggled against her bonds. Gianni found new strength and rushed toward her.

Hassell's entire awareness had been occupied by Gido. He couldn't help it. Their eyes had locked. Hatred shredded the air between them with knife-edged barbs. Hassell thought of Chloe and Gido's potential deception, the animosity and total lack of conscience an act of that nature revealed.

The criminal mastermind wore a black Gucci leather jacket with gold stitching across both shoulders, frayed designer jeans and gaudy gold and orange training shoes. His face was lean and clean-shaven and the curve of his mouth hinted at a smile. All this time, his gaze had been drifting from Hassell's face to his gun.

'You gonna shoot me now?' he asked Hassell. 'Marduk forced me to work for him. Nowhere else to go.' He spread his arms out.

Mason didn't dwell too much on the other three individuals: a wide brute of a man, the older guy and a shrewd, capable-looking woman. His entire being was focused on one burning question. *Where's Marduk?*

405

Hassell was continuing a conversation with Gido. 'You're terrified Marduk will come for you after this is all over.'

'Where's the book?' Sally snapped, on her knees by the side of Gianni's daughter. She looked like she wanted to say more but wobbled as her whole frame shook. 'Oh, my God. It's time!'

It was 8.59 p.m. The world turned on a knife-edge.

Disjointed cries then filled Mason's earbuds. '*We're not alone up here. Not alone . . .*' It was the voice of Dario, one of the men Gianni had sent upstairs to find his family earlier. '*There's a video camera, a desk, a—*' Screams followed amid an outburst of gunfire.

Mason whirled to Roxy. 'That was the guys Gianni sent to check the floors above.'

'Upstairs?' she asked.

'Upstairs. We walked right past the bastard.'

Together, they ran. Sally was quick to follow, Quaid on her heels. Mason glanced quickly back at Hassell. 'Have you got this?'

Hassell nodded. Three Swiss Guards backed him up. Mason flew across the gym floor, sprinted for the stairwell and pounded up the stairs. His chest started throbbing again. His forehead dripped sweat. Heads down, they ascended at speed, covering flight after flight. In their ears, the rattle of gunfire continued, the frustrating hiss of men pinned down while one of their number was out in the open, exposed and bleeding.

'On our way,' Roxy yelled into her comms. 'Thirty seconds.'

It was 9.00 p.m.

The white walls flashed by in a blur. The steps echoed back and forth in time to their sprint. Landings were taken at such breakneck speed that their feet slipped out from underneath them more than once, but they caught their falls and adjusted, forging on.

Mason hit the ninth floor and slowed.

Above, the stairwell door crashed open. Through the comms, a voice shouted that the enemy was escaping.

Mason leaned out, seeing two men – one bald, maybe in his late thirties, the other much younger and fitter. Neither could be Marduk. Both men carried weapons.

'Stop!'

Not expecting them to heed his command, he kept climbing, lungs burning, passing the tenth floor and approaching the eleventh. Above, the damaged roof access door was visible, blown off its hinges.

The younger man swivelled and laid down a lethal hail of gunfire.

Mason dived headlong, catching his head a glancing blow on the stairs. Roxy, Sally and Quaid ducked around him, the four of them falling in an ungainly heap.

It took one lull in the firing to get Mason moving. The reason was a magazine change, and when the bullets stopped, he rose to his knees, took aim and fired just one shot. The bullet passed through the shooter's face, dropping him headfirst down the stairs without a single sound. The bald man ducked back into cover.

Mason cursed. It was 9.02 p.m. Recklessly, he started climbing again.

When the bald man leaned out to take aim, Mason fired a merciless volley, blasting the man's skull to shreds.

Mason and the others raced up the last few steps, and came to the open door of the penthouse.

Looking inside, Mason kicked himself. It was there – *right there*. The others cursed. The astonishing Babylon tapestry that had adorned the back wall had been covering a door. That door now stood wide open. Through the gap, Mason could see an array of camera equipment and a stern-faced man, who could only be Marduk, staring earnestly into a computer monitor.

'Archgenerals,' Marduk cried, giving Mason the impression he hadn't started his broadcast yet. 'Stop them!'

Mason hit the floor as a man and a woman strode out of the room, unleashing their machine guns. Bullets shredded everything, the walls, the windows, even the ceiling.

The door was slammed behind the two Archgenerals as Marduk returned to his monitor.

Mason fired from a prone position. Their opponents didn't seem to care that they were exposed in the wide-open room. They didn't slow, just advanced past Marduk's desk with guns blazing. The huge wall of floor-to-ceiling picture windows gave incredible views of Rome to their left.

Bullets slammed into the door frame above Mason's head. A man cried out in pain. The onslaught continued.

And then ran dry.

Out of ammo, the Archgenerals didn't even try to replace their magazines. They threw the guns at their opponents, drew long, shining knives from their belts, and charged.

Mason fired one shot, realised he didn't have the time or space to get a certain kill, and rose fast to meet the attack.

He caught the thrust of a knife on the barrel of his rifle, deflecting it. His opponent, a broad man, snarled and jabbed three times in quick succession, pressing forward. Mason parried each lunge with the rifle, backing away.

To his left, Roxy engaged the other Archgeneral, a female with a confident, sardonic grin. Together, they feinted and parried, slipping aside and circling. Roxy drew blood with a jab of her rifle and then brought the stock around in a wide swing.

The gun flew from her hands as it smashed her opponent's nose. The woman snarled. Roxy sidestepped as the knife sliced her left shoulder.

Quaid was at their back. 'Step aside.'

Mason threw himself to the floor. Roxy landed on top of him. Mason grabbed Roxy's shoulders, pushing her aside.

'This really isn't the time!' he yelled and received a sharp elbow to the gut.

Their opponents faced Quaid's roaring machine gun. Bullets slammed into them, propelling them deeper into the room until they fell backwards across the great oak desk. Quaid was already sprinting for the door at the end of the room. When they reached it, Quaid made ready, stepped forwards and flung it open.

Mason saw everything through the gap. Marduk was holding the *Book of Secrets* in his right hand, holding it up to an unseen camera, pointing to the crest on the front page. His lips were moving, his left hand gesturing.

'No!' Sally screamed from behind.

Mason wouldn't let it stand. This wasn't the way. Without hesitation, he dropped to one knee, took aim, and fired a single shot. The bullet flew true, not penetrating Marduk's skull but hitting the *Book of Secrets* and smashing it out of the man's hand.

Marduk jerked in shock and then turned, screaming insults at Mason.

With Sally, Mason ran for the door.

Marduk abandoned his chair, his office, his broadcast, everything he'd worked for all his life and thousands of years of Amori cravings, to run. In the end, faced with death or capture, he stopped only to scoop up the *Book of Secrets* and sought to save his own hide.

Mason moved fast as Marduk and the cameraman disappeared through a rear door into what looked like a private stairwell that led upwards.

To the roof.

Mason charged across the room, kicked over the camera equipment and hit the stairs at a mad sprint, pushing as fast as he could. The carpeted stairs rose at a steep angle, the men they were chasing only ten risers ahead.

Seconds later, they vanished.

Mason heard the footsteps of his team at his back. This, right now, was where everything would be won or lost. This was where the world continued to turn on a steady axis . . . or changed for ever.

Mason dashed out onto the roof of the building.

There, illuminated by sporadic moonshine and the glow of streetlights, Marduk stood on the narrow, raised edge of the roof. Pounding drops of rain fell around him, and his long coat was unfurled by the wind, beating like black wings behind him. In his left hand he held a book the shape of a thick Bible. In his right hand he held only a mobile phone.

Mason slowed. Why would Marduk be standing there? Am I missing something?

That something made its presence known just seconds later.

A huge shape rose beyond Marduk and above the building, sleek and predatory. The sound of its engine and rotors surged across the rooftop, no longer drowned by the storm. Marduk looked up at the helicopter.

'The Amori will rise again!' he shouted, rocked by a blizzard of sleet. The chopper above him rose and fell as it battled the high winds. A rope and harness slithered out and were whipped by the gale, the black cable lashing the air above Marduk's head. Marduk reached out to grab hold.

Mason opened his mouth to shout a warning. The last thing he wanted was the book to go sailing off the roof and fall to the ground below, but then something forceful hit him from the left.

Caught by surprise, Mason staggered sideways across the roof, propelled by a heavy, strong man with thick arms. His dazed brain recalled there had been a cameraman with Marduk. Now, that cameraman was driving Mason quickly towards the roof's eastern parapet. In a few more seconds, he would be pushed over the edge. Mason let his legs collapse underneath him and fell to the ground. The cameraman tripped and sprawled across him. Mason kicked out, catching his assailant with a solid blow to the ribs. The man cried out in pain, giving Mason the chance to surge to his knees.

He saw Marduk, still clutching the book, reach for the slowly swinging cable and harness. The cameraman caught his attention again, rising like a mountain, clenching his fists and flexing his big shoulder muscles. Mason knew exactly what would happen next – the man would spread his arms and charge.

But then he saw he'd actually had no idea what would happen next.

A gunshot boomed out. Marduk stiffened, the left hand that held the book went limp, and the man swayed over the two-hundred-foot drop. The cameraman roared and started sprinting to the aid of his leader.

But more shocking for Mason was the sight of the woman holding the gun to his left.

Sally.

She held her Glock at arm's length, looking as surprised as anyone that her shot had struck true. The *Book of Secrets* fell to the roof, whipped and beaten by the elements and the rain. Sally dropped the gun and exploded towards it like a sprinter. Mason went half a second later, trying to keep up.

Marduk screamed as his arm pounded with pain, as the book fell away, and as the harness struck his body. It had quick-fasten-quick-release reins and he was able to buckle in with some effort. At his signal, the helicopter rose, dragging him off the top of the roof.

Sally fell to her knees in the rain, scooped up the book, and thrust it under her jacket. Mason aimed his Glock at Marduk's swaying, rain-battered figure, setting the front sight dead-centre upon Marduk's chest.

One squeeze and the Amori were done. One squeeze, and the threat was over.

His finger tightened on the trigger. He fired, but the cameraman rose up, taking the bullet in his wide chest. The figure blocked Mason's view of Marduk as the force of the bullet propelled him to the edge of the roof. Reaching out, the man found nothing to cling onto and fell backwards into thin air, screaming as he disappeared.

Beyond the roof, Marduk swung in his harness above the city, too far away to hit. Mason cursed and dropped the weapon. Sally stared after the Amori's leader as he swung away, her face a drawn, unreadable mask.

'Are we done, boss?' Roxy asked, appearing behind them.

Mason turned away from the escaping figure, from the rainswept rooftop and the turbulent skyline, which had now begun to clear as the storm abated.

'We're done,' he said.

Chapter 64

Hassell faced Gido, the air between them loaded with suffocating tension. The room dripped with menace, with weapons, with the potential for death, but for Hassell there was only one objective, and he was locked onto it.

'You gonna shoot an unarmed man?' Gido asked. 'Do it, or back off. I won't tell you again.'

To Gido's left, a woman stood. To his right, a man. Neither looked overly impressed at the guns two Swiss Guards were pointing at them.

Hassell studied Gido, this infamous leader of criminals, his boss for so long. His mentor. His . . . disgrace. 'Did you do it?' he asked.

'Do what? You walked out on me. Betrayed me. Because of you, and to honour my good name, I had to leave the boys back home and fly over to this shithole. Marduk offered me a choice – "either get Mason and his team off our backs or measure up for a coffin." Poor choice, if you ask me.'

'It's called Karma,' Hassell said. He wouldn't have been able to find the Amori's lair if Gido hadn't messed up and been forced to come to Rome. 'Did you do it?' he asked again, his finger straining against the trigger. One squeeze and his life would take on a different and far darker aspect.

'Do what, man? Did I save your ass – yeah. Did I give you shelter and meaning – yeah. Did I train you to be the best – oh, yeah.'

Hassel squeezed the trigger. The gunshot, deafeningly loud in the edgy silence, made Gido flinch and the gold chains around his neck rattle as it passed close to his right temple.

'Are you crazy? What the hell is wrong with you?'

Hassell was at the end of his tether. 'The next one's in your fucking skull,' he growled, voice charged with emotion. 'Did you do it? Did you arrange Chloe's execution to get your claws into me?'

Gido looked sideways. 'Ah, you finally figured it out, eh? All these years – working for the man who gave the kill order on your girl. You know why? Because that's what we do to cops. That's what we do to scum like you. You were fresh, eager, not yet jaded by cop work and politics, the perfect target, the perfect tool to mould as I wished.'

Hassell's world fell away. The floor receded. His knees barely held him upright.

'You feel me?' Gido said. 'I needed you to get rid of the opposition. Took me a while to find you after you went all blubbery.' Gido grinned like evil incarnate. 'Crying for that dead bitch. But I soon brought you around.'

Hassell fought to stay coherent. He sagged. He now knew that the man who'd engineered the murder of his childhood sweetheart had then befriended him and put him to work, getting a kick out of it every single day.

For the second time in his life, Hassell felt his entire world shift, perspectives altered by earth-shaking revelations.

In a way, this whole thing has been about revelation . . . The thought flitted through his brain and was lost.

'You really should shoot yourself,' Gido said. 'What do you have left to live for? And how could you ever live with yourself now?' Gido broke out into long, harsh laughter.

Hassell was aghast at the cruelty that spilled from Gido's mouth like poison. He faltered once more, and Gido took advantage, attacking from close range and battering him across the face with a bracelet-festooned arm.

Hassell staggered. Blood flowed down his cheek. He looked up and saw his boss and mentor rearing over him, the embodiment of evil, and squeezed his trigger twice.

The bullets thudded into Gido's chest. A look of surprise crossed the man's face, as if he'd considered himself immortal, but then he fell, already dead.

Hassell crawled away from the corpse, returned to the gutter once more, feeling the same now as he had back then when he'd lost her. Learning the truth had changed nothing, had improved nothing. Learning the truth had almost killed him. His soul was blighted, his heart withered.

Alone and lost, he kept his head down and edged away.

'Hey.'

The burden of Chloe's death and all the years since bore down on him like deadly thunderclouds, wrapping him in chaos.

'Hey, Hassell.'

He looked up. They stood there – Mason and Roxy, Quaid and Sally. They stood bathed in beams of glimmering moonlight that slanted through a window, and they were a beacon, something to cling to in the heart of darkness.

'What?' he managed.

'Are you coming with us?'

Hassell looked inward. *Am I?*

Chapter 65

Mason walked away from that night with nothing. No praise. No reward. No banked goodwill. He left the *Book of Secrets* in the capable hands of Gianluca Gianni and received barely a nod of thanks. The thought occurred to him that the recovery of that which is considered a great secret cannot truly be acknowledged.

Hell, he thought. *I didn't walk away with nothing. I walked away with a new purpose.*

In adversity, there was always a path for renewal.

Mason had never expected to meet Roxy, Sally and the others, nor feel a renewed sense of belief. His inner conflict wasn't gone by any means, but this was a start, something solid to build on.

After they went back for Hassell, they waited for Gianni to tend to his family, to comfort them and to see them safely to a police car. Gianni took his time. Nobody bothered them as they sat in Marduk's office around the great desk but, in the end, Gianni finally came up and extended a hand.

'I thank you for your help. Is that the book?'

It lay on the desk before them, about five inches thick, wrapped in a hard crimson cover bearing an old form of the

Vatican City's coat of arms. The cover was creased, the pages disorderly, and a hole the size of a marble had been blasted through it, singeing the papers where it passed through.

'Did you read it?' Gianni asked.

'Your secrets are safe from us, don't worry.' Sally shook her head and met his gaze. 'Did Marduk reveal anything world-shattering?'

Gianni shook his head. 'As we knew, he craved the limelight and was embellishing every sentence. You interrupted the broadcast while he was still describing the book. His entire dossier of proof was found inside a desk in his office, many pages relating to scientific results and expert testimonies. Even if he's got photographs and copies, it's nothing he can corroborate without having access to the actual book itself. To be believed, he needed to combine the modern results *with* the ancient book.'

'Which doesn't exist,' Mason pointed out.

'We'll talk to these experts and scientists,' Gianni said. 'See if we can spin something or convince them Marduk was constructing more fairy tales than Disney. But I have to know . . .' he gazed earnestly at them. '*Did* you read the book? Please tell me the truth.'

'Your secrets are not ours to keep,' Sally said firmly.

'And more importantly,' Mason said, 'how are your wife and daughter?'

Gianni's face broke into a wide smile. 'Oh, they are fine. They are home, not badly hurt in a physical sense, and resting. Mentally, it will be a long road to recovery and an experience that will plague them for ever. But our family is whole again. They are safe, we will soon be together, and that is what matters for now.'

Gianni nodded his respect to them and, before leaving the room, assured them that the wider Italian authorities were no longer looking for them, as Gianni had explained that they were friends not foes. Mason departed soon after, followed by the others, and they regrouped on the street. The wind had lost its strength, the storm had passed and the rain had stopped. Rome's slick streets glistened as if they'd been cleansed.

Mason cracked a smile. 'Drinks are on me.'

Roxy cheered. 'About time too. Hey, we deserve it. And I'm sure you meant *bottles* are on you. Lots of them.'

Sally linked arms with them and smiled. 'Thank you,' she said. 'Thank you for helping to lay my father's memory to rest. I'm content now, knowing that I did all I could for him.'

'He'd be proud,' Mason said. 'We all are.'

They walked for twenty minutes, rejecting two bars because Quaid wanted a particular kind of specialised ale. When they finally sat down, removed their coats and sat back, it was Sally who opened the conversation.

'So,' she said. 'What about Jesus Christ being a warrior king? Now *that's* a secret that should never be told.'

Mason caught the eyes of the other members of the group one by one, sharing a significant look with them. 'I have a feeling,' he said, 'that this isn't the end of our involvement with this particular Vatican secret.'